SMUGGLER'S
MOON

SMUGGLER'S
MOON

CHRISTINE KING

Published in paperback in 2019 by Sixth Element Publishing
on behalf of Christine King

Sixth Element Publishing
Arthur Robinson House
13-14 The Green
Billingham TS23 1EU
Tel: 01642 360253
www.6epublishing.net

© Christine King 2019

ISBN 978-1-912218-53-0

British Library Cataloguing in Publication Data. A catalogue record for this book is
available from the British Library.

Printed in Great Britain.

ACKNOWLEDGEMENTS

*Dedicated to all my family and friends for their unfailing love,
and support during the writing of this book.*

*In particular many thanks to Mr John McShane Senior for his unfailing
humour, encouragement and advice regarding many of the historical
maritime and nautical references throughout the book.*

A Smugglers Song by Rudyard Kipling

If you wake at midnight, and hear a horse's feet,
Don't go drawing back the blind, or looking in the street.
Them that ask no questions isn't told a lie.
Watch the wall, my darling, while the Gentlemen go by!
Five and twenty ponies,
Trotting through the dark --
Brandy for the Parson,
'Baccy for the Clerk;
Laces for a lady, letters for a spy,
And watch the wall, my darling, while the Gentlemen go by!

Running round the woodlump if you chance to find
Little barrels, roped and tarred, all full of brandy-wine,
Don't you shout to come and look, nor use 'em for your play.
Put the brishwood back again -- and they'll be gone next day!

If you see the stable-door setting open wide;
If you see a tired horse lying down inside;
If your mother mends a coat cut about and tore;
If the lining's wet and warm -- don't you ask no more!

If you meet King George's men, dressed in blue and red,
You be carefull what you say, and mindful what is said.
If they call you "pretty maid," and chuck you 'neath the chin,
Don't you tell where no one is, nor yet where no one's been!

Knocks and footsteps round the house -- whistles after dark --
You've no call for running out till the house-dogs bark.
Trusty's here, and Pincher's here, and see how dumb they lie --
They don't fret to follow when the Gentlemen go by!

If you do as you've been told, 'likely there's a chance,
You'll be given a dainty doll, all the way from France,
With a cap of Valenciennes, and a velvet hood --

A present from the Gentlemen, along o' being good!
Five and twenty ponies,
Trotting through the dark --
Brandy for the Parson,
'Baccy for the Clerk;
Them that asks no questions isn't told a lie --
Watch the wall, my darling, while the Gentlemen go by!

Rudyard Kipling

CHAPTER ONE

It was an inconveniently warm day to be holding a funeral. The morning sun shone down brightly onto the assembled mourners in the pleasant surroundings of the churchyard. The church clock struck eleven times, and as the coffin was lowered into the newly dug grave, a light breeze stirred the flowers planted all around the church, sending the scent of fresh roses and honeysuckle floating into the air. The sound of bees buzzing gently was heard as the bells stopped tolling; the whole scene was one of peace and tranquillity, a pretty, mellow stoned Norman church, well kept, well cared for – the perfect resting place for Sir Anthony Waverley.

The girl in black glared across the graveside of her recently deceased father at her stepmother who was even now, at the funeral of her husband, leaning on the arm of another man.

Lady Henrietta Waverley was dressed in widow's weeds. However, these were so artfully cut, so elegantly sculpted against her voluptuous curves, that if she had not been at the graveside of her late husband, her appearance would have been more suited to an evening at one of the more disreputable gambling clubs she was so fond of frequenting. She leaned heavily against her companion, dabbing at dry eyes with a tiny piece of lace. The gentleman whose arm she held patted her black clad hand in a gesture more proprietary than comforting.

Her stepdaughter, Charis Waverley, was more soberly attired in a simple black gown, covered by a short damask jacket and black beribboned bonnet. She bowed her head as the priest concluded the funeral rites and she held on to her Uncle's arm as, together, they stood beside the grave as the rest of her father's old friends

1

and few remaining family members returned to their waiting carriages. The murmured messages of condolences directed towards Sir Anthony's only child and his younger brother went almost unheard as she fought to control her grief.

Despite the warmth of the summer's day, Charis shuddered as she raised her head to watch her stepmother being assisted into the Waverley family coach by her companion. Her eyes narrowed and a tidal wave of ill feeling towards Lady Henrietta threatened to overcome her. She moved finally, throwing a single rose to land softly on top of the heavy oaken coffin holding the earthly remains of her beloved father.

"Goodbye Papa, God Bless," she whispered.

Wishing she could join her Uncle Frederick in his small carriage for their return to London, she reluctantly left him to follow her stepmother into the Waverley family coach, a solid, substantial vehicle, the liveried grooms in dark blue and gold displaying their funereal attire with black armbands. A footman assisted her into the coach and she settled herself opposite Lady Henrietta, sinking into the navy blue velvet of the seats and resting her head back against the well upholstered, padded squabs. Charis closed her fine wide green eyes, her thick eyelashes black against the pallor of her cheeks. She opened them again as the coach began to move, to find herself the subject of a particularly hard stare from the gentleman accompanying them. Sir Richard Hardy was seated beside the widow and the look he gave Charis was enough to make her turn her head away. The man was as loathsome as her stepmother and Charis wondered how long Henrietta had been having an affair with him.

Lady Henrietta's beautiful face was creased into a petulant frown. She sighed loudly and looked out of the curtained windows. "I suppose one has to invite everyone back to the house, but really it is a frightful chore. And most inconvenient – one should be left alone to grieve in peace, not entertain a host of boring old men."

Charis's eyes flashed with sudden fury. She was forestalled in her angry retort by Sir Richard's unexpected interruption.

"Now now, Henrietta. I know today has been difficult for you but really, you must bow to convention occasionally. You will welcome everyone most graciously and be the perfect grief-stricken widow and no one will ever be able to accuse you of not doing the right thing."

He smiled at the widow and was rewarded by the petulance leaving her face. As if only just aware of Charis's presence, Henrietta smiled at her stepdaughter.

"Of course, you are right. I must not leave myself open to any criticism. My poor dear Anthony had many friends, I must make sure they are looked after correctly."

Charis swallowed the remarks that came so easily to her lips. In her opinion, the only thing being taken care of at the moment was Henrietta herself. Silently she turned her head to watch the quiet country lanes give way to the noisier, bustling roads leading into London until finally, they glided into Curzon Street. They made their way along to a fine cream stone building, the tall, elegant town house that had been the home of the Waverley family for generations. The footmen hurried to help the ladies alight, placing a small footstool on the pavement for them to step onto. Charis thanked the young man who helped her and waited until Sir Richard assisted her stepmother from the carriage. She hated the possessive way Sir Richard looked at the well-proportioned, stylish house. As if he could read her mind he smiled at her.

"It's a lot older than my house, of course." He addressed himself to Charis, a conciliatory tone to his voice. "But very fine nevertheless. Your dear mama cannot help but be comfortable here."

"My Mama died several years ago, Sir Richard," she retorted. "But I am sure Lady Henrietta will find it extremely comfortable for the time being."

She left them on the pavement and entered the house. The house was not part of an entail, it belonged entirely to Sir Anthony and he told her many years ago that he was leaving the property to her in his will. The absence of a son meant that Charis was his sole heiress, the country estate would have to pass on to her father's brother, but the town house and his personal fortune would eventually be passed down to her.

As she removed her bonnet and handed it to her maid, she missed the glance exchanged by Henrietta and Sir Richard. She turned in time to see the slightest of smiles on the lips of her stepmother, as Lady Henrietta, divesting herself of the tiniest scrap of black passing as a bonnet, held out her hand to Charis.

"Ah, my dear," she sighed, her voice silkily insincere, "I fear I must disappoint you, Charis. I am afraid it is you who must make yourself comfortable for the time being!"

Charis stopped in her tracks to face her stepmother, looking squarely into the huge, limpid blue eyes that so ably deceived her father.

"Lady Henrietta? What can you mean pray?" Her voice was quietly polite, her feelings carefully masked. "This is my home. My father assured me it would always remain my home."

Lady Henrietta's shoulders moved in a shrug of black silk and lace. "I understand your Papa, my dearest Anthony, may have altered his will." She paused. "But of course we will not know until Mr Blackridge has attended upon us tomorrow."

"And who, Madam, is Mr Blackridge?" Charis enquired, as icily polite as her stepmother.

Henrietta smiled again, the warmth never quite reaching her eyes.

"Why, your dear Papa's solicitor of course," she replied.

"Our family solicitor is Mr Kielder; he has attended us for years," Charis protested.

"Oh, no Charis." Henrietta turned from her stepdaughter and moved away, into the high ceilinged room that they were to use for the wake. She paused briefly in front of a heavily gilded, ornate looking glass and smoothed the already impeccably styled golden blonde hair. "Your Papa and I changed our solicitors some time ago to Mr Blackridge. Did he not tell you, my dear?"

Charis and Sir Richard followed Lady Henrietta into the salon. A large elegant room, an Oriental designed Aubusson carpet covered the floor, the colours of green and gold picked up in the furnishings of the room. A huge Adam fireplace dominated, with sofas and armchairs covered in heavy green silken upholstery arranged tastefully throughout. A French door led onto the carefully manicured gardens of the house, open now, letting in the slight breeze that blew gently through the room, adding the scent of roses to the fragrance of the flowers that stood in huge bouquets on the occasional tables throughout the salon. A portrait of Sir Anthony Waverley looked down on them from above the fireplace and Charis went over to look up at her Papa, wondering what other surprises lay in store for her. A feeling of foreboding stole over her, but resolutely she refused to let either Henrietta or Sir Richard see her concern. She kept her expression neutral as she turned to face them. "No, Lady Henrietta, my father did not tell me. Which was most strange, Papa was always most punctilious in keeping me apprised of any changes that might affect me."

She managed a faint smile, determined not to let them see how much Henrietta's words startled her.

"I am sure all my questions will be answered in due course," she continued calmly. "In the meantime, I think our guests have arrived."

Charis followed Henrietta as the first of the mourners from the funeral arrived and were even now entering the large black and white tiled hallway. Sir Richard remained in the salon; he was nothing if not discreet. His appearance at the funeral had already raised eyebrows in some quarters and he stayed resolutely in the background whilst Henrietta and Charis greeted their guests. There were Sir Anthony's old friends from his club and his neighbours from both Curzon Street and the estate in Yorkshire. Some representatives from the country estate were also in attendance, the Steward and Estate Manager both greeting Charis with much sympathy and warmth. Their greeting of Lady Henrietta was much more restrained. She was polite but she showed no more interest in them.

Charis had no siblings. She had cousins whom she occasionally saw but her mother had died when Charis was a small child.

However, she needed no one but her dearest Papa. They had been close, sharing the same sense of values and humour, and she was delighted when her father informed her he had met someone at last who could take her beloved mother's place. Charis watched her stepmother now circulating the room, charming them all, and playing the grieving widow for all to see.

Her father so wanted Charis to love her new stepmother, but Henrietta Hunter was not pleased to have a budding beauty for a stepdaughter and Charis in her turn thought that Miss Hunter as predatory as her name.

Suspicion at the absence of the family solicitor, Mr Kielder, nagged at Charis for the rest of the afternoon, whilst she mingled amongst her father's old friends and colleagues. It was so unlike her father, so out of character, that she wondered what Henrietta could have said to make Sir Anthony change in this manner.

The arrival of her uncle roused her from her reverie. He was being greeted by Lady Henrietta as Charis made her way over to him. "Hello again, Uncle Frederick," she said. "Thank you for coming today."

Uncle Frederick bent and kissed his niece's cheek. "A sad day, Charis," he sighed, "very sad."

"Thank you, Uncle Frederick. I am sorry Aunt Elizabeth is too unwell to join us."

Frederick Waverley was the proud, if somewhat harassed, father of four growing children, all younger than Charis, all of whom her aunt (who suffered greatly from her nerves) allowed to run wild in the cramped accommodation of their York townhouse. A move to a large and prosperous country estate could not have come at a better time for the family.

"She sends her love and hopes you will visit us soon, my dear."

Lady Henrietta's sigh was most affecting, her large eyes sparkling with unshed tears.

"We will indeed, Frederick," she said, her voice melancholy in the extreme. "We must attend the estate very soon. I have a great deal of personal effects in the house that I must remove to make room for your dear family."

Frederick was slightly embarrassed, his cheeks reddening at her words.

Charis smiled at him. "I hope to visit my aunt and the children very soon, Uncle Frederick. Lady Henrietta is correct in saying we must visit the Manor soon though."

Frederick took his niece's hand and bowed slightly. "I realise there is much to discuss and many arrangements to make, my dear." His voice was low, but his meaning clear. "You would be welcome at any time. The Manor has been your home for many years, and I hope you will continue to think of it as such."

Henrietta's voice and manner were brittle as she was moved to retort, "We will be in touch soon, Frederick. Pray excuse me, I have other guests to attend to."

She moved away and Charis saw her making her way over to Sir Richard. Charis frowned as she watched Richard handing her a glass of wine and as she sipped it, Henrietta bent her head in Sir Richard's direction, whispering something that brought a brief smile to his face.

Sighing, Charis turned back to her uncle. "I expect you have much to discuss with your new Steward and Estate Manager, Uncle Frederick. Have you decided when you will move to Waverley?"

Frederick held her hand once more. "Charis," he said softly. "I wish you would come back to York with me." He too looked over at his hostess. "What Anthony ever saw in her …" He left the sentence unfinished and took a shaky breath. He forced a smile. "Listen Charis, I don't trust her – I don't like to think of you being alone here with her."

Charis's wide eyes cleared and her first genuine smile light up her face. "Darling Uncle Freddy!" she replied. "Pray do not worry about me. I would be delighted to accept your invitation to visit and will come to Waverley as soon as possible but I am not afraid of Henrietta." She glanced briefly at her stepmother, still standing close to Sir Richard, engrossed in a whispered conversation. "I have been alone with her for these last few weeks when Papa was ill – I am sure I can cope for a few more days whilst we sort out Papa's will and other matters."

Frederick frowned. He did not like or trust his brother's widow and as he accompanied his niece to speak to the estate staff, his concerns for Charis were increasing. He felt uneasy leaving her in the care of Lady Henrietta and he wondered again, not for the first time, how his brother could have been such an old fool to be so taken in by the wiles of Henrietta Hunter. A beautiful face and huge blue eyes could not hide the ruthless side to her nature for long and he wondered why his brother could not see through the façade she presented to the world. Charis had seen through her at once and it had only been her deep love for her father that prevented her from openly criticising the woman. Frederick kept Charis beside him, reluctant to leave her alone with the widow.

"Charis," he said quietly as they approached his Steward, "I will be here tomorrow for the reading of the will. When I leave, I would like you to come with me. Please my dear?"

Charis followed his gaze as they watched Henrietta circulating the room, dabbing a scrap of lace to dry eyes and accepting the condolences of her late husband's acquaintances. Charis felt a cold finger of apprehension touch her spine as Frederick's unease seemed to encompass her. She forced a slight smile to her face. "This is my home, Freddy," she said firmly. "Papa would not like me to run away and leave it – it is promised to me, and I will not let that woman drive me out!"

Her voice held a note of such determination that Freddy was quite disconcerted. However, his attention was then claimed by the gentlemen from his future home and soon he was deep in discussion about the estate. His obvious love and enthusiasm for the Waverley family estate pleased Charis, happy that her old family home was being passed to a custodian who would care for it as much as she and her father had done.

Eventually, as the guests departed, giving their final condolences to the bereaved wife and daughter of Sir Anthony, Charis found herself alone in the salon. She stood below the portrait of her father and stared up at him. She could not shake off the uneasiness Uncle Freddy's words had awoken within her and as she thought of Henrietta's remarks earlier, she wondered what, exactly, her stepmother was up to.

Henrietta's gasp was a harsh, jarring note in the solemn silence of the house. Charis whirled around to see Richard Hardy gripping her stepmother's shoulders and pull her roughly into his arms. Henrietta turned her head away but he put a finger under her chin and forced her head up before kissing her full on the lips.

They did not notice her standing in the salon and as Richard whispered something in Henrietta's ears, Henrietta nodded silently. Horrified at Henrietta's conduct, Charis' eyes followed them as they went upstairs, tears brimming at the insult they showed to her late father's memory. She had not thought Henrietta so unfeeling but something about Richard's behaviour disturbed her more.

•

Henrietta looked at herself in her dressing table mirror. Her maid had left a jewellery box open for her ladyship to choose the most appropriate item to wear today. Something discreet and simple, Henrietta decided, turning reluctantly away from the fabulous choker of emeralds her late husband presented to her on her last birthday. She picked up a string of gleaming, creamy pearls and as she moved them, her hand brushed against a plain gold locket.

She paused, frowning. The sight of the locket disturbed deeply buried unwanted memories.

Despite herself, she picked it up and unlatched the clip to open the locket. Her lips pressed together in a straight line, her vivid blue eyes clouding over as she gazed at the two portraits it contained. A handsome young man; with thick black hair, sapphire blue eyes and a strong, attractive face. He was smiling at her, all the confidence of youth and happiness of love vibrating out of every pore. The other was of a child. A curly haired, blue-eyed angel of a child. Unexpected tears sprang to Henrietta's eyes. True, heartfelt grief rippled through her body as she looked at the miniatures.

One dead in a pointless war; the other dead of pneumonia. She had done everything to save her child but it was not enough. It could never be enough. Her darling Lily succumbed to the illness that gripped her tiny body and she had been laid to rest in a small churchyard in Portsmouth.

Henrietta looked at the plain gold locket and dropped it back into the jewellery box, closing it with a decided snap. Determinedly, she turned her thoughts away from her old life. She had changed beyond recognition to the girl she was when those portraits were painted. Life had changed her.

Her thoughts turned again to Charis, her lips tightening as she considered the thought of how glad she would be to be rid of her stepdaughter. The girl had seen through her at once and disliked her on sight.

"Hold on a little longer..." she whispered to herself. "Just a little longer and it will all have been worthwhile and I will be the richest woman in London."

She fastened the simple pearl circle around her neck, took a last look at herself in the mirror and, finally satisfied, left her bedroom.

•

Charis emerged from her bedroom after spending the previous evening dining alone and seeing no more of her stepmother. She made her way to the dining room where she could hear Lady Henrietta already there, berating one of the footmen.

Charis entered the room to see Edward the footman hastily picking up the remains of a breakfast dish Henrietta appeared to have knocked to the floor.

Her eyes were flashing with temper and she turned swiftly as Charis entered. "I think a few changes around here are well overdue!" she snapped at her.

"Good morning, Henrietta," Charis said, calmly seating herself at her place. "How are you this morning?"

She smiled at the discomfited Edward, quietly thanking him as he placed a plate of her favourite scrambled eggs in front of her and filled her teacup from the teapot with hands shaking slightly.

He bowed and smiled gratefully at her as he backed away to stand beside the sideboard, in readiness for further orders.

Henrietta's turned an irritable face to her stepdaughter. "I am well enough, thank you," she replied, "except for the staff in this house who are trying my nerves and patience to the utmost."

"I am sure no one means to upset you, Henrietta," Charis replied coolly. "We are all still in a great deal of shock over my father's death – I think a period of adjustment is to be expected."

Henrietta took a sip of her tea followed by a deep breath to calm herself before speaking again. "I have asked Mr Blackridge to attend us this morning, Charis," she said. "Your Uncle Frederick will also be joining us shortly – he will need to be here for the reading of my dear Anthony's will."

Charis swallowed her egg and patted her mouth with the napkin as she considered her stepmother's words. Henrietta certainly did not seem her normal self this morning. Apart from being decidedly out of temper, she appeared nervous, almost jittery.

"When did Papa change his solicitor?" she asked, staring at Henrietta.

"It was some months ago," Henrietta answered her stepdaughter although she avoided Charis's direct gaze. "You were away in the North visiting the Estate."

Charis drank some more tea. Her mind turned to the events of earlier that year. She had been away visiting her Uncle and Aunt in York, spending time dealing with some minor estate matters on her father's behalf. Away from home for two months, she returned at the start of the Season, to find her father taken ill. Despite the temptations of the many entertainments on offer and her father's insistence she go and enjoy herself, she declined all invitations, remaining steadfastly at home, worried about his health.

She had been presented at court some two years earlier and being an attractive young lady as well as her father's sole heiress, she had been courted and sought after by many of the young men she came into contact with. Charis was a very down to earth young lady, prosaic and sensible. She was able to identify without much difficulty the fortune hunters from the more serious suitors but her heart was unmoved by any of them and it was with little regret that she gave up the rounds of balls and parties that year. At her presentation and subsequently, Charis was chaperoned by an elderly cousin of her father's. Aunt Emily however, happily retired on Sir Anthony's remarriage leaving Charis to be escorted by her new stepmother, an arrangement that delighted her father and absolutely appalled Charis. Charis swallowed her dismay however and accepted Henrietta's chaperonage to please her father.

Charis went to York that winter, partly to visit the estate and relatives, partly to absent herself from the company of the woman her beloved father had married. He remained besotted with his young and beautiful wife and upon Charis's return, he again encouraged her to accompany Henrietta to the various social engagements they were invited to attend. His illness prevented him from joining them and, when his health deteriorated, Charis refused to leave him, remaining with him and nursing him until his eventual death from pneumonia some seven days earlier.

Brought back from her memories by the rattling of teacups, Charis started and flushed slightly as she heard Henrietta's impatient sigh.

She stared at her stepmother. "Is Sir Richard returning today?" she enquired.

As she had heard Sir Richard leaving the house only two hours earlier, her annoyance was hard to keep from the coldness of her voice. Really, Henrietta was going too far. Her husband was barely buried and she was allowing her lover to spend the night already. The sooner she could rid herself of this woman the better! She could barely bring herself to be civil to Henrietta and longed for the moment she could ask her to leave!

Henrietta did not even have the grace to look embarrassed. She was staring at a mirror opposite the dining table, a strange, blank expression on her face. As she returned her attention to Charis, her expression hardened; her eyes narrowed slightly and the dislike she felt for her stepdaughter momentarily clouded her face.

"Sir Richard will be returning this evening," she said coldly. "He will be escorting me to the theatre."

Charis was genuinely shocked at Henrietta's announcement. "You cannot be serious," she said quietly. "You are in mourning, Henrietta – it would be in extremely bad taste to attend the theatre in the company of another man so soon after Papa's death."

Henrietta shrugged carelessly and, pushing her uneaten breakfast plate away, she stood. In the harsh morning light Charis could see the first fine lines of dissipation appearing on her stepmother's attractive countenance. Her huge blue eyes glared at Charis.

"My actions are of no consequence to you, Miss," she said coldly. "Pray do not presume to interfere in my affairs."

She moved towards the dining room door, waiting until the footman hurried to open it for her. "Be in the library for eleven," she snapped. "For the reading of your father's will."

She swept out in a flurry of black satin and Charis slumped in the chair, her shoulders sagging tiredly. Heartily sick of her stepmother's presence, she longed for Henrietta to depart. She had felt uneasy at Papa's funeral, Henrietta's words unsettling her. However, she knew her father too well to doubt him, she trusted him implicitly and even if his judgement was slightly impaired when it came to Henrietta, she knew he would keep his word when it came to taking care of his only daughter. His fortune would pass to her today and she would live comfortably in this house for the rest of her life.

She found herself considering the real possibility that she would have to engage a companion shortly. Once Henrietta left, Charis would need a suitable lady to live with her to give the necessary respectability a young lady in her position required.

She spent a pleasant half-hour alone, finishing her breakfast, drinking tea and considering who amongst her relatives would be most suitable. She had few relatives, dismissing most of them immediately as they were all too elderly to be interested in living with her, and although she was not as giddy or lively as many of her contemporaries, she still did not relish a completely sedentary, quiet life. No, she would find someone suitable once this business was concluded and Henrietta gone, out of her home and life as soon as decently possible.

CHAPTER TWO

It was market day in the town of Alnmouth, high up on the Northumberland coast. The weather had broken and the hot summer days of August were over for another year. Summer never lasted long in this part of the world but winter had not yet started and the long cool autumn days were upon them now. The fishermen squinted out to sea at the gathering clouds, measuring with seasoned accuracy the approach of the coming storms. They were weighing up how many more fishing trips they could achieve before the winter weather kept them ashore, unable to earn even a meagre living at the wheels of their small fishing boats.

The market was crowded with locals and visitors alike, buyers and sellers filling the town's main square, the noise of the vendors advertising their wares mingling with the calls of the local shopkeepers and the shouts of the townspeople. It was busy and bustling and an ever-changing scene of colour and activity. The rain fell on them intermittently; heavy one minute, then the clouds would be blown away until the next scudding clouds settled overhead, opening again on the damp heads of the people below.

The windows of the old coaching inn rattled with the force of the driving rain and a gust of wind caught the door as it opened to admit three figures, dressed in heavy greatcoats. The wind blew the door open with a crash and all present turned to look at the three strangers.

The landlord looked up at the newcomers and glanced to his right at the group of men sitting together, conversing quietly over the rough wooden table that served to hold the tankards of ale in front of them. The seated customers followed the landlord's eyes, observing the newcomers through slightly narrowed eyes before turning away and lowering their voices even more.

The three men entering the inn stared around them at the suddenly silent crowd. Ignoring the stares directed at them, they walked towards the bar. The tallest of the three men removed his hat and nodded towards the landlord.

Tall, broad-shouldered and narrow hipped, he wore no wig and his thick hair was cropped short. He had a military bearing about him and the landlord and customers eyed him warily. They had no love of either the military or the naval contingent that frequented the town and the three men were aware of the bristling animosity directed their way. The two older men glanced around the room cautiously, used to the effect they had on the local civilian population. Their Captain, however, was new to his role and although an intelligent and able man, he had never yet been in this position, and certainly it was his first foray into the heart of the smugglers' den that was The Schooner.

Captain Steele was a stranger to this part of the world. Born and brought up in rural Ireland, the younger son of English landowners, he was used to the hostility of country people towards strangers. Recently involved in skirmishes with the French during the wars, after facing battle-hardened French seamen during the various sea battles for the last few years, his posting to Northumberland seemed to be a welcome respite after his recent travails.

His eyes narrowed slightly as he gazed around the room, wondering if his first assumption that this posting was going to be an easy enough task had been mistaken.

The Captain was in charge of the newest, sleekest cutter the Navy ever built. He had been seconded to this part of England to assist the Revenue in their efforts to curtail the rampant smuggling going on under the noses of the few hard pressed customs officers battling against overwhelming odds in their efforts to enforce law and order. Militia from the towns of Newcastle and Berwick were often called upon to help but, as all the customs men knew, so far their efforts had been fruitless, few smugglers were ever caught. None of the local populace could ever be called upon to assist the militia – no one would testify against men who were, without exception, known to them as neighbours, relatives, and friends.

The arrival of The Scorpion in the waters off the Northumbrian coast was reported to the Captain by one of his erstwhile companions. The ship's name was known to him. Its captain likewise was known to him also, by reputation only. Luke Vincent was a legend in the Royal Navy – serving under Nelson himself until an injury at the Battle of Trafalgar ended his naval career. He had been a brave and upstanding officer and Captain Steele wondered what could have happened to turn this once outstanding man to the trade he now followed.

Captain Steele looked around the tobacco-fogged room, his eyes squinting through the smoke as he struggled to make out the features of the men sitting at tables and at the narrow bar. Most of them had their backs to him, others glared at him before turning away and gradually a low murmur of conversation started again following the silence his entrance caused. Thoughtfully regarding the groups of men gathered in the taproom he wondered if the elusive Captain Vincent was amongst them.

Steele made his way to the bar. The landlord's glare was unfriendly but the Captain's mouth lifted in a humorous smile. These people would not intimidate him.

"Landlord," he said quietly. His voice was pleasant. "Three tankards of your best ale, if you please."

The landlord looked as though he would have refused the request but his eyes glanced at the Captain and his two companions. They were only three but they carried pistols and swords and discretion overcame his natural reluctance and he served the tankards as requested.

They took their drinks to an empty table in the corner of the room and sat down, the Captain's back to the wall, his eyes scouring the crowded room.

"Well?" he asked. "Do you think Vincent is here?"

The two older men were also scanning the room. They were

seasoned veteran customs officers and they knew this part of the coast as well as any local seamen.

"That could be him," Jim said quietly. "Over there by the fireplace." He nodded over to where two well-dressed men were deep in conversation. Engrossed in their talk they had not moved to stare at the newcomers.

"Which one?" Steele asked, taking a draught of the cold beer.

"On the left," Jim replied. "I saw him once and think that could be him. The other man is Will Stewart, landlord of The King's Head, the Inn on the Newcastle Road. We've long suspected him of dealing in contraband but…" He shrugged, annoyance writ large across his face. "As usual there is never anything on the premises by the time we get there."

He took a long drink of his ale, wiping his mouth on the back of his hand. He turned back to Captain Steele and his other companion, another revenue man, as experienced and long-serving as Jim. Tom Evans nodded in agreement with his colleague. "Aye," he sighed. "We've made many a wasted journey to the King's Head. The day after a smuggling run and already too late. Everything gone. Disappeared!" He shook his head. "We know it goes there, we have informers and people watching the inn but we have searched and never found a thing."

Captain Steele leaned back in his seat, appearing for all the world to be at his ease, relaxed. Only his two companions recognised by the tightening of his knuckles on the hilt of his sword that he was alert and poised and ready for anything. They had heard stories about their new Commander, his history in the navy, tales of his adventures in the recent wars. Not yet thirty years old, his exploits and bravery were well known to them – this posting supposedly a reward for past endeavours. A respite against the horrors of war, of experiences the two older men could only wonder about and be thankful they had not been involved in. The new cutter, the sleek and fast Princess Charlotte, was their best chance yet to actually catch the smugglers in action, apprehend the villains as they landed their illicit cargoes along the Northumbrian coast. His commanders in the Royal Navy might have thought this posting a reward for one of their youngest Captains, the two experienced customs officers knew from experience that it was far from being the easy redeployment their new Captain might have wished for.

Steele himself surveyed the scene before him with a wary eye. Quietly pleased that this posting was not quite the sinecure he dreaded. He had survived some of the worst battles since Trafalgar but he was not ready, as he argued so vehemently with his Admiral, to go into semi-retirement.

"Come, gentlemen!" he said suddenly, swallowing the last of his ale. With a swift movement, he got to his feet and walked directly over to the two men by the fire.

"Captain Vincent, I presume?" he said as he reached them.

The whole taproom fell silent. The two men put their drinks down and turned to face Captain Steele. Then one of them stood to face the younger man. He was half a head taller than Steele, his hair was as dark and his eyes a deeper blue. The similarity ended there.

"And you are?" His voice was cold, a deeply timbered even tone.

"Your Nemesis, Captain," Steele replied. A slight, quirky grin lifted the corners of his mouth. "I am sure we will meet again soon." He bowed slightly and turned away, striding towards the door, his two companions following behind, worried at their impetuous young Captain's unexpected outburst.

Several of the men seated around the taproom got to their feet and made to follow the three men. A hand raised by the tall man beside the fire halted them in their tracks. A shake of the head and the men all returned to their seats.

A wry smile touched the lips of the man as he regained his seat beside Will Stewart.

"Arrogant young pup!" Will Stewart said, his face like thunder, his brows creased.

Luke Vincent lifted a glass of brandy to his lips and drank it down. "Easy, Will," he said softly. "He is young and foolish." He smiled. "As we all were at one time." His eyes strayed to the door, swinging shut behind the departing trio. A fleeting thought crossed his mind that the young man who just left could have been himself a few years ago. He was not so much older than the young Captain, but his life had taken a sharp turn away from the Navy after Trafalgar and his loyalty lay with no King now. His loyalty remained firmly with his ship, his men and himself and making as much money as possible in order to secure a comfortable retirement in the not so distant future. A shadow crossed Luke's handsome face. He had no love for his homeland; he had not been treated well after Trafalgar and felt no loyalty to England. He knew his days were numbered – he would give up the free trading soon – he knew that he could not outrun the Revenue men forever and plans were already set in motion for his future. He would give up soon, he told himself. Then he smiled to himself again, staring at the closed door between himself and the departing Captain. Soon. He promised himself. But not yet, you arrogant boy, not yet!

CHAPTER THREE

Mr Blackridge arrived at the Waverley town house promptly at eleven o'clock. Tall and thin, a pair of pince-nez perched upon his narrow nose. His shoulders were stooped and his attire was entirely black apart from the white linen cravat about his neck. His appearance struck Charis most forcibly of that of a vulture and she disliked him on sight. She disliked even more the obsequious manner in which he greeted Lady Henrietta, bowing over her hand and calling her a "dear lady" as he offered her his sincere condolences upon the death of her beloved husband.

Uncle Frederick frowned as he was introduced to the lawyer. He, like Charis, wondered why the family solicitor Mr Kielder was not in attendance and he resolved to investigate the matter further once these proceedings were over.

They took their seats in the library, Mr Blackridge behind her father's elegant old oak desk, the three of them facing him.

Charis felt unaccountably nervous and she shifted her seat slightly closer to Frederick. He smiled at her reassuringly and patted her hands, clenched together in her lap.

Mr Blackridge opened a large vellum envelope and took out a sheet of paper that he spread out over the desk.

"This is the Last Will and Testament of Sir Anthony Percival Waverley, lately of Curzon Street, Lord of the Manor of the Waverley Estate in North Yorkshire and Baron of Pickering and District," he intoned in his dry, rather reedy voice.

He looked over the top of his spectacles, observing the gathered company.

"Sir Anthony visited me in February of this year," he continued, "as he was desirous of making some alterations to his Will and he had some – concerns – with the dealings of his former lawyer, Mr – er – Kielder, I believe?"

Frederick and Charis exchanged a startled glance. "Mr Kielder has always served this family most honestly and punctiliously," Frederick protested.

Mr Blackridge shrugged bony shoulders. "That is as may be," he continued, "but Sir Anthony's doubts were genuine and he asked me to draw up a new Will."

Frederick glared at the lawyer; he obviously did not like the man seated before them in his brother's chair, behind his brother's desk.

"Get on with it then!" he ordered.

Mr Blackridge cleared his dry, raspy throat and began reading.

They listened in stunned silence. Stunned, that is, except Henrietta who remained stony-faced throughout and did not smile once.

Apart from a few legacies to old friends, retainers and servants, the estate and income thereof being entailed passed entirely to his brother Frederick and the rest of his homes and fortune, left to his wife, Henrietta. His daughter Charis was to remain in the care of his beloved Henrietta until she reached the age of twenty-five or such a time as she may marry, when she was to be given the sum of twenty thousand pounds and an annual income of three thousand pounds per year. Should Henrietta remarry then his fortune was to be passed to Charis. However, if Charis pre-deceased Henrietta then the fortune would remain with the widow.

Charis stared in disbelief at her stepmother. Henrietta's cold smile lifted the corners of her mouth.

"You can be assured, my dearest stepdaughter," she said softly, "I will respect your dear papa's wishes to the letter. I will look after you and you may remain living with me until such a time as you marry and have no fear that I will ever leave you – I would never dream of sullying the memory of my darling Anthony by ever remarrying."

Charis turned back to the lawyer, struggling to keep her voice from becoming hysterical.

"Did my father leave me nothing?" she demanded.

"You are to remain in the care of your stepmother until you reach the age of twenty-five or until you marry. Lady Henrietta is to have charge of you. She will decide what allowance you will be given and where you live." Mr Blackridge looked up from his perusal of the document before him. "I think apart from a few bequests to his nieces and nephews – your children, Sir Frederick, I believe – that completes the formalities."

Frederick's cheeks became redder as the lawyer continued speaking. At the end of the reading, his normally placid temper erupted.

"This is preposterous!" he exclaimed. "My brother would never have left Charis in such circumstances. Beholden to her stepmother for everything! What about pin money, her expenses, her clothing allowance? I know my brother was always very generous in these regards."

Mr Blackridge shifted uncomfortably in his seat. "I am sure Sir Anthony expected Lady Henrietta to continue with his wishes for his daughter's well-being," he said.

Henrietta's eyes were as cold as her smile. "But of course, Charis, I would not dream of depriving you of anything, my dear."

Frederick glared at her but as Mr Blackridge stood at that point, he was forced to return his attention to the lawyer. Mr Blackridge started to fold up the documents in front of him but was stopped by a gesture from Frederick.

"Please leave that here, sir," he said. "I would read this through once more with my own lawyer in attendance." His tone conveyed in no uncertain terms that he doubted the veracity of the Will.

Mr Blackridge bowed smoothly to the new Lord Waverley. "Of course, Your Lordship" he concurred. "I am sure, however, that you will find nothing untoward with his late lordship's wishes."

Frederick was not about to be placated. "I would like to verify that for myself," he said, and taking hold of the document, folded it back into its envelope before placing it inside his pocket.

Henrietta glared at her brother in law but she responded civilly.

"I know you will find everything to be completely above board, my dear Frederick. Now, may I offer you gentlemen refreshments?"

The lawyer murmured his regrets and with a bow to the gathered company he took his leave.

Charis remained sitting, her face almost as white as the envelope now safely in Frederick's possession.

Her world shifted beneath her feet. She could not believe her father could have left her in such a position and her eyes sought her uncle's for some reassurance.

"I will have this will checked, Henrietta," Frederick said, but Henrietta was unmoved.

"Check away, Frederick," she replied smoothly. "But it will do no good. I am Charis's legal guardian for the next four years or until she marries." Her gaze switched to her stepdaughter.

"I know of several would be suitors, Charis," she said. "Perhaps it is time you started to encourage one of them, my dear."

Eliciting no response from Charis, Henrietta continued. "In fact, I think I will arrange a few soirees where I can invite some suitable young men to meet you."

Charis was finally moved to reply. Her eyes, usually so warm and sparkling, flashed cold fire at her step mother

"Pray do not concern yourself with me, Henrietta," she said. "I have no wish to attend any parties for some time and in fact, I think I would prefer to join my Uncle and his family for a short holiday whilst I consider my future."

Frederick nodded in agreement. "A capital idea, my dear," he said. "Eliza and I would be delighted if you accompanied me home."

Henrietta raised an arched eyebrow. "But Frederick," she said smoothly, "as Charis' legal guardian you would need my permission for Charis to go with you – or anywhere else." She smiled once more, suddenly diverted by the way this morning had evolved. "I don't think I could bear for her to leave me just yet," she continued. "In fact, I think it would be better for all concerned if Charis were to remain with me for a few months before I allow her to go gadding about all over the country."

Charis stood, spots of red burning in her white cheeks. "You will not prevent me from going anywhere, I can assure you, Henrietta!"

Henrietta however, remained unmoved. "And how will you pay for your transport, my dear? Who will pay for your travel, your maid, your accommodation if you need to stay at a Hotel?"

Stunned, Charis was speechless.

"No," Henrietta continued. "I am afraid I could not permit you to waste the allowance you will be given on needless and unnecessary travelling!"

Frederick took a deep, steadying breath, calming himself before addressing his late brother's widow once more.

"Come now, Henrietta." His tone was placatory. "You must allow Charis reasonable visits to her family – she has always come to stay with us for a month every year – why should that stop now?"

Henrietta shrugged. "I may allow her to join you for her usual month at Christmas," she said. "But certainly not before then."

Charis and her uncle exchanged a long, silent look.

Uncle Frederick stepped forward and squeezed his niece's hands. "I will see Mr Kielder this afternoon, Charis," he promised. "I will see if this Will is legal and if there is any way we can overturn it."

Henrietta's laughter assailed their ears as she walked past them out of the study. "I fear you will find nothing untoward in the Will, Frederick – but please do not hesitate to come back and inform me if I am mistaken!"

Charis's hand trembled in her Uncle's firm grip. "Freddy," she whispered. "What am I to do? I cannot bear to stay here with that woman? It is she who should be leaving here!"

Frederick nodded, his brow furrowed, thinking hard. "I will leave you now Charis," he spoke quietly, urgently. "If indeed we can do nothing I will appeal to Henrietta's better nature to allow me to take you to Yorkshire."

Charis's shoulders drooped. "Henrietta has no better nature." She sighed bitterly.

Frederick placed his hands on his niece's shoulders. Bending slightly he kissed her forehead. "I will be back, my dear. And, if indeed there is nothing we can do, I will leave you with sufficient funds to enable you to travel in comfort to my home as soon as you can persuade Henrietta to let you leave her."

A tremulous smile lifted Charis's lips. "I will just have to be exceedingly objectionable to her, dear Uncle Freddy – she will be glad to be rid of me then, I dare say!"

She escorted her uncle to the front door and as she bade him farewell, she watched him walk away down the street in the cheerful summer sunshine.

She turned to look into the elegant interior of her home and for the first time in her life despite the heat of that bright day, she felt cold enough to shiver. Her warm and welcoming house suddenly seemed to have changed to one filled with hostility and dread.

Her feelings of foreboding had been well deserved but now she knew the worst of her father's plans for her future, she could not shake off that sense of real unease that had crept over her when Henrietta had smiled at her during the reading of the Will.

She could do nothing however until Frederick returned and with a heavy heart she went into the drawing room and sat down at her desk to continue writing to her father's friends and colleagues, thanking them for their concern and condolences. It occurred to her during the hours that followed that it should be Henrietta who undertook this particular task but she shrugged, realising Henrietta would too busy with plans for her own amusement to consider the more mundane role of running the household. That would surely still be left to Charis to organise and as she continued writing her letters in her fine hand, she tried not to let her grief and bitterness overwhelm her once more.

•

A month passed since that fateful day when the Will had been read and Charis had found out her father's wishes for her future.

She could not believe her father had been so deceived by his young and beautiful wife to such an extent that he would have altered his decisions so radically.

Mr Kielder and Frederick had been unable to find anything untoward with the late Lord Waverley's Will and it was, as Henrietta so confidently said, entirely legal. Mr Kielder expressed his concerns but with no idea why his esteemed friend and client Anthony Waverley decided to leave him and go to Mr Blackridge, he was at a loss to understand. A shocking business, he sighed, shocking indeed, but it was useless to try and contest it in any way. Had they done so it would have meant that Frederick would have to wait to take possession of his inheritance, leaving the estate and its tenants and other business concerns in a state of limbo. With much regret Freddy and Charis decided they could not do it, and Frederick returned to the North to take possession of his estates and settle into the role so recently vacated by his brother. Henrietta refused to allow Charis to accompany her uncle, conceding that she could visit for one month at Christmas, but not before.

As it was now only August, Charis viewed the rest of the year with some trepidation.

Henrietta wasted no time in earning the title of "The Merry Widow" in the short weeks after her husband's death.

Seen out with Sir Richard Hardy at every opportunity, although London remained sadly short of company during the heat of the summer, the gaming dens and less salubrious establishments were pleased to welcome the exceedingly rich and beautiful Lady Waverley.

Black mourning clothes were dismissed after four short weeks and Charis listened with growing despair at Henrietta's plans for a dinner party to be held in the Mayfair mansion. The guest list included none of Charis's old friends or any of her fathers'. They were all unknown to her and although some of the invitations were going to people she had heard of by reputation only, they were not the sort of people her father would have ever dreamed of introducing her to!

Henrietta had no such scruples.

"These are friends of myself and Sir Richard, Miss, plus Sir Richard has invited his son to attend," she told Charis. "I particularly want you to look after him."

Charis stared at her stepmother over her breakfast teacup. She swallowed down the retort demanding to know why Richard Hardy thought it appropriate to invite members of his family his cronies to her father's house. She knew Henrietta was in some kind of thrall to the man and witnessed on more than one occasion the propriety manner in which Richard spoke to her.

Charis was already dreading the evening ahead, coming so soon after the death of her father and scandalising those members of the Ton who still remained in London.

"Why?" she enquired. "I have no wish to attend this party, Henrietta. Pray do not ask me to be pleasant to people I would rather not meet."

Henrietta had managed to ignore her stepdaughter's caustic remarks for the past few weeks. Refusing point blank to go out with her, Charis remained quietly at home while Henrietta sought out those amusements still available in the capital.

"You will attend tonight, Charis, and I will brook no insolence from you!" she snapped. "I wish you to entertain Richard's son – the boy is pleasant enough. Besides," the widow smiled at Charis, "you may actually like him. He is extremely attractive."

Charis was immediately suspicious but, forced to attend the party that evening, she ignored Henrietta's instructions not to wear black and came down to the drawing room that evening wearing her black silk evening gown, simply embellished with velvet embroidery and black velvet ribbon trim.

Henrietta scowled at her stepdaughter but as the hour was late and the first of her evening's guests were at the door, there was no time to send Charis back upstairs to change.

Sir Richard Hardy was, as usual, the first of Henrietta's guests to arrive. His son accompanied him this evening and as Henrietta welcomed them, Charis curtsied politely to the young man. He was very handsome, however, with broad shoulders and narrow hips and as he bowed over her hand, he raised it to his lips.

"Miss Waverley," he said softly. "I have heard so much about you, it is a pleasure to finally meet you."

Charis regarded him coolly. "Thank you, Mr Hardy. Regretfully however I have heard nothing of you," she replied. "In fact, Sir Richard never actually mentioned he had a son."

Richard, listening to this conversation stepped in, slapping his son on the shoulder and smiling broadly at Charis.

"George has been rusticating, Miss Waverley!" he exclaimed. "He has been attending to some estate matters on my behalf."

George Hardy had a very winsome smile and Charis could imagine many a young lady being charmed by his engaging good looks.

"Indeed?" she replied. "Then we are very lucky to have you back with us this evening, Mr Hardy."

She did not see the look exchanged between Henrietta and Richard and the calculating expression on Richard's face.

The rest of the guests started to arrive and Charis was dismayed to find that out of the twenty or so people, most of them were men with only a handful of women amongst the company. The guests were certainly not the type of people Charis had ever entertained before in her father's house and she was aghast at the copious amount of alcohol consumed and the riotous nature of the dinner party. She was shocked by the language and manners of the guests, appalled as their behaviour became more outrageous as the evening drew on.

George Hardy was opposite her at the dinner table and she often found his eyes upon her, his amusement evident at the horrified expression on her face as two of the ladies decided to have a race around the table. Their skirts held up to afford freer movement, they were urged on by raucous cheering by some of the male guests. Henrietta, instead of calling her guests to order and returning some decorum to the activities silently watched the two ladies in their drunken endeavours to race. Charis glared at her stepmother who, intercepting the look, merely looked away and swallowed down more of the wine in her glass. The dining room at Waverley House had never seen such outrageous behaviour and Charis felt ashamed and sickened by the rowdy and unseemly display.

She longed to escape and leave Richard and Henrietta to their amusements but she remained totally motionless in her chair, horrified as the gentleman beside her started to pay attention to her.

He leaned close to her and filled her glass with ruby red wine, brushing her body with his arm as he reached across. She recoiled in her seat as he turned heavy-lidded eyes to her.

"Damn me, Madam." His voice was slightly slurred as he stared boldly at her. "If Henrietta wasn't right – you are a damned fine gal."

She glared at him. "My stepmother is very kind to say so," she said coldly.

"She said you were in need of a husband…" he continued, his eyes raking her slim figure, pausing to gaze directly at her partially covered breasts beneath the black lace.

"Did she indeed?" Charis wondered what else her stepmother had been saying about her.

He put the bottle of wine back down on the table and covered her hand with his own.

"She did," he said in what he obviously thought a conspiratorial whisper. "Said you were an heiress." He laughed suddenly, "but that the man who married you would need to school you – like a headstrong filly!"

Oblivious to Charis's look of disgust, her companion, a florid middle-aged man, winked at her. "I would love to be the man to take you in hand, m'dear…"

Charis threw her napkin on the table and pushed his hand away abruptly. Standing, she stepped away from the table but found her way blocked by George Hardy.

"Come, Miss Waverley," he said softly. "Allow me to escort you to the drawing room – the party is not to your liking, I can see."

She felt grateful for his words and accepted the support of

his arm as he bowed and led her out the room. Her cheeks were flushed and as they entered the drawing room, she pressed shaking hands to her face.

"How could she?" Charis was beyond being discreet. "How dare she turn my father's home into a – a bordello?"

She raged, hardly looking at her companion. Her pent-up feelings needing release, she walked away from him, pacing restlessly up and down the room.

"Who are these people?" she demanded. "How does Henrietta come to know such creatures?"

She suddenly realised that Mr Hardy watched her closely. He seated himself on one of the ornate sofas and crossed one impeccably clad leg over the other. One arm stretched out along the back of the chaise.

Her cheeks were red as she forced herself to stop and face him. "I apologise, Mr Hardy," she said. "I am being very rude – thank you for taking me out of there."

George stood and moved towards her. He was very tall and he took her hands in his, forcing her to look up into his eyes. "I could see how uncomfortable you were, Miss Waverley," he said.

"He said Henrietta had been saying I was in need of a husband…"

She was suddenly aware of how close he was and went to move away. He held her still and raised her hand to his lips once more.

"And are you?" he asked.

She felt unaccountably shy at being asked this question. She hesitated slightly before replying. "Well marriage would certainly be one solution to my current problem."

She gently pulled her hands from his and retreated to the seat he had recently vacated. She took a deep, steadying breath and sat down.

He raised an enquiring eyebrow and upon her nod, he seated himself beside her.

"How so, Miss Waverley?" he asked.

She frowned, not sure how much she could reveal to him.

Indeed, how much did he actually know about her straitened circumstances?

"My late father's wishes were that I remain with Lady Henrietta until I married or until I reached the age of five and twenty," she began, hesitantly.

George said nothing, waiting for her to continue.

"It may be no surprise to you, sir," she said, "but my stepmother and I have a – difficult – relationship."

She paused but as he remained silent, she carried on. "I am still in mourning for my father and want nothing more than to be allowed to leave here but unfortunately Henrietta will not allow it. "

She looked away from him, staring up at the portrait of her father above the fireplace.

"It seems my only alternative would be to marry to enable me to set up my own home and establishment."

"Are there no suitors waiting in the wings, Miss Waverley?" he asked.

She shook her head, her cheeks becoming rosy once again, with embarrassment this time, rather than temper.

"I was pursued by fortune hunters when my father was alive," she admitted. "And unfortunately I did not meet any other gentlemen whom I was remotely interested in marrying."

George considered her words carefully, a slight frown between his eyes.

"It is a shame I did not know you then, Miss Waverley," he said quietly. "Although," his sudden smile disarmed her, "you would probably have dismissed me, also, as a fortune hunter!"

She seemed surprised. "Your father does not strike me as being in any way impoverished, Mr Hardy."

His smile faded. "He is not," he replied. "However I very foolishly invested heavily in a business venture that failed quite spectacularly. I have been forced to remain at home in Devon for the last year to recover my fortunes. Hence my 'rusticating' as my father would have it!"

Her sympathies were quickly aroused. "I am sorry to hear it," she said.

He shook his head slightly. "My father was correct in sending me away," he admitted. "I am now happily solvent once more and ready to leave business to people with more sense than myself!"

She smiled at his easy, humorous manner. She could not recall ever having such a comfortable conversation with a member of the opposite sex. He was a charming companion and it was with regret that she looked up as the clock struck the hour of ten.

"I pray you will excuse me, sir," she said. "I do not intend returning to Henrietta's party. Would you mind telling her I have the headache and have retired?"

"Are you also depriving me of the only sensible company I have enjoyed for some time?" he quizzed her, not unkindly.

"I am sorry to leave you," she replied. "However, it is quite unseemly of me to remain here alone with you."

He laughed softly and his eyes sparkled. "Ah – of course – how remiss of me to keep you here with no chaperone!"

They stood and he once again possessed himself of her hand.

"Perhaps you would allow me to call on you again, Miss Waverley?" he asked.

She was silent as he lifted her hand to his lips once again. He held her gaze and she felt a strange fluttering in her stomach as he stared into her eyes.

"I – I would be pleased to see you, Mr Hardy," she replied hesitantly.

He seemed nothing like his father.

She disliked Sir Richard on sight, taking exception to the possessive manner in which his lecherous gaze lingered on Lady Henrietta and the way he had practically moved into her father's home. She had always been uncomfortable in his company and wondered how Henrietta could allow the man such control over her. She often intercepted a look, a gesture, a word, from Richard to her stepmother that she could only describe as being over familiar. He had some kind of influence over Henrietta as annoying as it was disturbing. She could hardly believe this attractive, amusing young man was related to him, let alone be his son!

"I will pay a very correct morning visit tomorrow." His voice a low, velvet murmur. "And perhaps Lady Henrietta will allow me to invite you to accompany me on a drive?"

His lips were soft on the back of her hand and she found herself looking at them, wondering for the first time in her life, what they would feel like pressing on her lips.

"I am sure she would raise no objection," she replied, banishing such wanton thoughts from her mind.

He stepped away from her but kept hold of her hand, threading her arm through his to escort her out of the room to the bottom of the stairs. He bowed most politely as she moved away from him and walked up to her room. She turned once as she reached the top of the stairs and saw him standing still in the hallway, looking up at her, a thoughtful expression on his face. He smiled up at her and nodded his head as she walked along to her bedroom door and slipped silently inside.

CHAPTER FOUR

The engagement of Charis Waverley and George Hardy was eagerly awaited by not only their respective families, but also expectantly by those members of fashionable London who could not remember Miss Waverley ever being so taken with any other gentlemen before now.

Certainly, George appeared to be genuinely serious in his courtship of Miss Waverley. From gentle drives through the London parks, to genteel parties at those respectable establishments her stepmother both scorned and was never invited to. Chaperoned by her elderly Aunt Emily, pressed back into service as a favour, Charis remained reluctant to attend any of the more extravagant events now returning to London as a pre-cursor to the next Royal Season. However, she went with Emily and George to Almack's where London Society watched and waited for the anticipated engagement.

George was nothing like his father, which as far as Charis was concerned, could only be a good thing. Charming, punctiliously polite, witty and amusing and he even managed to make her see the funny side of her situation with Henrietta!

She did not know if she was in love with him exactly, but he managed to make every other young man of her acquaintance seem impossibly immature and callow. He knew everyone in fashionable circles, and was exclaimed over by several society matrons as a welcome return after his year spent in the country.

Henrietta was strangely silent about Charis's interest in the young man, except to give permission for George to court her young stepdaughter. She kept out of the way and allowed Charis to continue unhindered.

That unnaturally hot August gave way to a cooler September and as the month progressed towards autumn, Charis accepted George's invitation to attend a ball at the home of the Duchess of Devonshire. It was the first major event Charis had been persuaded to attend since the death of her father and she quietly put away her mourning clothes in favour of a new gown not yet worn.

She looked enchanting as George arrived to escort her Aunt and herself to the ball. His fulsome compliments were sincere enough and he pressed a kiss onto the back of her satin-clad hand, exclaiming over her changed appearance.

She wore a rose-pink gown, trimmed with sparkling crystals that shimmered as she moved. Matching pink velvet ribbons were threaded through her hair and brought out the red lights in the thick brown curls tumbling over one shoulder. She carried a small ivory fan and a pink reticule. George's compliments brought a glow to her cheeks as he bowed over her hand.

Emily was utterly smitten by the charming young man and looked on fondly as her niece took his arm as he led them both out to the waiting carriage.

Sir Richard and Lady Henrietta were seated together in her drawing room as they watched the small party leaving. Henrietta's brows were drawn together in a frown as the front door closed behind her stepdaughter.

"Will he ask her tonight?" she asked Richard.

Richard smiled back at her. He seemed very comfortable as he relaxed in the padded armchair that once belonged to Sir Anthony. "I think so," he replied. "They seem very suited, do you not think?"

Henrietta's scornful glance raked his languid figure. "I certainly hope Charis thinks so!" she snapped. "He is the first young man she has ever shown any interest in so one can only hope she does the sensible thing."

"I am sure George will be very persuasive…" Richard remarked, sipping at a glass of red wine before sitting.

"I sincerely hope so," Henrietta responded and walked

over to the window to watch the carriage drive away from the house.

"Your stepdaughter has a considerable fortune, my love," Richard went on smoothly. "George will not let a prize like her slip through his fingers!"

Henrietta took a deep breath and a smile lifted her lips. "Of course he will not," she agreed. Turning, she held her hand out towards Richard and he stood at once, to step over towards her and taking it, pulled her into his arms.

"My son is no fool," he murmured against her lips. "He will not let me down."

•

Charis waltzed with George in the magnificent opulent surroundings of the Devonshire's ballroom. The room was filled with those members of Society seeking the entertainment still on offer in London, whilst most of their acquaintances retired from a summer in Brighton to their country estates for the rest of the winter season.

It was a tolerable crowd, and whilst not officially a 'crush' there were enough people present to please the Duchess.

Charis could not remember when she enjoyed such occasions more. The illness and subsequent death of her father prevented her from appearing much in Society that year, but with an attentive George Hardy escorting her to such pleasant and above all, respectable soirees she allowed herself to relax and mix with some of her old acquaintances and friends of her father.

George was aware that Miss Waverley was not to be rushed in the matters of romance. His father and Lady Henrietta might have planned his re-appearance in London and introduction to Charis but he knew she would not allow him any of the liberties he was used to taking with other, less scrupulous members of her sex.

George had led a rather chequered life before being forced to reside on his country estates for the last year. His father's threat of disinheriting him made him retire for the year and this sudden, unexpected summons back to the capital delighted him.

His arm encircled Charis's waist and, taking her small hand in his own, they danced together to the strains of the latest waltz music.

"Miss Waverley, I understand from my father that you are planning on deserting us in the not too distant future," he said as they spun around the ballroom.

"Not until December, Mr Hardy," she replied. "It is my custom to stay with my uncle in York for the Christmas season."

"Will Lady Henrietta be accompanying you?" he enquired.

She shook her head, smiling up at his handsome face rather than frowning at the mention of Henrietta's name.

"No. I think my stepmama prefers to remain in London."

He affected a sigh. "Ah, so you do intend to deprive me of your company for a whole month?"

"I am afraid so. I am sure there are plenty of distractions in London to keep you amused whilst I am absent," she replied.

He glanced around the room. There were several young married ladies of his acquaintance who, in the past, had been very welcome distractions. Even now they smiled coquettishly at him, the invitations in their eyes and demeanour only too evident. He shook his head, however.

"I regret to say that those 'distractions' which I would have enjoyed in the past no longer hold the same interest."

He whirled her around to the quickening tempo of the music. He held her imperceptibly tighter in his arms. Looking up into his twinkling brown eyes, she caught her breath.

"In fact, Miss Waverley, I regret to advise you that it is entirely your fault that my old distractions have no further appeal to me!"

She laughed at his words. She was getting used to his flirtatious manner and whilst part of her responded to his banter and his compliments, she could not help but hold a piece of herself back. She heard no gossip about the young man and was inclined to believe his story of a poor business deal forcing him to live quietly for the last year. In fact, she rather admired his dedication to recover his fortunes in this manner. It spoke of a man of character in her opinion.

The dance ended and he escorted her back to her aunt Emily, who even now happily gossiped with her old friends.

"Miss Waverley," he spoke quietly to her, urgently. "Charis…" He took hold of her hand and led her to a quiet window where heavy curtains were held back, revealing the landscaped gardens lit up by flaming torches.

They sat together on the window seat.

He turned to her and kept hold of her hand.

"Charis, would you allow me to speak to Lady Henrietta?"

For such a charming, forthright man – he suddenly seemed very reserved, diffident.

Charis caught her breath. "Why?" she asked.

He smiled. "Is it not obvious? I wish to have permission to marry you, my dear." He paused, taking in the surprised expression on her face.

"Marry me?" she whispered.

He stared down into her eyes, his expression earnest, and steady. "I have never met anyone like you before, Charis," he said softly. "You have truly enchanted me."

"But we hardly know each other…"

George nodded, still keeping her hand in between his own. "I know, and I have no intention of rushing you into anything, my dear," he said gently. "You are still getting over the death of your father and I would never hurry you but I think we are very well suited and you would make me the happiest man in the world if you would agree to marry me."

Charis gazed up into his eyes, totally mesmerised by the expression she saw there.

He raised her hand to his lips and pressed a kiss on it. "May I speak to your stepmother?"

She could not speak, bewildered by his words, but a part of her realised she had been expecting him to make his intentions known.

"I will certainly consider it…" she said softly.

In response, he stood and drew her to her feet. He did not give her chance or time to object. Charis found herself on the terrace, outside the French doors, overlooking the garden. The evening had cooled, the stars were out and the terrace was deserted. He stopped at the balustrade and turned her to face him. He placed his hands gently on her shoulders and slowly, carefully, he lowered his head and kissed her lips.

She stiffened, unsure, unable to move. He pulled her firmly into his arms, his kiss deepening. She did not know what to do, how to respond. His kiss awoke no hidden passion within her, yet it was pleasant enough and it did not alarm her.

He lifted his lips and drew away slightly from her. Her cheeks were flushed and her lips were rosy following his kiss.

His eyes glittered in the darkness and she smiled hesitantly at him.

"I will call on your stepmother tomorrow," he said and held out his arm to escort her back into the ballroom.

He took her back to her Aunt and left her while he went to secure fresh drinks for them. Returning, he flirted outrageously with Emily and made them both laugh before dancing once again with Charis and finally, when the evening drew to a close, he escorted them both back to the house.

Sir Richard was still in the drawing room with Henrietta as they returned. Emily was not fond of Lady Henrietta and stayed only as a favour to Charis. She waited until Charis said her goodnights to them before she also bade them a stiff, formal goodnight and accompanied her niece upstairs to their rooms.

George watched her leave, going upstairs with her Aunt after saying a shy goodnight to him. She had never felt awkward in his presence before, his sudden proposal had slightly unnerved her. She was still unsure what her answer would be and she decided she must think very carefully about this unexpected offer.

He went into the drawing room. His eyes roamed the room with that same gleam in his eyes reflected in Sir Richard's and went over to his hostess. He bowed over her hand, taking in with an appreciative eye the low-cut gown revealing rather more of her shapely bosom than was either fashionable or decent.

"Lady Henrietta," he murmured, intercepting a particularly sharp glance from his father. "I have the honour to request your permission to marry Miss Waverley."

A frown marred Henrietta's brow. "Has she accepted you, George?" she asked.

George turned away and walked across to the occasional table. As his father had done before him, he helped himself to a glass of brandy.

"Not exactly," he said softly. "But she will." He swallowed a mouthful of the spirit and grinned over to his father. "She is a bit too prim and proper for my normal taste," he drawled. He held up his brandy glass and took another sip. His voice hardened. "Far too prudish – for someone so pretty the girl is the most priggish creature I have ever met in my life!"

Richard, meanwhile laughed delightedly. "I am glad someone agrees with me!" He held out is own glass and George obligingly refilled it. "For God's sake, marry the girl and get her out of our way."

"What will you do, George?" Henrietta asked. "What if she hears some of the more lurid rumours about you and she turns you down?"

George appeared unconcerned with the question. He actually smiled. A slow cruel smile that sent a shiver down Henrietta's spine. "If she turns me down, I will abduct her. She will have to marry me once her reputation is ruined. I think a week in my company should be enough to persuade her. She would not dare to show her face in polite society again with the possibility of being pregnant!"

George seated himself opposite them, crossing his legs, relaxing and sipping his drink.

"In the meantime, I will carry on wooing the very proper Miss Waverley. I will convince her to marry me before Christmas and we will honeymoon in Devon. With a bit of luck that will be the last you, I or London, will ever see of her."

"Very well," Henrietta said softly. "As long as she is kept in Devon that is all I ask."

George smiled again. "The prospect of three thousand pounds a year is extremely tempting..." He laughed suddenly. "Until death do us part of course?"

"George!" Henrietta sounded genuinely shocked.

Richard and George exchanged an amused glance. "Now Henrietta my dear." Richard's voice was suddenly hard, his eyes narrowed as he surveyed the widow. "Do not worry your pretty little head about the details." He swallowed his drink in one gulp. "Just be reassured that you will never see her again and within a year the rest of her fortune will be legally yours."

Henrietta stood then, facing Richard, her eyes flashing with anger. "Richard, we have enough money. Anthony's fortune will suffice for many years. We do not have to resort to murder for the rest!"

Richard's hand took hers in a vice-like grip, squeezing it mercilessly. She bit her lip to prevent a sound from escaping.

"I said don't worry, Henrietta." He spoke quietly but the menace behind his words icily evident. "One day very soon you will have Anthony's entire fortune."

Henrietta pulled her hand out of his and rubbed it before turning away and, walking towards the table containing the drinks, she poured herself a drink with hands that shook slightly. She swallowed the brandy and turned back to face the two men.

"I have played my part, Richard. I married the man you chose for me and I was a good and faithful wife to Anthony. I dislike the chit but I will not condone her murder." Her voice was cold and she returned to her seat.

George raised his glass to her. "Please don't fret any further, my dearest stepmama to be. Once we are married, Charis and I will leave London and you don't have to consider her feelings ever again. An agreement is an agreement and I assure you the twenty thousand pounds dowry will be quite sufficient to ease the sorrow of a grieving bridegroom." George raised his glass to the ceiling. "A toast – to my future bride, the lovely Charis Waverley!"

•

Charis pressed shaking hands across her mouth to prevent herself from uttering a sound as she slumped against the wall outside the drawing room door.

The door had been open only a crack but their voices had carried through the silence of the house and she had heard every word.

She had only come back downstairs to retrieve a book from the library when she heard George's voice. Prim, proper and priggish was bad enough – she knew her natural reserve could be mistaken for aloofness in some people but he carried on and the rest of the conversation left her reeling with shock and horror.

They could not be serious. Surely she must be mistaken – but then she recalled the sheer venom in Richard's voice and the cold, calculated sneer so obvious in George's and she felt something inside her shrivel and die at the thought that she had been seriously considering his offer of marriage.

She heard movement inside the room and realised George and his father were moving, saying their farewells to Henrietta. Clearly Henrietta could not ask Richard to stay while Emily resided with them and their trysts had to be curtailed until Emily and Charis were both out of the house.

Stumbling, with legs that did not want to move, she forced herself away from the support of the wall and ran to the stairs. She fled up them just as the drawing room doors opened and she hid in the shadows at the top of the stairs, watching the two men taking their leave.

Henrietta closed the door behind them and leaned back on it, her head bowed momentarily. Charis heard Henrietta take a deep, shuddering breath as she pushed herself off the wall and started walking towards the stairs.

Charis moved as silently as she could towards her bedroom

and slipped inside as Henrietta reached the first landing. Charis shut the door tightly behind her and turned the key in the lock. She wanted no disturbance this evening, no interruptions as she moved to the bed and slumped down, her mind in turmoil, her brain searching for answers to what she could do to get out of the situation she now found herself in.

She stared sightlessly out of the window at the street, deserted now and with no sign of the perfidious Hardy father and son. Her mind raced, desperately trying to think, going round in circles. If she accepted his marriage proposal, she would be taken to Devon and never seen nor heard of again. If she refused she would be abducted by the black-hearted villain and forced to marry him. Her head went up and a flash of anger lit up her eyes at the thought. Charis came to the awful realisation that no matter what happened, marry George or not, Henrietta and Richard had been plotting to rid themselves of her. She remembered Henrietta's words, even her stepmother objected to the plot to murder her. Her companions, however, had no such scruples! Her fortune would pass to Henrietta if she died before the age of five and twenty and with four years left to go obviously they were in a hurry!

Her father's Will had been quite specific – married or not, if Charis died, Henrietta would retain control of all Sir Anthony's wealth, homes and assets. Charis's husband would receive a token amount but in the meantime, Henrietta became one of the wealthiest women in London. If her ears had not deceived her, Richard seemed to have some hold over her stepmother and despite Henrietta's objections, Charis realised Henrietta was powerless when it came to protecting her from Richard Hardy.

As she stared out at the dark London Street, a hardness crept over her face. So far, since her father had met Henrietta she had experienced every emotion from grief and disappointment to anger. Never before had she been gripped with such an ice cold rage that filled her now. She moved away from the window and paced the room. Her first instinct was to pack a bag and run, steal away in the middle of the night to the safety of her Uncle's home. However, having nothing in the way of funds prevented that course of action and she was forced to reconsider, her brain a whirl of restless activity.

Finally, almost two hours later, she went to bed. An idea came to her and, as she lay there, she went over in her mind the ways and means available to her to remove herself from her once beloved home as swiftly and as safely as possible.

•

Henrietta looked up in surprise as Emily and Charis entered the breakfast salon the following morning dressed in day dresses covered with jackets, wearing bonnets and walking boots.

"Are you going out, my dears?" she asked.

Emily glared at her cousin's widow but, carefully prepared by Charis, she merely sniffed.

"I need to return to my own home, Henrietta," she said coldly. "I will be back later, but in the meantime, I wish Charis to accompany me."

Henrietta smiled. "But Charis is expecting a visitor shortly," she objected.

"Nonsense!" Emily's voice was sharp. "We have never received visitors at breakfast, Henrietta, and if this is some new-fangled fashion to entertain at this hour, I am not convinced it is acceptable."

She turned to leave and nodding to Henrietta took Charis's arm.

"We will be back this evening. Tell Cook we will be eating at home, we have no social engagements to speak of so I believe a night at home is overdue."

Henrietta frowned. "You may have no engagements, Emily, but Charis and I have been invited to the theatre."

Emily's withering look at Henrietta was enough to silence the widow.

"You have asked me to chaperone my niece, Henrietta. If I do not think it is good manners to go out at every opportunity during this sadly unfashionable time of year, then I think it would do us no harm to remain at home occasionally."

Henrietta found herself in a battle of wills with the formidable old lady.

"Charis!" Emily turned to her niece. "Do you wish to go out or remain at home with me this evening?"

Charis lowered her head, hoping the rose colour flooding her cheeks would be seen by Henrietta as embarrassment instead of the amusement that suddenly assailed her.

"I think it best we remain at home, Aunt Emily," she whispered, and shrugged helplessly at Henrietta.

Before Henrietta could gather her wits, the two ladies swept out of the room and were out of the house in a matter of moments.

Charis smiled at her Aunt and squeezed her arm. "Thank you," she whispered as they made their way into the waiting carriage, ordered as soon as Charis had risen that morning.

They did not, as they told Henrietta, go to Emily's small London residence in nearby Chelsea. Instead, after a sharp order from Emily, their driver trotted the horse in the direction of the streets of the City of London.

An hour later the two ladies were seated before Mr Kielder, explaining the predicament Charis now found herself in.

"Much as I would like to keep Charis with me at my home," Aunt Emily said, "I fear it would do no good. She needs to get as far away from London as possible, and Chelsea is no distance for Henrietta and her cronies."

She sighed and squeezed her niece's hand as she continued. "I have no fortune to give her to allow her to travel abroad all I can do is give her a small allowance. Her Uncle Frederick is obviously the person to whom we should apply for help but we cannot wait long enough for him to transfer funds to her. We need some money now to enable her to travel immediately."

Mr Kielder nodded his head. "I quite understand, Mrs Andrews." He paused, regarding the ladies above his half-moon glasses. He appeared to be deep in thought. "However, this matter does seem extremely – fantastical." He seemed to be searching for the right words to say.

"Mr Kielder," Charis interrupted him, her voice low and urgent, and her eyes beseeching him to believe her. "I assure you I am not exaggerating. I fear for my life should I stay in London!"

Mr Kielder paused in his ruminations to smile kindly at the young lady opposite him.

"We also do not want to wait for Sir Frederick to come dashing down here to rescue you, Miss Waverley!" he continued pensively. "What I propose to do in these circumstances is this…" He had known Charis since she was a child and it grieved him greatly to see her treated so unfairly in the matter of his old friend's final Will. A decision no doubt influenced by the new Lady Waverley, now an extremely rich widow with a growing unsavoury reputation. He could not blame Charis for wanting to leave her influence as soon as possible.

"I will advance you sufficient funds to enable you to leave London," he said slowly. "I will write directly to Sir Frederick for reimbursement so that is not going to prove a problem. He will just be happy to have you with him, safe and sound."

Charis and her Aunt exchanged a glance. "I'm afraid I do not intend to go to my Uncle's house just yet," Charis said hesitantly.

"Indeed?" Mr Kielder raised an eyebrow.

Charis shook her head. "It is the most obvious place they will think to find me," she explained. "I intend to go elsewhere for a few months first to give myself time to consider my future properly and give Frederick time to arrange for my guardianship. Once you and he have made the necessary legal arrangements, I will go to him and remain there until I reach the age of twenty-five."

"But where will you go in the meantime, Miss Waverley?" Mr Kielder asked.

"I have a sister," Emily interjected. "Her name is Alice Embleton and she is somewhat of an eccentric."

"Indeed?" Mr Kielder repeated. "And where might this eccentric Mrs Embleton reside?"

Emily raised an enquiring eyebrow at her young charge but Charis nodded. They were reluctant to confide in anyone as to Charis's whereabouts, but if they could trust no one else, they knew they could trust Mr Kielder.

"She lives," Emily replied, frowning slightly as she recounted her sister's circumstances, "in a large, dilapidated property on the North Yorkshire coast. She has very little money and no family except myself, but she manages surprisingly well enough in her own way. We thought Charis could go to her as a companion. She is elderly now, and it would not be seen as unusual for a lady of her age to have a young lady to live with her. She only has a couple of old family servants so there would be no gossip about Charis suddenly turning up."

"How will you affect an introduction?" Mr Kielder enquired.

"I will write to my sister and Charis can deliver it in person," Emily said.

Mr Kielder seemed shocked. "Charis cannot travel all that way alone!" he protested.

Charis lifted a hand to prevent Emily from responding. Emily bridled immediately but remained silent.

"I shall travel on the Mail," she said quietly. "I have no fear of travelling alone and the Mail is the safest mode of transport available." She smiled at them both.

Mr Kielder shook his head. "No, no, my dear. If I do nothing else for you, please allow me to arrange transport for you. It will take a day or two but if you return here on Monday morning, I will have a carriage waiting, sufficient funds to allow you to travel in comfort and will arrange accommodation for you on your journey."

Monday remained three days away. Her eyes clouded over slightly as she considered the next few days. Then, taking a deep breath, she nodded. She rose and Emily stood with her. Charis held her hand out towards the old man, who shook it.

"Thank you, Mr Kielder," she said quietly. "I will return on Monday and take up your kind offer of transport."

The young lady before him seemed to have grown in maturity

since the last time he had seen her and Mr Kielder grasped her hand. "Until Monday, my dear," he replied. As the two ladies left his offices, the old gentleman sent for his clerk. With an energy and determination belying his age and infirmity he set about making the arrangements to ensure Charis Waverley's safe removal from London.

As they continued on their way to Chelsea, Charis and Emily discussed the immediate future. Emily frowned as she considered the thought the next three days were going to be the longest in their lives before Charis could leave.

Charis meanwhile smiled kindly at her Aunt. "It is such a shame you are unwell, Aunt Emily!" she said.

"Unwell? Nonsense, my dear, I am perfectly well!"

"No, dear Aunt, I fear you have contracted quite the bad cold. You cannot possibly return to Curzon Street and I, well, unfortunately, I must remain with you to nurse you!"

"Henrietta will be furious!" Emily chuckled.

"Henrietta may visit if she is so inclined!" Charis replied, well aware her stepmother had an aversion to illness and would never put herself anywhere near any possible danger.

"We will send for our maids and your clothes." Emily was thoughtful. "But you will not be able to take as much as you need to Alice's."

Charis squeezed her Aunt's hands. "I will not need much." She smiled. "I have no intention of socialising whilst at your sister's home! Besides which…" She smiled as she opened her small reticule to show Emily a carefully wrapped handkerchief containing several brooches, rings, earrings and one or two necklaces. "I think these might come in useful should the need arise for extra funds!"

Emily returned the smile and nodded, patting Charis's hand. "Good idea, my dear. However, as far as clothing is concerned, I think just a few decent hard wearing day dresses will have to do, I'm afraid!"

The two ladies gazed at each other in the gently rocking carriage. "I will miss you, dear Charis," Emily said softly.

Charis felt tears sparkling in her eyes. "And I you, dearest Aunt." She swallowed a suddenly large lump that appeared in her throat.

She looked out of the carriage at the fine old houses and the busy streets. She was going to miss Emily, her home and her life here in London.

However, she knew she had to leave. Her very life was in danger and tears spilled down her face as she thought of George. She genuinely had believed George cared for her – how could she have been so blind, so foolish? George obviously was ruthless enough to do his father's bidding for the very large price of a dowry and just charming enough to get away with it.

She wiped her eyes and sniffed prosaically. Turning to her Aunt, she squeezed her hands again.

"I can do this Emily," she whispered. "With your help and, of course, dear Mr Kielder – I will get well out of the reach of those who mean me harm!"

"Henrietta will be furious!" Emily said with some amusement and Charis's tears turned to laughter at the expression on her Aunt's face.

"I think I have more to fear from George Hardy," Charis said softly, remembering the malice she heard in his voice as he discussed her future with his father. Tears filled her eyes once more as she recalled his plans for her, abduction, forced marriage and pregnancy were bad enough should she have turned his proposal down but murder? She had not thought him so cruel. She had been genuinely surprised hearing Henrietta's horrified objections, but despite her new wealth and position, Charis realised Henrietta was as powerless against the two men as she was herself. Her brows knitted together as she wondered what hold Richard had over Henrietta. She knew Richard introduced her father to Henrietta, but as her father never said any more than he had met her at a private social event, she knew no more details.

She sighed and wiped her eyes once more. Emily reached over and took Charis's hand.

"You will be safe, my dear," she said softly. "We will get you away from them, and you will be safe."

Charis nodded and a tremulous smile lifted her lips. "I know, thank you, Aunt Emily," she replied. "I just wonder now what might await me in the North."

"Friends, my dear, and a quiet and secluded refuge," Emily replied. "A veritable haven of peace and serenity, if a little draughty, I believe!"

Emily chuckled softly, and Charis wiping the last of the sparkling tears from her eyes joined in with the older ladies laughter as they proceeded to the comfort and warmth of Emily's cosy home in the heart of unfashionable Chelsea.

CHAPTER FIVE

Clouds were starting to scud across the clear night sky, obscuring the stars and hiding the light of the moon. The winds had been favourable so far and the ship lying to anchor in the secluded cove had furled their sails, wanting to attract no unwanted attention as the business of the night was carried out.

Small cobles, manned by four strong sailors in each, shuttled backwards and forward between ship and shore, unloading the cargo, handing it over to the lines of men on the beach who awaited their bounty. The run tonight had been more than successful. A hold full of brandy, gin, tea, and bales of silk had been loaded in the Dutch port of Rotterdam, and was now being unloaded off the wild Northumberland coast. The Captain of the ship and the leader of the gang of smugglers were even now exchanging cash for contraband, the sight and sound of gold passing hands in a mutually satisfactory business deal. The ship, The Scorpion, was the finest smuggling vessel that operated on the coast. Captain Vincent was an experienced sailor; he had seen service under the great Admiral Nelson himself. Following his forced retirement at a ridiculously young age from the Royal Navy thanks to a French musket ball at Trafalgar, he avoided penury by taking his savings and investing in a share in The Scorpion. Now, almost ten years after Trafalgar his share increased to full ownership of the fastest, sleekest, most profitable smuggling vessel on the North Sea. It could outrun any Revenue cutter sent to apprehend it, and he forged relationships with some of the most notorious smugglers in England, concentrating his business dealings with his contacts on the Northumberland coast. The proximity of the English coast to Holland, as far as he was concerned, was the perfect distance.

Nights like this were also perfect; the long summer nights finally turned to autumn chills. Clear frosty stars shone down on the North Sea and the brightness of the moon aided The Scorpion's passage across the empty seas.

Empty that is except for the small ship that kept close to the coast, watching, waiting for the arrival of the smuggling ship. The Revenue cutter was smaller than the Scorpion, but light, fast, the government finally investing in some ships capable of capturing the smuggling crews so prevalent on the English coasts. The vessel loaded down with excise men and soldiers from the barracks at Newcastle, too often the smugglers escaped due to sheer force of numbers. The sympathies of the local populace lay with the smuggling fraternity as they provided them with the expensive contraband in return for their silence and tacit support.

The clouds were gathering, the winds were picking up, and a low rumbling in the distance told of an approaching storm.

The last of the contraband was unloaded onto the beach and Captain Vincent jumped back into the small shuttle boat to return to The Scorpion. With narrowed eyes, he finally noticed the approaching Revenue ship and with a sharp order to his men, they rowed frantically back towards the ship.

An approaching longboat heralded the arrival of heavily armed soldiers dispatched to shore, to capture the contraband and as many of the smugglers who remained to guard and fight for their loot. The cutter itself approached The Scorpion, intent on boarding and capturing the vessel, a valuable prize as well as ridding the coast of one of the most notorious smuggling ships around.

Vincent scrambled back on board just as the first heavy drops of rain fell onto the deck of his beloved ship. Shouting out his orders, the sails were unfurled and caught the wind as he raced to the ship's wheel, to guide The Scorpion out of that secluded cove.

The smaller ship raced through the water towards them as the crew ran around frantically following their Captain's orders. The storm approached faster than anticipated and as The Scorpion finally moved, a volley of cannon fire exploded across its bows and shouts were heard demanding the smugglers' ship heave to.

Vincent ignored the warnings and went on barking out orders to his men.

On board the Revenue cutter, Captain Steele watched the escaping Scorpion with frustration. His carefully orchestrated plans were unravelling; however, he could see his men on shore were engaging in a pitched battle with the smugglers. A grim smile lifted his lips; there were going to be quite a few arrests made tonight but the primary purpose of tonight's venture was the capture of The Scorpion – and he did not know if his vessel was going to prove fast and light enough to catch it.

His orders were carried out with swift efficiency, his men running to carry out his orders, bringing the ship about, chasing The Scorpion through the waves now growing higher in response to the swift-blowing winds and the heavy rain.

Out of the cove and south along the coastline, the cutter chased the larger ship, steadily increasing its speed until there was barely a ship's length between them. Mile after nautical mile they raced, leaving the Northumberland coastline behind them, passing Lizard Point where the small Souter Lighthouse gave off a dull light through the now raging storm. They passed the Bamburgh Light and on board The Scorpion, Vincent frowned as he realised he was about to enter unchartered territory. They reached the mouth of the Tees Estuary and passed the infamous North Gare; onwards, past the haunts of the famous Saltburn smuggling master, Mr John Andrews.

It fleetingly crossed Captain Steele's mind that he would dearly love to be the man who brought that particular lawbreaker to justice, but North Yorkshire was not his province. Mr Andrews had to be left to the local Revenue and the Militia – something not proving an easy task as despite his reputation and fame, he had never yet been caught in possession of any contraband.

Likewise, Captain Vincent, desperate to escape the determined little cutter passed the distinctive Saltburn Scar and saw lights on shore. The small inn owned and run by Mr Andrews would have been a welcome respite but the two men never met due to the unspoken honour amongst thieves and smugglers. They did not trespass on each other's patch of coastline and as Vincent had plenty of contacts in the more northerly areas he never ventured this far south.

Lightning suddenly lit up the skies, followed by the heavy rolling thunder. Heavy rain obscured his eyes momentarily, followed almost immediately by a loud explosion and the bright flash of cannon fire.

Captain Steele cursed quietly. The storm had been expected but not this sudden ferocious rush of rain and wind and the surging churning seas, forcing him to hold tightly onto the ship's wheel, straining to see through the night-darkened driving rain, the deck made slippery by the continuous downpour.

Visibility was minimal, and he cursed once more as he saw the larger ship unfurling more sails. Captain Vincent was behaving with reckless abandon – a more prudent man would never do this. He could destroy his ship, it could snap his mast in two, but The Scorpion ploughed on through the torrential storm. The Excise man realised Vincent was doing his best to outrun him, hugging the rugged coastline as even he did not dare to risk his men and his ship on the open seas, raging now with the wildest storm they had seen in months.

Cannon fire sounded again, and in the confusion, he could not tell if it was his own ship firing the cannon or The Scorpion. A sudden shudder was felt on the deck of the cutter, and a sharp crack heralded the collapse of the main mast. He leapt aside as the mast crashed down onto the ship's wheel and as he fought to gain his balance once more he could see The Scorpion lit up by a giant flash of lightning. His cutter was damaged, but The Scorpion was also in trouble.

He realised they had now sailed so far south they were now off the Yorkshire coast. This part of the coast was dangerous and rocky, the nearest lighthouse several miles south of their position. He watched as The Scorpion fought to avoid the rocky promontory it was being driven into by the force of the storm.

He had his own ship to worry about, however, and he ran back to try and control the wildly spinning broken wheel, to stop the ship lurching through the waves towards the same rocks The Scorpion was trying desperately to avoid.

A huge fork of lightning hit the deck of the Revenue cutter, breaking and splintering its decks. As its Captain was hurled into the mountainous seas, his last conscious thoughts were of how easily carefully laid plans could come to nought thanks to the vagaries of the weather.

•

Alice Embleton and her young companion, Charis Waverley, stood in Alice's tower bedroom and watched the two ships foundering on the rocks in the wild, turbulent seas below them.

The house resembled nothing less than a small Gothic castle, with two towers and mock battlements all around it. It had been built in an earlier age by Mrs Embleton's husband's ancestors and had once been considered a holiday home by the family at that time. A hundred years later gambling debts and poor investments had taken care of the family lands and fortune. The widow of the last of the Embleton's living her years in the crumbling house, all that was left of what was once a proud family estate.

Surprisingly, situated as it was on the high cliffs above the North Sea, open to the unpredictable weather and harsh winters of that part of the coast, most of the house was still habitable. Used now only by Alice herself and two servants, the addition to the household of a young companion meant that one of the musty old bedrooms in Cliffe House had seen a new lease of life as it was opened, cleaned, and made ready for the young lady. In the opposite tower to Alice's, Charis found it a warm and welcoming respite after her long and tiring journey from London. A letter despatched by Emily travelled by the Mail Coach and had arrived the day before Charis landed on her doorstep. Not much notice, but sufficient for Alice to grasp the urgency of the situation and be prepared for the arrival of the young lady from

London. A further, more detailed missive had been handed to her new employer, also written by her concerned Aunt Emily, and Charis filled in the gaps of the reason for her sudden departure from the capital.

They stood together now, a month after her arrival, watching as the lightning illuminated the boiling seas below them. It was the first time Charis had experienced the force and majesty of a storm at sea, and with heavy heart she offered up a prayer for those poor souls on the foundering vessels, plunging headlong through the gigantic waves.

She almost let out a scream as a massive bolt of lightning struck the smaller of the two ships and she watched in growing horror as the vessel split in half as it was hurled against the rocks.

From their vantage point in the tower on top of the cliffs, they could not see any of the seamen going into the water, but they both knew that few sailors would have survived in that vicious storm.

Mrs Embleton shook her head sorrowfully as they watched the two ships disappear under the waves.

"Those poor souls," she said quietly. Sighing, Mrs Embleton turned away from the window and sent over to the small padded armchair next to the fireplace. A log fire blazed cheerfully in the hearth and she held out her hands towards the heat.

Charis followed her. "Is this a regular occurrence?" she asked quietly.

Alice nodded. "Unfortunately, yes," she replied. "We will go down to the beach in the morning to search for survivors."

Charis brightened up at once. "Survivors? Even from such a storm?"

Alice nodded. She closed her eyes momentarily before opening them and turning her sharp grey-eyed gaze on her new companion.

"There will be other reasons for searching the beach, my dear," she said softly.

Charis turned her innocent eyes to her new employer. "Really? Why?" she asked.

Alice paused, her lips pressed together firmly as she weighed up her words carefully, unsure to what extent she could confide in the young woman. They had spent a month together. Charis had been polite, amiable and if her nerves had been stretched after her experiences, she hid them well enough and accompanied Alice to church on Sunday, meeting the vicar and the local people. Alice, carefully advised by her sister was prepared for the curious. Charis was the daughter of an old friend and following the death of her father she found herself in the position of needing to work and being an old lady's companion was considered a very respectable way to make a living. Why Alice never felt the need to employ a companion before now was a question that the vicar ventured to enquire. He had to be satisfied with a shrugged shoulder and the acid comment that she was doing a service for an old friend and had no need for anyone running around after her now or ever. Charis's employment was an act of charity, no more!

"Flotsam and jetsam," she said quietly, shaking her head. "There will be plenty of cargo washed up on the beach and the villagers will be down there in force tomorrow morning to see what they can recover from the wrecks."

"Oh, will we do the same, Mrs Embleton?" she enquired.

Alice sniffed. "Josiah will go down to the beach and see if there is anything washed up. We will look for survivors."

She observed the troubled look on Charis's face and smiled kindly. "Do not fret," she continued. "The people of this coast are not Wreckers – they do not lure ships to their doom and murder the crews. If anyone has survived, they will find them and do their best to save them. They are, however, very poor and if a cask of brandy or tea should happen to find its way into their cottages, who are we to criticise?"

Charis nodded slowly. In her sheltered life, so far, her only experience of the poorest members of society had been the villagers on her father's estate near York.

None of them, however, wore the thin, pinched look of people suffering from cold and hunger that she saw in the local villages near Alice's home. They were on a part of the coast between Whitby and Hawsker, and whilst most of the population of the local communities survived by farming and fishing, some families were truly impoverished.

Alice had taken Charis with her during her first week to visit some of the poorest families. Even though her employer was by no means a wealthy woman, Charis had been touched and impressed by the way Alice gave money, food and clothing to the widows and children she met. Charis felt ashamed of herself for fretting over the amount of clothing she had been forced to leave behind in London and resolved to sell some of the small pieces of jewellery she brought with her to help Alice and the families she visited.

She left Alice and returned to her own bedroom. She walked along chilly corridors, poorly lit except for the occasional candle gracing the few wall sconces. Charis hurried along the dark and gloomy corridor and, as she made her way down the tower stairs, along the landing and up the stairs to her room in the twin turret, she shivered, drawing her shawl more firmly around her shoulders. She reflected that perhaps, when she sold some jewellery, it might be sensible to purchase a couple of thicker dresses and warmer shawls to survive the coming winter months in this inhospitable environment.

The storm still raged as she made her way over to the long windows. The view was amazing from her turret room, and on a clear day she could see for miles up the coast and out to sea and at first, she had spent hours staring out at the ever-changing sea and the passing ships. Now she looked out as the lightning lit up the waves crashing against the cliffs below. A wild scene greeted her gaze. She shivered again as images of the poor souls aboard the two ships, battered and broken on the rocks, sinking below the mountainous waves, swamped her mind.

She murmured another prayer as she undressed and slipped under the heavy covers of her bed. Despite the warmth of her room and the crackling fire, she found she could not sleep. Only when the ferocity of the storm finally blew itself out did she manage to get some respite. Wide awake at dawn, she rose, quickly dressing and pulling on stout boots.

She was going down to the beach, the thought that there might be survivors needing help more than she could bear and she could not wait for Alice and the rest of the household to rise and go down with her.

She left the house and made her way along the road to the steps that led down a zig-zag path to the beach. Already she could see people down there, walking amongst the detritus of the storm. She could see them making up piles of barrels and wooden chests and going into the sea, dragging to shore the floating cargo from the drowned ships.

She shivered slightly, pulling her thick woollen shawl around herself as she picked her way over the slippery rocks towards the bay where the local villagers were hauling the cargo from the icy waters of the sea.

She had to walk out a little way to go around the larger boulders between her and the sea. Her stout boots sank into the soft sand and the hem of her thick dark blue dress picked up sand and salt water laying in small puddles left by the receding tide. Regretting her failure to don a warm hat, she pushed loose curls from her face as the wind caught at her hair, pulling strands from the simple braid that cascaded over one shoulder.

She walked between two large rocks and almost tripped over the body lying prone on the soaking wet beach, half in and half out of a shallow rock pool.

He was lying on his stomach, dressed only in torn breeches. He wore no shoes and whatever other clothing he might have been wearing when he went into the stormy seas had been ripped from his body by the force of the tide and, from the bruising evident on his back, the rocks onto which he had been thrown. She could see the signs of blood on the side of his head, and after recoiling in shock at the first sight of him, her natural desire to help made her crouch beside him to see if he was dead, as he first appeared, or whether life still existed. She put a shaking, hesitant hand out and touched him gently. His body was chilled and stiff, but as her fingers went to his face, she heard a faint, barely audible groan.

She moved then, scrambling to her knees she bent over him and pulled him over to lay on his back before standing up and getting her hands under his shoulders to pull him out of the shallow water onto the firmer ground of the beach. He was a tall man and no light weight. As she struggled to drag him clear of the rock pool, blood oozed from a deep cut on his temple and matted into dark hair. His eyes were closed, thick black lashes contrasting starkly with the pallor of his cheeks. A faint lifting of his bare chest the only evidence that he still breathed.

For a moment, Charis looked at the man, her brain taking in the broad shoulders and muscular frame, tapering down to a flat, taut stomach, marred slightly by signs of old wounds. She wondered vaguely how he might have acquired such scars even as she stood and pulled the thick shawl off her shoulders. Bending down again, Charis strived to lift him slightly to wrap the warm clothing around his bare torso. She gave no thought to anything but saving the life of this shipwrecked sailor and how to warm him as quickly as possible before the cold and exposure to the biting north winds made survival impossible.

He groaned again as her arms went around his shoulders and his eyelids fluttered. She drew back slightly, gazing anxiously into his face. Before she could react, his hand suddenly moved and fastened around her upper arm. With an unexpected burst of strength, he pulled her towards him, pulling her off balance so that she fell across him, her face only inches from his own. For a few seconds, she held her breath and found herself gazing into the deepest, bluest eyes she had ever seen in her life before. She watched as the strength left his body, his eyelids closing again, his hand falling limply to the ground once more.

Charis's breath caught in her throat and she let it out again, shakily rising back to her feet. Stepping back from the unconscious man, she ran around the large boulder and shouted with all her might at the group of villagers on the nearby beach.

Her voice carried on the wind and attracted the attention of a few of them. She waved frantically.

"Help me!" she shouted, "I've found someone alive!"

•

The fire crackled in the small hearth, warming the bedroom and giving off a rosy glow. The curtains were firmly closed against the cold October night, and Charis could hear the wind howling around the towers of the old building. She sat next to the bed, sewing a shirt given to her by Alice, repairing the small holes in it, neatly replacing lost buttons and making it ready for the bed's occupant to wear upon his eventual recovery. A slight rueful smile lifted the corners of her mouth as she recalled how six weeks ago she would have been horrified at the thought of being alone in a bedroom with any man – even when that man was unconscious!

The man from the beach lay still and silent beneath the warmth of the heavy covers. He had hardly moved since that morning when two strong young men from the village answered her calls for help and assisted her to carry the unconscious man from the beach up to the Embleton house. Alice sent for the local doctor at once and between them, Charis, Alice and Martha and Josiah, the elderly servants, put the young man to bed in another of the tower bedrooms. Martha swiftly readied it, lighting a fire and providing clean linen for the bed, airing the musty room as Charis and Alice bathed the blood from the young man's body, cleaned the sea water and sand from him and dressed him in one of Alice's late husband's nightshirts.

The urgency of their task overcame Charis's embarrassment as Alice in her usual no-nonsense manner stripped the torn breeches from the man's prone body. He had been wearing undergarments but these too were sea stained and ripped, and Alice would allow no missish vapours at the sight of a man's nakedness. Charis found she could not take her eyes off the way his muscles rippled under his skin as Alice washed the blood and sand from his body and she was almost relieved when Alice sharply ordered her to fetch the nightshirt whilst she attended to the man's wounds. They pulled the soft linen shirt onto him and laid him down onto the feather pillows of the bed.

He did not regain consciousness when the doctor arrived and examined him. The doctor inspected the head wound and declared that apart from a nasty headache the strange young man would awake with no other ill effects from the shipwreck. The doctor advised that he should not be left alone as he was bound to be disorientated when he finally awoke and arrangements were made that between them Alice, Charis and the two servants would take it in turns to sit with him.

The hours passed with him showing no signs of awakening and Charis stayed steadfastly by his side, occasionally rising from her seat beside the bed to put more wood on the fire or to stand beside him, gazing down upon his face. He had regained some colour by this time, his breathing deep and even. The open neck of the white nightshirt contrasted with the darkened, tanned skin of his chest and neck. A faint stubble was starting to darken his strong jaw and a frown appeared between his eyes, drawing his brows almost together. He moved now, and she heard again that low, almost growling tone of a groan as he shifted position in the softness of the bed.

Charis glanced towards the door, wondering if she should send for someone but it was late, and the rest of the household in bed. Martha's husband Josiah was due to relieve her at midnight, another two hours hence, and in the meantime, she was loath to disturb the sleeping couple.

She sat on the bed, reaching over and gently touched his forehead. He was cool to her touch, and she felt relief that he had not succumbed to any kind of fever.

She brushed his hair back from his forehead, startled when his eyes suddenly opened and she found herself staring once again into deep blue eyes. She caught her breath, hardly daring to move as his eyes slowly focused and gazed at her. His hand was above the cover and he lifted it slightly. Without thinking, Charis took his hand in both of hers and smiled down at him.

"Are you an angel?" his voice croaked, with the slightest hint of an accent she could not immediately recognise.

She squeezed his hand gently. "Indeed not, sir," she replied softly. "Just a beachcomber looking for flotsam and jetsam…" She smiled again. "And I found you."

A faint smile lifted the corners of his mouth. Asleep with his eyes closed he was a very good-looking man. When he smiled, slight creases appeared at the corners of his eyes. He was devastatingly attractive and she felt again that odd lurch in her stomach that she experienced earlier when gazing down at his naked form.

Without taking his eyes from hers, he lifted her hand to press a kiss against her skin. "You found me?" he whispered. "Then I must thank you for saving my life."

Her mouth suddenly felt dry. "I am happy we were able to find you in time, before the sea and exposure claimed you."

"How is your head, sir?" she asked. "The doctor said you might have a headache."

His brow furrowed as if trying to remember the extent of his injuries. "My head is indeed painful," he replied.

"I will bring you a drink of water," Charis said gently, strangely reluctant to remove her hand from his, reluctant to break the contact between them, reluctant to leave his side. "The doctor said it would help."

She stood and went to the dresser where a large jug of water and a glass was waiting for her attention. She poured him a glass and came back to the bed. He tried to sit up and she immediately went to him, to put her free arm around his shoulders to help him. He took the glass from her and drank down the water greedily. He sighed and handed the glass back to her before sinking back into the pillows.

"Can you remember what happened, sir?" she asked him, sitting on the edge of the bed, facing him.

He shook his head. "I cannot remember," he said. "My mind is fogged – my head still pains me."

Immediately contrite, Charis shook her head. "I must not

press you," she said softly. "You need time to recover. There will be time enough when you are rested to recall the events of the shipwrecks – and then we can contact your family to let them know you are safe and well."

He raised his hand to his forehead, closing his eyes and taking a shaky breath.

"Sir…" Charis said. "I will leave you to sleep now."

He opened his eyes again, and when she made to move away, he caught her hand in his once more. "No," he said, his voice suddenly urgent. "Please do not leave me." His eyes bored into hers. "Do you know who I am?" he asked.

She shook her head, soft brown curls shining almost red in the glow of the firelight. "No – you had no identifying papers on you when we found you. You were unconscious and unable to speak. Why? Should I know you?" She attempted to inject some humour into the seriousness of the question.

"I am not your husband?" he asked.

She shook her head, feeling a rosy blush stealing over her cheeks. "No – I told you we only found you today on the beach."

She saw the confusion cross his face and his hand clutched hers.

"I cannot recall my name," he said. "I do not know who I am."

CHAPTER SIX

Doctor Rutter was an old man with more years' experience of illness than anyone else Alice Embleton knew. She trusted no one as much as her old friend John Rutter and following his examination of their mysterious sailor, he joined the ladies in the cosy drawing room to partake in a small glass of sherry.

He sighed and seated himself in the comfortable armchair next to the fire, sipping his drink appreciatively

"Well, John?" Alice demanded, sitting opposite him with Charis hovering anxiously beside the window.

"A strange case…" John Rutter nodded his head. "He is very well spoken; I would say he is definitely a gentleman of some kind. He has no signs of any childhood disease that can affect the poor – no signs of malnourishment, scurvy or rickets – so I would surmise he has come from some kind of good, if not privileged, background." He frowned into his glass, considering his words, marshalling his thoughts. "He has scars that suggest he has lately been engaged in some kind of fighting activity. A bullet wound in his shoulder and a flesh wound on his chest – did you notice them yesterday?"

"We did," Alice answered, casting a sly glance at Charis whom she had noticed staring at the young man's chest rather longer than necessary the day before.

Charis felt her cheeks reddening again.

"But they have healed well and are several months old, I would suggest." Doctor Rutter shook his head once more, still deep in thought. "He wears no jewellery. He has no recollection of anything beyond waking up here yesterday. I have heard of such cases in the past but must admit this is the first time I have encountered such a phenomenon."

"Will he recover?" Charis asked, trying to keep her voice neutral, to keep the anxiety from surfacing.

John Rutter smiled at Alice's new companion. "I do not know, my dear," he replied. "I have heard this might just be a temporary state, brought on by a blow to the head, such as he received during the shipwreck. His physical health should return back to normal in a day or two but his memory – well, it could back in a day or two, or it could take weeks – or…" He sighed once more, taking another sip of the rich ruby sherry. "Or he may never remember who he is."

Charis and Alice exchanged a glance.

"Is there anything we can do?" Charis asked.

The doctor drained his sherry glass and stood, straightening his coat, and preparing to leave them.

"He will be physically fit enough to leave his room soon. Just let him rest and recover for another day or so and then, if his memory does not return, we must consider contacting the local militia to see if he is known to them. If he is from the Revenue cutter that sank then they will know him as one of their own." He paused as he retrieved his greatcoat and shrugged his way into the many-pocketed garment. "If he is one of the smugglers who did not perish with the sinking of the Scorpion, then the militia will be delighted to take him off your hands and hand him over to the relevant authorities."

Charis bit her lip, hesitant to ask but determined to know. "And if he is a smuggler?" she asked.

"He will be taken away for trial and, no doubt, imprisonment." Alice remained silent. She stood and escorted the doctor to the door, calling for Josiah to come with the doctor's hat.

"We will wait a while first, my dear," she addressed herself to Charis. "He must rest here for a few days first and then hopefully his memory will return before we need take any drastic action!"

They thanked the doctor and watched as he left the house,

mounting his horse, and trotting away through the grey, overcast day.

"Why don't you visit our castaway?" Alice asked. "I will ask Martha to take some soup up to him, and I have an errand for Josiah to run, so I need to speak to him."

Charis smiled at her, a smile that brought a light to her sombre eyes as she turned and lightly ran up the stairs of the tower towards the bedroom wherein their unexpected guest resided.

She did not knock but opened the door to let herself in. She was shocked to find him out of bed, clinging to one of the four posts, leaning heavily against it, to prevent himself from falling.

His face was as white as his nightshirt. She ran to him, taking his arm, and guiding him back to the bed before he could fall. He swayed slightly but held fast to her as she lowered him back into the bed.

"You might have injured yourself!" she scolded him, pulling the bed covers up over his legs.

He lay back on the pillows, his eyes closed and his hand pressed across his closed eyelids.

"I feel so useless just lying here!" he said.

"You will do no good if you fall and break something," Charis replied, sitting beside him.

He opened his eyes and stared into hers. A slight smile lifted his lips. "I might hit my head again and remember who I am," he said.

"Or knock yourself out completely," she replied, her own lips lifting in an answering smile.

"That doctor thought I might be an Irishman."

"'Tis the lilt in your voice, it has an accent that is definitely not from around these parts." Charis stood again, smoothing the bed covers. "Perhaps we should give you an Irish name until you can remember your own!"

She was smiling and only half joking, but he seemed to be considering her words seriously.

He nodded slowly. "Connor," he said. "That name seems to

have some kind of a meaning to me." He shrugged. "Don't ask me why."

"Connor," she repeated slowly. "It is a good name. Until you can remember who you really are, that will do well enough."

He frowned again, straining to force his brain to remember something, anything and failing. The fog around him as thick as ever.

"The older lady…" he continued. "Is she your mother?"

Charis shook her head. "No, a distant relative that is all. I am her companion and this is her house."

"Where is this house?" he asked.

"It is on the coast of North East England. We are close to Whitby. Have you ever heard of it?"

Connor sighed and shook his head, smiling a little ruefully. "In another life I probably do but not now."

Satisfied that he was comfortable enough, she moved away from the bed. "Martha will be here with some broth for you," she told him. "Get some sleep after you eat and then I will come back later."

Connor looked at her with a strange, deep intensity about him. "I wish you would not leave me."

She paused in her journey to the door of the room, looking back at him, that strange feeling overwhelming her once again. She realised that she did not want to leave either and would have been content to stay with him all day. Confused, wondering what was wrong with her, she smiled at him. "I am neglecting my duties towards Mrs Embleton. Stay here and rest and we will return later to discuss what is to become of you!"

"What is to become of me, Miss Charis?" he asked softly.

She laughed, attempting to lighten the mood between them. "We will find you a useful occupation, Mr Connor," she replied. "Until you recover your wits and your health. I am sure there will be plenty to keep you busy."

He grinned then, revealing white, even teeth. Lying back on his pillows he closed his eyes. "I am sure you will find me plenty to do…"

He did not attempt to restrain her further and she left the room, closing the door quietly behind her. He felt slightly dizzy and, resigning himself to the knowledge that he was not yet fit enough to get out of bed, he sighed and found himself slipping into an uneasy sleep once more.

To a well brought up, educated and aristocratic young lady, the menial tasks of the household came as something of a culture shock to Charis. All her life she was used to being waited on, her meals served, her clothes laundered and having to do nothing more arduous than decide which invitation to accept to fill her social calendar.

Aware that until her uncle sent for her, or she received news from Mr Kielder that he had succeeded in overturning her father's will, Charis felt compelled to remain in semi-hiding from the nefarious schemes and plans of her stepmother's cronies.

Correspondence from her Aunt Emily in which she described Henrietta's anger at Charis's leaving without permission sent a shiver of foreboding through her. Likewise, an impassioned letter from George Hardy, forwarded on by Emily, left her confused and upset. She started to wonder if she had been mistaken in what she had overheard but, in the cold light of a winter's day, walking along the cliff edge towards Whitby, breathing in the icy air to clear her thoughts, she knew she had made the right decision. She wrote back to both Henrietta and George via Emily, calmly assuring them both she was well and suffered no harm and was merely taking a little time to decide what to do with herself. She had no regrets about her impulsive journey and advised them that she had no plans to return to London just yet. She wished them both well and told George her only regret was that she had not seen him in person to refuse his offer of matrimony, wishing him happiness for the future.

As Mrs Embleton had been kind enough to offer her shelter and a position of sorts to keep her occupied until her future was settled, Charis offered to help around the house as much as possible. Mrs Embleton could only afford an elderly couple to look after her, and subsequently the house had taken on something of a slightly neglected air. Lack of funds reduced Mrs Embleton to living in a few modest rooms, and Charis, putting aside all thoughts of the luxurious life she left behind, found herself helping Martha in the kitchen. She made the beds, cleaned her own bedroom and volunteered to clean and air the rooms long closed.

Mrs Embleton currently had only one small drawing room that she used for all purposes from receiving visitors to her normal day to day activities. After Mrs Embleton expressed a desire to re-use the adjoining morning room, Charis spurned all offers of help from the elderly members of the household and set about the task of returning the room to its former glory. She donned her oldest dress and, covering it with a voluminous apron provided by Martha, armed herself with buckets of hot soapy water to aid her in her task.

She hummed to herself as she removed dust covers, swept, and scrubbed the hard-wearing wooden floors, dragging rugs outside to beat the accumulated dust of years of neglect out of their faded colours.

She dusted and polished the furniture and washed the windows inside and out, removing years of sea spray from their dull panes. She cleaned them until they sparkled with new life, letting the weak winter sun stream into the gleaming interior. The last thing to do was to light a fire in the newly cleaned hearth, and so it was that with cheeks streaked with coal dust, carrying a heavy basket of logs, Charis walked slowly up from the kitchen bent with her burden.

Not looking where she was going, she stopped abruptly as a tall figure halted in front of her. She almost dropped her basket as she looked up to see Connor standing before her, his face still pale but his eyes dark with concern.

"Let me take that from you, Miss Waverley," he said and before she could object, he seized the basket of logs from her and lifted them easily into his arms.

"Connor!" she protested. "You are not strong enough, you should still be in bed!"

He grinned at her, a mischievous, lopsided smile. "If I stay in bed another minute I swear I will go mad!" He strode down the corridor to the stairs leading to the first floor and the morning room.

"You have been busy," he said, gazing around at the room, taking in all the beautifully polished old furniture. "This is a lovely room."

He placed the basket of logs next to the fireplace and, kneeling in front of the hearth, picked up the tinder to light the kindling Charis prepared. He waited until a faint spark of flame started, and placed a dry log onto the coal to set the fire blazing. He sat back on his heels, banking the logs so that they were ready to catch fire, sending the warmth radiating out into the room.

"I didn't get the chimney swept," Charis admitted, coming after him into the room. "But Mrs Embleton assured me she had them all swept last year so we shouldn't have any problems."

Connor stood and turned back to her, grinning again as she pushed a lock of hair behind her ear. Charis was suddenly conscious of her unkempt hair, dirty hands, and face. "I repeat," she said crossly, "you should be resting, getting your strength back."

He sighed, running his hands through his hair as he did so. "I have rested enough, Miss Waverley," he said. "I need to do something, even if it is just going outside for some fresh air."

She looked at his tall frame, recognising the tension in the set of his shoulders. He was a man obviously used to activity and exercise. Days of resting and sleeping had helped him to recover, but he was edgy, needing to release some of his pent-up frustrations.

Charis surveyed the plain cord breeches and faded linen shirt he wore. An old but smart waistcoat covered the shirt, his outfit completed by a pair of stout buckled shoes, old and serviceable but not of the latest style or fashion.

"Where did you get those clothes?" she asked.

He looked down at his outfit, his eyes twinkling as he returned her gaze. "Josiah provided me with the breeches and shirt," he admitted. "Mrs Embleton gave me some of her husband's clothes and shoes. They fit me well enough, I think."

Charis busied herself with straightening the curtains and moving away from the intensity of his gaze. Her mouth felt dry as she forced herself to turn back to him. "If you will give me a few minutes to change, I have an errand to run for Mrs Embleton. Do you think you are strong enough to walk with me?"

"How far is it?" he enquired.

"Only a mile each way," she replied. "Do you feel able to walk that far?" She felt suddenly anxious at the thought the exertion might be too much for him.

He smiled again, the deep blue of his eyes sparkling at the idea of fresh air and the walk.

"I think so," he answered her. "I will see what kind of coat the late Mr Embleton has bequeathed to me!"

She smiled in response to his. She felt again, that strange lurch in her stomach as she looked into his eyes. She had never felt like this before, she did not recognise her own emotions and wondered what it was about him that brought these unfamiliar sensations to taunt her. She felt breathless and giddy and wanted, more than anything to reach out and touch him, to feel the firm muscles of his arm under her hand, run her fingers through his hair, and caress his face – his mouth….

Taking a deep breath, she turned her thoughts firmly away from him and walked briskly to the door. "I will not be long, please wait for me." She said and, leaving the transformed room, ran upstairs to her bedroom to wash and change.

•

Twenty minutes later, Charis came downstairs after washing the coal dust and grime from her face and brushing the dust of her day's labours out of her hair. Longing to immerse herself in the luxury of a hot bath, she resolved to ask Martha to help her fill a tub later so she could ease the aches caused by the unaccustomed exercise of such hard manual work.

Connor awaited her in the kitchen, where he was chatting amiably with Martha, drinking a mug of Josiah's home-brewed ale, and glancing up appreciatively as Charis returned. She looked charming in her winter bonnet and dark red velvet cloak over her old dress and short jacket. It was a cold day, and she wore a pair of warm leather gloves to complete her outfit. They were the oldest clothes she had brought with her from London, but even so, they were thick and richly embroidered and well-chosen to keep out the ravages of the north wind.

"Are you ready?" she asked him.

"Of course," he replied. "Where are we going, Miss Waverley?"

He, too, was dressed warmly in a thick coat over his borrowed outfit and he stood to join her.

"We are going to Mrs Jenkins's farm," she told Martha. "Mrs Embleton has asked me to buy some butter and see how the children are faring."

Mrs Jenkins farm was only a mile away, far enough for the first outing for a man who had been in bed for almost a week.

She smiled at Connor as he held the kitchen door open for her.

"Send them my best," said Martha as they were leaving.

They walked out into the kitchen yard, Charis leading them up the steps at the rear of the house. Connor followed her and they ascended the steps to the path leading along the cliff top in two directions. One led towards the small village of Hawsker, the other wound along the cliffs towards the larger town of Whitby. Charis took the Hawsker path, explaining to Connor that the Jenkins farm was not far and they would see the path leading off to the farmhouse shortly.

He stopped at the top of the path, pausing to gaze out at the view below them. It was a cold, November day and the north wind blew strongly against them, catching at her cloak, and blowing it out behind her. She had to hold on to her bonnet as the wind tried to loosen the firmly tied ribbons. The sea below was grey and choppy and looked extremely cold and uninviting.

There was something wistful about his gaze as Connor stared out to sea, something making him frown as he fruitlessly searched his memory to recall something, anything about his former life. Charis saw the concentration and sadness on his face, and her heart went out to him. She placed her hand on his arm and then, when a gust of wind caused her to stagger slightly, Connor's hand went out immediately to catch her. He threaded her arm through his to draw her close to his side, sheltering her small frame with his taller, broader body.

She clung to him, helplessly drawn in to the warmth of his body, holding on to him as they struggled through the battering winds. Despite the inclement weather, a broad smile lit up Connor's face, and he held tightly to her as they walked along the winding, muddy path, keeping well away from the edge as the wind threatened to blow them over. The wind made it difficult for conversation, and it was only as they turned off onto the path Charis pointed out that they could catch their breath.

The fresh air had put colour into Connor's pale cheeks and a sparkle in his eyes. Now that they were out of the strength of the wind, Charis would have removed her arm from his, but he held her fast.

"How do you feel?" she asked. "The walk has not tired you?"

He shook his head. "On the contrary, I feel invigorated!" he replied.

"Perhaps we can venture a little further tomorrow then?" she suggested.

"Will Mrs Embleton permit me to accompany you?" he asked.

A slight smile lifted her lips. "I think so," she replied,

"Is something amusing you, Miss Waverley?" he asked.

She shook her head. "Only just that a few short weeks ago, someone considered me a prudish bore. Too prim and proper for his tastes." She laughed. "And yet, here I am walking with a man who is virtually a stranger with not so much as a chaperone between us!"

"Prudish bore?" Connor was surprised. "Who is the blackguard who suggested such a thing?"

The smile left her eyes and lips. "Nobody important," she said and turning her head away, urged him onwards towards the farm.

Charis knocked on the farmhouse door, answered almost immediately by the farmer himself, Dan Jenkins, smiling as he recognised Mrs Embleton's young companion but the smile left his face as he stared up at the tall, dark-haired man beside her.

"Ma'am," he nodded to her and opened the door wider to let them enter.

"This is Connor, Mr Jenkins." Charis introduced her companion.

"Aye," Dan nodded at him. "You were the lad from the beach," he said.

"Dan helped us to carry you to the house," Charis explained.

"How are you, sir?" Dan enquired, no friendliness in his voice, just a cold suspicion.

Connor recognised the wariness and nodded briefly. "I am well enough now thank you. Miss Waverley and the rest of the household have been looking after me very well."

"I heard tell you'd hit your head and couldn't remember much," Dan went on.

Connor furrowed his brow and nodded. "True enough. I don't even know my own name," he said soberly.

He could tell from the farmer's manner that he didn't like or trust strangers and he was not about to antagonise him further.

Mrs Jenkins bustled into the kitchen just then, exclaiming over her unexpected visitors and inviting Charis to be seated by the fire. The children, likewise, recovered now from the influenza that had laid them low also proved to be a distraction. Fascinated by the stranger in their midst, they plied him with questions he had no hope of answering, but he answered them kindly and accepted a mug of ale from the farmer's wife as Charis purchased the butter Mrs Embleton had sent her for.

"Do you not even remember which ship you fell from?" the Jenkins' eldest son asked.

Connor shook his head but the boy grinned with delight.

"So, we do not know if you are a Revenue man or a Gentleman?" he exclaimed.

"Gentleman?" Connor turned puzzled eyes towards Charis.

She smiled at him. "Smuggler," she translated.

"There were two ships went down that night," Mr Jenkins continued. "The survivors of both were taken to the Customs House in Whitby – but as there was confusion as to who was smuggler and who was Revenue, they're still arguing about it now!" A rare smile lit his face. "The Militia are waiting for officers from Newcastle to get here to identify their men."

Charis turned at once to Connor. "They might know who you are!" she said excitedly.

Dan Jenkins frowned. "Aye, they might," he said slowly. "And if they recognise you as a Gentleman and not an officer, you'll be taken away to Gaol with the rest of them."

Alarm went through Charis's body as though she had received an electric shock. The excitement left her eyes, and she stared solemnly up at him. "Then you must wait with us until you remember who you are," she said quietly.

Connor meanwhile, after staring at the farmer for a moment or two, shook his head.

"No Miss Waverley," he said. "I need to know the truth. If I am indeed a lawbreaker, then I must hand myself over to the authorities. My conscience would not allow me to do otherwise."

Mrs Jenkins laughed suddenly, causing them all to turn towards her. "Spoken like an honest man!" she said. "I doubt any smuggler would be so anxious to hand himself in!"

Despite this reassurance, Charis still felt uneasy. "I am sure we can afford to wait a few more days to see if your memory returns, Connor," she said gently.

For a moment, he found himself gazing into her troubled green eyes. As he saw the concern there, he felt something inside himself falter, hesitating in his desire to learn the truth about himself. What if the truth were something he would rather not know, something that would force this girl to withdraw from him, unable and unwilling to be anything more to him than a mere acquaintance.

He caught his breath at the thought and suddenly conscious of his surroundings he forced himself to smile and nod at her. "Yes, I am sure a few more days would not hurt," he agreed.

They remained a little longer in the warmth of the farmhouse kitchen, but once the butter was packed away in Charis's basket and the health of the children verified and exclaimed over, it was time to go.

The light was fading, and Mr Jenkins walked with them to the cliff top path, holding a lantern to help them see their way through the rapidly gathering dusk.

Declining his offer of the lantern, the brightness of the new moon lit up their path as they said their farewells and started on their journey back to Cliffe House.

They walked in silence, each occupied by their own thoughts, both thinking the same thing. The wind was still blowing in from the sea and, as Charis stumbled slightly, Connor caught her. They stood locked together for what seemed like an endless moment.

"I'm not a smuggler, Charis," he whispered fiercely. "I can't be!"

He held her arms, and she gazed up at him, almost frightened by the passion in his voice. "I hope not," she replied. "I don't think I could bear to see you being taken away…" She shuddered, her head tipped back so she could consider those deep dark pools of his eyes, blazing now with the strangest of lights.

She saw his lips coming down towards hers, but her eyes closed against the intensity of his gaze and she lifted her lips towards his, almost of their own volition. His kiss was gentle at first, but then as he pulled her into his arms, as her hands crept up around his neck to hold him even closer, his kiss hardened, and for the first time in her life, she experienced the flaring of true passion. Desire, raw and unbridled, blazed between them. His lips crushed hers and she felt dizzy with the emotions rampaging through her.

A sharp blast of cold, North Sea air sent them both staggering slightly. She shuddered and reluctantly drew her lips away from his. He lifted his head and for a moment he seemed puzzled, disorientated almost. Then he smiled, a lazy, devastating smile that had her heart melting and her resolve weakening.

She pulled herself together, and pulled herself away from him, shocked by her own reaction to his touch and his kiss. "Pray do not do that again!" she said sharply and walked on, away from him back towards the house.

In two long strides, he caught up to her. "I apologise," he said softly. "I did not mean to offend."

She turned her head away from him so he could not see the colour flooding her cheeks, afraid that even in the deepening gloom he would be able to see her blushes.

"Let us get home before the rain starts," she said coldly and would have walked on but he caught her arm.

"I know I am not a smuggler, Charis," he said urgently. "I don't know who or what I am but I feel it in my bones that I am no miscreant – and I had no right to touch you or kiss you. Please forgive me."

She nodded her head stiffly. "I am not offended," she admitted. She forced herself to relax slightly and smiled, a wintry lifting of her lips. "Please let us continue home."

He offered her his arm once again and, glad of the shelter of his body against the cold and the bleakness of that evening, she accepted as they walked along together.

"We do not know who I am," he said to her as they approached the house. "But I also know nothing about you, Miss Waverley. Who are you?"

She shook her head. "I used to be a lady." She almost laughed. "With a fine home and a loving father. But he died, and I was left with nothing. I am Mrs Embleton's companion until my uncle sends for me and then I will no doubt be the ubiquitous poor relation, looking after my four young cousins and being at the disposal of my Aunt. She is a very kind lady but – of – a – sickly disposition, unfortunately."

To her amazement, Connor's eyes twinkled in the darkness, and he laughed aloud. "We are nothing but two waifs and strays,

Miss Waverley. Flotsam and Jetsam washed up on the beach of life!"

"Indeed Connor," she admonished him. "I heartily object to being called Flotsam!"

But her words were cut off and she was left breathless as he pulled her into his arms and deposited another swift, searing kiss onto her lips. Then she was released, as he strode away from her, holding open the garden gate that led down into the grounds of Cliffe House. As she passed him, he caught her hand, bowing slightly, and pressing another kiss to her fingers. She hoped that he put her shivering down to the chill wind of that exposed cliff top rather than the emotions flooding through her at his touch. Never in her life had she experienced these feelings.

Connor was a stranger. She knew nothing about him. Instinctively, as she watched his tall, strong frame open the door for her and stand silhouetted against the light of the kitchen, Charis knew she could trust him in a way she never believed she could trust anyone since her father died.

It was a comforting thought, and yet, that comfort was tinged with the first stirrings of real passion and desire Charis had ever known in her life. Connor was a stranger, but for her peace of mind, he was also the most dangerous person she had ever met.

•

Mrs Embleton looked up from her dressing table as Charis knocked gently on her bedroom door.

"Yes, my dear?" she smiled as Charis came into the bedroom.

Charis hesitated, but went over to her employer and drew a small item wrapped in silk from her pocket. "Mrs Embleton," she began, "I wish to sell this piece of jewellery. Can you advise me on the best place to take it?"

She unwrapped the silk to reveal a small ruby and pearl brooch.

"Do you need some funds, Charis?" Mrs Embleton quizzed her.

Charis smiled and shrugged. "I still have some money, but I

need some warmer winter clothing and thought this might help to purchase a few items."

Mrs Embleton studied the brooch for a moment and sighed. "I wish I could help you a little more financially, Charis, but as you know, my circumstances are quite straitened."

Charis sank to her knees in front of Mrs Embleton and clasped her hands. "I know, dearest Mrs Embleton. I would not dream of asking you. I am only too grateful you have given me a roof over my head for the time being. I brought a few pieces with me – items of no great sentimental value for just such an occasion. Can you advise me of an honest jeweller?"

Mrs Embleton stood and drew her young companion to her feet. "Of course, I will write a note for you to take to an old friend of mine in Whitby. He will give you the best price for your brooch. And there is a dressmaker I know of, a very talented seamstress who can make one or two day dresses for you – she is a widow and will be glad of the custom."

Relieved, happy not to have upset or insulted her new employer, Charis returned the brooch to her pocket.

"Thank you," she said quietly. "And Martha has sent me to advise that breakfast will be on the table in ten minutes!"

"We better go down then. Martha does not like her food to go cold!"

Mrs Embleton laughed softly and together the ladies left the bedroom and descended the stairs to the breakfast room.

Mrs Embleton watched with some interest the heightened colour of her companion as Connor joined them, uncertain as to his place in the household until Mrs Embleton summoned him into the small dining room.

"Come, young man," she said firmly. "Until we ascertain your true identity, you are a guest in this house, and as such you will join Charis and myself for meals."

Connor nodded his head in her direction. "I thank you, Ma'am," he replied. "However, guest or not, I will earn my keep and await your instructions as to how I may help you."

Martha brought in a platter of freshly cooked bread, ham

and eggs and Connor left his place at the table to assist her. She thanked him, and on her departure, Connor found Mrs Embleton looking at him with a thoughtful expression on her face.

"Charis tells me she wishes to go into Whitby today," she said as she poured tea from a large brown earthenware pot, more suitable for the kitchen than her fine dining room.

"Only if that is quite convenient, Mrs Embleton," Charis replied. "I can, of course, get any shopping you may want also."

Mrs Embleton passed over a brimming cup to her companion.

Charis's cheeks, already slightly pink from Connor's entrance, went a slightly deeper shade of rose as Mrs Embleton passed Connor a cup of tea and spoke.

"I would be obliged if you would escort Charis into Whitby," she said. "She will be carrying a substantial sum of money about her person, and I would feel happier if she had you to protect her."

Connor's lips twitched at the reddening of Charis's face. "I would be honoured to escort you, Miss Waverley. Thank you for trusting me with your confidence, Mrs Embleton."

He took a sip of tea, and a thought occurred to him. His lips tightened slightly, wondering if this was a test of his honesty.

As if reading his thoughts, Charis hastily intervened. "I must visit a jeweller and a dressmaker. I would be glad of your escort, Connor." She reached out and laid a gentle hand on his arm.

An electric shock seemed to go through her body as she touched him. He looked up at her, his eyes narrowing slightly, feeling the same frisson of excitement at her touch.

"I am entirely at your service, Miss Waverley," he said, his voice suddenly hoarse with the emotion this girl aroused in him.

She withdrew her hand hastily. Turning back to her breakfast, she found her appetite had almost deserted her but she forced down a small amount of the delicious freshly baked bread and drank her tea.

Mrs Embleton watched the exchange with a slight smile on her face and a twinkle in her eyes.

Charis had come to her a withdrawn, wounded soul, a proud

young lady brought low by the threats to both her sanity and her life. Over the past few weeks she had seen Charis draw on deep reserves of courage and emerge a stronger, calmer person. She surprised Mrs Embleton by the way she adapted to her new way of life without complaint or moroseness at the sudden drop in her standard of living and place in Society. Used to the life of a well-born, wealthy young heiress who was more at home in the salons and ballrooms of London, this move to the wild North East coast must have come as a shock to her, but she bore this change in her life without any sign of brooding over her old life and embraced the changes willingly. Now this enigmatic young man entered their lives, and Mrs Embleton wondered how events would continue to unfold.

As soon as breakfast was over, Charis went to her room to don her warmest jacket, her dark red bonnet and cloak, and came down to take the letter from Mrs Embleton addressed to the local jeweller she recommended. She also gave her the address of the dressmaker and Charis tucked the notes into her small reticule looped over her wrist.

"Is there anything I can get for you, Mrs Embleton?" she enquired, tying the long red ribbons of her bonnet underneath her chin.

"Not today thank you, Charis," Mrs Embleton replied, "Give my best wishes to Sally and tell her I will be visiting her in a week or so to order a new winter dress myself. I find the weather is affecting my poor old bones more than it used to and I think a new gown is well overdue."

They looked up as Connor entered the hallway, dressed as the previous night in the borrowed clothes, plus this time a small three-cornered hat, battered and old, donated by Josiah.

He grinned as he saw their faces. "I will be glad of its protection," he explained ruefully. "It's a cold day out there!"

They bade farewell to Mrs Embleton and left the house once more, leaving by the kitchen and going up the garden path that led out to the lane behind the house. Turning in the opposite direction to that taken last night, they walked quietly together along towards the fishing village of Whitby, some two miles away.

Connor paused, putting a hand out to prevent her from walking on.

"Charis," he said, "please forgive me." He seemed to be struggling with his thoughts. He was frowning, his deep blue eyes searching hers. "I had no right to kiss you last night." He took a deep breath. "I don't know who or what I am – I could be a married man for all I know…"

She put a hand out and took his arm. "Please, Connor – forget it." She forced herself to smile at him. "There is nothing to forgive. Please, do not torture yourself over something so… so … trivial!"

His frown did not lift. What happened between them had not been trivial, and they both knew it.

"You are obviously a man of honour, Connor," she went on. "Otherwise you would not be so troubled by your actions. I also think deep down, if you were married you would somehow be aware of it."

He relaxed slightly. "I hope you are correct," he said. "My mind and brain are firmly fogged, but I truly believe that if there was a wife or family in my life, surely I would remember something!"

She turned away and, after a pause, he followed her. He offered her his arm and, glad of the support along the muddy cliff top path she took it, and they walked along together towards Whitby.

It was a cold, bright winter's day. The tide was in, and they could see the fishing fleet out to sea, and also a sailing ship that appeared to be coming into shore. Not heading into the safety of the Whitby harbour but further up the coast towards them, into one of the inlet bays south of the town.

They paused for a moment, both thinking the same thing. It was unusual for a ship of that size to put to anchor outside the harbour, and it was too clear and too early in the morning for any vessel belonging to the free traders to sail so brazenly and so freely into one of the sheltered bays. Puzzled but unable to think of a reason for the ship's actions, they walked on, along the path, through the hamlet of Saltwick Bay and passing the ruins of

Whitby Abbey. Connor stopped to look at the Abbey, and Charis, although she had seen it in passing on other occasions, went with him to look around the ruins with interest. She had never seen it up close, and they wandered through it, discovering it together, marvelling at its age. Charis recounting the legend of Saint Hilda, who lived in the Abbey over a thousand years earlier. It had fallen into ruin during the reign of Henry the Eighth and remained a landmark for passing sailors ever since. The ruins were bleak and atmospheric and when she told him the ghost of St Hilda was supposed to appear at a certain window every morning, he laughingly hurried her away from the site, towards the steep steps that led down to the village, explaining he did not think he could cope with actual ghosts when he had phantoms of his own to deal with!

Pink-cheeked from the exertion of the walk, they half ran, half walked down the steps. Charis was laughing as they reached the bottom, holding his hand to prevent herself from slipping over on the steep path at the bottom of the steps.

"Where are we bound now, Miss Waverley?" he asked, punctiliously polite now they were back amongst the hustle and bustle of the busy streets below the Abbey.

Charis paused to consult the papers given to her by Mrs Embleton. "The jewellers are along here on Church Street," she said and led the way along the narrow, cobbled street. It was lined either side of the street with cottages and shops selling a variety of goods from meat, fish, jewellery made of the local stone, Jet, and an occasional tea shop that catered for the tourist who ventured to the town to climb the steep steps and see the Abbey. It was too late in the season to attract many visitors, but one or two of the small tea shops remained open, warm and inviting.

Connor appeared pleasantly surprised at how busy Whitby was. He expected a small fishing village, but what he found was a prosperous and bustling port, with a healthy fishing fleet, a centre of shipbuilding excellence and a whaling industry all existing cheek by jowl in this small North Yorkshire town.

The jewellery shop was soon located. It, too, looked a respectable and prosperous establishment and they entered together, Connor looked around at the premises with an appreciative eye as he escorted Charis inside.

The owner was summoned and, once appraised of their mission, and their connection to Mrs Embleton, he took the brooch away into the depths of the shop and returned a few minutes later.

He bowed over Charis's hand and made a very generous offer for the brooch. Whether it was because of her employer or because the little piece of jewellery was worth more than she realised, Charis was pleased with his offer and accepted immediately.

Waiting until Charis safely deposited the coins in her small bag, Connor held the door open for her, the pair leaving together.

"Where now, Miss Waverley?" he enquired.

She tucked her hand in the crook of his arm and squeezed it. "Would you object if we stopped for a moment? I would appreciate a drink if you would not object."

He grinned, his eyes crinkling at the suggestion. "I would greatly like some ale, Charis," he confided quietly. "However, I will not sully your reputation by taking you into a common inn."

Her eyes sparkled with mischief. "I would love to go to an inn," she replied. "I have stayed at quite a few hostelries over the years, sir!"

They found a respectable establishment not far from the jewellers and on entering Charis was privately relieved that the landlord was able to offer them a small parlour in which they could partake of a light luncheon, a tankard of ale for Connor and a hot drink for Charis.

"I must thank you," he said suddenly.

"Why?" she asked, surprised at his words.

"You and Mrs Embleton," he corrected himself. "You have taken me in, a complete stranger, with no knowledge of who I am, treating me with kindness and respect."

She sipped at the hot, reviving tea. "What would you have us do?" she enquired. "Send for the militia as soon as we carried you from the beach?"

He shook his head, thoughtfully. "Many would have done so," he admitted.

"We are not like that," she replied. "And you will regain your memory soon – I am sure of it!"

They sat together in the parlour, a merry fire blazing in the hearth, a small table set between them. Warm and cosy, protected from the cold wintry day outside, Charis found herself reluctant to leave, strangely happy to find herself alone with this enigmatic, attractive man.

Connor on his part also found some kind of peace from his ceaseless worry about himself in the company of this girl. He spent a sleepless night thinking about her, a longing to be close to her that he could not, with his limited memory, ever remember experiencing before. She was unassuming and pretty, and he found himself drawn more and more to her, hoping that when his memory did return it would not bring with it the knowledge of commitments and family that would spoil any chance of a relationship with her. He hoped he was a gentleman and worthy of the lovely Miss Waverley and not a low born miscreant enjoying the fruits of a life devoted to smuggling!

They continued their day together, and leaving the inn they found their way to the home of the lady recommended by Mrs Embleton. Connor waited patiently while Charis discussed material and styles with the dressmaker. He amused the young widow's small child as Charis accompanied Sally into a small bedroom to be measured up for her new clothing and once all the business of the day had been concluded, they made arrangements to collect the garments in a week's time. Charis paid the young widow before leaving, the couple walking back over the bridge and returning to Church Street, making their way to the steep steps that led up to the lane back to Cliffe House.

The afternoon was far advanced now and the sun beginning to set in the western sky. Few people lingered around the ruined Abbey as they ascended the steps. Charis shivered suddenly as a blast of freezing cold wind blew in off the wintry North Sea, and she put a hand up to her head to prevent her bonnet from blowing off her head.

Connor smiled and turned to face her. "Your ribbons have come loose," he said, and taking the ribbons, he tied them under her chin, his fingers brushing her cheek as he did so.

His fingers were cool against her skin, his closeness and his touch unbearable. She felt herself tremble slightly as she leant closer to him. She lifted her head to look into the sapphire blue of his eyes and found his eyes gazing at her lips. She could see a pulse beating in his cheek as he sought to master his churning emotions, his hands moving from her bonnet to her shoulders, as Charis felt herself being drawn imperceptibly towards him.

The sound of a gun going off close by made them jump apart in shock.

"What the devil?" Connor looked around in alarm. They could see nothing, but he held her close by his side as if to protect her from the unseen assailants.

"It is probably a farmer shooting rabbits," she said reassuringly although the follow-up sound of another volley of gunfire made her as worried as Connor.

"That does not sound like a farmer," he replied grimly. "Keep close to me, Charis." He drew her arm through the crook of his arm and they went together towards the cliff top path.

They went past the Abbey, and she shivered again as she looked at the imposing ruins, stark against the darkening skies, casting black shadows across the surrounding fields.

They climbed over the stile leading into the first field and walking quickly they traversed it together, still seeing no one with guns, but Charis was aware of how Connor's eyes scanned the fields and horizon, searching for the gunmen, holding her tightly beside him as if to protect her from any harm.

They passed Saltwick Bay where a movement on the beach below and a flash of red alerted Connor to the presence of a man in uniform, a soldier.

"Militia," he said grimly. "Come, whatever is going on here we do not want to get caught up in it. Let us hurry, Charis."

She needed no further bidding, holding onto his arm as they hurried along. The path was full of tortuous twists and turns and dips in the natural landscape of the cliff edge. He helped her over the narrow streams and up the muddy banks. She had been careful to avoid the muddier patches on their way into Whitby, but on this return journey, she splashed through them, little caring about the state of her boots and clothing.

They were only a few fields away, and they could see the towers of Cliffe House in the distance when they heard it. A groan, coming from the ditch at the side of the path. They stopped, looking around for the source of the noise. Following the sound they found him, a man with blood on his chest, clutching the wound with a bloodied hand, his face ashen white, lying in the ditch amongst the nettles and weeds.

Pausing only to glance at Charis, Connor knelt down in the ditch with the man.

"Easy," he said as the man clutched at his hand.

"Hide me," the man whispered. "If they find me, my family will suffer…"

Charis looked up and saw a group of soldiers coming towards them. She did not immediately recognise the man in the ditch but there was something familiar about him, and he looked up at her, his eyes beseeching for understanding and help.

Connor did not hesitate. He pulled the man out of the ditch and deeper into the undergrowth at the side of it. He rolled him in the long grasses and lay down with him, covering his body with his own, pulling weeds and the heavy undergrowth over them. He was loath to leave Charis alone on the path, but he need not have worried, she walked away from him, towards the platoon.

They paused as she reached them, their leader bowing his head towards her.

"Ma'am," he said, his voice clipped, cold. "We seek a wounded man – have you seen or heard anything on this path?"

She stared at him and shook her head. "I have just walked this way from Whitby," she told him. "I have seen nothing on this path – save for yourselves of course. Was that you firing the guns I have just heard?"

"Yes, Ma'am."

"Why are you here, Sergeant?" she asked him, recognising the epaulettes on his shoulders, realising what rank he bore.

"Smugglers, Ma'am. We had information that a ship was landing contraband today and we were lying in wait for them coming ashore."

Charis stared at the soldiers in alarm. "Smugglers!" she exclaimed. "Why I must get home immediately! I live over there…" She pointed at Cliffe House. "I do not feel safe walking home alone with desperate men abroad – may I rely on your escort, sir?"

He glared at her, but she looked up at him so artlessly, so helplessly, her face a study of horror and alarm that he felt he had no option but to concur.

"You have seen nothing, Ma'am? You are sure?"

"I am very sure, Sergeant," she said firmly, waiting for him to move and he bowed, standing aside so she could pass him and with a barked order to his men, they turned and walked back the way they came. The Sergeant was obliged to offer her his arm as she stumbled. Smiling, she accepted his help and, escorted by him and his four men, she led them towards Cliffe House.

"May I offer you and your men a draught of ale before you go on your way, Sergeant?" she asked as they reached the gate.

The Sergeant looked as though he would have agreed but a shout further along the path alerted him to the presence of his commanding officer. The Major marched up and with a perfunctory bow towards Charis directed his question to his Sergeant.

"Well?"

"Nothing, sir," the Sergeant replied. "The smuggler disappeared at the top of the cliffs. We could not find him – he was not on the cliffs between here and Whitby."

"And this young lady?" The Major turned his attention to Charis.

"Sir, my name is Charis Waverley, and your men were very kind to escort me home," Charis was quick to interject. "Why, I felt quite unsafe alone on these lanes with dangerous men at large!"

The officer narrowed his eyes suspiciously at the limpid green eyes turned in his direction.

"I am sure my men were only too pleased to assist, Miss Waverley," he said coldly.

Charis smiled at him and placed a hand on his arm. "Sir, may I offer you and your men a glass of something warm to help you on your way this winter's day?"

He looked over to the inviting warmth of the kitchen where an interested Martha stood on the hearth of the open door watching the exchange.

"Regretfully I must decline your very kind offer," he said, and in response to her grateful smile, he bowed over her outstretched hand and raised it to his lips. "However, if we should be passing this way again, I would be honoured to call in."

"We would be pleased to receive you, sir...?"

"Quinn," he replied at once. "Major Jonathan Quinn. My men and I will be based in Scarborough for the foreseeable future. No doubt we will be visiting this part of the coast quite often in the next few weeks."

Charis managed to look horrified at his words. "You are surely not expecting more smuggling activity, Major?" she exclaimed. "Why, I declare, we shall not feel safe in our own homes!"

Major Quinn sought to soothe the worries of the attractive young lady clinging so helplessly to his hand. "Do not fear, Miss Waverley. We shall be patrolling this stretch of the coast, and our friends in the Revenue service will be sailing these waters on a regular basis."

"I am relieved to hear it, Major Quinn. You certainly seemed determined to wipe out this menace!" She managed to put a great deal of admiration for him into her voice and attitude.

He preened himself under her innocent gaze. "There are reports of an infamous smuggling leader being seen in this area," he explained. "I am determined to bring him to justice."

Charis felt a cold shiver of alarm go down her spine at his words. Surely it could not be Connor to whom he was referring.

Forcing herself to be pleasant, she released her hand from his and bowed her head. "Thank you so much for your men's kind attention, Major. I hope we might meet again."

He bowed and waited until she descended the path, going into the house with Martha and closing the kitchen door behind her. She put a finger to her lips as she entered.

Alice Embleton came into the kitchen. "What has happened?" she demanded.

Charis looked out of the kitchen window as the soldiers marched off back the way they had come, away from Whitby and the hidden Connor with the injured man.

"We found a wounded man on the top fields," she explained. "The soldiers were hunting for him, but Connor hid him. He looked familiar, Mrs Embleton – one of the villagers, I think. I led the soldiers away, but we must go back to help them!"

She opened the door again and made to leave, but Mrs Embleton caught her arm.

"No Charis, wait. Martha get Josiah – he will know what to do."

"Yes, Madam," Martha said and with a sidelong glance at Charis hurried out of the kitchen.

Puzzled, Charis turned back to her employer. "Ma'am, we must not delay! The man was seriously hurt – it may even now be too late!"

Alice shook her head. "Josiah will know what to do," she repeated firmly. "Now come, you look chilled."

Taking Charis by the hand, Alice led her out of the kitchen and up to the newly restored sitting room. A cheerful fire blazed in the hearth, and Charis removed her cloak and bonnet, restlessly going to the window to look out at the deepening twilight.

Alice went to the side table and poured two small glasses of sherry. Giving one to Charis, she took a sip from her own glass before sitting down in the comfortable armchair next to the fire.

"Sit down, Charis," she ordered. "There is nothing we can do for the moment. Josiah will be back soon and will bring Connor with him."

Charis turned anguished eyes to Mrs Embleton.

"They said they were searching for a renowned smuggler seen in this area lately." She swallowed a sip of the sherry, glad of its warmth. "What if it's Connor they seek?"

Alice shrugged, her face calm. "Whatever happens, we will deal with it, my dear. Now come, calm yourself." She held her hand out to her young companion and Charis, despite her misgivings, took it and sat on the stool beside Mrs Embleton, gazing into the flickering flames and wondering what next would befall them.

CHAPTER EIGHT

Night had fallen, and Connor, half carrying, half dragging the badly injured man away from their hiding place amongst the heather on the cliff top felt the chill of the winter's evening penetrate his thin clothing. He wore only his cambric shirt and fine waistcoat, his heavy overcoat now wrapped around the wounded man to stop the cold and exposure from finishing him off completely. He had lost a lot of blood and Connor, despite his loss of memory and lack of medical knowledge, had no doubt that the man would be dead before morning. He just wanted to get him home to die in the comfort of his own home, before being found by any of the military still wandering around searching for their prey.

The man's name was Eli, and between bouts of unconsciousness, he managed to point Connor in the direction of a small farm lying half a mile inland from the coast. Connor rested when he could but Eli's life was slipping away, and when he was too weak to walk, Connor lifted him and carried him as far as he could.

He stumbled over a hidden rabbit hole and would have fallen if strong hands had not suddenly grabbed at him and pulled him back to his feet. Shocked, Connor turned to see Josiah beside him. A dark presence in black clothing, he appeared from out of nowhere, a silent, welcome help.

"Come on, sir," Josiah said gruffly. "Let me get the other side of him."

"Do you know where we need to take him, Josiah?" Connor was out of breath from his exertions, but between them they lifted Eli, managing to get his arms around each of their shoulders.

"Aye, sir," Josiah replied, "you're going in the right direction.

Just over yonder." He pointed to a farmhouse in the distance, silhouetted against the moonlit, frosty night. A dim light glowed in one of the windows, and a faint, misty trail of smoke snaked up out of one of the chimneys.

"Is that his home?" Connor asked as they slowly made their way across the muddy fields.

"Not exactly," was all Josiah would say.

Puzzled, but relieved to have someone to help with the dead weight of the injured man, Connor said nothing as, together, they trudged towards their destination.

They reached a deserted farmyard, no animals or chickens ran away at their approach, it was eerily silent, and Connor felt the first prickles of alarm as Josiah led the way away from the farmhouse itself towards the barn at the other side of the yard.

He paused at the doorway into the barn, glancing at Connor as if making his mind up and raised his hand to knock quietly on the wood.

A moment passed. Connor remained silent, his senses warning him that to speak now would not be a good idea. The door opened an inch, and an eye squinted out at them. Seconds later the door was wrenched open and strong hands relieved Connor and Josiah of their burden.

"Come in, sir," Josiah said.

Connor entered the barn. Looking around, he found himself under the interested scrutiny of a dozen pairs of eyes.

He stood straight, still and wary.

"Who is this, Jo?" one of the men asked, coming forward from the shadows.

"His name's Connor," Josiah replied. "He were one of the sailors washed up onshore a couple of weeks ago!"

"Smuggler or Revenue?" the voice asked.

Josiah shrugged. "He don't know. Lost his memory, he says."

Connor nodded towards the injured man, lying now on a makeshift bed of hay. "This man is dying – I think he should be taken to his wife and family."

A derisive snort greeted his suggestion. "Eli led the Revenue men away from the beach to give us a chance to get ashore. The military are crawling all over the countryside. We'll never get him home in time."

Connor turned to Josiah. "Would you please tell me what is going on here?" he demanded, his voice low and cold as he addressed the old man.

Josiah nodded at the man who had been speaking. "Captain?" The question was in his voice.

A man came forward into the light. He was short, stout and considerably better dressed than the remainder of the men. He looked from Josiah to Connor and snapped his order.

"Hold him!" Before Connor could move, two of the silent men came forward and grasped his arms. Connor struggled to get away, pushing one away before turning on the other. He faced the tall, burly man and struck out at him to prevent himself being captured. He did not know what was going on, but he was not going down without a fight.

"Stop it!" Josiah bellowed suddenly. "This man saved Eli!"

Connor's opponent reached for him and caught him, holding on to the fine material of the shirt, which ripped under the struggle as Connor fought to get away. Another man entered the fray, and it took three of them to subdue the enraged Connor.

They held him as he struggled against their restraining hold.

Their Captain faced Connor. "What happened on the cliff?" he demanded.

Connor glared at him, but Josiah nodded and he turned back to the Captain once more.

"We found Eli in a ditch on the cliff top. He was badly injured and asked me to hide him – he was concerned his family would suffer if the Military found him." He glanced again at Josiah and back again to the leader of the strange, disparate group of men. "Miss Waverly led the soldiers away from our hiding place, and once they were gone, I tried to bring him to safety."

The Captain nodded slowly. "They were hiding on the beach. Eli was look out and warned us when he saw them. He ran up the cliff path to distract them when they showed themselves and gave us a chance to go through the caves to get away. They shot him before he got to the top." His voice low, sorrowful. "Release him," he snapped. His men let go of Connor, pushing him slightly causing him to stumble before straightening.

His eyes gradually grew accustomed to the dim lighting of the barn. Connor looked around the room to see a dozen or so men, farmers and labourers by the look of most of them, local lads and friends of Josiah and the stricken Eli. He pulled the remnants of his torn shirt back onto his shoulders, his eyes raking the room, taking in the musty bales of hay. No animals were to be seen, and in the middle of the floor, a trapdoor stood open. His eyes narrowed. A passageway to the caves along the coast, he surmised. Two of the men were trying to help Eli, removing Connor's greatcoat and doing their best to staunch the flow of blood.

"What were you smuggling?" Connor asked, seeing nothing of any interest in the darkened shadowy corners of the barn.

"We had no chance to unload the cargo. The men on the boat rowed back to the ship before we could meet." He gave a short, humourless laugh. "We had a cargo to deliver too – he is still with us!"

A man, leaning carelessly against one of the supporting beams, pushed himself upright and stepped forward into the light. He was tall, his hair long and black, tied back in a careless bow. His face tanned dark by the sun, his eyes a brilliant blue. He smiled as he looked at the newcomers.

"There will be another opportunity soon, Captain Howard," he said; his voice low. "You will be well rewarded, have no fear."

Connor stared at him, feeling suddenly dizzy and disorientated. He closed his eyes and shook his head; it was almost as if a curtain in his brain parted slightly.

The newcomer turned then and stared at Connor, his eyes narrowing.

"Why," he said. "I know this man. He was one of my own good companions on board The Scorpion. Connor, my boy, I thought I'd lost you to the sea!"

He smiled showing white, even teeth.

Connor's eye's widened. "You know me?" His voice hoarse "Who am I, sir?"

The man grinned again. "I know you are one of my best men. Your name is Connor McQueen, and you have been with me for five years."

"I regret, I cannot remember anything. My fall into the sea has rendered my memory useless. And you, sir, may I know your name?"

That wolfish smile, the flash of white teeth, the laughter dancing in his eyes. The man came forward and grasped Connor's shoulders.

"I am your Captain," he said. "Vincent. Luke Vincent."

Connor felt the room swim. He closed his eyes briefly before opening them again and staring into the face of the man before him. He was lying. He was certain of it but could say nothing, could prove nothing.

"We are smugglers?" he asked.

Luke Vincent seemed to be enjoying himself. "The best, my boy. I commanded The Scorpion, the fastest ship on the North East coast." His humour faded. His face darkened. "The best ship I ever had under my command and sunk by the fiercest storm I ever encountered."

He stepped away from Connor and with an arc of his arm indicated the men sitting in the shadows of the barn.

"These kind men have been sheltering my men and I for the last couple of weeks – they have hidden us well, but we were betrayed." His voice hardened. "The Revenue were waiting for us – they knew we were leaving today – being picked up by an old friend to take us back to our home port!"

A noise, a gurgling sound and an anguished groan, distracted Connor away from Captain Vincent. He turned and seeing Josiah kneeling beside the stricken Eli, went over to join him. He looked into Josiah's eyes and the old man shook his head. He turned back to Eli and in a sad, gentle gesture, closed the dead man's eyes.

Captain Howard's head bowed. "I thank you, young man," he

said slowly. "You could have betrayed Eli to the soldiers, but you did not."

Connor sighed. He shook his head. "I did not want his family to suffer – Eli was distressed at the thought."

Howard nodded. "His family will be looked after, have no fear of that."

Silence followed his words. Connor turned away from the sight of the dead man, being covered now in rough blankets. Josiah handed Connor his coat back, stained with blood and mud. Connor stared at it, almost uncomprehendingly. He was a smuggler? He could not believe it, but Captain Vincent said he had known him for five years.

"What will happen to you now, Captain Vincent?" he asked.

"We cannot stay here indefinitely. The militia know we are in the area and will leave no stone unturned seeking us out. I must try and charter another vessel to get us away from here. You will come with me?"

Posed as a question, nevertheless the tone behind it brooked no disobedience.

Connor shook his head. "I must return to where I have been staying, Captain. I owe them an explanation. I cannot just disappear without a word."

Vincent stared coldly at Connor. "You are a wanted man, Connor McQueen. It will only be a matter of time before you are discovered. You will be arrested and tried for your misdeeds. If you are lucky, you will be transported. If not, you will hang! Go back to your lodgings if you must but say your farewells. As soon as I have a ship, I will send word, and you must rejoin us. Do you understand?"

White-faced with shock, Connor nodded his head. "I understand…" he whispered.

Josiah stood and gripped Connor's shoulder. "Come," he said, "Mrs Embleton will be waiting for us."

Connor laid his greatcoat over the still body of Eli. "I cannot wear it now," he said softly.

A movement in the rear of the barn made him look up, and

one of Captain Vincent's men came forward. He handed a rough jacket to Connor and Connor wordlessly nodded his thanks. The coat, although too large, was a thick woollen material, and Connor was grateful for its protection against the icy winds blowing across the open countryside as they stepped outside once again.

Captain Vincent stood in the doorway of the old barn and watched as the two men made their way towards the road leading away from the farm.

"A few days, Connor," he called after him. "I will send word soon."

Connor acknowledged his words with a brief nod of the head before turning away again and walking with Josiah back to Cliffe House. His thoughts were jumbled and confused and he was assailed by the sickening knowledge that he was a wanted man, a criminal. He might even hang, Vincent said.

Charis's face swam into his head briefly. He saw the clear, unspoken look of happiness and trust as she had gazed into his eyes earlier that afternoon. He recalled the softness of her cheek as he brushed it with his fingers when fastening the ribbons of her bonnet. He closed his eyes as he remembered their kisses the previous night. She may be only a poor companion, but she had been born a lady and would have no truck with a lowly law-breaking criminal, a smuggler no less!

•

It was midnight. The moon shone down clear and luminescent on the frost grazed ground.

Charis had been sent to bed by her employer. The two ladies had made their way to their respective bedrooms some two hours earlier. Charis dutifully undressed and climbed into bed but after half an hour gave up trying to sleep. She wrapped her heavy woollen shawl around her shoulders and put another log on her small fire to heat the chilly tower room. Her window overlooked the North Sea, and as Charis sat on her narrow window seat, she scanned the cliff top path for signs of movement. She watched and waited and finally two figures came into view.

They turned in from the path and made their way down to the kitchen entrance. A glow appeared on the frosty ground as the kitchen door opened. Martha must still be up and waiting for them to return and almost without thinking, Charis went to her bedroom door and wrenched it open. She flew down the stairs and along the corridor, halting abruptly as in the shadows the figure of a man suddenly appeared. It was Connor, and for a long, silent moment as their eyes grew accustomed to the darkness, they stared at each other. She could not help herself, some force stronger than her own free will compelled her onward. She ran to him and threw herself into his arms, hearing him groan as his arms came around her, holding her tight, bands of steel around her slim frame. His lips devoured hers, crushing them under his own. He shivered from a mixture of cold and delight at her welcome, and as their kiss intensified and became deeper, more passionate, he felt the weight of his recent revelations lift from his shoulders, replaced by his growing desire for her.

Finally, with a shudder, he came back to his senses and lifted his lips from hers. He cradled her face in his hands and shook his head, his eyes deep pools of sorrow and anguish.

"He died, Charis," he whispered. "We could do nothing."

Still clinging to him, she searched his face. "Josiah found you – where did you go?"

His head drooped then and with a supreme effort of will, he pushed her away and took her hands in his.

"He led me into Hell, Charis," he whispered, his voice as anguished as his face.

She went cold at his words, his attitude – all told her something was very wrong.

"I must leave you, Charis. I do not belong here, and I am not worthy of you. I am putting you all in danger by staying here, and I cannot bear to think of anything happening to you because of me."

"Connor! Please, I don't know what you mean – what has happened?"

His hands gripped hers, forcing his rampant emotions under control.

"I met a man tonight who knows me, he knows who and what I am and I must leave with him."

"No!" Her response was heartfelt. "I don't care who or what you are, Connor, you can't go, you can't leave now!"

"We will talk in the morning," he said, his voice low, hoarse. "Please go back to bed."

Abruptly he dropped her hands and stepped away from her. Bereft, bewildered, Charis stepped back as he brushed past her and went along the corridor to his own room. His eyes sought hers for one last lingering moment before he entered and closed the door behind him.

Tormented by a longing never before experienced, she wanted more than anything to go after him, to go to him, beg him to tell her what was wrong, what happened, but as she took the first faltering step to follow him, she stopped as a gentle voice called to her.

"Charis."

She spun round to see Alice Embleton, also dressed in nightgown and shawl, standing at the end of the narrow hallway, holding a candle.

Even in the darkness of the hall, Charis could see the sadness etched on Mrs Embleton's face.

"Go to bed, child," Alice said softly. "We will talk tomorrow."

"No!" Charis retorted. "I can't sleep. Something terrible has happened to Connor – please, tell me what is going on!"

Alice sighed, nodding and beckoning Charis to join her. Together they descended the stairs to the small sitting room Charis had so diligently restored only two days earlier. A small fire still crackled in the hearth and Alice added more logs, poking the embers to start a flame licking along the dried wood.

She sat down in the small armchair at the side of the fire and Charis followed, seating herself opposite her employer.

For a moment Alice said nothing. She stared at the flickering flames and closed her eyes briefly before opening them and smiling across to Charis.

"Would you pour us a glass of sherry each please, Charis?" she asked quietly.

Charis hid her impatience and did as she was bid. She filled two small glasses and handed one to Alice.

Alice smiled gently at her companion and lifted the glass of dark liquid, glowing ruby red in the dim light of the candle and firelight.

"This sherry, my dear, is from Portugal." She nodded over towards the small console table next to the wall. "The brandy is from France. Our morning tea comes from abroad, and we quite often receive gifts of game and meat. We are never without a healthy larder full of food."

Charis was puzzled. "Gifts from grateful villagers and farmers for your concern and charity, Ma'am," she said. "Surely no more than that? The sherry and brandy – why you said yourself you often get goods from shipwrecks."

Alice sighed and, shaking her head, sipped at the sherry. "You are a good girl, Charis. I did not wish to involve you in matters that may have disturbed you or made you wish to leave my home. I did not know your father well, my dear, we were distant cousins only, but Emily loved him, and for their sakes, I was happy to welcome you into my home and willing to give you refuge against the machinations of your stepmother." She paused once more, gazing over at Charis as she remained still, rapt by Alice's words. "I did not want to upset you, and I did what I could to protect you from the truth."

"The truth, Ma'am? Pray, please tell me what you mean!"

"I am not a rich woman, Charis," Alice continued. "I was left almost destitute when my husband died. If it had not been for the generosity of your father and my sister Emily, I doubt I should have survived for long without having to sell this house and eke out a very miserable existence."

Her eyes went from Charis to the flames as the logs in the

fireplace crackled and sent welcoming warmth to the far corners of the room.

"I was – approached – by certain people who once had dealings with my late husband. They offered me the same terms as they gave him. Goods and payment in kind for the use of our cellars to hide contraband smuggled into the country."

Charis's eyes widened at Mrs Embleton's words. "Smugglers? You are in league with them?"

Alice's smile was a little more forced, but her eyes held a glint of steel. "I am, Charis," she replied. "Underneath this house is a cellar with a tunnel that leads directly to the caves half a mile away. The cave is high enough out of the water for it not to flood too often and large enough to be accessible from a small boat carrying contraband. They land their cargoes here and leave it in my cellar until they can move them without being discovered by the Revenue."

She sat back heavily in her padded armchair. "Josiah helps the smugglers from time to time and Eli, the wounded man you found tonight, is one of the farmers from over near Robin Hood's Bay."

Charis was more shocked than she could say. Mrs Embleton always seemed to be the epitome of respectable gentility. It seemed impossible that she could be connected to such lawbreaking.

"Please do not judge me too harshly, Charis," Alice continued. "I do what I can to help the poor and sick; I share what I am given with the fishermen and whaler's widows. Whitby is a prosperous town, but there is a high mortality amongst the men. Their families receive little in the way of help once they are not here to provide for them."

Charis swallowed a mouthful of sherry and some spark returned to her eyes. "I do not judge you, Ma'am. I see what you do to help people – I see the result of poverty and sickness. I would not be here if it were not for your generosity in taking me in. I cannot condemn you for doing what you could to survive."

A thought occurred to her as she sipped her sherry in that dimly lit room.

"Mrs Embleton...." she began hesitantly. "Have I met any of the smuggling fraternity since I have been here?"

Alice chuckled softly to herself. "Everyone you have met has had dealings with them at some time or another," she replied. "Doctor Rutter is paid in brandy for some of his services." Her smile broadened, genuinely amused. "Even the vicar is not above accepting wine for turning a blind eye to some of his parishioners' more – nocturnal – activities."

"Mr Soames, the Vicar?"

As Mr Soames was a very pompous individual whose sermons were normally extremely boring and long-winded, Charis could not help but laugh at the thought of him accepting the smuggled wine from the same scoundrels he castigated every week from the pulpit!

She stopped the chuckle with an effort. Putting down her glass, she crossed the hearth to kneel beside Mrs Embleton's chair. She looked up at Alice and took her hand. "Thank you for telling me the truth," she said softly. "Thank you for trying to protect me from what is happening – I realise this must have been hard for you. You have had a difficult time, but you have welcomed me here and made me feel at home. I would never criticise you for your actions and would never betray you or your trust in me." She paused, squeezing Alice's hand. "Connor..." Her voice shook slightly. "He – he said he had to leave us – that he was not worthy of me..."

"Josiah told me he was recognised," Alice explained gently. "We have been hiding in the community a famous, or rather, infamous group of smugglers who came ashore during that same storm that brought Connor to our door. Their leader is called Luke Vincent. He claims to know Connor. He says our guest is a wanted man, and he is to leave with them as soon as another ship can be found for them."

Charis's eyes widened and she shook her head. "No, no – it can't be true!" she whispered passionately. "Connor can't be one of them – he is too good – too honest..."

Her eyes filled with tears and she let go of Alice's hand to raise her shaking hands to cover her face.

Alice reached out a gentle hand to smooth Charis's hair. "I will speak to Josiah again in the morning, Charis," she said softly. "Josiah said there was something about Captain Vincent he didn't trust, but he could say nothing at the time, he just wanted to get Connor out of there." Charis raised anguished eyes to Alice, her lips trembled, eyes wet with tears. "I don't understand what the matter is with me!" she whispered. "I know nothing about Connor yet the thought of him leaving fills me with dread!"

Alice smiled, her face softening in the firelight. "You cannot help what is in your heart," she replied. "All we can do is wait and hope Connor remembers who he is and that he is not quite the out and out villain, Captain Vincent says he is!"

The clock in the corner struck the hour. The two ladies looked up at it, startled to find it was two o'clock.

"Now, child," Alice said and, standing helped Charis to rise to her feet. "Now it is time for bed. Try to sleep, and we will talk to Connor in the morning. He is welcome to stay here for as long as he wishes. We will not force him to leave."

Charis wiped her eyes and pulled her shawl firmly around her shoulders. "We may not be able to keep him here, Ma'am," she replied sadly, following Alice towards the door.

They paused at the corridor and Alice bent her head slightly to kiss Charis gently on the cheek.

"Do not despair, child," she said softly. "Matters may well turn out well after all."

Charis forced a smile to her tremulous lips and taking her leave of Mrs Embleton returned to her bedroom.

That urge overwhelmed her once more – she found she could forget the constrictions of her upbringing and wanted to throw caution to the winds. She had never felt this reckless in her life. She wanted to go to Connor and seek comfort in his arms, seek forgetfulness in his kisses, seek happiness in his bed.

She shuddered as she finally climbed underneath the covers of her bed. She wanted more than anything to go to him, but she knew she could not. She could not let herself give way to this compulsion. She knew she had to wait, to be patient and hope that one day, despite all the odds against them, she and Connor might one day be together.

CHAPTER NINE

The fire blazed in the small crowded room. The bookcases groaned with the weighty tomes dedicated to all aspects of the Law. The large desk that dominated the small room was cluttered with similarly bulky volumes. Despite the snow falling heavily outside, the room was warm and cosy, and as far as the people gathered inside, perhaps slightly too overheated for their tastes.

Six people were crowded inside. Mr Kielder glowered at four of his visitors. Sir Frederick Waverley mopped his brow with his large white handkerchief as he sat at the side of Mr Kielder's desk, facing the gathered forces of Lady Henrietta Waverley, Richard and George Hardy, and Lady Henrietta's solicitor, Mr Blackridge.

"I can assure you, Mr Kielder," Mr Blackridge was saying, his voice smooth and calm. "There is nothing untoward about Sir Anthony's will. We can take this to the highest court in the land and waste vast amounts of your client's money if you wish."

"I am well aware of that!" Mr Kielder replied, his voice as raspy as his opponent's was smooth. "Miss Waverley, however, has no wish to dispute the Will. She merely wishes for some independence, a small allowance and permission to reside with her Uncle Frederick at their estate in Yorkshire."

George Hardy interjected at this point. His face was pale, his eyes showed signs of strain, and there was about him an air of desperation.

"Mr Kielder, I beg of you," he began earnestly. "Miss Waverley and I were engaged to be married. I am beside myself with worry over her well-being."

Despite his short stature Mr Kielder managed to look down his nose at George.

"Indeed?" he responded. "I understood from Miss Waverley that she refused your offer of matrimony."

George's face flushed slightly. "Miss Waverley was understandably reluctant to announce our engagement to the world so soon after the death of her father," he replied.

Henrietta stretched out her arm and patted George's hand in a gentle, consoling manner, before raising limpid blue eyes to Mr Kielder.

"Sir," she began softly, "I am desperate for news of my stepdaughter. Apart from one brief missive from her some four weeks ago, I have heard nothing, and I have no idea how she does, or what has befallen her!"

To the alarm of all the gentlemen present, tears sparkled in her huge blue eyes and she produced a lace kerchief from her reticule to dab delicately at her eyes.

"I promised my darling, Anthony, I would look after his dear sweet daughter and I cannot bear to think I have let him down."

She could not go on. Tears rolled down her cheeks, a break in her voice indicated the depths of her despair and only a man with the hardest heart could fail to be moved by her obvious distress.

"My dear Lady Henrietta," Mr Kielder replied, "the last time I received any word from your stepdaughter was a letter to assure me all is well and to ask if I succeeded in receiving permission to move to her Uncle's estate."

Lady Henrietta wiped her eyes. "Anthony would not hear of her leaving me," she sighed. "I want nothing more than the dear girl returned to our home."

She turned imploring eyes to Richard Hardy who immediately patted her hand and spoke directly to Mr Kielder.

"I think I might speak on Lady Henrietta's behalf gentlemen." He spoke quietly, with the utmost sincerity. "We must insist you tell us where Miss Waverley is currently residing in order that we may make immediate arrangements to return her to London."

Sir Frederick moved to speak at this juncture. "Miss Waverley will be spending a month with my wife and I at Christmas," he stated. "This was agreed with yourself Henrietta some time ago. I will speak to my niece upon her arrival and beg her to reconsider her decision to remain separated from her family. I assure you that all of us have the best interest of my niece at heart and I will attempt to persuade her to return."

He missed the sharp glance George gave Henrietta but Mr Kielder, elderly though he was, did not.

"We cannot force Miss Waverley to return," he said gently. "I understand she is quite comfortable in her present situation." He sighed. "However, I will add my voice to Sir Frederick's and implore her to return to London to take up her rightful place amongst Society."

Lady Henrietta nodded graciously at the lawyer and, standing, made ready to leave. "We can ask no more, Mr Kielder," she said softly and holding out her hand, shook hands with him.

Mr Kielder's young clerk hurried to open the door for their illustrious visitors and received such a glowing smile of thanks from her Ladyship that his cheeks turned quite pink at her graciousness.

The occupants of the outer office stood and bowed as the party left. Sir Frederick watched and waited until the door closed behind them before sitting down once again in his lawyer's office.

He shook his head at Mr Kielder. "Can they force Charis to return to London?" he asked.

Mr Kielder placed his fingertips together and studied them over the top of the glasses perched at the end of his nose. "No," he said softly. "As long as Charis remains where she is and does not attempt to join you for Christmas then I think she will be safe enough for the time being. I saw the way George looked at Henrietta. I think that young man is best kept well away from our young heiress. I thought Charis's fears were exaggerated. After today I can see she was entirely correct in her assumptions."

Frederick was appalled. "You really believe they mean her harm?"

"Indubitably," Mr Kielder replied. "Anthony was induced to change his Will, of that I have no doubt. Henrietta and Richard Hardy plotted together to get their hands on his money, and they will not let a slip of a girl like Charis come between them and a fortune."

His expression hardened. He no longer looked like a frail old man but suddenly someone far more dangerous. "We must ensure Charis remains where she is, out of harm's way for as long as it takes, Frederick! She is still four years away from inheriting her fortune and we must endeavour to keep her safe for that time!"

"In that case, I must go to her and warn her to remain hidden," Frederick replied, to be stopped by a gentle shake of Mr Kielder's head.

"No, Frederick, please do not attempt to visit Charis." He said. "I have no doubt Richard Hardy will be having us watched in case we do anything like that. I will send word to Emily Andrews to write to her sister advising her to keep Charis with her and not allow her to return to London for the foreseeable future, nor must she go to you for Christmas, Sir Frederick."

Frederick sighed once more. "My wife was looking forward to seeing Charis again," he said, somewhat mournfully.

As Mr Kielder had no doubt that Lady Waverley was more interested is Charis's usefulness with the children than any other reason, he resolutely shook his head.

"We will advance Charis and Mrs Embleton some further monies with your permission, Sir Frederick. I daresay their funds will be running fairly low now."

"Quite. Please do. Also if you are writing to my niece, please advise her that we look forward to welcoming her back into the bosom of her family just as soon as all this unpleasant business is sorted out!"

Mr Kielder was more worried than he cared to admit. Richard Hardy was acquiring quite a few gambling debts and although his family fortune was so far untouched, it would not be long before he would need to start selling off his land to repay them. Rumour had it that George Hardy too was in need of funds and what better way to acquire a fortune than by marrying one? A sad business, Mr Kielder was forced to admit, and he once again wondered at the foolishness of an old man seduced by the looks and charms of a beautiful young woman. Sir Anthony had never been a fool and it spoke volumes to the charms of Lady Henrietta that she managed to manipulate him so cleverly. Mr Kielder had doubted the urgency of Charis's need to escape them all, but he knew now she had been wise to get away when she had done.

Bidding farewell to Sir Frederick, Mr Kielder drew a sheet of paper towards him and wrote a long letter to Miss Waverley, urging her to remain with Alice Embleton, remain safe and do nothing until she heard from him. Summoning his clerk, he gave the boy the letter, a small purse of gold coins and sent him on his way to Mrs Andrews, urging him to go quickly and speak to no one.

·

The lad hurrying through the snowfall and frozen streets of London did not notice the tall, dark coated gentleman following him. Through the busy streets, they went, the young man intent on his mission, oblivious to any distractions.

The gentleman following him did not attempt to stop or delay the boy. His instructions were clear; he was to shadow anyone who left Mr Kielder's office in the aftermath of Richard Hardy's visit. He did not wait long. He lingered outside the office, warming himself on one of the braziers alight with a fierce fire, roasting chestnuts in the busy street. The party departed, and their carriage trundled away down the busy cobbled thoroughfare. The dark-coated man receiving a brief nod from one of the occupants of the well-padded coach as it passed.

The lad passed him, and the man hurried to keep up with him as he wound his way through the maze of streets in the city. His task was a simple one. Stop the boy and find out where he was going and his business there.

His opportunity came at last as the boy left the bustling streets and turned into a small, well-kept square. He paused to pull a letter from his pocket, and it was then the tall man acted. Moving quickly he came up behind the boy and raising a small cosh brought it down sharply on the lad's head. Blood spurted from the boy's head as with a groan he collapsed. The man caught him, and in seconds he had taken the letter and the gold from the boy's possession and dropped the child leaving him in a bloody, crumpled heap.

A passer-by saw the boy and seeing the tall man bending over the small heap on the floor, cried out in alarm.

The man glanced up quickly, and in seconds he had gone, running back the way he came, losing himself in the myriad streets, before a hue and cry could be started and he found himself the quarry in a hunt for the attacker of the young messenger.

The boy found himself being lifted and he opened his eyes to try and focus on the face of a stern-faced man dressed in the livery of a footman.

"Where were you going, lad?" the footman asked.

He shook his head to clear his vision. "The house of a Mrs Andrews," he whispered, and the footman wound his way through the gathered crowd and carried the boy up the steps where a couple of members of Emily's staff were standing, watching the drama unfolding outside.

They looked down in horror at the blood-streaked boy.

"Said he was coming here," the footman explained. "The footpad who did it ran off before we could stop him."

The boy, white-faced, struggled to release himself from the arms of his erstwhile rescuer. He swayed slightly and kept hold of the footman's arm. "Mrs Andrews," he whispered. "I had a letter and money for Mrs Andrews – from Mr Kielder."

Recognition passed between the two servants.

"Come in, boy," they said, and the maid put her arm around the boy's shoulders. "Thank you for your help," she said to the man before her. "We will look after him now."

Knowing they had been dismissed, the crowd started to disperse as the boy was helped into the house. He sat down on a hall chair and waited as the maid went to fetch water and a cloth to clean his wound. Moments later Emily herself came into the hall, summoned by her concerned servant.

The maid came back in and carefully cleaned the boy's face and head with a dampened cloth, wiping away the blood, leaving the child white-faced and trembling with shock.

"John, help the boy into my drawing room and bring him a glass of brandy," Emily ordered and led the way into her room followed by the two servants and the boy.

They made him comfortable on one of the small sofas, and he sipped the brandy, coughing slightly. They waited until a little colour came back into his cheeks.

"What's your name, child?" Emily asked, seating herself opposite him.

"Thomas, Ma'am," he replied.

"And you have been sent to me by Mr Kielder?"

A flash of real anger came from the boy's eyes. "I works for him, Ma'am!" he asserted. "I'm one of his best runners – he always trusts me with the best jobs."

"I'm sure you are, Thomas," Emily replied, soothingly. "Can you tell me what has happened?"

He swallowed a little more brandy. "Mr Kielder sent me with a letter and some money, Ma'am. He said the money was for you to put in your bank and send a note to Miss Charis."

"Ah," Emily nodded, understanding at once.

"I was just looking at the address on the letter, and then someone came up behind me and hit me over the head. Next thing I knows they're carrying me in here." Realisation dawned. He sat up suddenly, wincing at the pain in his head. "The letter – the money! They're gone, Ma'am!"

"Did you see your assailant, Thomas?" Emily asked gently.

Mortified, the boy shook his head.

Emily sighed. "No matter. I have a good idea who it might have been. John, get the carriage ready, we are taking Thomas back to Mr Kielder's, and I will be accompanying him. "

Emily smiled down at the boy and stood, her mouth set in a firm, straight line. She looked out of the windows at the swiftly gathering twilight, and a quickly suppressed surge of anger filled her. "Stay here and rest for a few minutes, Thomas, whilst I get ready. Molly will take good care of you."

She left the room, a sense of anger and foreboding filling her, knowing that very soon Henrietta and Richard Hardy would know Charis's whereabouts and it would be a race against time as to who could get to Charis first.

Richard Hardy paced up and down in front of the marble fireplace in the subdued elegance of the Waverley townhouse. His face contorted with fury. He shook with temper, and in his hands, he held a crumpled piece of parchment. He read the letter with growing impatience and anger. Mr Kielder was obviously not the old fool they had taken him for, and Frederick too was proving to be a distinct thorn in Henrietta's side. He refused to allow her access to the Waverley Estate and he resolutely refused point blank to permit her to keep any of the Waverley family heirlooms. She had reluctantly been forced to hand over the jewellery to Frederick's wife and had only been able to keep the several valuable pieces Anthony purchased for her during their marriage. His anger had been compounded by the knowledge that Charis had slipped through their fingers, the fortune remained untouchable, and George had failed in his attempt to charm the girl into matrimony. She was gone before he could carry out his threat to kidnap and marry her by force if necessary. A few more weeks and the entire fortune belonging to Anthony would have been Henrietta's and, by default, his. Instead, they were reading the letter so carefully penned by the old family solicitor warning Charis to remain with Alice Embleton and not to venture far from the safety of her chosen refuge. She was not to visit Frederick at Christmas and on no account was she to return to London!

"Richard, please calm yourself, my dear!" Henrietta tried to soothe her agitated lover. She hated to see him in this mood and felt uneasy as his face darkened with fury.

"Alice Embleton – who is this woman? Do you know her?"

"A distant cousin of Anthony's," Henrietta replied, her voice deliberately calm. "She is Emily's sister. All I know about her is that she lives in some God-forsaken crumbling castle hundreds of miles away. She was left impoverished when her husband died, and Anthony used to visit her when he went to his estates in the North. He used to give her funds occasionally, but she is a proud woman and refused to accept a pension from him."

Richard threw the letter at her. "That stupid old man is now telling her to remain where she is, out of harm's way! How dare he presume to interfere? How dare he warn her against contacting you?"

Henrietta went to him and put her hands on his arm, forcing him to stop his frantic pacing.

"Please calm down, Richard," she repeated. "At least we have some idea of where she is now living. We can make arrangements to travel there and…" She paused, a slow smile lifting her full lips. "Insist she returns to the bosom of her family. She must return home with us, she has no choice. Unless the chit has married someone in the last eight weeks, I am her legal guardian, and the law is on my side."

Richard's scowl lifted slightly. He moved away from her and went to the French windows overlooking the snow covered garden. Henrietta paused before following him and placed a placatory hand on his arm

"Unfortunately the weather seems to be conspiring against us, Richard," she sighed.

The gathering twilight made even darker by the snow-swollen clouds obscuring the weak winter sun.

Richard's scowl did not lift. His pressing financial affairs were sufficient to make him reckless but even he was not foolhardy enough to attempt a journey of some three hundred miles in such inclement and dangerous weather conditions.

"We will delay our journey for the time being," he assured her. "But we will go as soon as possible. In the meantime, there are more than enough amusements in the capital to keep us diverted until the weather improves!"

She was relieved to see a smile return to his lips and a glint in his eyes. She held out her hand, and he took it, raising it to his lips to press a gentle kiss upon it.

"Dear Richard!" she said softly. "You always know how to lift my spirits!"

In reply, Richard released her hand to pull his lover into his arms. He kissed her, and for the time being she allowed herself to be amused, putting Charis Waverley firmly out of her mind.

•

Word spread quickly. The ship was returning to port, fresh from the battles taking place out in the Atlantic and around the coast of the Mediterranean. She flew to the quayside, along with all the other women anxiously awaiting the return of husbands, sons and fathers. It was a cold, blustery autumnal day and she wrapped a threadbare cloak around her thin shoulders, bundling the child into her coat, a thick red woollen garment purchased by her doting daddy on his last shore leave.

She half carried, half dragged her little girl, desperate for the sight of her long-awaited husband, tales of the battles endured with the French coming to Portsmouth only in rumours and conjecture. She had not heard from him for months, she did not even know if he still lived and a mixture of anxiety and hope marred the fragile beauty of her face. They arrived at the quayside, and she fought her way through the crowds, carrying Lily and pushing their way through. She watched as the huge ship docked, her eyes searching the rails for a sight of that longed for, beloved face. It

took an hour before the anchor was dropped, the ropes played out and fastened to the capstans. Then, finally, the gangplank was produced, and the waiting crowd cheered as the first of the sailors started to disembark.

All around her, the joyous sounds of reunion mingled with the cries of despair as news came to those finding out that loved ones were not on board, were not returning. She searched desperately, but could not see him. She finally saw someone she recognised, a

117

friend of his – and she called out to him, pushing her way to stop him as he wound his way to his own wife and family.

He saw her, and his face changed. Happiness at the sight of his family altered to one of unutterable sorrow as Henrietta reached him. She did not need to hear him speak. His face told her everything she needed to know and as he silently shook his head an arrow of despair and anguish pierced her heart.

"No!" she screamed, joining in with the other bereaved and distraught wives. She dropped Lily, the child clutching her skirts as a wave of nausea and dizziness overcame her. She collapsed onto her knees on the cold flagstones of the quayside, she was sobbing, and a frightened Lily clung to her mama, her bewilderment evident as her eyes filled with tears.

His friend and family came to her, raised her to her feet, attempted to comfort her, but she could not be appeased. His friend tried to explain, her husband was missing, feared dead. He had been injured at Trafalgar and had not been seen afterwards. Intransigent hope flared briefly – no body meant he could still be alive, surely? The sadness and sorrow in his friend told her otherwise.

"I'm sorry, Hetty," he said softly. "If he were still alive he would be here now, nothing on earth would have kept him from you and Lily. You were all he talked about, all he lived for."

He turned to his own wife and family, and a sad smile crossed his dour features. He delved into his coat pockets and taking out a single gold coin pressed it into Henrietta's palm.

"Here, take this – it will last you until the Navy send you the rest of his wages," he said gently and taking her arm, led her away from the ship. "It will do you no good to stay here, Hetty." He went on, "He isn't here – take the child home and get warm."

She shivered as he spoke, the worn shawl no protection against the harsh wind blowing in from the sea. Lily was crying, and Henrietta struggled to pick her daughter up, holding her tightly against her thin frame. Grief, confusion and sorrow pierced her – distraught, she wanted nothing more than to cast herself on the floor and scream, shout to the heavens above, blame God for snatching her beloved husband from her. Instead, she slowly left the quayside, and with dragging footsteps wound her way back to the poor rooms she lived in with her child.

That night she lay shivering in her bed, holding Lily to her for both warmth and comfort. Memories of happier days flooded through her. Her wedding day in the little church overlooking the sea, running through the fields with him, letting him catch her and falling together in mutual passion, making love amongst the fields of golden wheat. Memories of walking hand in hand along the edge of the sands, their feet wet and cold and both of them too happy to care. His joy as his little girl was placed in his arms – his little Lily. How he had loved them both.

•

Henrietta awoke and sat up in her bed, beads of sweat dampening her brow, and a cry, quickly stifled, about to leave her lips. Her breathing was laboured and rasping, and she fought to control the emotions that threatened to overcome her. The nightmare troubled her less now but it was always the same, and she would awaken each time with a wave of horror and despair washing over her. Her beloved husband dead, her child dying and she herself left to find her own way in the world without family, money or hope. She had survived though, and as she looked down on the sleeping form of her lover, she took a deep, shuddering breath. Richard had saved her and now, with the help of Anthony's money and that wretched, wayward girl, Charis, she was going to save Richard.

She lay down once more onto her soft pillows and pulled the covers over her chilled body. She lay staring at the ceiling, waiting for sleep to claim her once more, knowing she would lay awake for an eternity, thinking, remembering, reliving those moments in her life that caused these nightmares. Finally, her eyelids closed and her final thoughts before sleep overcame her once more, was the memory of her husband, his roguish blue eyes twinkling at her as he kissed her goodbye on that long ago Portsmouth quayside.

CHAPTER TEN

The snow beginning to fall on the city of London was even now making the roads and pathways around Cliffe House unrecognisable. Thick swirling snowflakes fell constantly, covering the land until the bushes in the garden were strange alien shapes and the view from the windows one of unremitting whiteness, the turbulent grey seas a vague ghostly image through the heavy leaden blizzard.

Charis, wrapped in a heavy woollen shawl, dragged her gaze from the unrelenting bleakness of the view outside to turn her head as a knock on the door heralded the arrival of Josiah, carrying an armful of logs to stack beside the fire blazing merrily in her small bedroom.

"Thank you, Josiah," she said turning away from the window. "Is everyone up yet?"

It was early, barely seven o'clock, and from the dark shadows underneath her eyes, it was obvious Charis had not slept well.

"Mrs Embleton is not down yet, Miss," Josiah replied, unburdening himself of the logs. "Martha's preparing breakfast and no sign of young Connor yet."

"Thank you. I will go down and help Martha." She moved towards the door, and Josiah held it open for her.

He nodded his head at her. "He's a good lad, Miss," he said softly. "No matter what anyone says, he's no villain."

She smiled wanly at him. Nodding in return, she passed him and made her way slowly down the stairs towards the kitchen.

Martha was busy, moving around the large open fire warming the stone flags of the floor. There was a kettle boiling and a pot over the fire, the aroma of thick creamy porridge filling the kitchen as she sliced thick pieces of bread on the kitchen table. The room was warm and welcoming, and Martha smiled as Charis entered the room.

"Now then, lass, you sit yersel' down and I'll pour you a nice cup o' tea."

"Thank you, Martha. Is there anything I can do to help?"

"Nay, lass," Martha bustled around the table and placed a cup of strongly brewed tea in front of her.

"Get this down, you look fair worn out. Did you not sleep well, lass?"

Charis shook her head. "It was a strange night, Martha," she said, suddenly glad of the strong hot brew. She sipped it slowly, allowing the tea to revive her slightly.

"Aye." Martha's face darkened, in mutual sympathy over the fate of the unfortunate Eli. "Happen we'll have to pay a visit to Eli's folk later today." She sighed.

Charis nodded. "I'll come with you if I may," she said.

Martha nodded and returned to her bread, passing a slice of thickly buttered bread over to Charis who, suddenly aware of feeling hungry, started to eat. The events of the previous night still troubled her. Strangely enough, the knowledge that Alice was in league with the smuggling fraternity did not bother her as much as she thought it might. Alice had explained her reasoning and knowing the straitened circumstances Alice found herself in, Charis could place no blame on that lady for carrying on her late husband's association with the gentlemen of the night. No, what troubled her was the thought that Connor was now a wanted man. She could not believe his assertions that he was a criminal. There was something so intrinsically honest about him that she was troubled that her instincts could have been so wrong. However, she sighed, sipping once again at the reviving beverage, her instincts about George had been wrong as well. He had managed to convince her of his honourable intentions – right up until the moment she realised he intended to murder her!

A glimmer of dawn light was breaking through the grey

blizzard outside, and as Charis gazed unseeingly out of the kitchen window, a movement on the path outside startled her.

Two men were outside, and as she watched, one of them raised his hand and knocked softly.

Exchanging a puzzled glance with Charis, Martha went to unbolt and open the heavy wooden door.

Two men stood before them. One was a tall, ruggedly handsome man, a heavy dark cloak wrapped around him, a three-corner hat pulled low over his thick black hair. He removed his hat and stepped over the threshold, bowing his head toward the two women.

"Ladies," he said, his voice bearing no recognisable accent. "I regret this intrusion, but I have come to collect one of my men, currently residing here."

The second man followed him in and nodded towards Martha. "Morning, Mrs Markham," he said.

"Good morning, Captain Howard," Martha replied, bobbing a quick, respectful curtsey in the direction of the shorter man.

The Captain cast a wary eye over Charis who had stood upon the entry of the two men.

Charis stared at the tall man. "You refer to Connor McQueen?" she asked softly.

Her face and demeanour must have given away her feelings, and the tall man grinned at her, a wolfish smile showing white, even teeth and his dark blue eyes sparkled with barely hidden amusement.

"I do indeed, Miss," he said. "He is one of my best men, and I have come to take him away." He paused slightly, aware of the entrance behind Charis of the man himself. "I hope you are not another young lady to have fallen for my friend's undoubted charms?"

There was something in the teasing manner of his tone that caused Charis's hackles to rise.

"Why, whatever do you mean, Captain – Vincent, is it not?"

The tall man swept her another bow. "It is indeed, Miss. Yes, my Connor is quite the ladies' man – a girl in every port just like every good sailor!" He seemed to be enjoying himself now. His grin widened as Connor came fully into the room.

Connor's brow furrowed, a thunderous looked etched on his face.

"Captain! You are indiscreet, sir!" he said.

Captain Vincent's amusement seemed unabated. "I believe I may owe you an apology, Miss," he said, staring into Connor's eyes. "And you may thank me yet for removing him before he seduces and leaves you."

Charis's cheeks were stained a deep red. Connor started forward, looking fit to murder the man before him but before he could speak or move, Captain Vincent's attitude changed immediately.

"Connor, get your things now." His voice became harsh, authoritative, not one to argue with. "The military are searching every house and farm along this coast. They are leaving nowhere undisturbed, and we need to get you out of here before you are discovered."

Connor scowled, but Captain Howard interjected at this point. "He is right, we need to get you away, young man. You and the people who harbour you within their walls are all in danger if you are discovered."

The anger drained from Connor's face, to be replaced by genuine concern. "I would not put Mrs Embleton and her household in any peril," he said. His head drooped slightly. "I have nothing except a few clothes Josiah has given me. I will fetch a coat and join you, Captain."

He did not look at Charis as he turned on his heel and left the warmth of the kitchen, leaving the four people staring after him.

"Might I trouble you for some tea, Martha?" Captain Howard asked, settling himself down at the kitchen table. "It's a cold, raw day out there and I would be glad of a hot drink before venturing forth once more."

Martha glanced uneasily at Captain Vincent but did as she was asked and soon steaming hot drinks were placed in front of the two men. They waited in silence, Charis struggling to contain her feelings as the words spoken by Captain Vincent sank into her mind. Connor was some kind of womanising lothario. No better than the hedonistic George Hardy. She slumped into a chair at the side of the fireplace and, with her head bowed, gazed into the crackling fire allowing the sardonic words of the Captain to play with her feelings. A wave of shame overcame her as she recalled how last night she had been on the verge of giving herself to Connor. Pulling her shawl tighter around herself, she silently gave thanks that Mrs Embleton had intervened, preventing her from going to his room, and seeking the comfort of his arms, his lips, his body.

Movement disturbed her. Charis looked up as both Mrs Embleton and Connor came back into the kitchen.

Mrs Embleton was, as usual, composed and ladylike. She greeted Captain Howard and nodded at Captain Vincent as she was introduced to him.

"I understand you are about to relieve me of my house guest, Captain," she said coolly.

Captain Vincent stood, draining the rest of the tea from his cup as he fastened his great coat.

"Yes, Madam. I trust he has caused you no problems. I thank you for your care on his behalf. He has been with me for years, one of my best men. I thought I had lost him to the storm. I do not wish to now lose him to the army."

Alice seemed unmoved by his thanks. "Believe me, Captain, I have no love for the military forces currently abiding around these shores but I would have handed him over in an instant had I thought he was any kind of danger to me or my household."

Her voice was cool and composed. An imperceptible movement of her head brought Charis to her feet, and she went to stand beside her benefactor.

Connor carried the battered old hat Josiah had given him, wearing the heavy greatcoat which once belonged to the late Mr Embleton. He held nothing else as he stood in front of the two ladies.

"Mrs Embleton, Miss Waverley. I cannot thank you enough

for everything you have done for me." He spoke with a quiet sincerity.

Charis tried to avoid his gaze, her eyes inevitably drawn to his.

He captured one of her cold hands in his, bowing over it. "Charis, please forgive me, I had no wish to hurt you in any way."

His eyes seemed to hold an anxiety she suddenly could not bear. She pulled her hand out of his. "I assure you I have suffered no hurt from you, Mr McQueen." Her eyes flashed with a surge of temper. "I would wish you good luck, sir, but I fear your chosen profession has not served you well so far."

His eyes sought hers once more for a moment, and she saw a muscle twitching in his cheek as he fought to control his emotions.

"I bid you farewell, ladies," he said, bowing slightly before turning and joining the two Captains beside the kitchen door.

Captain Howard pulled open the back door, letting the howling wind blow a flurry of snow into the warm atmosphere of the kitchen.

"Mrs Embleton, Ma'am. Thank you for your hospitality," Captain Howard said as Connor joined him.

Captain Vincent slapped the younger man on his back, and with another nod of his head towards the occupants of the kitchen, the three men left, closing the door behind them with a bang as the wind caught it.

Charis stared sightlessly at the closed door. It was as though all the energy and happiness had drained from her as Connor left. She felt unwanted tears spring to her eyes and with an impatient gesture, she dashed away the moisture before they could fall.

Alice and Martha exchanged a silent glance before Martha reached for the empty cups and carried them out to the scullery.

"I'll get your breakfast in a minute, Ma'am," she called over her shoulder.

Alice sighed as she took in the stricken expression on Charis's face. "My dear," she said softly. "Whatever that man may have said about Connor, I simply cannot believe he is quite such a black-hearted villain as he is painted."

"No, Ma'am," Charis replied, her voice emotionless, cold.

"Perhaps not – but perhaps his amnesia was hiding his true character."

She went to the kitchen table and sat down in the seat so recently vacated by Captain Vincent. The faint aroma of tobacco and alcohol assailed her nostrils, the scent of the Captain still in the air.

A dozen thoughts swirled around her head. Connor on the beach the morning after the storm, Connor asleep and helpless when they rescued him. She recalled the strength of his body, the touch of his hands, the sweet caress of his lips teasing hers.

She hung her head and clenched her hands into fists in her lap to prevent them from shaking. She had never before allowed a man to turn her head in this way. Suitors in the past had been treated with a cool indifference; only George had ever come close to thawing her composure. But Connor – she had been ready to throw caution and morals to the four winds to be with him.

A hand on her shoulder made her lift her head and look into Alice's kindly, concerned face.

"Come, my dear, help Martha with breakfast then we must all prepare ourselves for a journey."

"A journey, Ma'am?"

Alice nodded, her eyes dark and expression sombre. "Eli's family. We must go over and take something to his widow and children."

A note of bitterness crept into Charis's tone. "Surely the smuggling fraternity will more than compensate them," she said. "After all, he sacrificed himself to save his comrades."

Alice squeezed her shoulder. "They will. However, it is our duty, my dear."

Chastened, Charis nodded. "Of course, Mrs Embleton. I will assist Martha now."

She stood and, giving herself a severe mental shake, went to do as she was bid, helping Martha with breakfast, finding solace in the ordinary things, forcing herself to turn her thoughts away from the tall, enigmatic man who had so recently entered, and left her life, with such a devastating effect on her peace of mind.

•

The wind howled around the four occupants of the small trap as, with head bowed, the elderly horse trudged along the road, guided by the hedgerow, other boundaries obscured by the thick fall of snow. The horse plodded carefully through the snow, each footfall sure and careful.

Mrs Embleton owned no horses and the old mare pulling them along the five miles towards Robin Hood's Bay was borrowed from another local farmer, harnessed to the old trap Josiah kept in pristine condition for just such a journey. Alice would not have been able to walk the miles to Eli's farm, but no power on earth would have prevented her from going.

Huddled under heavy coats and grateful for an old fur blanket, Charis gazed out over the blank white canvas before her eyes, her head heavy and her heart sore after the departure this morning of the man she had grown to care for.

The journey seemed interminable, but even in the inhospitable conditions, it took them no more than just over an hour to reach the turn in the road which led to the small farmhouse.

"What will happen to Eli's family, Ma'am?" Charis asked. "He is a tenant farmer, is he not?"

Alice grimaced as she wiped snowflakes from her face. "Hopefully his sons are of an age where they can continue with the tenancy. It all depends on the owner – and I'm sure he will be magnanimous." A note of bitterness seemed to pervade Alice's voice.

"Who is the owner, Ma'am?" Charis asked.

"Squire Lockwood. He bought these lands and farms from me when my husband died. I made it part of our arrangement that the families were to be well treated, so it is to be hoped he keeps to his side of the bargain."

As the small vehicle made its way along the rutted farm track, they saw a flurry of activity and people up ahead of them. Scarlet tunics denoted the presence of the military, and as they grew closer, Charis recognised some of the men from the battalion yesterday who escorted her home along the cliff top path after Eli had been shot.

"How on earth did they find out so quickly?" Charis hissed to Mrs Embleton.

Mrs Embleton frowned as if she, too, wondered the same thing. "No doubt from the same informer who told them about the landing yesterday," she replied quietly.

The soldiers were standing outside the farmhouse and they looked up with interest as the little pony and trap clattered into the courtyard. A warning glance from Mrs Embleton to Josiah and the older man put his head down, pulling his muffler further up his face as he drew the pony to a halt. He jumped down just as one of the soldiers came over to challenge them.

"You! What are you doing here?" one of them demanded.

Josiah ignored them and held his hand up to assist the ladies from the rear of the trap.

Mrs Embleton shook the snow off the fur wrap and turned to face the inquisitor. "I have heard about the death of an old friend, and we are here to offer our condolences to the family," she said, her voice as icy cold as the frosty air surrounding them.

Charis jumped down beside her, followed by Martha holding a basket filled with freshly baked bread, butter, a large pork pie and other delicacies considered suitable for the grieving family.

"We're to let no one in," the soldier responded, his demeanour as cold as Mrs Embleton but his eyes lingering on Charis long enough to make her feel uncomfortable at his attention.

Charis glared at him, in no mood for insolence. "Kindly tell your commander of our arrival," she demanded, her voice holding a note of her old, past life as mistress of a large establishment used to dealing with recalcitrant servants.

Glancing at each other, unsure now as they recognised that they were dealing with ladies of quality rather than the humble farmers and other visitors the grieving family had received that morning, the soldiers paused in their steadfast refusal to allow admittance.

"Who shall I say is calling?" one of them demanded, his voice still loud but slightly uncertain.

"Mrs Embleton of Cliffe House," Martha announced. "And be quick about it!"

The younger of the two sentries turned and knocked loudly on the farmhouse door, opened almost immediately by a member of the family. He glared at the soldiers but upon recognising the visitors, his face cleared and the door opened wider.

"Mrs Embleton, Ma'am," he said. "Come in out of the cold, please."

Without glancing at the soldiers, Mrs Embleton and Charis entered the farm, followed by an obviously annoyed Martha. They stepped sharply out of her way as she swept by them, sniffing loudly at their impertinence.

The small party paused as they entered the warmth of the kitchen. Mrs Harker, Eli's widow, was seated with one of her daughters beside her next to the fire. Her two sons were in attendance as were two members of the militia, a red-faced man in the uniform of a Sergeant and the officer from yesterday's incident.

He stepped forward on their entrance, smiling at the ladies. "Mrs Embleton, Miss Waverley, how very pleasant to meet you again, even in these – ah – unfortunate circumstances."

"Major Quinn," Mrs Embleton replied. "It is indeed unfortunate. I understand Mr Harker was shot by one of your own soldiers." Her voice was cool, composed and her eyes did not leave his as she spoke.

"My men were on duty and discovered what we considered to be a gang of smugglers attempting to land at Saltwick Bay, Madam."

"Did you actually apprehend these smugglers, Major?" Mrs Embleton went on.

Major Quinn did not seem in any way discomfited by her questions.

"Unfortunately no, Madam," he replied, "We did not. Mr Harker was shot trying to escape."

"My Eli was not a smuggler!" Mrs Harker's voice rang out. "He were on his way home when your men set on him and shot him – he were innocent!"

Major Quinn had apparently heard the widow's spirited defence of her husband already. She would not be moved, and from the tightening of his lips, they could see he was in no mood to argue.

Charis moved closer to him, laying a soft gloved hand on his arm. "Captain," she said gently. "I fear you are not going to get any further information from the family today."

He stared down at her hand and, blushing slightly, she removed it. He, however, caught it and bowed over it slightly. His eyes softened as he looked into hers and a smile lifted the corners of his mouth.

"I fear you are correct, Miss Waverley," he agreed. "We must continue our investigations another time."

He lingered a moment too long as he held on to her hand.

He raised his eyes from hers and looked over to his Sergeant. "Get the men ready to leave," he ordered, his voice brooking no further argument.

The Sergeant left the room, and Mrs Embleton removed her coat and bonnet to sit beside the widow. Martha put the basket down on the table and with the help of Mrs Harker's daughter in law, started to unpack it.

Seeing everyone else occupied, Major Quinn led Charis over to the door.

"Miss Waverley, I wonder if I might call upon you and Mrs Embleton tomorrow evening?" he enquired.

Puzzled but not wishing to alienate him, Charis returned his smile. "Why, if you wish, Major," she replied. "I am sure we would be happy to receive you."

"Thank you. I fear there is little in the way of civilised companionship around here and I find I am longing for a little feminine company."

Charis stared into his clear eyes and sincere expression and returned his smile. "We will look forward to seeing you again, Major," she replied.

Bowing, and kissing her hand, Major Quinn nodded his farewells to the rest of the gathered company and followed his Sergeant out of the farmhouse. A collective sigh of relief echoed around the room with the departure of the company of soldiers.

"Thank you, Charis." Mrs Embleton smiled at her young companion. "They have been questioning the family for hours about Eli's involvement with the smugglers."

She nodded towards the Harkers, the widow and her gathered family. "They were afraid the boys might be taken away to Scarborough gaol tonight for further interrogation."

"How did they find out about Eli?" she asked.

The boys were grown men, but from the expressions on their faces, the prospect of a night in the local prison was not a welcome thought. They were frowning as they too had wondered about the same thing.

"We have been betrayed, Miss," one of them said. "We reckon someone told them about Dad…"

"Major Quinn does not have the best of reputations, Ma'am," Mrs Harker said, glaring at the closed door. "Whoever it was told them probably got 'persuaded' by him. Thank you, Miss, for turning his attention away from us."

Charis removed her bonnet and gloves and seated herself next to Martha at the kitchen table. With a smile to the assembled company, she sighed. "If a slight intervention on my part can remove them from your home then an evening spent in his company will not be too high a price to pay."

Her eyes followed the departing soldiers as they made their way out of the snow-covered courtyard of the farm. Major Quinn was an attractive man, and despite the reputation he seemed to have, if a gentle flirtation with him eased her aching heart after the intensity of her feelings towards Connor then so be it. She could handle a man of his ilk and had no worries that anything more serious would ever develop between them.

Sighing, satisfied that she dealt with the situation as best she could, she turned her attention to the grieving family, gathered together to grieve as one over the death of their beloved patriarch, the gentle, brave, heroic Eli.

CHAPTER ELEVEN

Mrs Embleton observed with some little amusement as Charis presented herself for dinner the following evening wearing one of her rarely seen evening gowns last worn at a quiet family dinner in London.

It was a dark red, entirely suitable for a winter's evening, the colour bringing out the copper tones in her hair. Trimmed with scarlet ribbons, she wore it with a matching shawl, an item she would not have worn in London, but in the chilly climate where she now resided, she was only too glad of its thickness and warmth.

"What time may we expect the major for dinner, Charis?" Mrs Embleton enquired innocently, sipping a small glass of sherry.

Charis seated herself on the wide window seat, looking down on to the snow-covered road outside. The snow had stopped falling but lay thickly all around the isolated house. Josiah had cleared snow from the paths and the steps leading up to the lane, but she could see no sign yet of any visitors. The moon shone full and brightly down on the frosty landscape below and lit up the scene for miles around. In one direction she could see the lane, the road beyond and the open fields. If she turned her head, she could see the moon reflecting silver on the black, restless sea.

"He did not say, Mrs Embleton," she replied, resolutely turning her back on the white flecked North Sea below her. "I do not suppose it will harm to wait half an hour though, just in case."

"In that case take a glass of sherry, child. Your cheeks are pale this evening."

Charis did as she was bid and was about to return to her seat by the window when a movement outside alerted her to a horse and rider approaching.

"I don't think we need to wait half an hour," she murmured as the rider stopped at the front door.

The front doorbell rang loudly, and a few minutes later they heard Josiah opening the door to admit their visitor. He exchanged words with the Major and emerged from the house to take the rider-less horse around to the now disused stable. It was warm and dry enough for the horse to spend the evening there but his absence meant that Martha had to bustle upstairs to announce the visitor to the ladies in the drawing room. Major Quinn followed her in and went immediately over to Mrs Embleton to bow over her hand and thank her for her kind invitation.

She smiled at the officer. "No indeed, Major, it is us who should thank you. We rarely get visitors, and we are always glad to have news of what is happening in the world outside our small corner of Yorkshire."

He turned to Charis, and she curtseyed politely as he bowed over her hand. His manners were punctilious.

"Miss Waverley, it is a pleasure to see you again."

She smiled prettily up at him, blushing slightly at the warmth of admiration she could see in his eyes.

His eyes were a cool grey, his hair cropped short was fair but with an auburn redness to it. He had high cheekbones and a thin face, but he was attractive, and Charis could feel herself thawing towards him. Her initial desire to keep him from harassing Eli's family eased now to a faint interest in the man himself. Her recent experiences, first of all with George and latterly with Connor, had served to make her cautious when dealing with members of the opposite sex. Her normal cool judgement had been sadly lacking in both instances. George had been an out and out fortune hunter and Connor – her heart had been badly bruised by Connor, more so than any other man she had ever met. His friend's assertion that Connor was nothing more than a womaniser had hurt her more than she could ever comprehend and so it was that she greeted the Major with a cautious civility.

"Major Quinn," she replied. "Thank you for coming out in such inclement weather."

"The promise of a good dinner in such convivial company was too much of a temptation to let a few snow flurries deter me."

"Charis, please get our guest a glass of sherry. You do partake, do you not, Major?"

The Major accepted a glass of the ruby rich drink and sipped it appreciatively. Raising his eyebrows at its quality, he smiled over at Mrs Embleton.

"I am sure you are well looked after at your barracks, Major. However, we are delighted to offer you a home cooked meal this evening."

"If the food is as fine as this drink, Madam, then I am sure I will be very well looked after."

A knock at the door heralded the arrival of a dour-faced Josiah.

"Dinner's ready," he said, eliciting an exasperated glance from his employer.

She stood and smiled graciously at their guest.

"I think dinner is served, Major," she announced and, dismissing her servant with a nod of her head, she led the way down to the dining room.

Charis and the Major followed her into the dining room where another cheerful fire awaited them. Martha had set the table for three and had produced the best tableware for the occasion, eliciting a slightly raised eyebrow from Mrs Embleton to Charis as the two ladies smiled at each other in joint amusement.

The Major held Mrs Embleton's chair for her as she sat down and the three were just settling down as Martha came bustling in with the first course of a hearty soup accompanied by thick slices of freshly baked bread.

She ladled the soup into three bowls, and Mrs Embleton passed them to her guest and then to Charis. Martha left the room, and they started to eat.

"Tell me, Major," Mrs Embleton said, "how long have you been stationed in this part of the world?"

"I arrived only a few weeks ago, Ma'am," he replied. "However I have been well looked after since my arrival."

He smiled over the table towards Charis. "I have been twice to the Assemblies in Scarborough thanks to the kindness of my Commanding Officer and his wife. I do not recollect seeing either of you ladies there though."

Mrs Embleton shook her head. "Unfortunately I no longer keep a carriage, Major. I dare say it is a little boring for Charis here but we will be attending the Christmas soirée in December. The Vicar very kindly escorts me every year, it is something I very much enjoy."

"I understand there is a Ball at the Whitby Assembly next week." The Major ate his soup, smiling at his hostess but his eyes went to Charis.

"Indeed?"

"If you would permit me, I would be delighted if I may escort you both?"

Mrs Embleton smiled once more, careful to hide any dismay she might have felt at the thought of further social interaction with the military.

"Charis?" she enquired.

Charis looked up from her studious buttering of the slice of bread on her side plate.

"If the Major has no objection to coming out of his way to collect us, I am sure an evening at the Assembly would be most agreeable."

She looked up at the Major and smiled, answering his own smiling countenance.

"It is some time since I danced," she said quietly. "I fear I may be rather clumsy."

"Nonsense." The Major was nothing if not gallant. "I am sure you will be delightful, Miss Waverley. When did you last attend a Ball?"

Intercepting a warning glance from Mrs Embleton, Charis lowered her eyes and crumbled a piece of bread between her fingers.

"It was some time ago, I'm afraid, Major."

Major Quinn took in the quality and richness of her evening gown, admittedly not of the latest style currently being worn in the capital, but it suggested it was being worn by a lady who had once known comfort and, if not a luxurious lifestyle, a certain degree of prosperity.

He saw what they were at pains to project: a young lady fallen on hard times forced to make her own way in the world, to make a living as a paid companion to Mrs Embleton.

He wondered at the relationship between the two women. Finishing his soup, he accepted a glass of wine from his hostess.

"May I ask if you ladies are related?" he asked.

Mrs Embleton sipped at her wine and rang the bell for Martha. "Charis is the daughter of a cousin of mine," she explained, "Sadly my cousin passed away earlier this year and Charis came to live with me."

The Major turned to Charis, and his eyes swept over her face, coming to rest on her lips.

"My condolences, Miss Waverley," he murmured. "I hope your bereavement will not prevent you accepting my invitation to the Ball."

An imperceptible nod from Mrs Embleton and Charis returned his smile. "I think that would be rather agreeable, Major," she replied.

For a moment, the Major held her eyes, and she felt unaccountably nervous under the intensity of his gaze.

Martha and Josiah offered a welcome interruption as they entered, Josiah clearing the plates and Martha to carry in the main course of a golden roasted chicken with accompanying vegetables.

Josiah nodded at the window. "Blizzard's started."

They followed his stare and watched as the swirling snowflakes obscured the scene outside.

"It seems you picked an unfortunate night for travelling," Mrs Embleton commented dryly.

The Major stood and walked to the window. The blizzard was

fierce, the snow settling deeper and the roads outside becoming impassable.

He sighed, and his shoulders slumped. "I fear I must trespass on your hospitality a little longer than anticipated, Ma'am," he said, turning back to face them.

Mrs Embleton did not miss a beat. She smiled at her unexpected guest. "Of course, Major, it would be extremely foolish to try and ride back in this weather. Please sit and eat your meal. Martha, would you please prepare the guest bedchamber for the Major?"

Charis turned to him. "Will you not be missed tonight, Major?" she enquired.

He returned to his seat and thanked Mrs Embleton as she handed him a plate filled with chicken. Martha followed with a tureen of vegetables and served them to him as he turned his attention once again to Charis.

"Not tonight, Miss Waverley," he replied. "However, if I do not report for duty by tomorrow I think the alarm will be raised. I am grateful for your hospitality tonight, Ma'am, but I will not intrude on you any longer than necessary."

"You are very welcome," Mrs Embleton added. "And Josiah will make sure your horse is well cared for." With a sharp glare at her servant, Josiah nodded at her and left the room, followed by his erstwhile wife.

"I take it your retainers have been with you a long time," the Major commented, amused by the sullen glances cast his way by Josiah. Privately he thought the elderly man impertinent, but he was prepared to overlook the slights directed towards him to enjoy the company of the very attractive young lady he dined with.

"Too long," Mrs Embleton admitted with a smile.

The evening continued in a convivial manner. The Major was charming and erudite, having recently returned to England following his adventures abroad on the Peninsular. He had not, however, been at Waterloo. A situation, he admitted, which grieved him greatly, to have missed the battle that defeated

Bonaparte. He had lost a good few friends that day, and his eyes clouded over at the memory as he described how he had been forced to remain at headquarters and missed the momentous day. His posting to the North East of England was something of a sinecure, he admitted. However, after several years of service to the Duke of Wellington, he laughingly advised he was very happy to be chasing smugglers rather than the murderous Frenchmen he had been used to.

They returned to the drawing room where they drank coffee, and the Major accepted some of Mrs Embleton's fine brandy. The quality of the alcohol aroused his suspicions, but Mrs Embleton sighed and regretted the bottle of brandy they were currently drinking was the last one given to her by an old friend as a Christmas present last year.

"Indeed, Ma'am?" The Major was no fool. He had drunk enough fine French brandy over the years to recognise it when he tasted it. "You have a very generous old friend."

She nodded her head in agreement. "Yes, the Vicar and I have known each other for many years. "

Charis hid a smile but allowed herself to talk as naturally as possible to the Major, being careful not to give too many details away about her past. Unlikely though it was that the Major would know anything about her family connections, she did not want any gossip regarding her whereabouts to reach London and be passed on to any interested parties.

As far as the Major was concerned, she was nothing but an attractive but poor girl. Companion and poor relation, she did not warrant any particular interest, except as perhaps a flirtation to pass the time away whilst stationed in this remote corner of England.

He drank quite a lot of Mrs Embleton's last bottle of brandy and Charis could see a slight glaze in his eye as he swallowed the remainder in his glass.

Martha advised them that a bedroom had been made ready and a fire lit for their guest, and as the evening drew to a close Mrs Embleton informed him that as they did not keep late hours and would be retiring as the clock struck ten.

If he was surprised at the early hour, he made no demur when accepting a candle from his hostess and followed the two ladies out of the drawing room and up the stairs to the first-floor landing.

"This way, Major," Charis advised him, leading him towards the room recently vacated by Connor.

Wishing Mrs Embleton a fond goodnight, she kissed her before walking away, the Major following her. Mrs Embleton watched them leave, the tension she had been feeling all evening still not leaving her. She did not like or trust the man she had been entertaining all night. There was something about him that did not sit well with her, and she did not like the way he had been paying attention to Charis.

She had no fears his behaviour would deteriorate in the few minutes it would take to escort him to his room, but his presence troubled her. She would be glad when the morning came, when he would leave them, and she looked forward with some foreboding to the promised Whitby outing.

Charis meanwhile led him along the corridor to the room made ready for him. She opened the door and let him into the warm and welcoming room, a merry fire blazing in the hearth.

"Thank you, Miss Waverley."

"You are very welcome, Major," she replied. "Goodnight, I hope you have a pleasant night's sleep."

She nodded her head to him and turned to continue walking away, to the steps that led up to her room in the tower.

A movement and a hand on her arm restrained her.

"Wait," he murmured softly.

She froze as his other hand rested on her shoulder and turned her round to face him.

She suddenly found herself being pulled close to his body. Too shocked to struggle, she felt his breath on her face, the brandy fumes almost making her eyes water with his proximity.

"Major!" she remonstrated.

"One moment if you please, Charis," he whispered. He might have been drinking but his voice was clear with no slurring. "I know about the smuggling," he continued. "I know your employer is involved."

Her eyes widened in surprise, but she remained silent, waiting for him to continue.

He smiled then, a slow, sensual smile and he lowered his head to kiss her. She struggled then, pulling back away from him.

"You have no proof, sir!" she protested as she pulled her head away from his.

"The wine, the brandy, the sherry – the food. The rumours abound about your mistress, my dear. I can soon find proof, have no fear." His voice was low, seductive, and it sent shivers of apprehension down her spine.

He held her close. She struggled but found herself suddenly pinned to the cold stone wall. Her candlestick flew out of her hand, the flame extinguished, plunging the corridor into darkness, lit only by the glow of the fire from the open doorway.

The whole weight of his body pressed against hers, his hands holding her prisoner, his lips a furious, demanding force crushing her mouth. She struggled and tried to scream for help, but he was relentless.

He lifted his mouth from hers briefly, and she saw the strange glitter in the cold grey of his eyes. His smile was cool and mocking. She was too shocked to speak as the words continued, slowly and menacingly into her ears.

"Say nothing of this, Charis," he said. "I have no wish for an unwilling partner. But take note – next week – after Whitby, I shall stay the night here once more, and you will come to me willingly."

"Never!" She found her voice at last.

"Then you and the lovely Mrs Embleton and her impertinent servants will all be arrested for being in league with the smuggling fraternity."

"You would not dare!" she hissed at him.

His smile was positively reptilian as he ground himself against her rigid body.

"Oh, I would dare, my dear. After all, an impoverished

gentlewoman with a poor relation as companion – who would support you against my accusations? You will find your virtue is meaningless if it were to save your Aunt from hanging."

Charis was appalled. She could hardly believe what she was hearing.

"That is blackmail, sir!" she retorted.

"Of course, it is, my dear. But I so much prefer you to come willingly to my bed. And make no mistake, I can and will carry out my threat…"

He lowered his head and kissed her once more and, finally galvanised into action, she struggled helplessly. Her actions only excited him further as, with a groan, he pulled the scarf from around her shoulders revealing her throat, and partially exposing her body. His hands moved to her breasts, squeezing them as she continued to struggle, roughly kissing and holding her, but she fought him and, with a supreme effort she took advantage of his slightly inebriated state and pushed him away.

As he stumbled back, Charis turned on her heel and ran, towards her room, up the stairs, terrified that he would follow her, not feeling safe until she closed that stout door behind her and turned the key in the lock.

Panting, trembling, she pulled her dress back onto her shoulders and moved over to her bed before collapsing onto it.

A mixture of fear and fury coursed through her. Fear of what the Major could and would do, fury that he had so assaulted her. Never had she felt so helpless. He thought her a powerless, impoverished poor relation. She had never felt the need for her father's fortune and presence so much in her life. Not for the first time, she cursed the day Sir Anthony met and married the fortune hunter who became her stepmother.

CHAPTER TWELVE

The cold sea spray drenched his face as Connor stood in the bow of the ship, holding on to the rigging that reached down from the main mast. He stared out at the open seas, no other vessels obscuring the view before him. His eyes were narrowed against the glare of the bright winter sun as he searched the far horizons. His thoughts were in turmoil at this further change in his circumstances. A few days ago he had been lost, confused, not knowing who or what he was. One thing he had learned in the last few days, however, was that he was a natural sailor. He fitted in perfectly with his companions, none of whom were known to him but whether because Captain Vincent had ordered it or whether they were old friends and shipmates he did not know, but they treated him with respect and a certain amount of caution.

He had an innate air of authority about him, and on questioning Luke Vincent about his role on the ship, he was told he had been one of the Captain's right-hand men. He did not know or recognise the vessel and nothing about his quarters or his shipmates stirred his memory, but this was explained by his Captain that this was because his original ship, the ill-fated Scorpion had gone down in the storm. The same storm which had washed him up on the beach where Charis had found him. It d so long ago now – only a matter of a couple of weeks – but her face swam before him at any given time of the day. He ached when he remembered the softness of her lips, the sweet tenderness of her kisses. Their mutual passion had been stirred, and he was only glad that he had not spoiled that sweet purity and trusting innocence.

He might have been the callous womaniser his Captain had laughingly asserted, but he could remember nothing of any other women. He could recall no adventures, amorous or otherwise with members of the fair sex. His vague recollections, coming to him through a haze, a fog of insubstantial misty half memories was of a Ball, he wore a uniform, and he was dancing with elegant, beautiful young women. The uniform was not clear, nor were the faces of the young women, but it was somewhere sumptuous and opulent. The decorations were lavish, there was champagne and laughter. Then – nothing – he could remember no more, and his frustrations grew with every glimpse of his forgotten past.

He shook his head as if to clear his mind and bring him back down to that task in hand. Droplets of seawater were dislodged from his hair. It grew now, the short crop starting to give way to thick raven curls over his ears that were beginning to cover his neck.

The ship was heading north, back to the Captain's home port on the Northumbrian coast. Their progress was agonisingly slow. The vessel Captain Vincent had procured was old, not the smart, swift sailing vessel that had been his pride and joy. The Scorpion lay in a million shattered pieces at the bottom of the North Sea. Vincent's only consolation was the fact that he had been on his way to pick up the cargo of contraband and it had not been filled with the tea and brandy and other riches he had been due to collect. His own personal fortune had been safely stored ashore, and he had lost nothing else of value. This leaking old hulk was a far cry from The Scorpion, but at short notice, it was the best he could lay his hands on until he could get home and consolidate his position.

The problem was, as they skirted the coastline, they were forced to pause in secluded coves to avoid the curious eyes of the Revenue cutters and military platoons still scouring the coastal paths and villages north of Whitby. The weather was both a curse and a blessing to them. A boon in that the swirling snow and fogs of the winter season kept them well hidden from the authorities, and a curse in that their journey was a sluggish, protracted voyage which tested the nerves and tempers of every man aboard.

Connor's eyes strained as he sought movement out on the

open sea. The sun was setting, and soon the twilight would turn to deepest black, only the bright, harsh silver of the full moon would light their way to a safe harbour. He could see nothing, and with a sigh he turned and signalled to the helmsman. The wheel turned slowly, and the great ship veered towards land, towards the sheltered inlet they had been seeking.

The shelter of the cliffs represented safety to the men on board, but Connor felt oppressed by their overpowering darkness. Restless and on edge, his instincts were screaming out to him that something was wrong, but with the blackness of his memory he could not understand what or why.

The elderly ship moved slowly but with a surprising grace into its shelter. Connor gave the order, and the anchor dropped, halting their progress. He waited until the vessel settled and he could hear the gentle slap of the calm waters against the hull. All was silent around, and as he gazed once more out at the blackness of the seas, his mind filled with the image of the hurt expression in her eyes as he thought again of Charis.

A loud crack rent the silence of the night, followed by a shout.

One of the masts had fractured, and he started forward as it slowly toppled towards him. One of the other men on watch had called out in alarm, and as Connor reached him, they halted the fall as best they could, getting tangled in the ropes and the smaller sails as it fell around them.

It came down with a lighter crash than if Connor and his shipmate had not broken its fall. Nevertheless, it fell onto the side of the ship, and smashed the wooden balustrade around the bow as it came to rest, dangling precariously over the side, only the two men and the tangle of ropes and sails preventing it from sliding over and into the depths of the icy North Sea.

"Hell and Damnation!" the voice of their Captain exploded behind them. "This worthless hulk is going to ruin me!"

Captain Vincent strode up the stairs to the deck, followed by several other sailors, disturbed from their suppers by the sudden crash above their heads. Moving forward, they lifted the broken spur from the bow, cutting through the ropes to release it from its moorings.

Connor gathered the stiff cambric of the sails together as the other men dealt with the ropes and the broken mast.

"What now, Captain?" he asked as Captain Vincent held his lantern aloft to inspect the jagged edge of the broken mast sticking up out of the deck.

Vincent frowned. "We need to get back to Whitby," he said. "This ship is not known in that port, and we need to get the repairs done before we can get home. Whitby is the closest, and the best shipwrights in the North work from there. We can get the work carried out and be back at sea within a week."

"Wouldn't that be dangerous, Captain?" Connor asked. "The port is teeming with militia."

Vincent shook his head. "No, Howard assures me the Revenue men are scouring the coast around Scarborough. The weather is so bad at the moment there is little movement of the military, so I think a private merchant ship should be safe for a few days at least."

He kicked the broken spur with pent-up frustration and a string of expletives followed. Turning back to Connor, he lowered the lantern once more.

"Come on," he said shortly. "Let's go below while the men clear this mess up. I need a drink!"

•

The ship sailed sedately into Whitby Harbour the following afternoon. The snow fell heavily, the November day grey and overcast. The fish quay was deserted, fishing boats anchored for the day, their catch unloaded and sold on to the fishmongers to sell in their shops and cooks to serve in their inns and hotels. The shipwrights, however, were still busy. The place was a hive of activity and as Connor guided the elderly ship into its berth, Captain Vincent was already ashore, negotiating the repairs to the mast and the broken rails around the bow. Connor could see from his Captain's face as he returned to the ship that he was not a happy man.

"Bad news, Captain?" he asked as he gave the order to drop anchor and settle the ship into its mooring.

"Not good, Connor," came the reply.

Indicating with a sideways nod of his head, Vincent called Connor over to his side. "We are stuck here for at least a week," he said in a low voice. "The men are restless enough as it is. We have a cargo to pick up from Holland and no way of getting there this side of Christmas with the bad weather and now this!" He frowned. "I'll give the men a bit of shore leave. We can't let them all go ashore together, that would attract too much attention but a few each night shouldn't be a problem. The weather has kept the Revenue men and the militia at bay for the time being, but there are still some about."

Connor nodded. "Aye, Captain. I'll stay aboard tonight if you and some of the men want to go ashore."

Vincent smiled at his young shipmate, a crooked, lopsided grin that made his handsome face even more attractive.

"Not tonight, Con," he grinned. "You and I are going together tonight. I know a tavern where the ale is strong, and the women are wicked. It's been quite a while since we let our hair down!"

"But the ship, Captain?"

"We'll leave the first mate in charge. Don't worry, he'll have his turn tomorrow!" He slapped Connor's shoulder. "Go and get ready, lad. I'll sort things here with Will and then we'll be away."

Connor nodded, wondering exactly how long it had been since he and his Captain had actually been out together in any taverns, good or bad! His memory was still hidden behind a wall of blackness, and no matter how hard he tried, he could recall nothing prior to his rescue from the cold beach below Cliffe House.

He went below to freshen up. With not much in the way of clothing, he could only change into a clean linen shirt given to him as part of the bundle of clothes from Mrs Embleton. The scent of lavender triggered memories of his days in Cliffe House, coming back to him in crystal clear detail and not for the first time he wondered how Charis and the rest of the little household were faring since his departure.

An hour later the sun had set, and the two men walked through the streets of Whitby. It was still busy enough that they could blend in with the crowds of revellers out this night. They made their way along Church Street and at the sight of a redcoat in the distance, an urgent tug on his arm pulled Connor off the street and into the Board Inn, the tavern at the foot of the steps leading up to the Abbey, last frequented by Connor on that day two weeks earlier with Charis on their visit to the jewellers and dressmakers.

The landlord passed over two frothing tankards of ale. He nodded at Connor as though he recognised him from that day. "Evening, sir," he said. "Are you well? We haven't seen you here in a while."

Connor took a swallow of his ale, passing the other tankard to Luke. "I'm very well, thank you." He looked around the crowded taproom. "Business is booming, I see," he remarked.

The landlord frowned, shaking his head. "It could be better," he said darkly. "We'll all be better off when the Revenue men leave town."

He squinted across the tap room bar at the two men. "Aren't you the lad stopping at the Embleton place?"

Connor's senses were immediately alert. "Not now, but is all well with Mrs Embleton?" he asked.

The landlord sighed heavily, wiping the wooden bar with a grubby cloth. "Nay, sir, Josiah has been in complaining about that Major from the fort up at Scarborough."

"The Major?"

"Aye sir, Major Quinn. He's been sniffing around that young lass Mrs Embleton has stopping with her."

Connor could feel his hackles starting to rise. "Really?" he asked. "And is Miss Waverley welcoming his advances?"

The landlord shook his head. "Nay, sir, Josiah reckons not. Not surprising though, if rumours about him are true."

Luke caught Connor's arm. "Come away, boy – it's nought to do with you anymore."

"What rumours?" he asked, his voice cold, pulling his arms from Luke's grasp, his eyes boring into the landlord.

The landlord looked around as if to ensure no one else was within earshot.

"He's got a bad reputation, sir. Rumours of ill-treatment of prisoners, a bit too heavy-handed if you like."

"And Miss Waverley?" Connor asked, his voice icy, his gaze unwavering.

"He has a bad reputation with the ladies as well," the landlord replied. "I've seen his handiwork with a couple of the girls from Mrs Brady's."

Connor's eyebrows snapped together in a frown. "Mrs Brady?"

Luke drank a long draught of his ale. "Bawdy-house…" he said. "Prettiest girls in Whitby."

The landlord sighed heavily. "Two of them needed the attention of a medic," he said quietly. "They're good girls, never cause any trouble and go about their business without harming anyone else. He were a bit too rough with one of them, and Mrs Brady wasn't going to let him back in, but he waved a purse full of coin at her. She let him have Bella, one of the younger girls and… well, put it this way, she won't be earning much for Mrs Brady for a while."

Connor listened with growing unease. "And this man has turned his attentions to Miss Waverley?" he asked.

"Aye, sir, and Josiah said he is taking Mrs Embleton and Miss Waverley to the Whitby Assembly tonight." The landlord turned away to serve another customer but not without a final shake of his head. "Let's just hope the fact he is dealing with ladies of quality improves his manners."

Luke watched the play of emotions over the face of the younger man. "It is nought to do with you anymore, Connor," he repeated, moving away to sit at one of the side tables.

Connor stared into Luke's eyes, his gaze straightforward and unwavering: "Sir, you claim to have known me longer than any other man."

"I do know you, Connor. I do not claim to!" Luke's voice held a note of amusement at his young companion's words.

"Then why, if I am such a rake, why do I feel this unease on behalf of Miss Waverley? Surely I should be able to shrug my shoulders and turn away?"

The amusement left the eyes of Captain Vincent. He took a long draught of the cool ale and wiped his mouth. "She is a sweet young thing, boy," he said carefully. "And a lady to boot. I do not care for the thought of her being ill-used by the likes of Jonathan Quinn." He paused as if debating whether to continue but he went on. "I have also heard of Quinn's methods." He spoke carefully. "He has, like the landlord says, a bad reputation and many a confession has led to good men being hanged whilst in his charge. Confessions made…" His voice lowered, and his eyes hardened. "Confessions made under torture at the orders of Major Quinn. In fact, it is said he has been known to personally enjoy inflicting pain on his captives."

"Surely his Commanding Officers would not permit this to happen?" Connor was outraged.

Luke shook his head. "They never get to know. They are too pleased with his results to care!" He looked down at his tankard, his fist curling around the pewter. "From what Captain Howard tells me, your Mrs Embleton is a good friend to the smuggling fraternity. I can only guess that rumours of her involvement have reached Quinn's ears, which is why he is so attentive to the ladies at Cliffe House."

"And his attentions to Charis?"

Luke shook his head. "She is a poor companion. Without influential friends or relatives, she is as helpless in his hands as those poor girls at Mrs Brady's."

A growing sense of horror filled Connor, and he raised anguished eyes to his Captain. "Sir, I cannot let this happen." He took a swift gulp of the ale in the tankard before him. "Do you know where the Assembly Rooms are, sir?" he asked.

Captain Vincent's gaze never faltered. "You will never be allowed in boy," he said shortly. "You are not dressed for the occasion."

A grin split Connor's face and his eyes danced with sudden merriment. "But you, Captain, can surely loan me something suitable?"

"My wardrobe went down with the Scorpion," Luke retorted but, his sense of humour, as well as his sense of adventure, was suddenly piqued. "However, an evening spent at such a convivial event sounds slightly more diverting than the taverns of Whitby. Especially as Mrs Brady seems to have lost a couple of her young ladies. We will find no entertainment there tonight." He swallowed the last of his ale. "Drink up, boy." He grinned back at Connor. "We will have some sport with Major Quinn, I think!"

Connor finished his drink in one swallow and stood, replacing the three-cornered hat on his head. He followed his Captain out of the tavern with an eagerness brought on as much at the thought of thwarting whatever the Major might have been planning as the thought of seeing the lovely Charis Waverley again.

CHAPTER THIRTEEN

The carriages pulling up outside the doors of the Whitby Assembly Rooms disgorged their passengers onto pathways cleared of the fallen snow, lanterns lighting the way and footmen in attendance to escort the revellers into the festively decorated ballroom.

Charis and Mrs Embleton accompanied Major Quinn into the rooms, leaving their cloaks with the maidservants as they did so. Both ladies were elegantly dressed for the occasion. Charis had brought an evening gown with her from London, and she wore it tonight, finer than anything she had previously worn since her arrival at Cliffe House. She wore it in defiance of the belief held by Major Quinn that as a poor relation she would have nothing suitable to wear. She did, in fact, outshine most ladies present that evening.

Her gown of rich rose coloured silk was embroidered with dozens of tiny seed pearls that shimmered and sparkled under the lights of the chandeliers. Alice had been taken aback by her appearance and smiled with satisfaction as Charis attracted the attention of most of the young men in the ballroom.

Major Quinn had seemed disconcerted when he arrived to collect the two ladies, but he complimented them both on their appearance and was charm itself as he escorted them to his waiting carriage.

Their appearance in the Assembly Rooms caused more attention than he had been anticipating and it was with hastily averted annoyance that he watched as Charis went to dance with the son of the local Mayor. Manners and custom prevailed upon him as he offered his arm to Mrs Embleton and they joined in with the dancing.

Mrs Embleton was well known to everyone in the Assembly, and as several members of the militia were also there that evening, the Major was separated from his party. He was afforded the sight of Charis dancing with several young men, but he held his temper and reminded himself grimly that it was of no matter. If she did not want her employer and servants to be taken to the fort for interrogation – and he had no scruples about what methods were used to question old men and women – she would accede to his demands later that night.

She had been cool towards him ever since that night outside his room. Her demeanour had been icily polite on their meeting again the following morning over breakfast and tonight, their next meeting, she had been civil and cool but no more. He smiled to himself at the thought of melting that ice maiden exterior later.

The music swelled and came to a halt, and an intermission for supper announced. He made his way over to Mrs Embleton who was deep in discussion with a man he recognised from the fort. It was a doctor who had been summoned to attend to one of his commanding officers.

He bowed politely. "Doctor Rutter, I believe," he said.

The Doctor returned his bow with a slight nod of his head. The Major was also known to him, and he was not enamoured of the man.

Charis came back from her dancing, slightly pink-cheeked and out of breath. Dr Rutter smiled warmly at her. "Charis, my dear," he said, bowing over her hand. "How are you tonight? You look radiant!"

She returned his smile and pressed a hand against her breast. "I am rather warm Doctor but very well thank you."

"May I get you a drink, Miss Waverley?" the Major asked.

Her smile faded, but she nodded. "You may, Major," she replied.

He bowed his head, and the smile did not leave his face as he moved away from them to acquire drinks for himself and the ladies.

The doctor lowered his voice as they watched the Major speak to one of the footmen bearing a tray of champagne. "I do not care for your companion, my dear Alice," he said.

Alice Embleton's smile did not waver, nor did it reach her eyes as she fanned herself with ornately large ostrich feathers.

"Nor do I," she replied. "But he seemed to have developed rather a penchant for Charis here, and I am loath to discourage his attentions."

Charis turned away from looking at the Major, and her demeanour one cold, bristling anger. "We discourage him at our peril," she said shortly. "The man is dangerous, Ma'am, make no mistake."

She could say no more as the Major returned, accompanied by the footman, and offered champagne to them. Charis accepted a glass, swallowing the alcohol carefully. She was thirsty but aware that she could not let the alcohol dull her senses. She was going to have to keep her wits about her tonight.

She had not told Alice about the threat from the Major. She had no idea how she was going to extricate herself from the position she found herself in but if she could outwit Henrietta and her murderous cronies then the Major might not be such a challenge.

She forced a smile on her face as she finished her drink. The orchestra started the strains of a waltz, and as the Major bowed to her, she took his hand and they walked together out to the dance floor.

They made a striking couple as they danced. The tall, handsome Major in his full regimental dress and Charis, stunning in her fine gown and sparkling jewellery.

"May I say how well you look tonight, Miss Waverley?" he said as he held her closer than etiquette allowed. She could feel his hand firm and hot through the thin material of her silk dress, pressing the small of her back and drawing her closer towards him.

"Thank you, Major," she replied.

"Jonathan," he replied, his voice low against her ear.

She pulled her head away from his. "Thank you, Jonathan."

"You are indeed the belle of the ball," he continued. "You are attracting a lot of attention."

"Not all of it welcome," she retorted.

He smiled, a lifting of the corners of his mouth as his eyes continued to bore into hers. "I look forward to paying you a lot more attention, Charis," he said softly.

"As indeed other men have thought," she replied, staring back at him, not missing a beat as they circled the dance floor.

"You have had other admirers, Charis?" he enquired.

"A few when I lived in London," she said calmly. "One man wanted to marry me, but I decided I would rather go and live with a distant relative than agree to a match I did not care for."

He smiled then, disconcerted slightly.

"I am not quite the poor helpless woman you think me, Major," she went on, her eyes steady, her whole bearing suddenly one of confidence and a haughtiness she had, so far, kept hidden.

If he was unsettled by this sudden change in her manner, he hid it well. "And where are the rest of your family now?" he asked.

"They remain in London, but I will be joining my Uncle in York for Christmas," she said.

The music swelled and stopped.

Standing together on the dance floor, Charis turned to rejoin Mrs Embleton. She could not see her nor Doctor Rutter, and for a moment she hesitated. It was a moment too long. She felt his hand on her arm, steering her to the doors that led to the balcony. He pulled the curtains to one side and despite her gasp of protest, she found herself outside on the balcony, the frosty night air causing her to catch her breath.

"What do you mean by this?" she demanded as he turned to her, grasping her shoulders.

"I want you to know exactly what I mean," he replied and without another word he pushed her against the wall next to the balcony door and pressed himself on her.

With one arm around her shoulders, his other hand went to her breast and squeezed it hard. She let out a scream and started to struggle.

His mouth silenced her scream, his hands hard and ruthless against her skin.

She pushed him and pulled her head away from his, letting out another cry for help. She heard a rip as his hands pulled the flimsy material of her dress from her shoulder.

"I could take you now," he snarled, his voice a harsh whisper, "but your surrender will be made all the sweeter in the warmth and comfort of your bed…"

He seemed then to be lifted from her stiff, unyielding body in one swift, fluid movement. In a moment of confusion, she watched as two men pulled him away from her and although the darkness prevented her from seeing clearly, she looked on as one of the men struck the Major with such force he fell across the stone balustrade surrounding the balcony. The Major shook his head and started to his feet, his hand going to the sword at his side, but the movement was stalled by a kick and another blow to the head that sent him reeling once again.

Charis was shaking and pressed a hand to her mouth to prevent another scream from escaping her. The man beside her held her arm to stop her from moving away into the ballroom and alerting any of the people inside.

The Major had rallied, but his opponent was relentless. He hit the Major again and again until blood spurted and blended in with the redness of the Major's dress uniform. The man beside Charis moved then and pulled his companion away from the Major's prone body.

"Connor!" His voice was sharp. "Enough – you will kill him!"

Connor breathed heavily, his hair and clothes askew following the exertion of beating the man on the floor at his feet. He pulled his arm away from the restraining hand, but he bristled with fury, anger emanating from every pore.

"Connor?" Charis's voice was a hoarse whisper.

Connor turned, and in the light of the full moon, she could see his face clearly for the first time. In four strides he was beside her, his hands gentle on her shoulders, lifting her face, seeing the tears sparkling in her eyes.

"I – I'm sorry, Charis. I heard you scream for help and I could not help myself."

"Connor!" she said again and threw her arms around his neck, pressing her shaking body into his arms, feeling their strength as they went around her, holding her close, murmuring her name over and over again.

"He will not hurt you again tonight, Miss Waverley." The other man spoke then, and she turned her head to see Luke Vincent beside them.

Connor was pulled away from her.

"Come, boy," Luke said, his voice grim, unrelenting. "Let's get away from here now. Miss Waverley, pray give us two minutes to leave and then return to the ballroom – scream for help and tell them inside that you were attacked. The Major here came to your assistance and was overpowered."

"Indeed I will not – you saved me!" she retorted.

Connor held her face between his hands, his anguished eyes staring into hers. "If you accuse the Major of attacking you, you will not be believed, and his revenge will be ruthless." He pressed a quick, hard kiss on her trembling mouth. "He will not dare to harm you and will take a while to recover, I hope. Use that time well, Charis. Try and get away from here."

"Connor!" Luke's voice was urgent now, movement from the other side of the window alerting him.

He strode over to the balustrade and looked over at the garden some ten feet below them. "This way, boy!" he demanded and climbing over, he dropped silently to the snow-covered ground below.

Connor kissed her once more before stepping away. The Major groaned, regaining consciousness and Connor paused long enough to deliver a final furious kick in his ribs before vaulting over the stone balustrade and joining Luke.

Charis ran to the edge of the balcony and watched as the two men ran to the gates leading out of the garden into the street. She waited until they disappeared into the night before turning back to kneel beside the injured Major Quinn.

"Help!" she screamed. "Help us!"

The balcony door opened then, and two burly footmen burst out of the crowded ballroom.

"Help us!" she repeated, "We have been attacked. The villains have killed the Major!"

The Major chose then to regain consciousness and groaned loudly the two footmen ran to help the injured man and the obviously distressed young lady beside him.

Taking in her torn dress and dishevelled hair, they saw no reason to doubt her story, and when Mrs Embleton appeared in search of her companion, Charis flying to her arms, sobbing loudly and hysterically, they were only too pleased to pass her over to her family to deal with.

The Major was taken back to his quarters in the fort to be attended by the doctors there as Charis gave the military and authorities the version of events Luke Vincent had advised. As the streets were scoured for the two hooded, masked men Charis described, the hysterical young woman was allowed to go home, safely escorted by friends and neighbours, leaving the Assembly to resume once the dramatic interruption had calmed down and the evening's conviviality continued unabated.

CHAPTER FOURTEEN

The majestic old ship departed the Whitby shipyard three days after the night of the Assembly. Physically restrained by the Captain from leaving the vessel to go ashore again, Connor could only wonder in agonised frustration what was happening to Charis after his attack on the Major.

A surge of fury had gripped him as they followed Charis and the Major out of the ballroom that night. He had heard her scream, heard the rip of material as the Major had forced himself on her, and saw her futile struggles as the man held her against her will. A red mist had descended, rage lending him strength he had not known he possessed. Vincent had felt it too, and the two men had flown together to save the girl from the Major's unwanted attentions.

Connor had to force his thoughts away from what might be happening ashore as the ship sailed away, not north to Alnmouth as he expected but south and east towards the Continent. Harried by Captain Vincent, the shipwrights of Whitby had responded to the extra coin waved under their noses and the new mast was installed and fitted in record time. Vincent could afford to wait no longer. There was a cargo in Rotterdam awaiting collection, and he had customers becoming impatient for delivery.

As they sailed away from England, Connor felt a lowering of his spirits, and as he kept vigil at night, watching the coast slipping away over the horizon, his thoughts never far away from Charis. He cursed his memory, relentlessly trying to get the fog in his brain to clear, to remember his life before these last few weeks. Agonisingly just out of reach, he experienced occasional flashes of clarity. A summer's day, a child playing in a tree and falling, the screams of a mother, the laughter of another child, a sibling? Was he the child, was he the brother laughing or was he the father of the two children? The memory seemed an old one, the mother's clothing dated and a faded scar on his shoulder could be the result of a childhood fall. He felt cold at the thought that perhaps he had a wife and family somewhere he could not recall… were they awaiting his return? Surely Captain Vincent would know his history, but all Luke would do was shake his head and say Connor's memory would return in its own good time. In the meantime, he must put out of his mind all thoughts of another woman and concentrate on the journey ahead.

As the coast of England finally slipped over the horizon, Connor breathed in the cold November air and looked up at the millions of stars in the clear, frosty night sky.

"Keep her safe," he whispered. "Until I return."

•

On a cliff top path walking to the edge and staring out to sea, Charis felt tears filling her eyes. She watched as the ship glided into the glow of the moon, its sails unfurled, a stark black silhouette against the silver. It moved slowly, gracefully, but with a purpose, sailing away from Whitby, away from England, away from her.

She had no idea if Connor was on board, whether it was his ship or not. All she knew was that he had saved her and then had gone. As mysteriously as he had appeared, he had left her. Perhaps this time she would never see him again. She watched as the ship in the distance gradually faded from her sight until there was nothing but the moon and the stars and the empty glittering black waters of the arctic North Sea.

"Goodbye, my love," she whispered. "Until we meet again."

•

The small drawing room was a quiet haven where Charis and Mrs Embleton sat after dinner, warmed by the crackling fire.

Charis sat on the window seat, listlessly turning the pages of the novel she had picked up to read, not taking in the story, pausing every few minutes to look out at the darkness of the night beyond.

The three sharp knocks on the door downstairs echoed loudly throughout the house. Charis looked down at the front door and saw a figure standing there, dark against the banked up snow either side of the path. He was wearing an overcoat and muffler and had a hat pulled low down on his forehead. Mrs Embleton stood at once at the sound and went across to the window to look outside.

"Do you know him, Ma'am?" Charis asked.

Alice was frowning. She had been expecting this call, but with all the militia interest over the last few weeks, she had hoped it would not come just yet.

"I don't want you getting involved any further, Charis," she said quietly. "I will go down to see to him."

"Involved?" Charis was puzzled. "Why, who is it?"

Mrs Embleton said nothing, but she pulled her shawl tighter around her shoulders and turned to leave the room. Charis forestalled her. Standing up, she followed suit and pulled a warm paisley shawl around her shoulders. She walked over to the candlesticks and lit a large white candle with a spill from the fireside.

Resolutely she waited by the door. "If it's the smugglers, Ma'am, then I will help you in whatever way I can. If it is someone else, then I do not want you answering the door alone."

"Josiah will be downstairs, Charis," Mrs Embleton replied. She opened the door, and the two of them went out into the corridor and descended to the hallway. Crossing the wide tiled floor, they found Josiah coming from the kitchen to join them.

Without a word he walked ahead of them and pulled open the heavy oak door. The man outside raised a lantern to his face and pulled the scarf from around his mouth.

"Five minutes away, Jo," he said, his voice low and guttural.

"Aye, Sam, I'll be right there," Josiah replied. "I'll just get my coat." He turned to Mrs Embleton. "I'll lead them to the caves if you can open the gate, Ma'am."

He glanced at Charis and raised his eyebrow to his employer, but Mrs Embleton nodded. "Don't worry, Josiah," she said quietly and taking Charis's arm, she led her away towards the kitchen.

They watched as Josiah pulled on a greatcoat and scarf, his clothes dark and matching the man waiting outside. The two men walked away down the path, closing the front door behind them.

Mrs Embleton walked quickly then, into the kitchen, followed closely by Charis. Martha stood beside the table and as the two ladies entered, she pushed the table out of the way and pulled back the heavy rug covering the flagstones. There was a wooden trapdoor in the floor that Charis had never seen before. Mrs Embleton took a bunch of keys out of the pocket of her dress and, crouching, unlocked it. She pulled the iron ring, and it lifted silently, revealing by the light of the kitchen, a set of stairs leading down into the cellar.

Charis was astonished. She'd had no idea the cellar even existed. Martha had readied a lantern, and handed it to Mrs Embleton who thanked her with a silent nod of the head, her face set and cold. Charis had never witnessed Mrs Embleton in such a stern and purposeful mood. She exchanged a worried glance with Martha, following Mrs Embleton down into the darkness below.

The steps were steep leading down into the cellar. Charis looked about her with interest at the large, dry and empty room. She had no time to linger however and followed Mrs Embleton across the cold flagstones to a door at the other side of the room. Mrs Embleton inserted another one of the keys on the ring. It turned smoothly, unlocking it with a loud click.

She pulled it open, and Charis stared along a lengthy tunnel, dimly lit by the light of her candle and the lantern. The walls were lined with oak timbers, and the path was hard packed sand. Mrs Embleton led the way and, taking Charis's candle she lit a torch attached to the wall by an iron holder. As they walked down the tunnel, a biting wind blew in at them, and Charis felt the sand under her feet start to become damp. She shivered at the sudden drop in temperature and seeing a faint glow in the distance realised she could see the light of the full moon illuminating the end of the tunnel.

They reached the end at last and were faced with a solid, cast iron gateway, hammered into the frame around the entrance to the tunnel. Mrs Embleton took the third and final key and unlocked the gate, letting it swing inwards, whereupon she handed Charis the lantern and secured the gate to the wall by means of a small hook.

A chill wind blew back their skirts as they watched a lantern bobbing towards them, held high by a dark figure. His face became clearer as he neared the illuminated entrance to the tunnel. It was Josiah and behind him walked others, each carrying a large barrel or wooden crate. Next to him, holding another lantern to lead the way was another man, shorter, stouter and as they reached the tunnel Charis could see it was Captain Howard, last seen some weeks ago in the morning warmth of their kitchen, the day Connor had left.

He bowed and held his hand out to Mrs Embleton. Taking hers, he raised it to his lips in an old-fashioned, courtly gesture.

"Madam," he said softly. "A pleasure to see you once again."

Mrs Embleton did not return his smile but rather withdrew her hand to hold her shawl more securely about her shoulders.

She nodded at him. "Captain Howard," she said. Her voice was cold, the bleakness of her face and tone at odds with her tone. "You are, as ever, welcome here. May I ask, how long may I expect to be custodian of your goods this time?"

They stepped back and returned to the shelter of the tunnel as the first of the long line of smugglers walked through and along to the dry room. Charis recognised several of the men who passed her. They were local farmers and fishermen, people she saw regularly, men who would speak politely to her in passing, men she saw in church every Sunday with their wives and families. She said nothing however, acknowledging their nodded greetings with a nod in response. No one spoke.

The whole operation was carried out in silence. They passed

her, they deposited their cargo in neat piles in the storeroom and returned to the beach to collect and bring more contraband ashore from the waiting longboats.

At a quiet word from Mrs Embleton, Charis returned to the storeroom, as Captain Howard and Mrs Embleton remained in whispered conversation at the entrance to the tunnel. Charis stood by the door to the storeroom, holding her lantern and lighting the way for the smugglers as they walked surefootedly along with their cargo, load after load until the room was filled to bursting with only a narrow passageway allowing access to the door leading out of the cellar.

Finally the last bolt of silk deposited, the final barrel of brandy added to the pile of others, the men returned to the beach, as quietly as they had arrived. Charis watched as they dispersed along the beach until even the brightness of the moon could not distinguish them from the deep shadows of the overhanging cliffs.

Captain Howard bade a quiet farewell to Mrs Embleton and with a final bow he, too, walked away down the beach and boarding the waiting longboat, was rowed out to sea to the ship waiting at the entrance of the bay.

Josiah came through the tunnel and, together, he and Mrs Embleton locked the barred entrance to the tunnel, joining Charis in the storeroom. They secured the outside door and stood together for a moment surveying the crowded room.

"How long, Ma'am?" he asked in lowered gruff tones.

Mrs Embleton sighed and looked around the room. "It is a larger cargo than normal," she said, her own voice as hushed as Josiah's, as if they were both wary of raising their voices even though they knew no one could hear them. "Captain Howard requests that we look after it for a few days only until he can arrange forward passage. We are permitted to take whatever we desire, within reason…" she added. "Please bring up a cask of sherry and brandy as usual, Josiah."

"Some tea, Ma'am?" he asked.

"If you please, Josiah. But hide it well – the military is

everywhere. Not only looking for smugglers but for their cargoes. There is more activity than ever up at the fort." She turned to look thoughtfully at the silent Charis. "They are still searching for the men who attacked you and the Major, Charis. Apparently Major Quinn is convinced one of them was the infamous Luke Vincent."

Charis had confided to Mrs Embleton the truth about the night of the Assembly. Despite the coldness of the room, her cheeks flushed, with anger as much as embarrassment.

"Does he indeed?" she retorted. "Well, I wish him luck in finding the gentlemen concerned! They are well gone by now, no doubt."

Mrs Embleton smiled, her first genuine show of emotion that night.

"Charis choose one of the bales of material – we will take it to Sally in Whitby and have her make us up some new gowns for the Scarborough Assembly. It will be amusing to flaunt our contraband under the eyes of the military!"

Even Josiah managed a grim smile as he did as he was bid and picked up a small barrel under each arm, going over to the stairs leading to the kitchen.

"I think I will save that pleasure until tomorrow, Ma'am," Charis responded. "I am cold, and you are very pale. I think a small glass of sherry might be appropriate now."

Mrs Embleton shivered in the chill air of the cellar. "Yes, my dear, I think we have spent enough time down here for one night."

Turning, she followed Josiah. With one final thoughtful look around the crowded cellar, Charis joined them and returned to the warmth of the kitchen, carefully locking the doors and covering the trapdoor behind them, making certain no outward signs remained on show of their disturbed night and clandestine midnight visitors.

CHAPTER FIFTEEN

Henrietta stared out at the snow-covered fields as the carriage trundled carefully along the Great North Road. She pouted at the frustratingly slow progress of their journey, leaning back in her seat, closing her eyes and resting her head against the navy blue padded squabs.

"Will this interminable journey never end?" She sighed, drawing the ermine-trimmed edges of her velvet cloak tighter around her slender frame and shivering slightly.

Richard Hardy was as tired of her complaining as he was of the lengthy journey. He tried, however, to placate her.

"It will be worth it, my dear," he reassured her. "Once we have our runaway miss home with us we can put all our plans into action."

"I think you mean when my fiancé and I are reunited..." George Hardy drawled from his position in the corner opposite Henrietta.

She smiled at him, the dimples appearing on her cheeks. "Run away with her to Gretna Green George," she said. "We will not be too far from the border once we reach Alice Embleton's home in that God-forsaken corner of the world she has chosen to hide herself in!"

"It will take us at least a week to get to Gretna." He smiled. "I think my reluctant bride will be only too happy to agree to an anvil wedding after I have completely ruined her reputation by spending several nights together."

Henrietta was diverted at last. "My dear George," she declared, "with your undoubted talents of seduction she may not be quite the unwilling bride we all anticipate!"

She laughed along with him whilst Richard observed his lover and his son from beneath lowered eyelids. The sooner his dissolute son disappeared with the lovely Miss Waverley, the better he would like it. George and Henrietta were becoming far too familiar in his opinion.

"You never know, George," he joined in with the conversation. "Perhaps you will be so enamoured of your wife you will not want to rid yourself of her quite so soon! "

"You may possibly be right, father," George drawled. "She is a fine looking filly after all. I may not be too averse to schooling her!"

Henrietta's laughter was stifled. "You will be bored in a month, my dear!" she exclaimed.

Turning her attention back to the passing scenery, she looked out at the snow-covered fields stretching into the distance. Sighing again and tired of teasing Richard with her flirting with George, she closed her eyes and tried to get comfortable. The carriage was luxurious and well-padded, but they had been travelling for several days, and she was exhausted.

The weeks leading up to this journey had been ones of increasing frustration. Despite having access to wealth she could never have in her life imagined and, having persuaded Anthony to change the Will in her favour, she found herself thwarted by her late husband's brother in accessing all of the funds she required. Her clothing allowance was miserly, and he even questioned the wisdom of keeping a stable of horses and carriages.

Somehow, despite the best efforts of the lawyer Mr Blackridge, Frederick had succeeded in demanding an enquiry and her inheritance had been blocked.

Safely ensconced in the Waverley lands in the North, Frederick had allowed enough time to pass to ensure the smooth running of the estate before turning his attention to the matter of his late brother's wife and that perfidious Will. He, along with Mr Kielder and several other members of the legal profession, suspected Sir Anthony had been coerced into changing his Will in Henrietta's favour, and he had finally been moved to contest it in a Court of Law. The wheels of justice were turning far too slowly for Lady

Waverley's liking. Confident that she would win any case against her, she was nevertheless forced to make economies unthinkable a few months ago.

Charis's inheritance had suddenly become more and more necessary! Even Richard with his title and estates had very little in the way of tangible wealth. He too was feeling the pinch, hence his suggestion that as there had been a break in the weather, they attempt to find Charis and bring her and, more importantly, her money, back safely under their control once more.

The likelihood of Charis finally becoming his wife had galvanised George into insisting he accompany them. As their plans all hinged on his marriage to the heiress, Richard had agreed to his joining them. However, George's determined flirting with Henrietta was becoming increasingly tiresome. There was something about his lover and his son that played on his mind and his suspicions that theirs was more than a flirtation began to take root.

A sudden spurt of speed roused Henrietta's interest and made her sit up sharply. She looked out of the window once again to see an empty stretch of road ahead of them. The snow had been cleared, and the horses were now able to gain a solid foothold on the frost-hard mud covering the road.

"Where are we stopping tonight, Richard?" she asked turning back to the man beside her.

"The King's Head, my dear," he replied. "It is a very well appointed coaching inn not far from Leeds. We will be there directly, I dare say, now we have picked up speed."

Henrietta's moods were always mercurial, but she bestowed a dazzling smile on him. "A hot bath and food, my darling, and I will sleep a happier woman tonight."

His own face lightened, and he returned her smile, squeezing the hand she held out towards him.

"I think a good night's sleep will do us all good," he replied.

"And one night closer to our quarry," George added, a dark, sardonic smile playing on his lips.

•

To Henrietta's chagrin and George's disgust, the coaching inn took them another two hours to reach. Stepping down from the coach, grateful to stretch her limbs and breathe in the sharp cold evening air, Henrietta took Richard's arm as they entered the warmth of the welcoming establishment.

The landlord bustled forward and directed one of the inn's serving maids to escort Henrietta to her room.

Her temper improved somewhat when she found a blazing fire awaiting her, and on requesting hot water for a bath, the maid went to attend to it immediately. Sighing, Henrietta removed her cloak and hat and warmed her chilled hands in front of the fire.

A discreet knock on the door alerted her to company. Thinking it would be Richard, she called out for him to enter.

George came in and quickly walked over to her. Seizing her hands in his, he drew her towards him and pressed a swift, hungry kiss on her lips.

She drew back sharply. "George, your father will be here in a minute!"

"He is busy ordering our dinner, my sweet. I could not resist seeking you out for a moment. "

With that, his arms came around her and he pulled her towards him, crushing another long, passionate kiss on her lips.

She melted against him and returned his kiss with as much ardour as his own.

"Enough!" She pulled away from him. "Go to your room now, George. We will see each other at dinner."

Reluctantly he stepped back, releasing her and executing a mock bow in her direction. "And after dinner, my love?" he whispered.

Her smile was almost as calculating as his own. The prospect of an ardent young lover almost too much for her to contemplate. "We must be discreet, my darling," she replied, suddenly very serious. "Richard would kill us…"

He laughed then, a short bark of amusement. The thought of his middle-aged father, already starting to run to seed, being able to best him in any kind of physical combat quite ludicrous to him. However, he acquiesced to Henrietta's wishes and kissing her hand once more, he left her alone to go along to his own room and ready himself for the evening.

•

Dinner that evening was a restrained affair. Prevented from dining in private due to the influx of travellers, they were forced to eat in the public rooms, much to Richard's dismay and annoyance.

Henrietta however quite enjoyed the ambience of the dining room. She received several admiring glances from the gentlemen present, and the compliments from George as he flirted outrageously with her caused her eyes to sparkle and her laughter to ring out several times that evening.

They could not, however, discuss their plans in any great detail. Their scheme to go to Mrs Embleton's home and force Charis to leave with them was as far as they had gone. Following Henrietta's comments earlier, George was all for taking the heiress to Gretna Green and marrying the chit, whether against her will or not. The fact that she had spent several nights in his company would be enough to ruin her reputation in the eyes of the world should they not marry.

Richard was inclined to be more circumspect in that he wanted to remove Charis from Mrs Embleton's protection and return with her to London. His feeling that once back under their control, there would be no need for an anvil wedding and Henrietta would be seen as the loving stepmother she always purported to be. There would be a Society wedding for all the world to see that they had done their utmost to look after and cherish the only daughter of Sir Anthony Waverley. No hint of any further scandal could be allowed to sully the reputation of the lovely Lady Henrietta.

George kept his father's wine goblet filled all evening, encouraging him to eat heartily of the heavy meal presented before them and as they retired to their rooms for the night,

Richard was obliged to lean against his son as they made their way up to their rooms.

He escorted his father to the room Richard shared with Henrietta and, exchanging a look of barely suppressed excitement the younger couple assisted Richard to undress and into bed. Within a few minutes, he was asleep, snoring heavily.

George, taking Henrietta's hand in his, bowed over it and kissed it gently. "It is up to you what happens with Charis," he said softly. "Either London or Scotland, whatever you wish will be my command." He held her hand up to his lips and, turning it pressed another kiss against her palm. "I hope to see you later, my lady," he whispered.

A shudder of excitement coursed through Henrietta. Apart from Richard and then Anthony, it had been some time since Henrietta had experienced the thrill of a new lover.

"Give me an hour, my sweet," she murmured and was rewarded by a swift, ardent kiss before he left her to return to his own room.

Henrietta undressed and slipped her nightdress on. Covering herself with her lacy robe, she sat at the dressing table, removing her jewellery and brushing out her long fair hair.

She regarded Richard dispassionately, not for a moment concerned that she was about to be unfaithful to him. No, her heart was closed, cold and unfeeling. All her finer emotions had died long ago in a tiny cottage in Portsmouth along with her child. Her husband, dead in some long-ago sea battle was the only man she had given her heart and soul to and the only man she had ever truly loved.

She had felt nothing but contempt for the men who came afterwards, in that house in London. She had been rescued by Richard, and she would be forever grateful to him and equally grateful for the good fortune of being introduced to Sir Anthony. She had developed excellent acting skills and not for a moment did Anthony ever suspect she was anything but his loving, devoted spouse.

Charis might suspect she had something to do with Anthony's

death, but apart from neglecting her husband to follow her own selfish desires, she had done nothing to speed his unfortunately early demise.

Yes, gratitude was all very well, and she recognised her incredible good fortune in meeting Richard. Tonight, however, just for once, she wanted to feel the urgency of a virile, handsome young man and, for a little while, lay the ghosts of her past to rest in a few snatched moments of passion.

She smiled to herself as she carried a lit candle to the door of their room. Pausing only long enough to ensure Richard still slept the sound, snoring sleep of the truly inebriated, she slipped out of the chamber and along to the room next door where George waited.

She went into his eager arms, and they fell together into the downy softness of his bed with barely a thought for the man next door. She returned his kisses with a passion she had all but forgotten and gave herself over to his body, blotting out all memories, all sorrow, all conscience with a ruthless disregard for anyone but herself. Tomorrow would come soon enough, but for tonight, she was lost to the hedonistic delights of a young man's hands and body caressing her and the shuddering diversion of a few snatched hours of pure, unbridled pleasure.

•

The messenger, head down against the biting wind and snow, battled through the night on the powerful stallion. He had made good progress from London, but his destination was still many miles away.

Armed with papers and money, the messenger's next stop was a posting inn on the Great North Road, the road deserted, due to the inclement weather and terrible travelling conditions. Only the hardiest of travellers were out this night, and the swiftness of his horse carried him past many known trouble spots. No highwaymen impeded his journey, however. He was armed, and the urgency of his mission had meant only the hardiest of messengers was chosen for this particular journey. His physical presence alone was enough to deter any but the roughest of adversaries, and so far he had met no one to delay him.

The lights of the posting inn ahead were a welcome sight, and it was with a heartfelt sigh of relief that he handed his horse over to the livery grooms and went inside to the warmth of the tap room.

Taking a long draught of the cool ale provided by the landlord, he looked around the open rooms. The smell of hot food coming from the dining room reminded him of the emptiness of his stomach, and it growled hungrily as he made his way through.

The sound of female laughter stopped him in his tracks. He paused and cautiously looked through the door at the diners within. One particular table drew his attention to a stunningly beautiful woman dining with two men. His hackles rose as he recognised the three customers. He backed out and went to find the landlord.

A discreet enquiry was enough. He settled himself on a bench next to the roaring fire in the tap room and waited patiently until one of the serving maids was able to bring him hot soup and sandwiches. Refreshing himself with the repast, he watched until all the diners in the dining room had finished and the majority had made their way to their rooms.

He dozed fitfully for two hours before rousing himself. It was after midnight now, but the snow outside had stopped, and the roads were clear, cold and sparkling in the frosty night.

Taking more food from the obliging landlord, he settled his bill and returned to the stables. His horse refreshed and rested, contentedly ate at a bale of hay hanging beside his stall.

"Sorry, boy," the messenger said, stroking the head before him. "No time to rest up any further. We need to get back on the road."

Half an hour later, he was saddled and mounted up, and the horse's hooves clattered against the cobbles of the courtyard as they left. Heading northwards the messenger returned to the Great North Road and rode on, past the signpost pointing in two directions, London one way and York, still some fifty miles off. He smiled grimly to himself as he pulled the thick woollen muffler up over his mouth and nose. He had the advantage now. Lady Henrietta might be travelling hotfoot to the north, looking for the runaway heiress but he had papers and letters to deliver to Sir Frederick Waverley which he knew contained some unwelcome information Henrietta would be most anxious to keep from her stepdaughter.

All he had to do now was reach Sir Frederick to advise him of the news he carried. Then it would be up to Sir Frederick to go to Whitby to appraise Charis of the latest developments in London. Bleakly he realised he had only a slim advantage over Charis's enemies and despite his tiredness and the lateness of the hour, he rode on, the horse striding powerfully over the frozen landscape, onward towards their ultimate destination.

CHAPTER SIXTEEN

They were being watched. The watchers were hidden, discreet, but they were there. The patrols had lessened. Which, as Mrs Embleton remarked dryly, was suspicious in itself. Since the night of the Assembly and, further, the visit by Captain Howard and his band of smugglers, the patrols by both the militia and the revenue men had become less frequent, less obvious.

Nevertheless, the contraband stayed hidden in the cellars below Cliffe House, and despite herself, Mrs Embleton grew increasingly nervous about it remaining. Normally, as she explained to Charis, it stayed there for two or three days at the most, being collected in the middle of the night by a band of men with wagons and horses and donkeys, the barrels strapped across the backs of these sturdy animals before being led away over the moors to the main road leading to Scarborough and Whitby and all the villages in between. There the cargo would be dropped off to customers impatiently waiting delivery of their goods.

A sharp rap on the front door one morning early in December alerted the occupants to the arrival of visitors.

Charis, going down the stairs from the drawing room, witnessed Josiah opening the front door to the unwelcome sight of Major Quinn and another uniformed man.

Forcing a smile to her face, Charis descended and walked over to the Major. "Major Quinn, how are you, sir?"

As his face still bore the marks of his beating and his arm still resided in a sling, she had the satisfaction of knowing he still suffered for his assault on her.

He was unsmiling, his face severe and stern. "I am recovering from the attack I thank you, Miss Waverley," he replied.

"To what do we owe the pleasure of your visit today, Major?" she asked, her face innocent and free from all artifice.

"Official business, Miss Waverley," he responded.

Mrs Embleton arrived from the kitchen then, alerted by the sound of the knocking on the door and voices in the hallway. She held out her hand to the Major.

"Major, please come in and take some refreshment with us, sir!"

His expression did not soften, but he bowed slightly in her direction. "Madam, it is with regret that I must decline your invitation. As I was just explaining to Miss Waverley, I am here on official business and must advise you that we need to search your premises."

Mrs Embleton's gaze did not waver. She smiled at him. "Of course I have no objections, Major, but may I ask why?"

He was icily polite as he stared at the two women. "We have received information that smugglers have visited your property and have deposited goods."

Charis's face was a mask of sheer indifference, but she managed a pale smile. "Smugglers, sir?"

She moved over to Mrs Embleton. "What is he talking about, Mrs Embleton?" she asked.

Alice patted her hand reassuringly. "There is no need to worry, my dear," she responded. "We have no truck with smugglers, Major, but you are welcome to search my house."

He turned to his companion and nodded. The Sergeant went to the front door and opened it. Four soldiers in full scarlet uniform, carrying muskets over their shoulders, entered at his signal.

Alarmed now, Charis held on to Mrs Embleton's arm as the five men split up, three walking upstairs, and they listened as the heavy boots trod through the rooms, up into the towers and through the chambers on the first floor.

The other two marched into the drawing room, the sitting room and finally, they moved towards the door leading to the kitchen. Major Quinn followed them, with the two ladies in his wake. Josiah and Martha were sitting at the kitchen table and did not move as the soldiers searched the pantry and the scullery. The Major stood silently watching as Martha calmly continued peeling potatoes at the table, not moving.

His eyes narrowed slightly as he observed the calm tableau before him.

"Where is your cellar, Ma'am?" he asked suddenly.

Charis fought to keep the fear from showing in her eyes, lowering her gaze from his. Before she could answer, Mrs Embleton moved away from her to the corner of the room to a small door beside the scullery. She opened it and beckoned the Major forward. Charis knew it led to nowhere more exciting than the coal cellar.

"This is the only cellar we have, Major Quinn," she told him calmly.

He poked his head inside and withdrew it after seeing nothing more than the piles of kindling sticks and lumps of coal.

"I have heard you have another below the house, Ma'am," he said, his voice icily cold. "Pray, where is the entrance?"

Mrs Embleton's smile and voice were as cool as his own. "Those cellars were flooded years ago, Major. There is no entrance from the house, unfortunately. If you would care to go outside onto the beach at low tide, you might see the entrance there, but I can assure you it leads to nowhere. A cave-in some years ago prevented us gaining access, and there are no longer any cellars below this house, I'm afraid."

She stared calmly into his eyes, but he turned to his men and barked out an order. The two nearest the door moved to obey him and left the kitchen. Charis could feel her heart pounding but, taking her cue from Mrs Embleton, she smiled again at the Major. Moving to the table, she sat down beside Martha.

"Would you care for a hot drink, Major?" she asked. "Martha, would you kindly make us all some tea?"

She smiled sweetly at Major Quinn and had the satisfaction of seeing him discomfited.

"I thank you again, Miss Waverley, but no."

"I think Mrs Embleton and I would appreciate a drink though. Please sit down, Major."

Conciliatory and sweet, she looked at him with such admiration that for a moment he wondered at her demeanour; this was not the terrified innocent who had so vehemently fought his advances.

Before he could respond, his two men came back into the room. Their boots were caked with sand and seawater and Martha, huffing in annoyance, went to get the broom from the corner of the room.

"Well?" he asked.

"We found the entrance but it's as she said, there's been a cave-in – there's no way through from the beach."

Anger and frustration clouded his attractive face. However, forcing a politeness to his features that he was far from feeling, he bowed to them. "I apologise for disturbing you, Mrs Embleton, Miss Waverley. We have obviously been given unreliable information."

The soldiers left, and he remained alone in the kitchen with them.

Mrs Embleton's anger flashed momentarily onto her face. "Then I suggest you check your information before barging in on innocent gentlewomen in future, Major. Good day to you."

She went to the kitchen door and held it open for him. Frustrated, he could do no more than bow again, manners coming to his aid, and he marched out, bristling with unresolved anger. For a moment, before he left, his eyes sought and held Charis's. It was only a moment, but the coldness and anger in his eyes bored into hers. Josiah followed them out and as they left, they heard the slam of the front door as he vented his own fury at this unwarranted and unwanted intrusion.

Charis realised she was trembling as Mrs Embleton's legs seemed to give way beneath her and she collapsed into the seat next to her.

She raised anguished eyes to Charis. "Josiah must go to Captain Howard at once," she said. "We cannot hold their goods any longer!"

The colour had drained from her face, and Charis became alarmed at the normally robust and serene Mrs Embleton's sudden loss of composure.

"We must surely wait a little while, Ma'am," Charis replied. "They will be watching the house, watching our every move. We cannot afford to put ourselves in any more danger. Major Quinn has revenge on his mind," she finished, a note of bitterness in her voice. She covered Mrs Embleton's hand lying on the kitchen table. "Send Josiah to fetch Captain Howard, but it must be to just start planning the removal of the contraband. We must be very very careful."

Her voice was low, calm, soothing. Her very tone seemed to reassure Mrs Embleton who sighed and patted Charis's hand. "Of course, you are right, my dear. "

She calmed down a little, colour coming back into her pale cheeks. She did not seem herself though, and as she stood, she swayed a little. Charis stood with her and held her arm. "Come, Ma'am," she said quietly. "Let us go up to the drawing room. You need to rest."

She led the unprotesting older lady out of the kitchen and with a smile to Martha, she sought to reassure her. "Would you bring us that tea please, Martha. As Major Quinn has managed to quite spoil our morning, I think we all need some refreshment."

As Josiah returned at this moment, his rejoinder that it wasn't tea they all needed but something stronger made Charis smile.

"Josiah," she said, "Mrs Embleton is desirous that we fetch Captain Howard as soon as possible. Do you know where he can be found?"

"Aye, Miss," he replied. "I'll just have tea, and then I'll go fetch him."

Charis nodded her thanks and, keeping hold of Mrs Embleton's arm, she led her into the hallway and up the flight of stairs to the cosy drawing room where the fire blazed and warmed the small room.

She helped Alice to sit down and, before the tea arrived, a

worried Charis took Josiah's advice and poured her a small glass of sherry.

Alice sipped the sherry appreciatively. "Thank you, Charis," she said softly. "That was more of a shock than I anticipated."

Charis seated herself on the footstool beside the armchair. She frowned as she looked up at Alice.

"This is my fault," she said thoughtfully.

"Nonsense." Alice's voice still slightly faint.

"It is," Charis responded. "He is angry with me. I rejected him, I fought him. Connor and Luke Vincent rescued me and attacked him. He wants his revenge."

Mrs Embleton sighed and leaned back in her armchair closing her eyes.

"I fear we have made a dangerous enemy, Charis," she said quietly. "We have never before been subject to such scrutiny." She sipped her drink. "I have met the Commander of the Scarborough Garrison in the past, and he has always been a most affable and upright gentleman." She paused again. "Obviously Major Quinn is out to prove himself and bringing to justice the local smuggling fraternity is one way to gain a reputation with his superiors."

"Could we go to him, Ma'am?" Charis asked, a sudden light appearing in her eyes. "Could we go to see the Colonel and bring the Major's behaviour to his attention?"

A shake of the head and Mrs Embleton opened her eyes again, finishing the sherry in one swallow.

"They would close ranks, Charis. The Major is set to make a name for himself, and the Commander from what I can remember of him is only too happy to let other people take charge. He will reap the rewards of anything Major Quinn may achieve, and the Major will be rewarded with promotion and his own command. No…" She paused, some of her old resolve coming back to her. "No, we can do nothing yet except empty the cellars of the contraband. I have a feeling Major Quinn will not give up so easily next time." A small smile appeared on her lips. "And next time his soldiers may find the true entrance to our caves and not the false one Josiah has rigged up for any casual intruders."

Charis smiled at the subterfuge the soldiers had so easily accepted. The Major, however, would not be so easily fooled in the future. She had a bad feeling about the whole business, and despite the heat of the fire, she shivered. Drawing her shawl tighter around her shoulders, she stood to open the door for Josiah as he entered carrying the tea tray.

"The Captain's in Whitby, I understand, Ma'am," he said, putting the tray down on the side table. "Do you need anything else when I go fetch him?"

Mrs Embleton shook her head, quite composed again once more. "No, Josiah. Ask him to come here. We need to organise how we are going to dispose of his contraband as soon as possible. I will not have my home, my family and friends put in any further danger."

A little of her old determination had crept back into her voice, but Charis was still alarmed at the older lady's pallor.

Not for the world would Charis add to Mrs Embleton's worries but the way Major Quinn had looked at her before leaving had sent a shiver of apprehension down her spine. He had been frustrated in his plans for her, and he would not be so easily thwarted in the future.

"Mrs Embleton," she began almost hesitantly. "I think – once we have emptied the cellars, perhaps the time would be right for us to leave Cliffe House for a little while. We could go to my Uncle Frederick's. He is expecting me to join him for Christmas anyway. We should go together."

Mrs Embleton's smiled at Charis. "I think we are in somewhat of a predicament, my dear! We are indeed caught between the devil and the deep blue sea, it would seem The deep blue sea being your wicked stepmother, and the devil – why the devil himself would be proud of Major Quinn!" She roused herself and poured two cups of tea, handing one to Charis. "Once this business is settled with Captain Howard, I will write to Frederick and enquire how matters are progressing on your behalf. I should be sorry to lose you, Charis, but I feel matters will shortly be coming to a head and we must be prepared for you to take your rightful place back in Society."

A few weeks ago Charis would have agreed wholeheartedly with Mrs Embleton's words, but she now felt strangely reluctant at the thought of leaving the sanctuary that was Cliffe House, the people she had come to care for and her life here on this wild Northern coast. Her only thought now was to protect and care for them, and she wished with all her heart that she could keep them all safe from the dangers that seemed to be encroaching on their very existence.

Taking Mrs Embleton's hand, she pressed it gently. "I will go nowhere until I am sure you are all safe and well cared for," she said softly.

"Bless you, child," Mrs Embleton replied and kissed Charis's cheek.

Quietly they sat, either side of the warming fire and sipped their tea, each lost in their own thoughts but both of them only too aware of the gathering storm starting to surround them.

CHAPTER SEVENTEEN

The gentle rocking and the sound of waves splashing against the wooden hull of the ship awoke him as he stretched in the narrow bunk. He opened his eyes, and for a moment his thoughts were jumbled and disorganised as memories filled his mind demanding to be recalled and put into some kind of order. He scanned the small cabin, and as the morning sun illuminated the porthole, he struggled to remember where he was and what he was doing there. He sat up and looked around before remaining still, closing his eyes and waiting for the chaos in his mind to settle.

Images swirled around his brain, no longer the nebulous ethereal thoughts of just a few days ago – these were more real, more solid now. Frowning, he stood and looked out of the tiny round window. They were at anchor in a secluded bay, the sun just appearing over the horizon. A slight, grim smile lifted his lips, and leaning his head on his arm, he stared out at the sea, watching as the December mists eddied around the gentle waves embracing the creaking timbers, dispersing slightly as the weak sun warmed the icy waters.

A shout from above roused him, and he prepared himself for the day ahead, pulling on rough warm clothing and stout long boots. Brushing the black curls from his face, he opened the cabin door leading out to the narrow passageway.

Going up the wooden stairs he climbed out onto deck, breathing in the sharp icy air. The Captain was up before him, standing by the wheel, talking to the helmsman. Vincent saw him emerge and raised a hand in greeting. Connor raised his hand in reply, his mind suddenly swirling with more thoughts and visions and a grim wintry smile lifted his features once more.

He joined the Captain on the quarterdeck and followed the direction Vincent was looking.

An ominous weather-front was gathering over the horizon, and as fast as the sun rose, the darkness of the cloud seemed to follow on behind. Connor squinted as he looked at the dawning sun.

"Trouble, Captain?" he asked.

"Storm, Connor," Vincent replied. "Just where we need to be heading."

He frowned, and Connor could see the indecision in his face as he scanned the far horizon. "Do you want to wait until it's passed?" he asked.

They were due to set sail that morning, their hold full of the cargo being transported to eagerly awaiting customers. It was an expensive load, the Captain and his crew standing to make a small fortune upon delivery. Vincent had confided to Connor that it was his first shipment since the storm several weeks ago when his ship The Scorpion had gone down off the coast at Whitby. At the mention of the ship's name something had stirred in Connor's brain but, just as briefly, it had passed. The explanation given that he had been thrown from the ship and hit his head on the breaking timbers of the deck had been accepted and verified by other members of the crew.

Luke grinned at his young companion, his mood lifting, a sparkle lighting up the deep sapphire blue of his eyes with an almost mischievous glint. "Can we outrun it, Con?" he asked, his voice alive with suppressed laughter.

His good humour was infectious. "In this old lady?" Connor grinned back. "Not a hope – but we can give it a good run for our money!"

Luke let out a shout of laughter and slapped him on his back. "Unfurl the sails, Connor! We're on our way back to England!"

Connor went to do his bidding, shouting out orders to the sailors milling about above decks. One or two of them shook their heads at the folly of attempting to outrun an approaching storm, but they knew their Captain was one of the best, foolhardy but brilliant, and they trusted him with their lives.

The anchor heaved, the sails unfurled, the ship creaked and groaned and slowly started its long journey north-west towards the coast of England.

Connor took the telescope from the Captain and held it to his eye to see better how far away the storm was brewing. A flash of lightning in the distance jarred him, and he almost dropped the eyeglass.

"What's wrong, boy?" the Captain asked him, noting the sudden paling of Connor's tanned cheeks.

Connor shook his head. "Nothing, Captain. Just a headache is all. Too much rum, I fear."

Luke laughed again. Their meal last night had been a merry one, with drinks all round after the final loading of the cargo and the battening down of the hatches, everything and everyone safe and back on board.

Connor rubbed his eyes and for a moment that sudden vision came back to him in all its clarity. An image of a storm, of forked lightning bouncing off the tempestuous seas, gigantic waves raging around two ships, racing each other, one battling to stay ahead of the other as lightning struck the smaller of the two vessels and split it in half.

"How did we lose the Scorpion, Captain?" he asked, handing the eyeglass back to Vincent.

A frown and clouding over of his eyes were the only clues to the Captain's pain at the loss of his beloved ship. "Rocks, Connor. In that bay near Whitby where your lovely Miss Waverley's house sits."

"Not a lightning bolt then?" Connor asked as he recalled the scene in his head.

"No – that was the fate of the Revenue cutter," Vincent replied shortly. "The winds drove us on to some rocks – we couldn't avoid them."

He retook the wheel and spun it, bringing the ship hard about, facing now towards the darkening skies.

"The lightning hit their gunpowder stores, the ship exploded and split in two, and it went down. We ran aground and sank shortly after. We were lucky to have survived – many did not."

His mood was in danger of lowering once more, but he grinned at Connor. "You were washed ashore, boy, and very lucky you were to have been found."

Connor smiled then, recalling in vivid detail the moment he had opened his eyes and found himself looking into a pair of fine green-tinged eyes, gazing down at him on a cold and windswept beach.

He recalled the touch of her hands, how she had pulled him from the cold of the rock pool onto the sands, the way she had wrapped her shawl around his shivering body. He allowed himself the luxury of remembering the softness of her lips as he had kissed them. Then he recalled the disdain in her eyes as Vincent had told her that she was but one of many women in his life. He had redeemed himself somewhat by rescuing her from the hands of Major Quinn, but her response could have been fuelled by no more than gratitude and relief.

With something akin to despair, he put Charis from his mind and turned his attention to the job in hand and went about his duties on the ship, watching the gathering storm with the same cool eyes as Captain Vincent. Vincent was a reckless but superb sailor, Connor was brave and resourceful. The men looked to both of them for guidance and, in Connor's case, he felt a grudging respect had been earned over the last few weeks.

He grinned then as the men around him started to sing. They were facing the dangers of a storm, the winds filling the full sails and hurtling the ship through the deepening swell of the sea, the rains beating down on their heads, the words of the sea shanty echoing and resonating through his brain even as he moved amongst them.

"I've been tae the nor'ard cruising back and for'ard
I've been tae the nor'ard cruiing sair and lang
But I dare not gang ashore for fear of Bover and his gang…"

He watched as lightning lit up the horizon. A shiver went through his body which had nothing to do with the icy wind blowing in from the cold air streams of the north. More memories began forcing their way through the mists in his brain and a sharp moment of clarity caused him to gasp out loud and hold on to the ropes to prevent himself from falling, a giddiness almost overcoming him. He shook his head to clear his mind and went over to the water barrel.

He took the cup and drank a long draught of the cold fresh water, blaming the rum from the night before for this feeling of disorientation. He knew, however, in some deep-rooted part of his brain that this feeling was more than that. This was no mere hangover. This was the beginning of realisation of the truth.

He looked up and stared at Captain Vincent. Vincent caught the look and grinned at the younger man.

Smiling to himself, Connor turned away, running slightly shaking fingers through his unruly curls and fastened back his hair to prevent the wind from blowing it into his eyes, obscuring his vision.

"No, not yet Captain Vincent," he murmured to himself. "Not just yet!"

•

The rain lashed down on the northeast coast. A small group of men were leading their horses slowly along the snow packed roads, the rain turning the ice and snow into slush that made the ground treacherous underfoot. The horses had sacking tied onto their hooves which muffled the sound but which, in turn, made it difficult for the animals to get a secure grip. The men were covered in heavy coats and hats that were quickly becoming sodden with the weight of the deluge, however, they did not pause in their steady tramp, nor did they speak, except to quietly encourage their horses to keep going.

Behind the packhorses a wagon rolled along, pulled by two more horses, the wagon draped in heavy material, meant to cover its eventual contents.. Fewer men than usual were out this night. The lure of the reward they each would receive a strong incentive, but many had decided this trek across the moors at midnight was not one they cared to participate in.

It was, however, a perfect night for moving contraband. Clouds covered the moon and heavy rain silenced any noise of their movements. They made their way carefully along over the badly rutted moor road towards Cliffe House, no lanterns lighting their way, just the faint light from the house itself giving a weak pinpoint to lead them onward. Lookouts had gone ahead, and so far no one had signalled to them to stop, disperse or run away. So they continued on, alert, aware of any movement, cautious and careful. They were well used to this journey but the urgency on this particular night was something new, something unexpected and most were feeling a heightened tension. Each man had a loaded pistol in his belt although every man prayed to God that it would not come to any kind of a battle with the military or Revenue men. They had always avoided such a confrontation in the past, but the Embleton family had never sent for them before. They had had time in the past to plan their movements slowly and carefully. True, they were simply moving the goods to a safer destination, but each man was on edge this night – each aware that this was enough out of the normal for them to be anxious and every one of them felt jumpy and ill at ease.

•

Josiah came limping into the kitchen, soaking wet from being outside, holding the muted lantern on the coast road, a weak signal for the men making their way over the moors towards them.

"What's wrong with your leg, Josiah?" Charis asked, instantly concerned at the elderly man's demeanour.

"Nowt," Josiah replied with a scowl towards his wife.

"He's got gout, Miss," Martha said. "His foot has been

troubling him all day, but he's too blessed stubborn to rest up."
She returned the scowl without demur.

"You must rest now, Josiah," Charis said, and standing up from
her warm place beside the fire, she directed him to her vacated
seat.

"Sit and let your wife bring you a drink," she ordered him. "I
will fetch my cloak and signal the men on the moors."

Both Josiah and Martha looked horrified. "Nay lass, t'isnt
safe!" Martha exclaimed.

"Well, it won't be safe for any of us soon," Charis retorted.
"It's a wicked night. They will never find their way here without
some kind of signal."

She made her way over to the kitchen door, a renewed
determination in her face and demeanour. Over the last few days
she had assumed control over the household. Mrs Embleton's
health had deteriorated, anxiety and stress over possible discovery
had aged her, and she was even now in bed, tucked up with a hot
toddy and a blazing fire. Josiah and Martha had rallied around
their employer but it was Charis who had negotiated with Captain
Howard, and it was she who had arranged the collection of the
smuggled goods from their cellar.

He had predicted the cloudy night and the bad weather. When
she had asked why he thought it such a good omen, he had
merely smiled at her and said that a cloudy moon was an excellent
smuggler's moon.

Going upstairs she put on a warm jacket over her sensible dark
blue day dress and tied a bonnet tightly over her hair, tucking
stray curls behind her ears. Taking her heaviest winter cloak, she
dressed and returned down to the kitchen.

Taking the lantern from Josiah, she listened to his instructions
on where to stand to emit the lowest possible chink of light and
opened the kitchen door. The wind howled once more around
the room, blowing snow and rain onto the flagstones.

"Be careful, Miss!" Martha's voice was filled with anxiety.

The smuggler's visits to Cliffe House in the past had always
been tinged with the worry something might possibly go wrong

but never had they felt such apprehension as they did on this occasion. They knew the dangers inherent in hiding the smuggled goods but the rewards were always worthwhile and they justified their assistance in the knowledge that their involvement kept Mrs Embleton safe and warm in her own home.

Charis acknowledged Martha's remark with a nod and, clutching her cloak around herself, she stepped outside into the pouring rain.

With her head down, she battled up the path onto the back lane. She held on tightly to the lantern, keeping it sheltered as much as possible to save the light from blowing out. She walked along the cliff top path and around the side of the building to the lane leading to the coast road.

A sound alerted her. At first she thought it was something blowing over. She looked around, her cloak swirling in the wind as she turned. She saw movement behind the hedge on the cliff top path. A glint of metal caught her eye, and she struggled to see through the gloom what it was. At that moment the clouds parted, and she saw, quite clearly, the shape of a man crouching behind the bushes with the faint glimmer of moonlight shining down on his highly polished bayonet. A man, moreover, in uniform. He ducked down again, she turned away, her heart pounding, her brain racing. An ambush! She wondered how many other men were in hiding around the house and along the pathways.

She knew then what she must do. Gathering her skirts up, she started to run around the house towards the coast road. She started running down the road, casting away the lantern as it hindered her progress. She had to run, had to get to the smugglers, had to warn them and get them away before they were ambushed, before the soldiers caught them or, worse, shot them as they tried to escape.

She heard movements behind her, but she was as surefooted as any native born in this wild inhospitable place. She ran, ignoring the wind that caught at her clothes, ignoring the rain beating into her face and eyes and tearing the bonnet loose. She saw dark shapes in the distance and ran towards them, knowing they would be the men sent ahead to look out for danger. She did not dare shout out, the wind would have carried her words away, and they would not have heard her anyway. The shapes were tall, black silhouettes against the moonless sky. The men were on horseback, and as she raced towards them, she heard faint shouting in the background. The militia had seen her and were following her, running after her, stumbling through the moorland heather and the long grasses, mercifully not finding the same paths she had followed.

She reached the men on horseback, and she found herself looking up into the face of Captain Howard's second in command, a man she had met briefly at her meeting with the Captain.

"Jed, the militia have surrounded the house. They have laid an ambush." She was out of breath and panting as she blurted out her news.

Jed raised his shrewd eyes up to the direction from where she had been running. Leaning down he offered her his hand. She took it and found herself being half hauled, half lifted onto the back of his horse.

"Come on, Miss," he said. "This is no time to be caught out in the moors!"

She held on to his waist as she straddled the horse behind him. He wheeled the horse around and dug his spurs into the horse's flanks. They set off at a gallop, the other lookout following close behind.

They heard the shouting then, the military men, who without horses could only run, following them, realising their ambush had been discovered.

Within a few minutes, Charis and her erstwhile protectors had reached the men.

At the sight of the lookouts and Miss Waverley seated on the horse, they realised their apprehension had been justified. A few short, terse orders from Jed and they turned their horses around, pulling off the silencing sackcloth and mounting them with nervous haste.

The thunder of horses' hooves could now be heard in the distance and Charis saw other military men riding towards them, still a good way off but getting closer. The men looked to Jed who shouted out to them, and they started to ride away from the way they had come, the wagon taking an age to turn in that difficult rutted road.

Charis could feel her heart pounding in her chest as Jed kicked his horse once more and they set off, riding over the moors towards the main Whitby road. The chase was on, and Charis hardly dared to look around, but when she did so, she saw the men on horseback, the scarlet red of their jackets black against the dark stormy sky.

Jed rode on, galloping over the moors, harrying and encouraging his fleeing men. They stopped once, the wagon faltering on the uneven ground, its wheel caught in the mud and together, Jed and his fellow lookout took the horses' bridles and pulled them, trying to assist the driver get the wagon going again.

The delay was their undoing. The shouts of the militia ordering them to stop rang out across the barren landscape. Charis whirled around on her precarious seat as a musket shot whistled past her ears. The horse reared, and with a scream, she lost her hold on Jed and fell backwards into the rain-soaked heather.

Jed fought to keep the nervous animal under control, but it was frightened by the gunshots and bolted, riding wildly across the moors. Charis sat up, winded and soaked by the rain and the mud, and watched in despair at her companions attempting to escape. The wagon driver was the first to be apprehended, and a couple of the other men on foot were captured. Charis turned her head and found herself staring into the barrel of a musket pointed at her head.

Her bonnet had gone, blown away during that wild ride across the moors and her hair tumbled down about her face and shoulders, a heavy wet curtain plastered to her face by the unrelenting deluge.

Silently she scrambled to her feet, shivering as the biting wind and rain permeated the damp clothing.

"Get that gun out of my face!" she demanded.

The soldier, surprised by the imperious tone of her voice stepped back, but he was joined a moment later by his commanding officer seated on a bay coloured horse.

"Bind her!" he ordered, and the soldier shouldered his rifle to tie her hands in front of her with a length of rope he had over his other shoulder. She watched the captured men receiving the same treatment.

A length of rope was handed to the Sergeant on horseback, and she was pulled unceremoniously along behind the horse, stumbling over her skirts and falling once more. Struggling to her feet, she pulled her skirts up and walked behind the horse, soaked through to her skin, her feet freezing in the unrelenting rain.

If the Sergeant recognised her, he made no comment. He made no consideration for the fact she was a woman, and when she stumbled again, he raised his horsewhip and brought it down across her shoulders. She screamed at the sharp sting more in shock than pain and her eyes blazed with anger at the effrontery of the attack.

They trudged across the rain-flattened moor, skidding and slipping in the melting snow, no shelter offered or given against the harshness of the landscape.

They reached the road at last, and the walking became slightly easier. Charis saw at least six of the men who had been on their way to Cliffe House, bound and being pulled along, as she was herself. They stopped at the captured wagon.

The Sergeant threw his rope towards one of the other soldiers. "Get the prisoners on board the wagon. We'll get there quicker!"

The dispirited group of villagers and farmers scrambled up onto the open back, helping to pull Charis on board.

"Are you all right, Miss?" one of the men asked her, and she recognised Dan Jenkins, one of the farmers who lived close to Cliffe House.

He helped her to sit down next to him, and she shivered, pushing her wet hair out of her face. Glad of the warmth of the other bodies around her, nevertheless she looked around in dismay at the other captives.

"Thank you, Dan," she replied. "Did everyone else get away?"

"Aye, Miss." His voice low.

"They cannot hold us, surely," she said quietly. "We have done nothing wrong, and there was no contraband to take from us."

"No, Miss," he said. "But they will want to know what we were doing out on the moors at this time of night with all the packhorses and the wagon."

She lurched back suddenly then as one of the soldiers whipped the horses to start the wagon moving, trundling slowly along the winding road. She gazed out at the passing scenery, seeing in the distance the light in the towers of Cliffe House. She sat with her back against the rough wooden side and pulled her knees up, wrapping the damp cloak around herself to try and ameliorate some of the cold and shelter from the icy wind.

"Where are they taking us, Dan?" she whispered, a cold grip of fear suddenly seizing her, knowing the answer before he replied.

"Scarborough Fort, Miss," he said.

She lowered her head to her knees and sighed. She prayed then. Prayed that the soldiers even now searching Cliffe House once more would find nothing, that Mrs Embleton, Martha and Josiah were safe and unharmed. Then she prayed for herself – and for what might await her in Scarborough Fort.

CHAPTER EIGHTEEN

The welcoming lights of the harbour beckoned them in. It had been a long, tiring and arduous journey. They had battled through a night of storms to their eventual destination and had, thankfully, been greeted by their customers at the secluded bay on the North East coast south of the Flamborough lighthouse. They unloaded their cargo with a sense of relief, and continued into the local harbour, the holds emptied, their pockets full.

Captain Vincent leaned on the rails as the old ship moored up and tied to the harbour side capstans by his crew. All were tired, but all were well satisfied by the result of their labours, and he sighed with the satisfaction of a job well done.

His eyes screwed up against the glare of the rising sun and watched with some concern at the sight of a stout, well-dressed man making his way hurriedly along the harbour. He stepped over the ropes and fishing baskets and made his way towards the ship with a decided air of determination about him. The man paused, raising his eyes to the vessel and, on seeing Captain Vincent raised his hand in greeting.

"Who is that, Captain?" Connor asked as the man made his way to the gangway.

"A colleague from Whitby," Vincent answered. He frowned, wondering what had occurred to send one of Captain Howard's aides all this way to seek him out.

"Let's go and find out what he wants!" he said and, pushing himself away from the rail, he walked towards where the gangway met the ship.

Connor followed him, intrigued and curious as to what had sent the emissary to seek out his Captain.

The small man came bustling up onto the ship.

He came towards Captain Vincent and held out his hand in greeting. "Captain Vincent," he started, shaking the Captain's hand. "Captain Howard sends his felicitations and would ask a favour of you, sir."

Vincent stepped back and motioned for his guest to accompany him. "I am, of course, indebted to my friend Abraham Howard. In what manner may I assist?"

The man took a large handkerchief from his pocket, mopped his brow, sweating after his rush through the port, and replaced his three-cornered hat.

"There has been an unfortunate development with regards to some cargo currently residing in the cellars of his good friend, Mrs Alice Embleton."

"What kind of development?" Connor asked, his senses alerted again, concern for Charis uppermost in his mind at once.

"They are under investigation, sir. May we discuss this in private?" The emissary looked up at Connor in some suspicion.

Vincent smiled at the two men. "Come, let us go to the mess room. Connor is in my confidence, Mr Culley. You may speak freely in front of him."

Mr Culley nodded towards Connor. "Of course, of course. My apologies, Connor. If Captain Vincent can vouch for you then I can have no problem in discussing the matter with you."

Vincent's blue eyes sparkled as he led the way through the ship and down into the small mess room. The cook was clearing away the remains of that morning's breakfast, and at the Captain's order, he brought in tankards of frothing ale to refresh them and cool down the red-faced Mr Culley. Vincent could sense an adventure with an element of danger about it, and as he smiled at Connor, he saw an answering gleam reflected in the young man's eyes.

"Now, Mr Culley," he said, taking a sip of the refreshing ale. "How can we help?"

•

Charis and the other prisoners were taken to the dungeons of the fort and, without ceremony, were thrown into a large, dank and malodorous cell. It held several other prisoners – all men and all who eyed the newcomers with curiosity and not a little interest when they beheld the bedraggled but finely dressed lady with them.

Charis shivered and instinctively moved closer to Dan and the other men with her. Dan was a tall, solidly built man, and he and the others glared around at the occupants of the cell as they formed a protective circle around the young lady. She had tried to warn them and thanks to her the majority of their friends and compatriots had escaped capture. They were going to do their best to protect her, and it would take more than a handful of gaol rats to overcome them to get to her.

They moved towards a corner of the room and clearing away some of the fetid straw from the floor, they sat down on the flagstones. Charis's cloak was still damp, but she took it off and folded it so she and a couple of the others could sit on it. A faint glow from a barred window provided the only light, and as her eyes became used to the gloom, she looked around at her fellow prisoners and could only be grateful that she was not alone with the original occupants. The sound of scratching rats horrified her, and she held her knees up close to her chest as Dan and the others settled themselves around and beside her.

"What will happen to us, Dan?" she whispered.

"Jed will have got to Captain Howard," he replied. "He is a magistrate and has powerful friends. They will not be able to hold us for long once we get taken to the Assizes."

Feeling only slightly comforted, Charis sagged against the harsh stone wall. "We ran away, Dan," she said quietly. "They will want to know why…"

"Say nothing, Miss," Dan whispered back fiercely. "They caught us with nothing. We held no contraband. They have nothing to hold us for!"

Charis nodded, wishing she could feel as confident as he

197

sounded. "Very well," she said. "I only hope nothing has been found at Cliffe House."

Dan made a noise almost of a guttural laugh. "There has never been a soldier yet who could get through Josiah's caves!" he said. "And tonight's storm will have kept them off the beach. They won't know where to look until the storm abates and the tide is out – and even then, there are so many caves to get through they won't know where to start." He nodded at her, reassuring her. "Don't 'ee worry, Miss." He smiled. "Abraham Howard is a wily old fox. He won't let a valuable cargo like that fall into Revenue hands!"

A faint sparkle of humour momentarily lit up Charis's eyes. "How on earth did I end up falling in with a bunch of villains and smugglers?" She almost laughed. "A few months ago, Dan, I would have been firmly on the side of the Revenue and militia – but now…." She looked around at the dark and disgusting cell. She shook her head. "If Henrietta could see me now…" she whispered.

"Henrietta, Miss?" Dan was puzzled.

"My stepmother," Charis replied. "She's a money hungry adventurer who hates me, but even she would never have imagined I could end up here."

She shook her head again, and suddenly all the adrenaline drained out of her. She felt unutterably tired, and she closed her eyes. It had been a long and weary night, and she was exhausted. She did not notice Dan and the others glance at each other and, without a word they moved then to make room for her to lie down. Too fatigued to care, she fell asleep with her head on Dan's shoulder, and he held her as tenderly as one of his own daughters, not moving all night as she slept on.

•

Major Jonathan Quinn slapped his leather booted leg with his riding crop in growing frustration as his men waded through the receding tides searching cave after cave in a fruitless attempt to find the contraband their informant had assured them was, at this very moment, residing underneath Cliffe House.

Mrs Embleton had very graciously allowed the soldiers to once again search her home. They had left no stone unturned this time, and every nook and cranny was thoroughly inspected, every cupboard emptied, every bedroom searched in their fruitless quest to find some kind of illegal booty. Apart from a bottle of French brandy and some tea, they found nothing suspicious and certainly not the contents of a hold full of foreign contraband!

Josiah had been frogmarched to the beach and, on the tide turning and starting to recede he was ordered to show them the cave that led into the cellars. He obeyed and led them to the same cave network they had searched previously. Again they found nothing but rock fall and blocked tunnels. Satisfied, Josiah watched as the soldiers tried fruitlessly to dig through the rubble and he sat on a rock on the beach with his arms folded, a smile on his face as the increasingly angry Major Quinn harried his troops.

Finally, Quinn had had enough.

"Fetch the prisoner!" he snapped as the soldiers were forced back onto the beach.

The freezing rain was turning to snow, and Josiah's battered three-cornered hat soon became covered in the heavy snowfall. He watched with narrowed eyes as two of the soldiers left the beach and made their way up the steep zigzagged path to the top of the cliff overlooking the bay.

They reappeared a few minutes later, dragging a man with them. His hands were tied behind his back, and he was struggling with them to try and prevent being taken down to the beach. Josiah watched in growing consternation as the man was hit with the butt of a rifle to prevent any further dissent. As they approached, the man saw Josiah and halted, fighting again to stop going on. The soldiers were having none of it and almost lifted him off his feet to carry on down that steep path.

His face was battered, his clothes torn and Josiah could see that the man being borne down towards the beach had put up quite a fight.

Josiah recognised him at once. It was Eli Harker's eldest son, and from the look of him, he had been severely beaten. He knew though that Bill Harker would take the severest of beatings and not betray anyone – they must have some other hold over the lad.

Bill's eyes sought Josiah's in a mute plea for understanding. Josiah got up from the rock and walked over to him.

"They've taken Ma and the lads, Jo," Bill said despairingly. "They're going to hang if I don't tell them…"

Josiah turned to Major Quinn and spat on the ground next to his feet. "They've done nowt wrong. You have no right to hold 'em!" he growled.

Major Quinn looked bored, a faint smile lifting his dour features. "I have every right. They are the family of a known smuggler and several illegal items were found at their farm."

"'e put it there, Josiah. I swear it…"

Josiah had no doubt Bill was telling the truth. A kick in Bill's back propelled him forward.

At a nod to two more of his troops, Josiah suddenly found his arms held by two strong young members of the red-coated dragoons. Neither of them gentle with him, he looked up in surprise at Quinn who, almost lazily drew his pistol from his belt.

He held it to Josiah's head and smiled, a gentle winsome smile, as though he was passing the time of day with an old friend.

"Now Mr Harker…" he said softly. "We already have your mother and your brothers – who will hang if you do not cooperate further with us. I will also shoot this repugnant old man in front of your eyes if you do not now escort us to the correct cave which will lead us to the cellars beneath Mrs Embleton's house…"

The soldiers were expressionless. They knew better than to remonstrate with their commanding officer and they held onto Josiah with an iron-fast grip.

Bill's head drooped. "I'm sorry, Jo…" he said quietly and, without another word, led the redcoats to a tiny crack in the side of the steep cliffs.

They followed, the crack appearing too small to allow a man to enter but as they got closer, they found it quite large enough and wide enough to let them through one at a time. Curious, the soldiers advanced into the mouth of the tunnel, and a few minutes later one of them emerged, carrying a burnt-out torch. He waved it at Major Quinn who immediately returned his pistol to his belt and followed them. He almost ran over the pebbles and soaking wet sand to get to the tunnel entrance. His eyes were alight with glee, and he pushed the unfortunate Bill out of the way to be first down the long tunnel ahead.

His men followed him, each of them as curious as their commander and when they reached a barred gate they watched as he once again removed his pistol, this time to shoot off the padlock.

Pulling the gate open, they continued down the tunnel to a locked door. At Major Quinn's command, two of the redcoats ran at the stout oak door and threw their weight against it. It took several attempts to break the door open but finally, it splintered, and they fell through into a huge, dry, sandy-floored room.

Apart from a broken set of stairs in the corner leading up to a blank and bare ceiling, it was totally, completely, empty.

Back on the beach, the Major's shout of anger and frustration could be heard. The soldiers left on the beach looked at each other in dismay at their Commander's screams of fury. The two men who held Josiah loosened their grip slightly, and the old man pulled his arms from their slackened grip. Josiah's eyes screwed up against the glare of the sea and the wintry sun shining weakly through the falling snow. He looked out at the far horizon, as a soft, throaty chuckle escaped from his lips.

CHAPTER NINETEEN

The hotel was certainly not the best Sir Richard Hardy and his party had ever frequented, but it was a step up from the posting inns and other hostelries they had stayed in over their week of travelling along the Great North Road. The hotel had three excellent rooms plus staff available to attend the weary travellers.

Lady Henrietta was able to finally sink into a deep hot bath and have a serving maid prepare her clothes and assist her in attending to her toilette that night. Satisfied at last, knowing that their quarry in the shape of her elusive stepdaughter was only a matter of an hour away, she was able to relax and enjoy all the luxuries the hotel had to offer.

Finally, she emerged from her room. Dressed beautifully, hair coiffed to her satisfaction and the warmest of shawls protecting her from the chill of the evening, she joined Richard and George as they descended into the smart dining room. The staff were satisfactorily obsequious and fawned over them as they were escorted to a table and when the head butler produced an outstanding bottle of wine for their delectation, Richard, for one, was more than happy.

Taking a sip of the ruby red wine he sighed and nodded to the butler to pour more for the other two guests.

"Tell me," he spoke to the butler as the wine was drunk. "Do you know the Embleton family, of Cliffe House?"

The butler's face did not alter as he straightened after completing his task. "I do, sir," he responded. "May I ask if you are related to the Embleton family?"

His tone was respectful, but Richard did not appreciate his

reply. Henrietta recognised the signs and hastily placed her hand on his arm, smiling charmingly up at the butler.

"My stepdaughter is currently residing with Mrs Embleton – she is a cousin of my late husband," she explained.

The butler's shrewd eyes weighed up the situation and directed his reply to the attractive lady.

"I regret to inform you, Madam, that there have been some disturbances at the Embleton residence."

Henrietta exchanged worried glances with both Richard and George.

"In what way, may I ask? We were desirous of calling on my cousin and daughter tomorrow."

The butler was nothing if discreet. "I understand Mrs Embleton has been visited by the Revenue Militia from Scarborough Fort with rumours of her being in league with some local smugglers."

Genuinely surprised, Henrietta's hand fluttered to her throat. "And my stepdaughter?" she asked faintly.

At a sign from Richard, the butler placed the bottle of wine on the table. "Unfortunately I cannot confirm what has happened to the young lady who was staying with Mrs Embleton. However, rumours have reached us that she has been taken to Scarborough Fort for questioning regarding her involvement with the smuggling fraternity."

The three travellers looked at each other, shocked at the news. "Well, it looks as if our visit is very opportunely timed," George drawled as he swallowed the wine.

"Indeed," Henrietta said faintly.

With a nod, Richard dismissed the butler who bowed and left the party to their discussions.

"It also looks as though fate has intervened on our behalf." Richard smiled at the other two. "Miss Waverley, the thorn in our sides, may be removed without us needing to do a thing after all!"

He raised his glass. "Cheers." He smiled and drank deeply.

•

They passed a convivial evening. Henrietta flirted with both Richard and George, laughing at their jokes and exchanging meaningful glances with both men. Richard, mellowed with the consumption of a large amount of the red wine supplied by their solicitous waiter, followed by a heavy meal and copious amounts of brandy, smiling indulgently at the younger couple as their flirting became slightly more outrageous.

The news of Charis's arrest and imprisonment had improved Richard's mood considerably. George, however, was more concerned at the possible loss of his promised dowry.

"Don't worry, boy," Richard reassured him. "You will get your money whatever happens."

With a raised hand Richard summoned over the obliging butler who attended to them immediately.

"Yes, sir, how can I be of service?" he enquired.

"My companion here is worried about her stepdaughter," Richard began. "Whilst we are sure this arrest is a misunderstanding, what are the penalties around here for such a crime should she be found guilty?"

The butler stared stony-eyed at the lady who, far from looking upset, was actually pink-cheeked and very merry.

"I regret, sir, that if she is indeed found guilty of smuggling the young lady may actually be hanged. However, she would have had to be found in possession of the smuggled goods. Being in the company of known smugglers would bring about a lesser sentence if she were found guilty."

The three travellers looked at each other.

George was the first to speak. "The Colonies?"

The butler nodded and, bending, removed the empty wine bottle from the table. "I understand that is normally the punishment meted out to those found guilty of such a crime."

That answer did not seem to suit the party, however. George's expression changed from one of amusement to one of anger. The last thing he wanted was his future wife to be spirited away where they could not touch either her or her fortune.

Henrietta too, saw the effect this news was having on George.

"We can only hope my dearest Charis is found innocent," she said, her voice almost breaking on the words and the merriment gone from her eyes.

The butler seemed satisfied the party were taking the news a lot more seriously.

"May I ask if there would be anyone available to escort us to my cousin's home tomorrow?" Henrietta went on.

The butler bowed in her direction. "Of course, my lady," he replied. "I will ensure one of our staff is put at your disposal in the morning."

She smiled at him, and on his departure, she turned to Richard. "Well, Richard?" she asked. "What do we do now? If she is sentenced to death, we get her fortune. If she is sent for transportation, how does that sit with the legalities?"

Richard, however, was not perturbed. He smiled. "Charis Waverley will die," he said quietly. "Whether by a hangman's noose or a well-paid jailer on board the transport ship, have no fear, my love. Her fortune will be ours very shortly." He turned to his son. "I am only sorry you will lose your sport, my boy." He went on. "She would have been a fine wife for you to school, albeit for the short time she had left to her!"

George forced a smile back on to his face. He looked from his father, older, red-faced and going to seed and then to the glowing beauty of Lady Henrietta. Perhaps his future may not be quite so bleak after all.

"Whatever happens, Father, I am sure you will do your best for her ladyship." He bowed his head in Henrietta's direction.

Attractive, sure of himself, all he had to do was bide his time. He raised his glass in the lady's direction and winked at her.

•

A discreet tap on her bedroom door alerted Henrietta to a visitor. The maid had left, and she sat alone next to the fire, tired and satiated after her meal and wine.

Her head rested against the high backed settle, her thoughts wandering to what may await them in the morning when they would be travelling the final few miles to Alice Embleton's home. She thought of the indignities heaped upon women when in prison and wondered if Charis even now wished she had accepted George when she had chance. He, at least, would have been gentler with her than the type of man Charis was likely to encounter.

She roused herself as the tapping continued. Drawing her white lace negligee around her nightdress, she opened the door, expecting to find Richard seeking entry.

George leant on the threshold.

Alarmed, Henrietta glanced up and down the corridor.

"What do you want?" she hissed.

George smiled lazily and stepped inside. Without a word, his arms circled her waist, pulling her towards him, pressing his lips down on hers as he held her tightly.

"You drive me mad..." he whispered when she finally pulled her lips away from his. "I could not bear to retire without seeing you once more." His lips sought the pulse beating in her neck.

She closed her eyes as desire swept through her.

His embrace excited her more than Richard's had ever done but even as she returned his kisses with equal ardour, she was alert to any sounds of movement. Groaning, she gave herself over to the touch of his hands, the passion in his kiss, revelling in the feel of his hands against the smoothness of her skin.

The bed was tantalisingly close and even as George attempted to steer her towards its silken splendour, the soft noise of a door opening and closing was enough to make Henrietta pull away from him.

Taking a deep, steadying breath, she smoothed the rumpled night clothes and returned to her seat on the settle by the fire. George followed her and sat in the armchair opposite just as Richard appeared in the doorway.

His eyes narrowed at the cosy scene before him, but as he had only left his son moments earlier, he had no reason to believe either his son or his lover had been indulging their senses in anything but discussion.

George rose to his feet as his father entered the room. Bowing to Henrietta, he took her hand and kissed it in a courtly gesture. "Goodnight, my lady. I am, as ever, at your service. Goodnight, father." He paused as he passed his parent. "We were discussing the journey tomorrow," he explained. "I wondered if it might be as well to go directly to Scarborough Fort."

Richard shook his head. "No, I think our original decision to go to Cliffe House should stand."

"Very well, I bow to your decision." George smiled and nodding again in Henrietta's direction he left the room.

Henrietta stood and came over to Richard. Snaking her arms around his neck, she kissed him. "Are you joining me tonight, my love?" she whispered.

Richard's eyes softened as he returned her embrace. "You should not let George bother you, my dear," he said.

She smiled. "He amuses me, my darling; that is all." She kissed him again. "Stay with me," she murmured against his skin.

Richard kissed her before turning to lock the door. Henrietta's smile did not leave her face as he returned to take her into his arms once more. She closed her mind to the thought that tonight, just for once, she would have appreciated being left to enjoy the comfort and silence of her bed completely alone.

•

The rain beat down relentlessly, horse's hooves and carriage wheels leaving deep furrows in the road rapidly filling with the deluge.

The girl could feel the water soaking her thin slippers, and her bonnet was soaked through so that her hair hung in bedraggled curls over her shoulders and around her face. The shawl over a faded blue dress was scant protection against the downpour, and she shivered as she paused outside the millinery shop.

Attempting to wipe her face with a damp scrap of lace handkerchief, she pushed a wayward curl back underneath her bonnet and pushed the door open.

She knew she did not look her best but a day spent tramping the streets of London had worn down her body. Her spirit, however, refused to be beaten, and she held her head high as she walked in.

The shop had only two customers, an elegant lady sitting next to a small counter upon which a shop assistant had laid out for her inspection an array of lace and beading. Next to her a gentleman stood smiling down at the lady, amused at the transaction taking place.

They stared at her as the girl hesitated inside the doorway. An older lady standing at the rear of the shop came forward.

"May I help you, Miss?" she asked.

Henrietta hesitated slightly but smiled at the woman. "I would like to speak to the proprietor," she said quietly.

"That is myself," she replied.

"I am seeking employment, Madam," Henrietta said. "I have worked as a milliner and seamstress in Portsmouth and have references as to my skill and reliability."

The woman smiled, not unkindly, but shook her head. "I am sorry, my dear, but I have no situations at the moment. Have you tried Madame Renoir's establishment?"

Henrietta felt her shoulders droop. "She sent me here, Madam," she said. "Is there anywhere else you can recommend?"

The woman looked thoughtful. The girl looked tired and by the look of her pale face and shabby damp garments she had been tramping the streets for hours. She was a very attractive girl though. She had never seen such a natural beauty, a heart-shaped face, huge blue eyes and damp tendrils of rich golden hair. Aware of her other two customers watching the exchange with interest with a deep breath attempted to avert their attention.

"Wait here, my dear. I will write down the address of another shop. You may have more success with them."

Henrietta smiled her thanks and sat down upon the chair next to the front door, one normally used by maids and servants accompanying their mistress to the shop. She was aware that she was the subject of scrutiny for the two customers examining the fripperies on the shop counter and a blush suffused her cheeks.

She had grown used to such interest over the past few weeks. Since leaving Portsmouth, she had arrived in the capital with little more than a portmanteau of her belongings and a little money raised from selling everything she owned. She had found lodgings in a small back street tavern and had slept with all the furniture piled against the door to prevent unwanted night-time intrusions.

Days had been spent walking the streets seeking employment. Starting at the grand houses of Mayfair, she had gone from door to door looking for work of any kind. Whether it was her looks or her refined voice, but she had been turned away from every establishment she approached.

Born to a good family and brought low by circumstances beyond her control, she had arrived in London determined not to let her sorrow over the deaths of her husband and child prevent her from moving on with her life.

She had finally decided to try the dressmakers and milliners. Shops she had once upon a time visited as a customer with her mama in that far off time of her childhood and youth. Ostracised from her family for marrying the man she loved, she had turned to them only once and when they had even then rejected her, she had turned her back on them with a cold finality.

Unnerved at the stares from the tall man in the corner, she shifted uncomfortably in her seat and looked at the floor.

A swish of skirts and she found herself staring at a pair of highly polished boots and a gown of the finest dark purple satin. Looking up, the customer who had been seated stood before her, a smile on her face.

"My dear," she said kindly. "Am I to understand you are seeking work?"

Henrietta stood and faced the lady before her. "Yes, I am," she replied.

The woman looked at her. She smiled again. Producing a small white card, she presented it to Henrietta and nodded.

"You are a very attractive young lady," she said softly. "May I ask how old you are?"

Slightly disconcerted at the question, Henrietta stammered, "Three and twenty, Madam."

The woman nodded. "You are slightly older than my other girls, but then, none of them are as beautiful as you, my dear. You would be a very welcome addition to my establishment."

Henrietta looked down at the white card. It was engraved with the name 'Lady Anne Courtney' and an address in a part of town unknown to Henrietta.

It meant nothing to her.

"Are you recently here from the country, my dear?" Lady Anne asked.

"Portsmouth, my lady. Two weeks ago."

"Are you married?" she asked

"Widowed. My husband died at Trafalgar."

"I am so sorry, my dear. Have you no family, no relatives to help you?"

Henrietta stared at Lady Anne, wondering why she was being questioned. However, she swallowed the retort that sprang to her lips and shook her head. "No," she replied. "No one."

Before the questioning could continue, the proprietor returned and, seeing what was happening hurried to intervene.

"My Lady," she said to her customer, "I have just brought out more Brussels lace for you to inspect." She indicated with her hand the additional wares on the counter.

Turning back to Henrietta she pushed a scrap of paper in her hand. "Go to these addresses, my dear," she said in a low voice. "One of them may be able to help."

Confused, wondering why the shop owner should want her out of the shop so quickly, Henrietta thanked her, curtsied at Lady Anne and, pulling her shawl tighter across her shoulders, left the shop.

Tired and hungry, Henrietta decided that she would go back to her rooms. She needed to rest and dry her clothes before trying once more to find work. She did not look her best and was puzzled as to why Lady Ann Courtney would be so interested in her. She pushed the card and the piece of paper into her reticule and made her way through the rain to her lodgings.

Her stomach rumbled, and she felt faint from lack of food. She could only afford to eat once a day, and even then it was just a bowl of broth and some bread from the tap room of the tavern. She normally took the food to her room, uncomfortable at the stares of the men in the tavern and on more than one occasion she had been forced to repulse unwanted advances.

Making her way through the downpour, she shivered with cold and walked the long journey back to the tavern. She was used to being propositioned by the drunken men near the inn and had ignored their calls and demands that she satisfy them for the pennies they offered. The streetwalkers had eyed her with suspicion, worried that a new and beautiful girl on their patch would rob them of their custom. Henrietta had always kept her head down and avoided contact with any of them. Running into the tavern out of the deluge, she stopped to shake the water off her shawl before going through the tap room to find the landlady. Even the landlady mistrusted the girl, and though she took her money and fed her a decent bowl of bread and broth, she was as suspicious as the rest of the local people.

Henrietta hesitated, but she hoped the landlady might be able to enlighten her.

"Mrs Briggs," she began. "May I ask if you have ever heard of a Lady Anne Courtney?"

Mrs Briggs' eyes narrowed. "How do you know of that lady?" she demanded.

"Why... I met her today, and she gave me her card."

Mrs Briggs looked at her tenant from the wet slippers to the bedraggled bonnet. A broad smile suffused her face. "She runs the most exclusive whore house in London. If she wants you, then you are a fortunate girl, my dear!" Laughing at the suddenly horrified Henrietta's face, she shook her head. "She caters for Lords and suchlike. If you are lucky enough to be taken in by her, you will never have to sell yourself on the streets around here."

"But… I would never…" Henrietta was mortified.

Mrs Briggs stopped laughing. "Not yet – but how much money do you have left and how long can you go on living here? We don't take in strays, and if you can't afford your rent, Mr Briggs will soon be sending gentlemen to you to pay your way."

Henrietta shivered again at the implied threat. No, not implied. Mr Briggs was rough and unpleasant, and Henrietta was afraid of him. She had caught him staring at her more than once. Her first night at the tavern she had been so frightened she had placed a chair underneath the door handle after she had locked it. A sensible move as it turned out when a low curse had been heard followed by the turning of the handle shortly after the tavern had closed for the night.

She went to her room and, once again, counted out her remaining coins. She had enough to last her a few more days and if she was not lucky enough to find employment soon, she had little alternatives left to her. Prostitution or the workhouse. A grim choice lay before her.

She wept bitter tears into her pillow that night. Images of the strong laughing face of her beloved husband danced before her eyes and she awoke wondering for a few seconds where she was and where he had gone. Then realisation set in and pain pierced her heart once more.

•

Henrietta moved away from the window and looked down at the sleeping figure of Richard Hardy. Memories assailed her this night, triggered by the ceaseless, constant hail beating against the panes of glass. The hail had reminded her of that day, that relentless rain on the day her life had changed forever.

Ten years had passed since that night. Ten years had passed and so much had happened. So much had changed. So many memories crowded into her mind and caused her to rise from her bed in restless agony.

She remembered the men. She had finally given in to poverty

and hunger and fear and had gone to Lady Anne's establishment. She had been welcomed and well treated but oh, at what cost?

The gentlemen had been many and varied, and she had only survived them all by closing her heart and eyes and imagining it was him, the man she loved. He had been dead these last ten years, yet she still held him so firmly in her heart that she could close her eyes and see his image in all its rugged, handsome detail.

Then along came Richard and yet again, her life had changed. He rescued her, took her out of the brothel, set her up in her own home and, always with an eye to a fortune, had introduced her to Anthony. She was his puppet though. He owned her. He had held over her head the threat of exposure to her husband, society and her stepdaughter, so she never dared disobey him.

As she slipped back into bed beside Richard, she touched the gold locket around her neck. It contained those images most precious to her even now, and she prayed that when her time came, the Angel of Death would come in the shape of the laughing blue-eyed boy she had loved and married and lost all those years ago.

•

The loud knocking on the heavy front door of Cliffe House roused Mrs Embleton from her seat by the fire to go over to the window. Hoping that finally, Captain Howard had received her urgent missive, she drew the brocade curtains back to peer through the darkness to the path outside.

Angry and anxious following Charis's arrest, she had sent word immediately to members of the local gentry, calling them to her aid. The Captain had not been easily found. He had been engaged further up the coast with various other members of the smuggling brotherhood, disposing of the hastily removed contraband that had so nearly fallen into Revenue hands.

It was the Captain, but he was not alone. Standing with him, hidden from her view were two men. Both taller than the Captain, and by his stance, she recognised Connor immediately. He looked up at her window, and in the clear moonlight, she could see his face was drawn and haggard. Apparently the news of Charis's arrest had caused him as much anguish as it had her.

She left the room and went down the staircase where Josiah was taking the hats and cloaks from their visitors. The cloaks were heavy with the dampness of snow, and she saw Connor run his hands through hair that had grown longer in the recent weeks. Josiah was welcoming them in, although he was still regarding Luke Vincent with some suspicion. Captain Vincent, however, said nothing and only the slight glint of amusement in his eyes gave away his feelings towards the elderly retainer.

Captain Howard stepped forward as Mrs Embleton came down the stairs. He took her hand in his and, bowing, kissed it in an old-fashioned, courtly gesture. "Ma'am," he said softly, "We came as soon as we heard."

"It was good of you to come so promptly, Abraham," she responded. "Please come up to the drawing room while Josiah brings us some brandy." With a nod to her servant, she led the men upstairs.

Connor, however, stopped her with a hand on her arm. "Mrs Embleton, Ma'am, has there been any news of Miss Waverley?"

Gently she shook her head and carried on up to her cosy room. She seated herself in her usual armchair and indicated to her guests that they should sit.

Connor, however, could not settle, and he went over to the wide window seat, sitting uneasily while Mrs Embleton explained what had been happening.

"How long has Miss Waverley been incarcerated in the fort?" Captain Howard asked.

"Three days," she replied.

The door opened, and Josiah entered, bearing a tray with four glasses and a bottle of the finest French brandy liberated from the contraband some days earlier.

She did not miss the horrified glance between Luke Vincent and the younger man.

Mrs Embleton sighed. "I sent word to all of my friends and

your good self, Captain Howard, to advise everyone of what had happened and requesting their help. Luckily the goods in my cellar were removed before the militia could find them.

. "Charis went in Josiah's place that fateful place, She knew the risks involved, but I doubt she would have expected there to be so many militia around on the moors. The men were caught with nothing and their explanations of going for a night of poaching was accepted by the magistrate when they appeared before him the following day."

"The Reverend Soames was the magistrate, I presume, dear lady?"

"Yes, he was. I had already advised him of what had happened, and he fined them all for poaching and set them free. He did not, however, see Charis. When I went to the fort to demand to see her, I was refused and the only thing I learned was that she had been removed from the general cell with the rest of the prison population and taken to a separate room." She raised troubled eyes to the three men. "Dan Jenkins told me she was safe and well the last time he saw her but that was two days ago, and I have no idea what has befallen her since then."

Captain Howard glanced over at the two silent younger men. "And what of this Major – Quinn, is it?"

At the mention of Quinn's name, Connor's eyes darkened and his face flushed with fury at the thought of that unscrupulous officer's designs on the helpless young woman.

"Well…" Mrs Embleton allowed a slight smile to briefly lighten her countenance. "He was in a foul temper when he left here earlier. Their searching was fruitless. Thanks to you gentlemen all they discovered was an abandoned cellar and nothing else. He had to admit defeat yet again and for a man like that – well, it could be dangerous."

"For Charis…" Connor spoke at last. His voice was little more than a harsh whisper.

"Could the magistrate do nothing, Ma'am?" Luke Vincent asked.

"He was told charges were being brought against Miss Waverley for being in league with the smuggling fraternity and she had been found in possession of stolen goods. Totally trumped up, of course, but the Harker family are still in gaol on the same charges." Alice swallowed the last of her brandy. "I have arranged to go into Whitby tomorrow and seek assistance from Lord Wentworth. I was hoping you would accompany me, Abraham."

Captain Howard nodded his agreement. "Of course, of course. James Wentworth and I are old friends. I am sure between us we can expedite Miss Waverley's release."

Connor stood, bristling with anger. "And in the meantime, Miss Waverley remains incarcerated with that – that – monster." He started to pace the room. He stopped and stared at Luke Vincent. His gaze hard and uncompromising. "I'm going to the fort." He said. "Tonight."

•

She had been allowed a single candle that, when night fell, was the only light in the meagre room she had been taken to.

She had been moved from the cell when her companions had been taken up to face the magistrate, but for two days they had looked after and protected her from the lascivious comments directed her way from their fellow prisoners.

She had not heard what their fate had been nor had she been informed if anyone had enquired about her wellbeing. She could only hope Mrs Embleton had been working on her behalf to try and get her freed from incarceration. However, no news could be elicited from the surly guard who had removed her, and the sour-faced officer who brought her a plate of inedible food barely glanced at her before leaving her alone and locking her into the tiny room.

She had hardly slept. Despite her resolve, a few tears had escaped from eyes gritty with tiredness over the long night and a day she had been alone. Her courage had almost deserted her when Dan and the others had been taken out of the general prison cell. She had shrunk against the cold, damp walls of that dismal room, wondering what strange twist of fate could befall her now. The lustful glances she received and the ever bolder remarks had terrified her, but she had remained stoically silent and ignored them all. Then as night fell, her name had been called, and hope had momentarily flared in her heart.

She had scrambled to her feet from the rough straw-strewn floor and made her way to the door. Her hopes had been dashed immediately when the churlish guard had grasped her arm and pulled her roughly along the dimly lit corridor and up the spiral stone staircase to the floor above the dungeons.

He had unlocked the door of her new cell and had pushed her inside. She had stumbled and fallen onto cold flagged floor, and found herself in another chamber. It had no more comforts than the cell below but a rough sack and a blanket lay in the corner, not clean but they did at least offer a barrier between herself and the cold stone floor.

She had wrapped herself in her cloak and the blanket and shivered through the night, thinking longingly of the blazing fire in the comfort of Mrs Embleton's drawing room. Her thoughts wandered to the drawing room of her home in London, a far more formal and grand affair and she realised with a jolt that she did not miss the Curzon Street house as much as she used to. It had been her home for over twenty years, but with the advent of Henrietta, her home had stopped being the haven she had once thought it. The wild and windswept environs of Cliffe House had become more than a refuge these last few months – it had become her home and she missed Mrs Embleton and the two elderly retainers more than she could have imagined.

She fell, eventually, into a fitful sleep and awoke, still shivering as the icy coldness permeated through to her bones. Her dreams had been tortured images of her friends being taken away and hanged; interspersed with the laughing figure of Connor. He was holding her hand, and they were running along a cliff top path – then he pulled away from her, and she could not move as he walked away – she called after him, but he could not hear her. She awoke with a start with tears drying in streaks on her cheeks.

She endured another full day of silence. The tiny window at the top of the wall was too far up for her to look out and let in only the grey, dismal light of that dark December day. She received only one interruption during that interminable day when the door opened, and a tray of dried bread and cheese and a cup of water was pushed onto the floor in front of her. Thankful that she had not been forgotten entirely, Charis tried to stop the soldier with a question but she was ignored and the door closed and locked once again.

Frustrated but realising how hungry she was, she chewed on the bread and cheese and forced it down with sips of the cold water. The food and drink revived her a little, but she was so cold she could not stop shivering as the sun finally set and the room plunged into icy darkness.

Time dragged but finally when the moon shone through the sliver of the window, the door of her cell was opened.

The light from the corridor blazed into the room, and she squinted to see who was standing there.

"Get up!" The order was sharp.

She scrambled to her feet, brushing the straw and dirt from her creased and stained dress. She pulled her cloak around her shoulders once more and walked towards the man standing there. It was the Sergeant who had arrested her that night on the moors. Was it only three days ago? She was losing track of time.

"Where are you taking me?" she demanded. Her voice sounded weak to her own ears, but she managed to summon up some of her old autocratic manner.

The Sergeant looked down at her, distaste at her appearance very evident in his attitude.

"Come with me," was all he said.

He stood aside as she left the room. There was another man with him, and as the Sergeant led the way, she followed with the soldier behind her. Obviously worried she might make some attempt to escape, she thought, amused at the very idea. The fortified castle was a myriad of passageways and corridors, and even if she had the strength to run from her captors, she had no idea where she was or where she would go.

She was led upwards, out of the dungeons, up the spiral stone stairs until they gave way to a courtyard. She was led into the main rooms of the fort, into a hallway alight with torches and candles. Suddenly acutely aware of her dishevelled and dirty appearance, she straightened her shoulders, lifting her head in an imperious gesture as the Sergeant led her across the hallway and up a broad set of stairs.

She followed him up to the first floor and along a carpeted passage. He stopped outside a door and knocked sharply.

"Come in!" came the voice inside.

The Sergeant opened the door. "The prisoner, sir!" he said, not moving from the doorway.

Charis went into the room and stood stock-still as the Sergeant stepped away, closing the door behind her.

Her first impression was one of welcome warmth as a log fire blazed cheerfully in the hearth. She realised she was in a well-appointed dining room, with heavy damask curtains shutting out the winter night beyond.

Major Jonathan Quinn stood in front of the fire. He had his hands behind his back, and he stared over at her with the same distaste in his eyes as the Sergeant had displayed.

"Miss Waverley." His voice was cold.

She nodded her head gracefully at him. "Major Quinn," she said, her voice equally as icy. "I trust you have come to release me and return me to my home."

A thin smile crossed his features. "Please come in, Miss Waverley. You look chilled."

Reluctant to move, Charis nevertheless walked slowly towards him. He indicated a chair beside the roaring fire, and she sank into it, trying not to continue shivering as the heat slowly began to warm her frozen body.

"Has Mrs Embleton been to seek my release?" she enquired.

"I have just returned from Cliffe House," he replied. "Mrs Embleton did not enquire about you." He left her side and walked to the dining table where a bottle of wine and two glasses rested. "Allow me to pour you a warming drink, Miss Waverley."

He poured wine into a glass and returned to her side, handing her the rich ruby liquid. She sipped at it. The fiery liquid burned its way down her throat, but she welcomed the warmth that spread through her body.

She had begun to think she would never feel warm again but gradually as she sipped her drink, the wine and the fire worked their magic, and the shivering stopped.

"Why am I being kept a prisoner, Major?" she asked, keeping her voice steady.

Ignoring her question, he smiled at her, the lifting of his lips more of a grimace than a smile, and it did not reach his eyes.

"May I take your cloak, Miss Waverley?" he asked.

Warily, she stood and removed the cloak, handing it over to him. He placed it across the back of a dining chair before returning to her side. She sat back down on the chair and watched him as he brought another chair over to sit facing her.

"You are not looking your best, Miss Waverley," he said. "I dare say a bath and a change of clothing would be welcome at the moment."

She stared at him, no smile of gratitude in response to his words. Instead, her instincts started to prickle, and she wondered what he was leading up to.

"I would be grateful to be taken home where both those things could be provided," she replied.

She sipped at the wine, welcoming the reviving of her spirits as she swallowed the rich liquid.

"I thought we might be able to accommodate you better here," he replied.

"I have done nothing wrong, Major Quinn," she went on, slight nervousness adding an edge to her voice. "I must insist you allow me to leave."

He smiled again, genuine amusement on his face this time. "Oh no, I think not." He leaned forward but made no attempt to touch her. "Your Aunt is in league with a number of well-known smugglers," he said softly. "We have been unable to apprehend them, and we have been unable to catch your Aunt with any of the goods we know have been taken to her home."

Charis remained silent.

"As you know I am determined to bring these wrongdoers to justice. I also know you were prepared to do anything in your power to save your friends. I am offering you the opportunity to leave here a free woman if you will just agree to help me."

His voice was low, hypnotic. She found herself unable to look away from his eyes, boring into hers.

"How could I possibly help you, Major?" she replied.

"Just a bit of information, my dear." His voice remained so quiet it was almost a whisper.

"You are asking me to be an informer?"

He shrugged, a slight nonchalant lifting of his shoulders. "There are worse things in life." He smiled. "You are alone with me now. There are no friends to run to, no gallant rescuers to save you. You can scream all night long. No one would hear you, and none of my men would dare to come in."

She remained perfectly still, mesmerised, as he reached out and gently tucked a stray curl of hair behind her ear.

She stared into his face, seeing the lines that were forming around his eyes, at the cruel set of his mouth, at the fading bruises inflicted by Connor on that balcony only two weeks earlier. She thought briefly of Connor then closed her eyes. Opening them again, she stared down at the glass in her hands.

In one swift, fluid motion she threw the rest of her glass of wine into his face and before he had time to react she stood and raced towards the closed door.

She had only just reached the door when he caught her. Spun around, the blow to her face caught her by surprise, her head snapping back as the force of his fist against her jaw sent her reeling.

The red wine dripped from his face, and as she fell to the floor, he wiped his face with his open palm. She had no chance to recover as he bent down, pulled her to a sitting position and hit her once more, the full force of his body behind the blow. She did not have chance to even scream as a wave of blackness overcame her and she slumped down on the floor with a stifled groan of pain.

CHAPTER TWENTY

It was approaching midnight as the carriage wheels clattered on the snow-cleared courtyard of Scarborough Fort. The Sergeant at Arms, alerted to the arrival of the carriage and its occupants, left the comfort of his quarters and came outside just as the carriage doors were opened and the first of the two occupants descended. He knew neither of the men who stood before him, however, from the air of authority which emanated from them, he realised that they were here on a matter of some importance. One of the men seemed extremely annoyed to be there and the Sergeant, eyeing him shrewdly, came to the conclusion that he was not happy to have had his evening interrupted in this manner.

The taller of the two men addressed him in tones that brooked no argument.

"You there, Sergeant. Take me to your Commanding Officer at once."

The Sergeant bridled. "My Commanding Officer, sir? Do you mean Major Quinn or Colonel Hewitt?"

"I mean Hewitt, man. He is the overall commander of this garrison, is he not?"

"He is, sir. May I ask who is enquiring?"

The tall man looked down his nose at the Sergeant. "Lord Wentworth," he advised. "The Colonel will know who I am."

Even the Sergeant at Arms recognised the name of the local Justice of the Peace and friend of his Commander.

"Certainly, sir. The Colonel may have retired, however."

Lord Wentworth's patience was stretched extremely thin. "Sergeant, this matter is urgent otherwise I certainly would not be here!" The look he gave his companion was filled with exasperation. The Sergeant guessed that his Lordship had been persuaded to leave the comfort of his home with great difficulty and he was not about to brook any insubordination.

"Come in, sir. I will send for the Colonel immediately."

He stepped aside and indicated the two men enter the hallway. There were very few people around at this hour as he led them into the Colonel's library. A cheerful fire burned in the hearth and comfortable armchairs beckoned, as he despatched one of his men to the kitchen to bring refreshments to the two men.

"Your name, sir?" he asked the second man.

"Howard," the other man replied, "Colonel Hewitt knows who I am."

"I regret the Colonel may be asleep. If you would not mind waiting, I will endeavour to summon him as soon as possible."

The door opened, and a servant entered with a tray of drinks. The Sergeant left them to go rouse his Colonel. He would not dare send another man to summon his commander.

The door closed behind the Sergeant and the orderly. The two men looked at each other.

"How long have we got?" Connor asked, striding over to look out of the window.

He could see Josiah turning the horses in the courtyard. The elderly man raised his eyes to the window and nodded brief acknowledgement.

Luke went to the door and opened it slightly. The hall was once again deserted. He had counted only two men on guard as they had entered.

"According to Howard, the dungeons are on the floor below this, but Dan said she had been taken out, probably upstairs. We don't have long to search, boy."

Connor joined him at the door. "Come on then." His voice was grim but determined. He would tear the castle down a brick at a time to find Charis.

They left the warmth of the library and back out into the hallway. No one stirred as they ran up the stairs to the first floor. Connor held a sword by his side, making sure it made no noise as he ran silently to the passageway lined with doors either side of the main landing.

They glanced at each other and Luke indicated he would go one way and Connor the other. They started opening doors quickly glancing inside each room before moving along to the next.

Connor halted as one door would not open to his touch. Pressing his ear to the wood, he listened intently, but no sound came from within. About to move on, a noise halted him in his tracks. It was the sound of a soft groan, followed by the unmistakeable sound of a slap and a muffled scream. His blood ran cold as he tried the door handle again. It did not budge, and with an oath, he drew back his foot and kicked the lock with the full force of his body. The noise of the wood splintering made Luke Vincent start in alarm, and he ran back along the corridor to see Connor kicking the door again.

The door gave way, and the sight that met their eyes caused Connor to let out a roar of fury.

Charis was tied to a chair, blood pouring from swollen lips, her eyes half closed with black bruising already starting to show and her hair hanging down in a tangled mess over a torn and bloodied dress.

Quinn faced him, disturbed from the torture of his helpless victim by the splintering door and the shout of anger. His fists were bunched, and he leapt for his discarded blade as Connor sprang at him, a red mist of rage in his eyes, and murder in his heart. Quinn did not quite reach the sword as Connor brought him to the floor in an eruption of fists that pounded into his face and body. Quinn recovered however and rallied, pushing the enraged man away far enough to bring his own fists into action. The two men grappled together, a heaving furious mass of bloodied faces, knuckles and torn clothing.

Luke ran to the half-conscious Charis and cut the ropes that bound her. He lifted her into his arms and at a shout from Connor to get her out, he obeyed their previously discussed arrangements and ran with her to the door just as reinforcements in the way of a handful of surprised guards roused from their sleep started down the corridor towards him.

He wasted no time in trying to help Connor – they had foreseen this might happen – and he did what Connor had asked. He ran down the stairs with Charis in his arms and out of the building towards the waiting coach. At a shout to Josiah, he threw Charis inside and jumped in after her, just as Josiah whipped the horses and galloped over the slippery cobbles away, out of the castle grounds.

They drove at a frantic pace through the streets surrounding the castle and emerged onto the Whitby road before any of the soldiers were able to set off in pursuit. Josiah kept the horses at full gallop and Luke found himself having to hold on to Charis for dear life as they were thrown around the carriage interior.

They drove on through the night and passed the turn off for Cliffe House just as Charis roused from her faint. She looked up into Luke's eyes and struggled to comprehend what had happened. He held her in his arms, holding her still, preventing her from falling to the floor of that wildly swaying carriage.

Luke grinned down at her. "Have no fear, Miss Waverley," he said softly. "I am taking you away from danger."

Comprehension dawned, and she tried to sit up, still clutching at his coat sleeves. "Where are we going?" she asked faintly.

"To my ship," Luke replied. "It will be safer for you there than with Mrs Embleton."

"And Connor?" she whispered. "Where is he?"

His smile disappeared as he helped her to sit upright. He pulled his white cravat from around his throat and gently wiped the blood from her face. Her lips were swollen, and he dabbed carefully at the cut on her lips where a ring had caught her tender skin.

"It was he who came to rescue you. He is probably even now in Scarborough Gaol in your stead."

Tears sprang unbidden to her eyes. "No!" Her voice was raw with anguish. "Quinn will kill him!"

Luke's face was grave as he continued to clean her face and wipe away the tears sparkling on her cheeks.

"Did Major Quinn hurt you in any other way, Miss Waverley?" he asked gently.

She felt a rush of heat to her face as he realised his meaning. She shook her head and raised a shaking hand to his. "No, sir. Although no doubt that was probably next on his twisted agenda."

He steadied her once more as the carriage hit a pothole and bounced along the highway.

"Tomorrow morning there will be Sir James Wentworth, Captain Howard and the local magistrate at the castle intent on securing his release. Connor knew what would happen and he ordered that whichever one of us had chance, we were to get you out of there. He was prepared to take that risk to ensure you were out of harm's way so we must now abide by his wishes and get you away to safety."

The dizziness left her brain, and she sat upright, Luke surprised to see a look of determination hardening on her face. This was not the helpless prey he had snatched from the depravity of a madman. She changed before his eyes into a composed, proud and extremely angry young woman.

"I too have connections, Captain Vincent," she replied. "I will accompany you to your ship, and from there I wish a missive to be sent to my Uncle."

Luke sat back against the padded squabs of Captain Howard's town carriage. "Your Uncle, Miss Waverley?"

That old light of amusement sparkled in his eyes once more, Connor's troubles momentarily forgotten.

"My Uncle, sir. Lord Frederick Waverley. Baron of Pickering. He should even now be in his York residence so a messenger should be able to reach him within a day of hard riding."

Despite himself, he was impressed. "You do, indeed, have connections, Miss Waverley."

She did not think it prudent to disclose any further information to the Captain. He might have rescued her but he was a rogue and a smuggler, and she was wary of revealing any details of her own fortune, locked away though it might be.

"He has many friends. The weight of the combined pressure from him and the gentlemen you mention should be enough to influence Connor's release."

Luke's eyes narrowed slightly. Connor's fate might not be so easily resolved, especially if Quinn had his way.

"I pray we are just not too late, Miss Waverley," he replied, his voice sober once more, no trace of amusement in his tone.

"Major Quinn had best pray if it is," she said, her voice colder than he had ever heard it.

He took her hand in his and squeezed it gently. "Connor is like a cat, Miss Waverley," he said grimly. "He still has a few lives left in him, I think!"

She smiled gratefully up at him, a faint lifting of her mouth he saw briefly in the moonlight coming through the window of the carriage.

They travelled in companionable silence until the carriage rattled its way down to Whitby Harbour. He helped her from the coach, and they waited as Josiah turned the horses around and trotted away, a much slower pace to allow the horses to recover from their gallop across the moors. Josiah waved once, and Charis returned his wave before, shivering with cold, they made their way up the gangplank to the safety of the stately old ship, just as dawn touched the icy cold darkness of the horizon.

•

Shaking with rage, Jonathan Quinn stood over the man who had dared pummel him to a bloodied heap on the floor of his own room. Held down by chains, Connor was imprisoned in the dungeons of the old castle. It had taken three of the guards to drag the incensed man off their commanding officer, and they had held him as Quinn had climbed back to his feet, blood from a split lip oozing down onto his white shirt. His eyes had been icy, his face set with an anger that made the guards' blood run cold –

they had seen it before and were glad that on this occasion his ire was not directed at any of them.

He had not paused as his men held down the furiously fighting man and had struck Connor in the stomach, winding him and causing him to cease in his struggles. As Connor straightened and glared at Major Quinn, his face held all the contempt and hatred he felt for the man torturing an innocent girl.

He had seen Luke pick Charis up and run from the room with her –an arrangement planned on their way to the castle – and was heartily relieved that the Captain had kept to his promise. All Connor had to do now was to give them time to make good their escape. He had heard the carriage leave the courtyard whilst he was being dragged off the supine body of the Major.

Despite the situation he now found himself in, he smiled. A slow, wicked smile guaranteed to enrage Quinn even more.

"Take him to the cells!" Quinn had snarled, and he had been dragged, fighting and struggling all the way down the two floors to the dungeons below the castle.

An hour later and Quinn faced him, but they were not alone. The gaoler stood in the corner beside an array of instruments used to extract confessions from the most innocent of men. Connor had dismissed him and his variety of tools with a contemptuous smile and looked up at Quinn.

"I suggest you release me now, Major Quinn," he said quietly.

If Quinn was surprised by the cultured tone of the man before him, he hid it well.

"Release you? Are you mad?" he sneered.

Connor smiled again. "Did you catch up with the carriage?" he asked almost casually, knowing from Quinn's temper that they had not.

"They made good their escape – but we will find them, have no fear of that."

Connor raised his head and stared directly into Quinn's eyes. "Then you have let escape one of the most notorious smugglers ever to have plied his trade around this coast."

"I have you – and you will tell me where and when the next

smuggling operation will land and where he has taken Charis Waverley."

Connor shook his head. "Again, I suggest you release me before you go any further."

His confidence and tone enraged Quinn even more. "You do, do you?" He could not understand how his prisoner could sound so composed. He was used to inciting terror into men by his mere presence yet this man had bested him twice and twice snatched his prize away from him. His anticipated night of pleasure reducing the reluctant Charis Waverley to a quivering broken shadow of a woman had been curtailed all too soon. He had been looking forward to her warming his bed to stop the brutality from continuing. This man had interfered with his plans once too often, and he was going to pay for his meddling.

"Yes, I do," Connor replied, maddening his tormentor even more by the coolness of his tone.

Quinn let out a short bark of laughter. At the same time, he hit Connor in the face with his fist, snapping Connor's head back.

Connors lip, already bruised, split open and more blood splashed on to the formerly white shirt Quinn wore.

Connor's eyes narrowed, but he held Quinn's in a steady gaze. "Release me, you moron, before you get yourself into any more trouble."

Quinn laughed again and hit the chained man again and again until his knuckles were sore.

"You idiot, Quinn!" Connor roared. "I'm on your side!"

Quinn paused as his fist raised again to strike the prisoner. He glanced over at the gaoler as if to confirm he had heard correctly.

"What?"

"My name is Captain Oliver Connor Steele," Connor replied. He paused and spat blood onto the floor. "I am a member of His Majesty's Royal Navy deployed to the North East coast to bring Luke Vincent to justice. My vessel, The Princess Charlotte, sank in a vicious storm several weeks ago, and I was injured."

He stopped speaking, looking over from the gaoler to Quinn. The former looked uneasy, Quinn looked even angrier.

"My father is Admiral Lord Tristan Steele, of County Clare, and Equerry to His Majesty King George. Now let me go or bring one of the Revenue Captains here to verify who I am."

Quinn paused momentarily before his fist connected to Connor's stomach once more.

"If you are telling the truth, why did you not reveal yourself before now?"

Connor dragged his head upright and glared at him. "I was ill. I have only recovered my health these last few days."

"You could have stopped him earlier – instead of attacking me."

The hatred emanating from Connor was palpable in that small, dark, dank room. "You were torturing the woman I love," he snarled. "How was I supposed to react?"

Quinn stared uncomprehendingly at the seated man.

"The woman is little more than a servant – guilty of aiding and abetting the same crew of smugglers you yourself were working with. If you are who you say, why would you care about a lowly paid companion?"

"I repeat – she is the woman I love, and as soon as I find her again, I will be asking her to marry me. I don't care who or what she is." The words were ground out of Connor between gritted teeth.

Quinn was unsure what shocked him more. The revelation that this prisoner purported to be a member of a well-born family or that he intended to find and marry the chit.

"I think you are lying," he hissed. "And I will find out the truth eventually." His smile was as cold as his eyes.

"Sir…" the gaoler interrupted nervously.

"What is it?"

"Sir, if the man is telling the truth, we can soon verify it," he went on. "There was a Captain Steele lost at sea in September when the Charlotte went down off the coast near Robin Hood's Bay."

"He's lying!" Quinn repeated.

"But there are Revenue men here who can identify him," the gaoler insisted.

"Silence!" Quinn was beyond angry. The thought of the prisoner being snatched away from him before he had repaid him for the indignities suffered was unthinkable.

Bending, he raised his fist and struck Connor on his back, at the tender spot above the kidneys. Connor flinched but bit his lip to prevent a sound from escaping.

The assault carried on, Quinn beside himself with rage, and it was only when the chair toppled to the side with the unconscious man still chained to it did he stop, breathing heavily, his fists bloodied and sore.

The first light of dawn appeared through the windows.

"Leave him!" he snapped as the gaoler would have lifted the seat upright. "We have not yet extracted a confession."

He fastened his loosened shirt and straightened his clothing. "We will come back later, once I have bathed and rested."

His eyes narrowed as he watched the gaoler move to unlock the cell door. "And you – do not summon anyone until I have finished with this lying scum."

Knowing full well the consequences of disobeying an order from Major Quinn, the gaoler nodded. "Yes, sir."

They left, locking the heavy door behind them, leaving Connor alone and unconscious on the blood splattered stone floor.

CHAPTER TWENTY-ONE

Mrs Embleton reflected – as she heard the loud knock on her front door – that her life had been a lot quieter before the unexpected arrival of Charis Waverley. Unobtrusively going about her business and drawing no unwanted attention to her quiet lifestyle, she had seen everything turn on its head since that day several months ago when a pretty young lady had sought refuge in her household.

Shaking her head but with a slight smile, she remained beside the fire in her drawing room and listened as Josiah answered the door.

Knowing Charis was safe had set her mind at rest and she had been comforted by the thought that Sir James Wentworth and Captain Howard would leave no stone unturned to ensure the release of young Connor.

Josiah had returned at dawn, exhausted, lines of tiredness creasing his face. He had not shirked though, he had taken the carriage and horses back to their owners before advising her that Charis had been rescued and was even now setting sail with Luke Vincent to a safe harbour. He did not say where they were going, he had not been told and had not wanted to know. The fewer people who knew her whereabouts, the safer she would be.

Hearing voices in the hall below, she put down her embroidery and stood. She had heard a woman's voice, and with a frown creasing her forehead, she opened the door to her drawing room. There were three people in the hall below, and Josiah was asking their names and business with his mistress.

"Our business is nothing to do with you," the younger man retorted, his voice betraying his contempt at being questioned by a mere servant. "Kindly inform your mistress that Miss Waverley's Mama and Betrothed have arrived."

Josiah's face was stoical, and his expression did not change. "Miss Waverley is not here," he replied.

Henrietta was tired and Richard's dislike for everything he had encountered so far sounded in his voice.

"Take us to your mistress immediately," she snapped.

Mrs Embleton stepped out onto the top of the stairs. "Lady Waverley, I presume?" she said as her presence caught their attention.

Henrietta looked up, and Mrs Embleton had to admit she could see why that old fool Anthony had fallen so hard for the lady's beauty. Dressed in a dark blue velvet cloak with a matching bonnet, the colour enhanced the sapphire of her eyes and the paleness of her cheeks. Artifice had added colour to Henrietta's lips but her mouth was set in a hard line, and Mrs Embleton smiled to herself. Desperation had brought this woman to her door, and she was not about to be turned away by an insolent butler.

"Pray come up to my drawing room," she said graciously. "Josiah, ask Martha to provide drinks for my guests. I am sure they must be cold after their journey."

Removing their hats, the two gentlemen below followed Henrietta up the stairs and followed Mrs Embleton. Returning to her seat beside the fire, she waited until they joined her.

"I am happy to make your acquaintance, Mrs Embleton," Richard said smoothly. "Pray allow me to introduce myself and my son, since Lady Waverley here is known to you."

"Oh, she is not," Mrs Embleton replied, smiling serenely at her guests. "She is known to me by reputation only."

The slight edge to her voice was enough to make Henrietta's eyes widen. Careful to hide her annoyance, she managed a smile and curtseyed prettily to her hostess.

"My dearest Anthony often spoke of his cousins," she said. "This is my friend, Sir Richard Hardy and his son George. George and my stepdaughter were engaged to be married."

"Really?" Mrs Embleton raised her eyebrows at the younger man. "I understood Charis refused your offer, Mr Hardy." She smiled at him.

"No indeed!" George was eager to speak. "There was a slight misunderstanding only, Mrs Embleton. She left before we had a chance to remedy things between us."

Mrs Embleton leaned back in her chair, smiling, entirely at ease with her visitors.

"Charis informed me she had overheard a plot to kill her, Mr Hardy. I hardly think that was a slight misunderstanding."

The shock of her words resonated through her three visitors. George looked dumbfounded and Henrietta's pale face blanched even more. Only Richard appeared unperturbed by her words.

Interrupted by the entrance of Josiah and Martha carrying a large tea tray, Mrs Embleton indicated with a wave of her hand that her visitors be seated.

Henrietta sat down on the sofa opposite Mrs Embleton, for once in her life at a loss for words.

Richard waited until the servants left and Mrs Embleton poured tea for all four of them before he broke the silence that had fallen.

"I can assure you, Mrs Embleton, that what Charis overheard was nothing more than idle jest. My son adores Charis and would not harm a hair from her head. We have come all this way to make things right between them and restore Charis to her rightful place in the world, in Society."

"As my wife..." George added.

Henrietta took a sip of the tea that has been handed to her. "However," she said, her voice suddenly colder than either of the gentlemen present had ever heard. "However, we are led to believe that my stepdaughter is currently incarcerated within Scarborough Gaol. Charged with being in league with the smuggling fraternity?"

Mrs Embleton looked over the rim of her teacup at her visitor. The lovely Henrietta's demeanour was slipping, the coldness of her voice reflected in the hardness of her eyes. Even her face, shaded as it was by the edge of her very fetching blue velvet bonnet did not seem quite so attractive in the harsh icy winter's sunlight streaming through the window.

Mrs Embleton glanced at the clock. It was already past midday. Even if they rode their horses hard, it would take them the rest of the day to reach Scarborough, almost twenty miles away.

She smiled, as calm and as tranquil as ever. "You are quite correct," she replied. "Charis is even now being questioned as to her involvement with a group of men accused of being smugglers." She took another sip of her tea before continuing, aware of the sudden air of interest her words aroused. "But as the men themselves have all been released, it is quite likely that Charis will also be released. She will have to appear before the magistrate at the next Assizes of course, but I have every hope she will be released soon."

She saw no reason to tell them of Charis's dramatic escape the previous night. The less this harpy and her entourage knew what was going on, the better she liked it. Let them drive to Scarborough on a wild goose chase. The longer they were haring all around the country, the safer Charis would be. For all his faults and reported villainy, she knew Charis would be protected to the death by Luke Vincent, for her own sake if not for Connor's. Quite a friendship and rapport existed between the two men, and although she suspected Vincent's motives, she could not doubt the way he had supported them these last few days and the way he had unhesitatingly agreed to help Connor rescue Charis from the clutches of Major Quinn.

She did not miss the look exchanged between Henrietta and Richard Hardy.

Richard turned to her.

"Do you think it would help if we were to go to Scarborough and try to expedite Miss Waverley's release?" he enquired. "Surely they would consider releasing her into the care of her stepmother if we were to vouch for her good character."

Mrs Embleton seemed to consider the idea, slowly drinking her tea and nodding slightly. "It certainly would not hurt," she said. "But you must agree to whatever Charis decides to do," she added. "If Charis wants to return here, you must bring her back to me."

A slight smile lifted the corners of Henrietta's mouth. "But of course, we will take Charis' feelings into consideration, and if she truly does not want to return to London with us, we will bring her here."

Mrs Embleton's smile was a false as Henrietta's. She knew they had no intention of returning the runaway heiress to her home; if not London then they would be driving further north to the Scottish border for a forced marriage over the anvil at Gretna Green. A quick glance at George Hardy confirmed her suspicions as he fought to keep the light of triumph out of his eyes.

She sighed. "Well, that is certainly a relief," she said. "And I am sure Charis's fears over what she overheard was nothing more than nervousness brought on by the recent bereavement she had suffered. That you both suffered," she amended, looking once more directly at Henrietta. "Although," she smiled up at George. "I would suggest that in future you refrain from making such jesting remarks regarding the death of your future wife. It does not bode well for a happy union."

George smiled happily at their hostess. He mistook the sparkle in her eyes for sympathy rather than shrewdness. "You are too kind Mrs Embleton," he thanked her. "I will never say anything quite so crass in the future."

He sounded almost sincere.

They finished their tea and, thanking her most profusely, they departed, setting off once again in search of the elusive Charis Waverley. Henrietta groaned as they re-seated themselves in the carriage. She was heartily sick of travelling and wanted nothing more than to return to the comfort of her home in London. What started off as an adventure to bring home their reluctant heiress, had turned into an epic, uncomfortable inconvenience and she could not wait for it to be over.

Mrs Embleton and her servants watched from the drawing room window as the carriage set off again. Sighing, she turned to them. "I finally understand why Charis came here," she said softly.

Martha collected the used crockery, sniffing loudly. "She was certainly no lady!" she said. "And that so-called betrothed – he was as slimy as a toad!"

Mrs Embleton chuckled softly to herself. By rights, she should be reprimanding her servants, but as she thoroughly agreed with Martha's summation, she could not bring herself to chastise her.

"What do you think they'll do when they find her gone?" Martha asked.

Mrs Embleton shrugged, pulling her warm shawl more firmly around her shoulders. "I don't know," she admitted. "We can only hope that they give up and go home. Charis, however, is safe for now and we must only pray that our friends can arrange the release of young Connor. If what Captain Vincent says is correct, I have a terrible feeling that our Major Quinn will not let him go quite so easily!"

Soberly they went about their duties. Mrs Embleton remained by the window, staring out at the restless seas and watching the carriage drive away along the coast road, disappearing over the hill in the distance. She wondered what their reaction would be once they reached their destination and, despite herself, she smiled.

•

The chill wintry day dawned with a deep red sun coming over the far horizon. Charis was already up and out on deck of the creaking old ship. She leant against the rail, looking out to the land in the distance and listening to the gentle slap of the waves again the hull and the creaking of the wood and ropes and sails. It was a soft, comforting sound and she felt almost peaceful as she gazed out over the icy blue of the North Sea. They were sailing off the coast of Scarborough, and she could just make out the castle atop the hill in the distance. Her peace was tinged with anxiety as she thought about her rescue and how Connor had thrown himself onto Quinn. She remembered his shout of fury as he launched the first of several blows to the head and body of her attacker.

Her head drooped as unexpected tears sprang to her eyes. She had no idea what was happening back on shore, and she only hoped the messenger Luke despatched would reach her Uncle in time.

A movement behind her caused her to straighten and hastily wipe her eyes. She turned her head to see Luke coming towards her. A faint smile lifted her lips as he joined her leaning on the rail.

He could see the telltale tracks of tears on her cheeks, and his eyes darkened with compassion for her.

"We will get him out, Charis," he said softly, knowing the cause of her distress.

She nodded and, in an entirely natural gesture, she linked her arm through his and leaned against him.

"He's young and strong, and he will survive this, don't worry." He paused, knowing that the time had come for complete honesty. "He was never one of my men, Charis."

Startled, she stared uncomprehendingly into his face. "What do you mean?"

He shook his head. "It was my idea of petty revenge. He had lost his memory and had no idea of his identity, and I took the opportunity to play a twisted game of vengeance against him." He sighed. "He was never a smuggler, Charis. He's the Captain of the Revenue ship which went down in the storm."

She faced him then, dropping her arm from his. "A Captain?" she repeated.

He nodded. "Steele, Oliver Steele. He is from a good family, Irish aristocracy. His father is an Admiral loyal to the Crown."

Hope suddenly blazed in Charis's eyes. "Well, we must go back at once, Captain Vincent! We must go back and tell the authorities and get him out of there!"

His eyes twinkled, and a smile crossed his face, some of his old spirit returning to his demeanour.

"He had recovered his memory, Charis. He deliberately let me get you out so I would not be arrested."

He watched as the joy on her face faded suddenly. "Why would you do such a thing, Captain Vincent?" she asked. "Why would you put him through such an ordeal and take him away from me where he was safe and recovering?"

Luke's face darkened in response. He had the grace to look shamefaced. "A stupid whim, Charis. A foolish moment of revenge against a young pup who had the temerity to challenge me and dare to hunt me down." He turned away from her and leaned on the railing once more. "He chased me a hundred nautical miles in the worst storm I have ever sailed through, and I lost my ship. He would not give up even when his own ship and life was in danger. He carried on and followed me through the hell of that night." He turned his head once more, and his eyes bored into hers. "He is the bravest man I have ever met." He went on. "Brave, dogged and foolish. We both lost our ships, and he almost lost his own life, but he was doing his duty and refused to give up. I have known him these last few weeks and grown to like and admire his courage and his determination. I am ashamed that I have put you both through this ordeal. He recovered his memory a few days ago, but he would not let me give myself up to save you. He thought of the plan to rescue you, and he insisted I get you out. Connor said he would reveal the truth of his identity and Quinn would have to verify what he claimed before anything happened."

Charis looked into his face and saw nothing there except regret and honesty. She swallowed a lump in her throat and put out her hand to touch his arm once more.

"He sacrificed himself for both of us," she whispered. "We must go back and make sure he is safe."

He put his hand over hers. "If anything has gone wrong," he said softly, "I will give myself up to ensure his release."

She smiled, happiness returning to her eyes. "It will not come to that, Luke," she said. "If Connor – Oliver – was willing to take your place, he must have a very high opinion and regard for you. He would not want you to hang."

He threw back his head and laughed out loud at her words. "Neither would I, my dear!" he said. "I have not survived all this time to let the likes of that jumped up popinjay Quinn get the better of me!"

She returned his laughter, hope bubbling through her at his words.

She re-linked her arm with his, and in companionable accord, they leaned on the ship's rail together.

"What is your history, Captain?" she asked him hesitantly.

He sighed, and she watched shadows chase across the fine planes of his rugged face. "I was a sailor under Nelson," he said. "In ten years I was promoted through the ranks from able seaman to an officer. I was happy and content with my life. I had a family, a home and a career I loved. "

He paused for a long time, memories clouding his eyes. Charis hardly dared breathe, the intensity about him palpable.

"I was injured at Trafalgar," he finally continued. "The surgeons saved my life, but it was a year after the Battle before I could return home."

"Your wife?" Charis asked, hesitantly.

"Dead," he said shortly. "Both dead and buried in a pauper's grave with no marker save a simple cross inscribed with their names. A token gesture by her family, I imagined."

She was curious but could ask no more. The pain etched on his face was so deep, so real it was as though the events he described had happened yesterday.

explained. "They disowned her when she fell pregnant with my child. We were married without their permission or blessings. When our child became ill, she went to them – telling them I had perished at Trafalgar. She was penniless and starving, and our child ill. They turned her away." His voice was soft, but the hatred and venom tangible. "They disowned her and would not help her in her darkest hour. They both died less than a week later, and I never saw either of their sweet faces again."

241

Charis felt tears spring to her eyes as he spoke, unable to bear the deep pain that emanated from his husky voice.

"I had money by then," he went on. "Money the Navy should have sent to my wife to help her, but they failed her, just as her family and I had failed her. I used it to buy a ship and took to free-trading. I felt no loyalty to the people who had let my family perish and decided then that I needed more to enable me to get away from this country and all its hypocrisy. After a couple of years, I had enough to buy land out in Virginia. I have a tobacco plantation over there, and if I survive these next few days, I will be sailing for the New World with a pocket full of gold and a heart full of memories."

He started then, as if just remembering her presence.

"I'm sorry, Charis," he said softly, seeing her tears. "Please do not feel sorry for me. I am content with my life and as soon as I restore you to Captain Steele, I will leave you with him, and you will never see me again."

She bowed her head and raised her eyes to his again, sparkling with unshed tears.

"And for that I will be heartily sorry, Luke," she replied.

He lowered his head and kissed her gently on the cheek. "Thank you, Charis," he said, his voice as gentle as his lips. "'Tis a shame young Connor met you first!" He grinned suddenly at her. "I have been known to charm a few ladies over the years."

Her mood lightened then. "And if I had not fallen so helplessly in love with a stranded, amnesiac stranger then you might have charmed me too, Captain Vincent!"

He moved away from her then and with a courtly bow, he raised her hand to his lips and kissed it. "What a team we would have made, Miss Waverley!"

He left her then, shouting orders to bring the ship about, to return them to the quiet bay near Scarborough, and Charis remained by the rail, drawing her shawl tighter around her shoulders as the bitter wind scoured the decks.

She gazed at the land drawing closer and despite the lifting of her spirits at the newfound knowledge of Connor's identity, she shivered at the thought of what revenge Major Quinn might even now be planning.

•

The cold of the prison cell permeated into his very bones. Tied now, facing the stone wall, chained to two iron rings, he fought not to shiver as the shirt was ripped from his back.

The gaoler stood back, keeping out of the way of Major Quinn who stood beside the prisoner, his face very close to the shackled man.

"Confess, and I will go easier on you," Quinn said, his voice almost gentle.

A good sleep and a hearty meal had restored Major Quinn's equilibrium. His injuries had been attended to. One eye was almost closed, and the bruising around his face would take some time to heal, but his anger still bubbled under the surface. This man had attacked him twice, humiliated him twice and frustrated his attempts to make Charis Waverley his mistress. Charis had not been willing, true, but that would have made her surrender all the sweeter. He had no time for enthusiastic lovers. He could buy any amount of willing women in the various bawdy houses he frequented but someone like Charis, a well-born girl, brought low through circumstances, someone who would have once expected to marry an officer like himself, her shame in becoming his mistress would have pleased him enormously.

Except for this man in front of him now. He felt his anger starting to rise and bent his head close to Connor's ear once more.

"Confess…" he repeated.

Connor glared at him. "I am an officer in His Majesty's Navy," he repeated through gritted teeth. "Bring someone to identify me and release me at once!"

The gaoler was wracked with uncertainty, but he did not dare remonstrate with the Major. Better men than he had felt the wrath of the unstable humours of Major Quinn.

Quinn smiled at his prisoner. "You are a liar and a thief," he said coldly. "I do not believe your claims that you are any kind of a Gentleman." He stepped back. "No Gentleman would have truck with such scum as the smugglers you associate with." His mercurial mood had changed. "Now confess to your crimes, tell me the name of your accomplices, the good people of Yorkshire who are helping hide your contraband, and I will go easy with you."

Connor's eyes did not waver as he stared Quinn full in the face. "I have nothing to say to you. Except you, sir, are making a huge mistake."

"And you, sir, will confess or hang," Quinn snarled back at him.

He bent and took up a whip from where it had lain on the icy flags of the cell floor. Stepping back, he drew back his right arm and brought the whip across Connor's back, leaving a thick red welt where the leather struck his skin.

Connor flinched with the pain of the flogging, but he bit his lip and did not cry out. Frustrated, Quinn struck him again, putting all his strength behind the blow. He wanted to hear his prisoner scream in pain and beg for mercy, but Connor would not give him the satisfaction.

Again and again, the whip found its target. Connor's head fell forward against the stone wall as his body jerked from the blows. The skin on his back split open, and the blood ran down his body, mingling with the sweat that broke out from the force of the flogging.

Quinn breathed heavily, and raised his arm once again to bring the heavy leather strap down onto his helpless prisoner.

"Sir!" The gaoler could stay silent no longer. "Sir, the man is unconscious – he has fainted!"

Quinn reached up and pulled Connor's head back. Connor's eyes were closed, his breathing laboured.

Cursing, Quinn pushed Connor's head away in disgust. He could get no information from an unconscious man.

"Release him. If he will not confess then tomorrow morning he will hang."

The gaoler hurried to unfasten the metal cuffs around Connor's wrists. "But... sir, he hasn't been tried or convicted..."

Quinn's eyes blazed with fury. "I do not need to have this man tried. He is a smuggler, he assaulted me and has been captured whilst in the company of a known criminal, Luke Vincent. His guilt is without doubt!"

He watched as the gaoler lifted the unconscious man down from the wall and placed him on the rough straw pallet in the corner.

"My word is law in this castle!" Quinn continued. "I will order the scaffold to be prepared and inform the Colonel that an execution of a captured smuggler is to take place. I want this man bound and gagged and brought to the scaffold tomorrow at noon!"

Flinging the whip away in disgust, he turned and stormed out of the cell.

Connor groaned and opened his eyes. "Thank you," he whispered to the gaoler.

The man fetched water from the jug on the table and raised Connor's head to help him drink. "He's mad. He would have flogged you to death if the pleasure of watching you hang hadn't been greater."

"Can you get word to the Revenue of where I am?" Connor asked, struggling to sit up, wincing as a stabbing pain went through his back.

The gaoler brought a rough blanket and gave it to the prisoner to wrap around his freezing torso.

"I'll try, sir," he said. "I am no traitor to my commanding officer but what he's proposing is murder. Even if you are a smuggler, you deserve a trial with judge and jury – not this lynching he is ordering."

Connor took another long drink of the water before handing the jug back. "Thank you for this," he said.

"You just lie down, sir, and try to sleep," the gaoler replied. "If he thinks you are unconscious he will leave you alone. He knows he can't get a confession out of you, so he just wants you dead now."

Connor nodded and leaned gently against the cold wall of the cell, shivering as the wounds on his back touched the solid surface. He could feel the blanket sticking to his skin already, but he refused to think of the pain he had endured. It had been worth it to see Charis rescued and taken away from the sadistic Jonathan Quinn. He watched as the gaoler gathered up the whip and other implements.

"I'll do my best to contact the Revenue authorities, sir," he said, leaving the cell.

Connor watched him leave and leaned his head back. As usual his mind filled with the memory of his brief time with Charis, and he wondered how he could feel this deeply so quickly. He knew he was not the womaniser Luke Vincent has said of him, he knew he had no sweetheart or wife or children waiting for his return. He was part of an aristocratic family, and his parents and brother would even now be mourning his loss at sea. He smiled to himself as the pleasant daydream of introducing Miss Waverley to them as his intended wife filled his mind. They would overlook the fact she was a penniless companion if she made him happy. She was well mannered enough to please his mama, well-bred enough to please his father and beautiful enough to make him the envy of his brother. He was not the heir to his father's estates, his elder brother had that honour. He had followed his father into the Navy, and, until the unfortunate incident last September, had been thoroughly enjoying his chosen career. He frowned now as he thought of the pain his supposed death would have imposed on his family, especially his beloved mother.

Shivering again, he tightened the thin blanket around his naked chest and groaned softly as it rubbed against the open wound on his back. Biting his lip to prevent any further sound escaping, he closed his eyes and thought once more of Charis, refusing to acknowledge that Quinn would do anything to avoid his eventual reunion with the woman he loved.

CHAPTER TWENTY-TWO

"Why Captain Howard, you are such a frequent visitor these days, I should have a chamber prepared for you." Mrs Embleton's words were quietly spoken, but the irony behind them was not lost on the Captain.

He bowed over her hand and raised it to his lips.

"It is, as usual, a pleasure to see you, Alice," he replied.

His visits to the widow had, indeed, been frequent these last few weeks but he had never known such circumstances before. The storm back in September unsettled more than the status quo he and his companions had been used to.

He had to admit however that she was a handsome woman and he could remember her as a beautiful bride the day she married his friend Gabriel Embleton. Jealousy had gone through him thirty years ago when she chose Gabriel over him, and his admiration for her had never wavered in all these years. They had always remained close, and when Gabriel died, she had reluctantly carried on helping his friend. Reluctant because of the risks involved but Captain Howard was discreet and circumspect, and had never in all the years placed her in any danger of discovery. The funds she earned for helping him enabled her to carry on living in her home, and she always felt comfortable in the knowledge that Captain Howard and his friends were looking out for her.

She led him up to her drawing room and poured him some brandy before seating herself down opposite him.

"What news of young Connor?" she asked. Anxiety sounded in the sharpness of her voice.

Howard shook his head. The rumours were grave coming out

of Scarborough Fort. He had spies everywhere, and they had wasted no time in updating him of the latest developments.

"Quinn has gone too far this time," he said. "He is taking matters into his own hands and has ordered the scaffold to be readied for tomorrow at noon."

Mrs Embleton was appalled. "What about the Colonel? Surely he has authority over the Major?"

"The Colonel has let Quinn more or less take over since his arrival in Scarborough. He has the connections and the family name behind him and, of course, the Colonel is an old man. He is looking for an easy journey to retirement, and he is allowing Quinn more power than is good for him."

She shook her head in dismay. "What on earth is a man like Quinn doing in such a backwater at Scarborough?"

Howard swallowed his brandy and settled back in the armchair, his eyes dark, his features stern.

"His family needed somewhere to send him," was the terse response. "He disgraced himself in battle, and the Duke was all set to have him court-martialled."

Mrs Embleton raised her eyebrows, waiting for more information.

"He led his men into battle at Waterloo and abandoned them. His entire troop was killed. He was found by one of his brother officers in hiding and would have been shot as a deserter had his father not intervened with the King. The man is a braggart and a coward and is not welcomed anywhere in Society. His father arranged to have him sent here until the scandal died down. He is not well liked, his men despise him, and he has a reputation for being an ill-tempered bully who enjoys inflicting pain on anyone weaker than himself."

Mrs Embleton recalled the torn dress and marks on Charis's skin the night of the Whitby Assembly. The Major had tried to force himself on her that night, and it had taken intervention by Connor to prevent her companion from being attacked. She knew from Josiah that he had beaten Charis while she was his prisoner and she prayed that the girl had not suffered anything worse.

"Poor Connor," she whispered.

"I have some good news though, Ma'am," Howard went on. "I have been to see James Wentworth. He has given me this." He drew a rolled up scroll of parchment from his pocket and handed it to her.

Addressed to the Colonel at the Fort, it was unsealed, and Mrs Embleton unrolled it.

It was an official order to release the man known as Connor McQueen until such time as he could stand trial for the crime of smuggling.

"It will stop him from being hanged," Howard went on. "The Colonel will not dare disobey Lord Wentworth. Quinn would like to, but even he must obey the Chief Magistrate of the North."

Mrs Embleton stood and rang the bell for her servant.

"We must leave tonight, Abraham," she said resolutely. "Scarborough Fort is twenty miles away, and the weather is closing in. If we go now, we should get there before noon tomorrow."

"We?" he queried as Martha entered the drawing room.

"Yes, we. Charis would never forgive me if I failed to do everything in my power to prevent this heinous crime. Connor may be a smuggler, but he deserves a fair trial, not this – this – travesty!" She turned to Martha. "Martha, please prepare some warm soup and hot bricks to be put into Captain Howard's carriage. I will be accompanying him to Scarborough."

If Martha looked surprised, they were all three even more surprised when a loud knock on the front door disturbed them all.

Leaving the drawing room, they saw Josiah open the heavy oaken door and admit two gentlemen, one of whom was well known to Mrs Embleton.

"Frederick!" she exclaimed. "What on earth are you doing here?"

Frederick removed his hat and looked up to her. "Hello cousin!" he exclaimed. "We have come to the rescue!"

•

Heavy overnight snow made the roads leading to Scarborough almost impassable. Heavy wagons and carriages laboured slowly through the snowdrifts towards the town, the drivers pausing regularly to dig stuck wheels out of ditches.

In her carriage, despite the fur rugs, Henrietta shivered and put her feet on the hot bricks thoughtfully provided by the landlord of the small inn they had been forced to seek shelter in the previous night. They realised, an hour after leaving the shelter of Mrs Embleton's home, that their journey to Scarborough would not be as easy as they first envisaged. Snow started to fall once again, and they were unable to carry on any further. They took rooms in the first inn they had come to and despite Richard's distaste at the small chamber and mean furnishings, Henrietta had been nothing but grateful for the warm fires and cosy bedroom she had been shown into. The inn had been small but busy, and as they had only two rooms, Richard and George had been forced to share, and she had felt relief that she was able to pass the night undisturbed. Exhausted from all the travelling, the last thing she needed was to engage in any amorous activities with either of her lovers.

"How much longer?" she asked Richard as he returned to sit next to her after investigating the state of the road.

"There's a clear stretch up ahead, but a wheel has come off a wagon and the driver's gone to help get it back on the road. We should be moving soon and then Scarborough is just another couple of hours away."

His face was etched with tiredness and he, too, felt the ill effects of endless days of travelling.

"Thank the Lord!" Henrietta declared. Putting her gloved hands inside the fur wrap, she shivered again.

"Are you feeling unwell, Henrietta?" George asked from his corner of the carriage.

"I am merely cold and tired of this interminable journey," she responded, a faint smile lifting the corners of her mouth.

Richard settled himself next to her and pulled some of the fur rug over his knees. "Don't fret my dear," he reassured her.

"Another few hours and the girl will be back where she belongs. Or ..." He paused, frowning. "The driver tells me rumours abound on the road that there is to be a hanging at the fort today." He smiled, but the smile did not touch his eyes, a cold, calculated smile, which sent a shiver down Henrietta's spine that had nothing to do with the plummeting temperature outside.

"You don't think it could possibly be Charis?" Henrietta was genuinely shocked.

"They don't know – it is just a smuggler apparently." Richard shrugged. "It is not known whether the ne'er do well is male or female so we will not know until we reach our destination."

Henrietta stared at him – she could hardly believe the news. A gamut of emotions played through her mind, shock at the thought the thorn in her side would be removed permanently and dismay that a well-born lady of Charis's stature should end her life in such an ignominious manner.

"Well, it will be a shame if it is my betrothed wife," George complained. "I was looking forward to my wedding night with the little prude."

His disgruntled face set the tone of the rest of the morning, and when they started at last on the last leg of their journey, none of them spoke, each wrapped up in their own thoughts.

•

In another carriage on the same road, the four occupants were discussing the very same young lady. Armed with the order from Lord Wentworth to release Connor, Sir Frederick and Mr Kielder had decided to accompany Captain Howard and Mrs Embleton to Scarborough Fort. Wherever Charis was, she would not be far from Connor, and they needed to find her before Lady Henrietta and her companions caught up with her.

Mr Kielder was explaining to Mrs Embleton the new evidence, which had come to light regarding the late Sir Anthony's wife.

"We can refute the legality of the new Will Sir Anthony signed. We can now prove he was coerced into making a new Will during the absence of his daughter when she visited Sir Frederick here."

Mrs Embleton was intrigued. "How was he coerced?"

"He discovered Henrietta Hunter had been taken out of a brothel and introduced to him by Richard Hardy as a well to do lady, a little down on her luck. When he found out the truth, he was horrified and had decided to divorce her when he became unexpectedly ill. We understand and believe he was being poisoned. Whether Henrietta or Richard were responsible is a little vague – we do know however that Lady Hardy suffered and died from a similar unexplained illness some two years ago. Richard Hardy is a gambler and his debts are large enough to make him desperate enough to try anything to get his hands on the Waverley money." Mr Kielder lay back upon the quilted squabs of the carriage. "We have been able to ascertain that certain items had been procured and administered to Sir Anthony without the knowledge or permission of his doctors."

Captain Howard was as fascinated by the story as Mrs Embleton. "Ascertain how?"

"Lady Henrietta's servants were happy to talk once certain inducements were put before them," the enigmatic Mr Kielder disclosed. "However, we also found out that Mr Blackridge visited Sir Anthony late one night and he signed a new copy of his Will under duress. There are witnesses who will swear to it."

"What kind of duress did my cousin suffer?" Alice asked faintly.

Frederick and Mr Kielder exchanged a look as if wondering how much they dare tell a lady of Mrs Embleton's delicate ears.

"He was told Charis had been taken to the brothel Henrietta had worked in. He was also told she would be killed if he refused to sign. When he refused to believe them, he was taken to the brothel and allowed to look into a room where a young lady dressed in Charis's clothes lay bound and gagged. He was ill, with the poison making him delirious, but he believed the girl was his daughter and he gave in to their demands. He signed the

Will and the following day Charis returned from her holiday with Frederick knowing nothing about the incident."

Captain Howard was fascinated. "And he never asked Charis about the so-called 'kidnapping'?"

"He did not. By the time she returned home, he was so ill he did not have chance to discuss it with her. She nursed him to the end, but he was never able to send for me and reinstate his original Will."

Captain Howard shook his head in disbelief at the story. "How did you find all this out?" he asked.

Sir Frederick smiled at his companions. "Mr Kielder has contacts in some very dubious circles," he said with a slight chuckle in his voice. "I have been finding out things about our esteemed Solicitor here which would bring a blush to your cheeks, dear cousin."

Mrs Embleton did not doubt it. Mr Kielder, mild-mannered, softly spoken and slightly portly, seemed for all the world to be perfectly innocuous and harmless. However, she saw the glint in his eyes as he spoke of Richard Hardy and Henrietta. She heard the hardness creep into his voice as he told the tale of her cousin's illness and she felt the anger in him as he described Anthony's death at the hand of his wife's lover. No... appearances could be deceptive, and there was a lot more to Mr Kielder than the face he presented to the world.

Something she, too, knew all about.

•

The stately old ship sailed gracefully into a bay off the coast south of Scarborough. The occupants of the small rowboat lowered over the side held on tightly as they reached the heaving waves crashing against the hull. Charis was thrown to the edge of the boat and was pulled back into her seat by Luke Vincent. Two of his men were rowing them to shore, and Luke held the tiller as they battled through the high seas and the bitterly cold wind.

Snow was in the air, and Charis was glad of the heavy hooded cloak Luke presented to her. She did not ask where it came from but it was an embroidered brown velvet, the hood trimmed with a thick border of fur. The swelling on her mouth and the bruising on her cheek had reduced, and she was left with a faint mark around her eye from the beating she had endured at the hands of Major Quinn. Her cheeks, however, were rosy, and her eyes sparkled with the joy at the thought of finally reuniting with the man she loved.

The two seamen rowed vigorously through the waves, and despite the wind blowing against them, the small boat pulled up high onto the beach to allow Charis to step onto the dry sand. Luke paused to speak to his men and waited until they set off back to the ship before turning and together with his companion started up the shallow paths leading to the road.

Scarborough was a mile south of where they landed and holding onto his arm for support against the icy roads and bitter winds, Charis set off with Luke at a smart pace, eager to get back to the fort. She expected to find Connor waiting for her either in Scarborough itself, reunited with his Revenue forces or back at Mrs Embleton's. A doubt crossed her mind briefly that he would already be gone, back to his command, back to his men and away to sea on a new ship but she closed her thoughts to that possibility. After all they had gone through, surely he would wait to see her before leaving.

She knew she and Luke had to be discreet, to be careful. As far as Quinn was concerned the two of them were escaped criminals, and she would not feel safe until she saw her Uncle, come to ensure her safe passage home.

The snow fell quickly, covering their tracks as they walked towards the town. Despite the bleakness of the December day, there were lots of people about, all going in and out of Scarborough. They reached the town in half an hour after landing on the beach. The weather was in their favour as they walked through the narrow streets of the harbour towards the road that led up to the castle. No one lingered outside in the cold weather, and even soldiers on their regular patrols were hurrying to their destinations, pausing occasionally beside the warmth of braziers roasting chestnuts to thaw out before carrying on. No one spared them more than a cursory glance, the tall man in a three-cornered hat pulled low down over his eyes and a cloaked lady, arm in arm heads down against the wind and snow.

They walked steadily onward, not stopping to warm themselves, passing the shops and fishermen and soldiers and only pausing once to look around them before starting up the hill towards the castle.

Other people were on the road, and with some alarm, they realised there was an air of excitement pervading the atmosphere. A smuggler was being hanged, and with a sideways glance at the suddenly pale face of his companion as they overheard the animated conversations, Luke hurried her onward, not pausing to ask any questions.

They entered the courtyard along with the rest of the crowds and pushing through, Luke led her through the gates to the inner yard where they could see the scaffold had been prepared.

Carriages were being unloaded at the main gates, and the occupants were following the rest of the crowds into the castle keep.

A troop of soldiers surrounded the scaffold and faced the growing throng. They had muskets readied to prevent any interference and Luke noted with alarm a group of men dressed in the unmistakable uniform of the Revenue.

"What's going on, Luke?" Charis was suddenly gripped with a fear she could not put a name to. Terror coursed through her.

"I don't know," he replied, his voice low and urgent. "But something is wrong…"

The day darkened, the sky heavy with snow and it fell relentlessly upon them, covering their clothes in its icy embrace.

It was almost noon as the black masked hangman mounted the platform and adjusted the noose. The crowd surged forward, the air of suppressed excitement almost palpable.

A priest was next to climb the scaffold steps, carrying a bible, his head bowed in prayer.

As the drumroll started, Charis's eyes widened in horror. A single prisoner escorted between two armed soldiers was being led towards the scaffold.

The man had a hood over his head, disguising his face, and his arms were tightly bound behind his back. A simple white cambric shirt hung loosely over blood-stained breeches.

His height and stature were enough for Charis and Luke to recognise Connor, and they watched helplessly as he was marched towards the platform leading up to the scaffold standing bleak and stark black against the white, swirling snow.

CHAPTER TWENTY-THREE

Charis and Luke stared at each other in shock. Thinking quickly, Luke nodded his head in the direction of the Revenue men. "They will know him!" he said in an urgent whisper. "Get to them while I distract the soldiers."

"No, Luke!" She caught his arm. "Don't give yourself away – I can do it alone."

She moved away from him and pushed through to the front of the crowd. Major Quinn stepped onto the platform behind Connor. Charis, taking a deep breath, shouted over the hum of voices.

"Murderer!" Her voice carried across the courtyard as she pointed to the Major. "This man is innocent!" She turned to face the small gathering of Revenue officers. "That is your Captain – Oliver Steele!" she cried out as she walked towards them. "The Major covers his face so you will not recognise him!"

The crowd were silenced by her outburst, and Major Quinn stepped to the edge of the scaffold. "Arrest her!" he shouted down. "And get on with the hanging!"

The group of Revenue men stared from her to the hooded man. One of the group called out to the Major. "Uncover his face, sir!" he shouted. "Captain Steele went down with his ship months ago, but if he survived, we demand to see this man."

A murmur of assent grew in the crowd, and Luke looked on silently, smiling at Charis's interference. She was a brave woman, but as he saw two of the guard start towards her, he forced his way through the crowd to get to her.

Before he had chance to reach her side, he watched in horror as two very well dressed gentlemen lunged at her and pulled her away. She screamed and fought to release herself while at the same time shouting out to the men around the scaffold, "Release him, he is innocent!"

Pandemonium broke out. The Revenue officer ran towards the scaffold, held back by the troop of guards around the base. Major Quinn was shouting to the hangman to do his duty, the priest remonstrating with the Major, demanding the hood be taken from the prisoner's face.

Luke started after Charis, who was being dragged, screaming and protesting, out of the courtyard. To his relief he saw Captain Howard descend from a carriage, accompanied by Mrs Embleton and two gentlemen totally unknown to him.

He ran to them. "Charis has managed to stop the hanging, Abraham," he said urgently. "But get in there quickly and stop Quinn from killing the boy. Charis has been taken…" He pointed over to the gentlemen bundling her into a carriage outside the castle grounds.

"Richard Hardy!" Mrs Embleton exclaimed. "Stop him, Captain Vincent. They mean Charis harm."

He nodded, not understanding why anyone would want to harm the girl, but she had been taken unwillingly and he could not stand by doing nothing.

One of the older gentlemen stopped him with a hand on his arm. "She is my niece and is very precious to me – bring her back safely."

Vincent grinned at him, remembering the missive Charis had insisted be sent. "I am at your service, my lord!" His eyes were already sparkling with the adventure of the chase but time was against him. He nodded at them and ran towards the gate leading out of the castle.

He could see the carriage had already pulled away and, cursing that he had no horse to chase after them, he set off at a run, following the coach as it careered down the hill, the driver taking little care in his eagerness to get away with their prize. The body of the coach swung from side to side as it racketed downwards and Luke, slipping on the icy cobbles, ignored the danger of falling and ran after them. The town would still be busy, and he knew they would not get far through the narrow streets surrounding the harbour.

On he ran, banking on the coach slowing long enough for him to catch up. He had no idea who these people were or what danger Charis could be in but judging from the way she struggled with them, her screams of protest cut short by a hand across her mouth, he could only surmise she was in very real and immediate danger.

He caught up with the carriage as it turned a corner leading out of the harbour. Slowing down to avoid crashing into a group of passers-by, the coach driver hesitated just long enough to allow Luke to reach it. Keeping his head down, he caught the straps that held the luggage at the rear of the vehicle. He jumped up and held on tightly as the carriage rounded the corner and picked up speed again. He had no time to think where they were going, he just knew he had to stay with them and get Charis away from whoever these people were who meant her harm. Hooking his legs around the trunks to give himself a firmer foothold, he kept his head down and tried to listen to the argument taking place inside the carriage. Grinning, he found himself wondering what it was about this girl that attracted such trouble.

Hoping that Connor had avoided the lynching by the enraged Major Quinn, he put him out of his mind and concentrated on not falling off.

Raised voices were coming from inside, Charis vehemently ordering them to stop and release her, a man remonstrating with her, and another man telling her to be silent. He heard the low tone of another woman in the carriage, and he strained, listening to what she was saying, but her voice was too soft to hear anything clearly. The icy cold penetrated his hands, and he was grateful for the thickness of the gloves he had donned earlier that day. He hoped the carriage would not go too far as he had no idea by this stage how far he was away from the castle and Scarborough.

To his relief, twenty minutes later the carriage turned into the bustling livery yard of The Sun Inn. It was apparently some kind of staging post as the ostlers hurried out to catch the heads of the steaming horses and led them into the yard.

Luke dropped down from his perch at the rear and moved quickly to hide behind a neighbouring coach. He watched as Charis was taken out of the carriage and, being held firmly by one of the men, was escorted into the inn. She was followed by another man and a lady in a dark blue brocaded cloak, the hood up and her face protected by a veiled bonnet against the vagaries of the wind and weather.

An idea came to him, and he followed the carriage into the stables where the grooms were busy changing horses. Summoning one of the grooms, he spoke to him in an urgent whisper.

"I need to delay the people in this carriage," he said quietly. "There is a guinea for you if you can see to it that they do not leave yet."

The groom looked about him to see if they had been overheard. Pocketing the golden guinea, he grinned back at Luke. "Leave it to me, sir. Is two hours a long enough delay?"

They had travelled for roughly an hour from Scarborough. He calculated that if Captain Howard had anything to do with it, Connor would be released by now and would even now be following them. He needed to keep the party from leaving for at least two hours to enable Connor and the others to catch up with him.

Or, he thought grimly to himself, if they could not get to him, he would need to do something to get the young lady out of their clutches before any further harm befell her.

Nodding his thanks to the groom, he made his way across to the inn. The party he'd followed had been shown into a private room, and he was unable to get any closer to them. He welcomed the warmth after the snow and ice outside, and he bought a tankard of ale before settling himself in a quiet corner of the taproom. He ascertained there was no other way in or out of the private parlour and he waited, watching the door for any signs of movement, wondering what their plans for Charis would involve exactly and why she was so important to them. His brows furrowed in concentration as he pondered the mystery of the lovely Miss Waverley.

•

At the sound of Charis's voice shouting out his name and accusing Major Quinn of being a murderer, Connor took his chance. His guards had loosened their hold on him once they had escorted him to stand before the noose and as he heard the calls coming for his face to be revealed, he stepped back away from them. His movements were careful, he could only see faint light coming through the sack-like hood, and he knew the steps were behind him but other than that he was disorientated. The guards were distracted by the uproar coming from the enraged crowd and wasting no time, he turned and ran towards the steps. The guards tried to rally and stop him but as one of them approached them he bent down and butted the man in the stomach. He reached the steps and, having counted seven climbing up, he stood on the first one and jumped the rest of the way, hitting the ground and rolling on the hard-packed ice, the fall forcing the air out of his body.

One of the Revenue men ran to his aid and with a loud curse ripped the hood from his face.

"Captain Steele, sir!" It was Tom Evans, his second in command and companion from the Princess Charlotte.

In moments he was pulled to his feet and the cords tightly binding his hands and arms behind his back were cut free. Searching the crowd for Charis's face, he was in time to see her being dragged away by two unknown men and, further back he saw Luke Vincent start after her. Satisfied for a moment, he grasped Tom's hands.

"Sir, we thought you dead!" Tom exclaimed, his delight at his Captain's reappearance evident in the smile on his face. In moments the two men were surrounded by the other Revenue officers, all exclaiming over his appearance, others turning on the Major, standing on the scaffold, his face scarlet with rage.

"What happened to you, sir?"

Connor turned to see Jim, another one of his men beside him with others from the Charlotte.

"It's a long story, Jim," he replied, grasping the man's hand and turning to return the handshakes and welcome from his men.

The commotion had attracted the attention of the senior Colonel from the Castle, and as he marched into the courtyard accompanied by a retinue of his men, Captain Howard approached the scaffold carrying a scroll signed by the Lord High Lieutenant of Yorkshire to demand the immediate release of Connor McQueen.

"Major Quinn!" The Colonel was angrier than Quinn had ever seen him. Used to having his own way and having the Colonel leave him to his own devices, this sudden interruption was as unexpected as it was unwelcome. "What is the meaning of this?" He read the scroll presented to him and glared up at his second in command.

"We have evidence to believe this man is a smuggler, sir!" Quinn replied.

"You do not hang a man without trial in my command, sir!" the Colonel continued, his voice sharp with undisguised loathing. "Captain Howard, my apologies, this should never have happened. I understand, however, that this man is not in fact, Connor McQueen?"

"I am not, Colonel," Connor replied directly. "My name is Captain Oliver Connor Steele of His Majesty's Navy. It is a long story and one I will be honoured to explain to you, but I have a pressing matter to attend to first. Jim, I need a coat!"

Jim laughed and divested himself of the heavy navy coat he wore. "A pleasure, sir!" he responded.

"And a horse?" Connor continued, fastening the greatcoat over his blood-stained garments.

The Colonel turned to his guard. "Fetch this man a horse immediately," he ordered. The Colonel looked at the bruising on Connor's face, the tell-tale wincing as he pulled on the coat, the blood on the man's breeches and boots. His eyes narrowed at the obvious ill-treatment the man had received. "And when your business is concluded, young man, I will be waiting to hear a full explanation of what has been happening in my castle." The Colonel addressed his next command to his men. "Take Major Quinn to his quarters immediately. Post a guard outside," he said coldly. "And Captain Howard, if you and your companions would care to accompany me, I would be delighted to offer you refreshments."

Captain Howard, Mrs Embleton and the two gentlemen who accompanied them accepted his invitation as Connor embraced Mrs Embleton briefly. "Charis?" he asked.

"Richard Hardy and her stepmother Henrietta have taken her," she said shortly. "She is in grave danger, and Luke is following them. He will probably need your help."

He nodded and, following the Colonel's guard, went to the stables to be presented with a high spirited attractive black stallion.

"A fine horse!" he remarked as he swung himself up into the saddle.

"Major Quinn's animal," the soldier grinned up at him.

With an answering grin, Connor swept his unruly curly hair back from his forehead, wheeled the horse around and rode out of the castle. As there was only one road leading down into the town, he galloped as quickly as possible down the hill. Through the harbour he reached the crossroads at the edge of the town. Pausing, cursing, he looked around and saw in the distance a carriage with the unmistakable figure of Luke Vincent clinging to the straps holding on the luggage. The light of adventure was in his eyes, and he reflected as he kicked the willing horse ever faster in pursuit, that he would miss the Captain when the time came for them to finally go their separate ways.

●

The taproom was crowded but the Captain, in the settle beside the fire, had the best vantage point in the room. He could see both the front door and the door leading to the private parlour where Charis had been taken. He removed his hat and coat and settled himself down, resting and thawing out after the rigours of his journey clinging to the back of the carriage. He drank a long draught of the cool ale, letting the liquid refresh his parched throat. He declined the food offered by the landlord. He was hungry, but he did not dare to partake in the heavy foodstuffs coming out of the kitchen. His stomach growled, but he ignored it. If he were to become involved in any kind of altercation he wanted a clear head and his reflexes as sharp as possible.

The room was too noisy to be able to hear anything from within the parlour. The Captain bided his time. He knew one of the men would be out as soon as the landlord informed them of the problems with their carriage. He would use that time to attempt a rescue. One man and a cloaked woman would not be too onerous to overpower. He smiled to himself as he considered Miss Waverley. He knew that if it came down to it, she would prove herself a useful ally in any kind of fight. Her angry struggles and the raised voices he'd overheard in the carriage testament to that.

He looked up as the taproom door opened and he smiled broadly as the tall, imposing figure of Connor stood in the doorway, looking around the crowded room. His eyes lit upon the Captain, and he made his way over to him, an answering smile on his face. Luke stood, and the two men grasped hands in a firm handshake.

"You escaped the gallows then, pup?" Luke demanded.

"As you can see, Captain," Connor replied, his eyes twinkling. "Is Charis safe?"

Luke sobered at once. "She was taken into that parlour about twenty minutes ago. I have heard nothing yet, but I have been waiting for one of them to leave before I storm the room."

Connor nodded. "I am ready when you are, Captain."

Luke took in the paleness of Connor's face. He had been badly beaten when in gaol and his mistreatment at the hands of Jonathan Quinn would not be so quickly recovered from. Connor had ridden hard to catch up with him so soon, and he indicated the seat opposite the settle.

"Sit, boy," he said. "Get a drink and rest for a moment. They will not dare to harm her here. She is safe enough."

His shrewd eyes did not miss the pain creasing Connor's face momentarily as he divested himself of the heavy great coat. The white linen stuck to the younger man's back, and Luke could see the faint strips of blood staining the shirt. His eyes narrowed in anger at the thought of the sadistic Major. If he could do this to an innocent man such as Connor, he wondered what sort of fate would have befallen Charis Waverley. The girls at the bawdy house in Whitby had suffered at his hands, and they were experienced worldly women. Someone like Charis, a well-born lady, not used to the darker side of life, would have been no match for a man with his dubious reputation and evil streak.

A frown creased his forehead as he raised his hand for the landlord to bring Connor a drink. He wondered what secret Charis was hiding if she was so valuable to the people in that parlour. He strongly suspected she was not quite what she seemed. Well-born certainly. Down on her luck? Somehow he did not think so.

Connor accepted his drink gratefully, but his eyes did not leave the parlour door. Luke knew the younger man was poised, ready to go crashing in there, but he held his nerve and drank down the ale, easing his dry throat and preparing himself mentally and physically for whatever would come next.

"You really care for the girl, do you not?" Luke asked as the two men sat together, awaiting their opportunity.

Connor turned his head towards Luke, his eyes leaving the parlour door for a moment. He seemed surprised Luke had asked the question.

"I care very deeply for her," he responded. "When my memory had gone, and my brain addled I could say nothing to her in case I had a wife or sweetheart awaiting my return." He paused, took another swallow of his drink and raised eyes brimming with mischief to Luke's. "And when we met, you told me I had a girl in every port."

Luke did not look abashed. He grinned in response. "A cruel

jest, Connor," he admitted. "For which I apologise – and I have already made my apologies to Miss Waverley."

"What did she say?"

"I think it safe to say she feels the same way about you, Connor."

A smile curled up the corners of Connor's mouth. "The way she spoke up at the scaffold," he said. "I knew then. I just want to find her and keep her safe." He sighed.

"She certainly has a knack for getting into trouble," Luke said. "There is more to that young lady than meets the eye."

He chuckled softly, and Connor smiled in response.

"Do you think she will have me?" Connor asked him.

"Do you want a poor relation? A penniless companion forced to make her way in the world by living with an elderly aunt?"

Connor looked shocked at the very suggestion. "She may be in straitened circumstances now, Captain, but she is and always will be a lady. I wish to marry for love. I do not have need or ambition to marry well, and if she will have me, I have enough for both of us."

Captain Vincent hid a smile behind the tankard he rose to his lips again.

"You are very well born yourself, young Connor," he remarked. "Or do you prefer Oliver?"

"My mother always preferred Connor. It will do well enough," came the reply.

"Will your family accept a penniless, unknown girl?"

"They wish me happy, and I think Charis will make me very happy." His eyes went back to the parlour door, the urge to go in so strong Luke felt compelled to lay a restraining hand on his arm.

"Wait…." he counselled.

"But they might be doing anything to her in there!" Connor's voice betrayed the anguish he felt.

Luke's amusement showed in his face. "If Miss Waverley were in any danger, I assure you we would be hearing it by now," he said.

They watched as the landlord and one of his serving girls walked over to the parlour, carrying a large tray of food. They saw them go into the room and a few minutes later leave. The landlord had a scowl on his face, apparently disgruntled by what had occurred in that room.

Some five minutes passed when the door opened again, and a man emerged. He was young and good-looking, bare-headed and very well dressed. He glared around the taproom, his displeasure evident as he stalked through, going out into the snowy yard towards the stables. Connor's buoyant mood evaporated as he watched the man leave.

"Do you know who he is?" he asked Luke in an undertone.

Luke shook his head. "The landlord has no idea. They just stopped to change horses and rest for half an hour. The wheel of their carriage has met with a mishap so unfortunately they have been delayed for longer than they wished."

A slow smile crossed Connor's face. The Captain was nothing if not resourceful.

Leaving his seat, he went to the taproom door and watched as the man walked over the courtyard and went into the stables. He came outside, and Connor watched as he and one of the grooms appeared to be having an argument. He turned on his heel and returned to the inn, his face reflecting his displeasure. He reached the doorway of the inn and stared at Connor, the arrogance in his bearing evident as he pushed his way past. Connor let him go, staring after his figure as he went back to the parlour.

Connor had felt the anger, and it caused in him an answering anxiety. Instinct told him that if Charis were to cross this man while he was in this mood, she would be facing even more danger.

He returned to the table and, picking up his tankard, drained the rest of his drink.

Luke raised his eyebrows.

"Time, Captain," Connor said.

CHAPTER TWENTY-FOUR

The occupants of the private parlour were continuing the argument that had started as Charis had found herself unwillingly dragged onto the Waverley family travelling coach.

"I will not marry you, George!" she protested vehemently. "You cannot force me, and you will certainly never make me return with you to London!"

"Don't be ridiculous, Charis!" Henrietta exclaimed. "You must return to London and take your rightful place in Society!"

"George loves you dearly." Richard tried to be patient and attempted to soothe the enraged girl. "You can have the Banns called and be married at Christmas."

"We can have the Society wedding of the year, my darling." George tried to persuade her. She stood beside the parlour window, looking out at the gardens beyond. He stood with her and took her hand in his, ignoring her icy glare.

"No," she replied, snatching her hand away. "I want to return to Mrs Embleton's home and remain there until I can receive my inheritance." She turned her eyes to Richard and Henrietta. "I never want to live with either of you again," she continued, her voice cold and even.

George and his father exchanged a glance, heavy with menace.

"If you refuse to return to London with me," George smiled at her, "we will continue our journey northward, and we will be married at Gretna."

Charis refused to be intimidated. "You will still need a willing bride, George. Even at Gretna no one can be married against their will."

George took another step closer to her. He reached out and

grasped her by the shoulders. Pulling her towards him, he held her struggling body tightly. "You will marry me," he hissed. "You will be willing enough by the time we reach Scotland."

To his amazement, she stopped struggling and laughed in his face. Her eyes crinkled with merriment.

Puzzled, he released her and pushed her away from him. She stumbled backwards and fell down on the padded window seat.

"What is so funny, my dear?" Henrietta glanced at the two men.

"I have fought off the advances of a man far more threatening than you, George." She laughed. "I think I could actually kill you if you tried to rape me." Charis stopped laughing and glared at the three of them. "I have been threatened, beaten, thrown into prison and kidnapped." Her voice was steady, her face cold and a new hardness had crept into her eyes. "I have sailed with smugglers and am proud to call them my friends. In fact," she smiled at them, standing up and moving towards the table where Henrietta sat, "I am very sure that even now they will be searching for me."

If Richard felt any unease at her words, he hid it well enough. As suave as ever, he sat beside Henrietta and smiled at the girl. "I am sure everyone will be most anxious over your whereabouts, my dear," he said smoothly. "However, with all the chaos we left behind at the Castle, I doubt if anyone will have had the presence of mind to organise a search party just yet."

Charis tried not to let the dismay she felt show in her expression. She removed her cloak and seated herself opposite Henrietta and Richard.

"In that case, I trust you have no objection to providing me with refreshments while we await our change of horses." Her voice was still cool, and she fought to keep calm in the face of the truth of Richard's words.

Frantically trying to think, she knew she had to remain calm, she could not afford to antagonise any of them. They were quite capable of tying her up or rendering her unconscious should she try to fight them. She knew she could not win against them all and even though she'd felt no fear when George had held her, she knew that alone in a bedroom with him she would only be able to fight him off for so long. As she stared at him, at the signs of dissipation already starting to appear around his eyes, she knew he could not possibly be as much of a threat as Major Quinn had been. However, she had no doubts that between them, the Hardy men would very likely be quite capable of working together to ensure her complete and utter surrender.

Suppressing a shudder at the thought, she accepted a glass of wine poured for her by George and sipped it tentatively. Her mind raced. In all her recent trials, this was potentially the most dangerous situation she found herself in. They had meant her harm months ago in London, and if they had followed her hundreds of miles north, they were obviously in a worse state financially than she had imagined. She closed her eyes briefly, wondering how much of her father's fortune Henrietta had actually squandered.

As if reading her mind, Henrietta tried to be conciliatory. She reached forward and put her hand on Charis's hand on the table top. "My dear," she said softly. "I wish only to carry out your dear Papa's final wishes and look after you as he would have hoped."

Charis looked in her eyes and a small cold smile lifted her lips. "My Papa," she replied, "wanted me to marry a man of my choosing when I was ready. He would never have countenanced a forced marriage to a man I..." She sought a suitable word. "...I dislike."

George flushed at her words. His eyes darkened with anger, and he would have retorted but for the knock on the door interrupting them.

The landlord opened the door, and his serving girl followed him inside, carrying a tray of food. There was a tureen of soup, bread and cold meats, and she placed it on the table whilst the landlord deposited soup bowls and spoons in front of them.

He bowed to Richard. "My apologies, sir," he said. "The Head

Groom has reported there is a problem with your carriage. The wheel is loose, and they will need to fix it securely before you carry on your way."

Richard was not pleased. His plans had not included spending any length of time in this posting-inn.

"How long will it take to repair?" he demanded.

The landlord was used to gentry being demanding but this man's tone and attitude bordered on the insulting.

"My men are working as hard as possible, sir," he replied. "It won't be much longer."

He bowed and they left, closing the door quietly behind them.

Richard glanced around the room at the increasingly angry George and the silent women. Henrietta, he knew, was tired of all the travelling but Charis was harder to read. He knew that any delay would only give her an opportunity to plan her escape from them once more. He wanted her safely married to George as quickly as possible. Or – his eyes narrowed as he observed his future daughter in law – dead. Whatever happened, Henrietta would soon be a wealthy woman and ripe for re-marrying. He knew her history, after all, he had been the one to rescue her from her former life in a brothel. He had no qualms about her background, especially where a large fortune was concerned. What her feelings were on the matter he did not care. He knew she would be the target of every fortune hunter in London once Charis was out of the way and he was determined that the only man to take advantage of the lovely Lady Henrietta would be him.

"Father…" George's urgent whisper interrupted him. "We have to get going." George reiterated his own thoughts. "Charis is likely to try and run away from us again if we linger here too long."

Richard nodded. "Go and see if there is any other carriage we can hire. Scotland is still two days away, and we must set off now," he replied quietly.

George turned and left the room, Charis's eyes following his movements. Richard walked over to the table and set about ladling the soup into the bowls left by the landlord. "Come along, ladies," he said. "Eat before this gets cold."

Henrietta broke off a chunk of bread and chewed on it before swallowing some of the soup. "Is it imperative we continue today?" she asked.

"Of course it is!" Richard snapped. His nerves were stretched as far as her own. He had seen Mrs Embleton in the company of Lord Frederick Waverley and the lawyer. He knew they had no time to lose. They were very likely in pursuit already but having no idea which way they had gone, he could only hope the pursuers had gone south, thinking them already back on the road to London.

Charis sipped a spoonful of the hot broth, swallowing it appreciatively. She was hungry after her early start this morning with Luke and the exertions of the day. If she had learned anything these last few days, it was to eat whenever she had chance as she had to keep her strength up for whatever may befall her next. Her examination of the room told her there were two doors and one window. One door led back out to the taproom and the other she knew not where. The window overlooked the garden, and beyond the garden, there were snow-covered fields as far as the eye could see. Even if she could climb through the window and run away, the deep snow and heavy drifts would hamper any escape attempt.

Despite the urgency of her own situation, her thoughts turned once again to the scene earlier that afternoon. She prayed that she had been in time, that her intervention had been enough to save Connor from the hangman's noose. Whatever his true feelings for her were, all she knew was that twice he had risked everything to save her. Her feelings for him had hit her with unimaginable force the day she found him half dead and half-naked on that windswept beach. She had never believed in love at first sight, assuming it to be girlish nonsense. But this sailor – this brave, courageous man who had fought to save and be with her – had swept away all her sensible down to earth feelings, replacing them with such desire and longing that the thought of anything happening to him filled her with dread.

George came back into the room, his greatcoat and bare head covered in a dusting of snow. He brought the cold in with him, and Henrietta shivered slightly.

"The coach will be ready in half an hour," he said shortly. He was scowling, and it was obvious from his demeanour he was not pleased with the reception he had encountered in the stables.

He turned to Charis, his face thunderous. "We will be driving to Pickering tonight. We will be sharing a room at the White Swan Hotel and tomorrow we will turn northwards again for Scotland. You will be my wife by the end of the week."

He was angry.

She almost quailed at the venom in his voice. "I have told you, George," she replied as calmly as possible, "I will never marry you."

He strode over to her and, closing his cold hand over her wrist, pulled her from her seat and held her shoulders in an iron grasp.

"You will marry me. If I have to put a child in your belly to make you then so be it!" His voice was a hiss and cold with undisguised menace. There was an unpleasant undertone to his words.

"And you would kill your child as well as your wife?" she demanded, not caring what she said.

The sneer in his voice was evident to all in the room. "I could kill you now, Charis," he said. "No one would stop me, and Henrietta here would get your money."

"And you would hang for murder!" she retorted.

His eyes narrowed and slowly, as if of their own volition, his hands went to her throat.

She stood perfectly still as his fingers started to squeeze, putting her hands up to his to try and ease the growing pressure. Her head swam and she closed her eyes, struggling then against the strength of his hands.

Henrietta was first to object. "George!" She stood and flew to him, pulling at his fingers. "Stop it!" She turned frightened eyes to Richard. "Stop him, Richard!"

Richard stepped in then. "George release her!" he thundered. "When Miss Waverley dies, it has to look like an accident, you fool."

No one noticed the door open. The two men who stood in the entrance were shocked by the tableau before their eyes. Connor swore loudly as he launched himself across the room, knocking the older man to the floor as he sprung at George.

Luke did not move. He was frozen on the spot as he stared at the scene before his eyes and the woman who was trying to prevent George Hardy from throttling Charis.

Connor dragged the man away, pushing the other woman to one side and with a hard blow to George's stomach winded the shocked attacker.

Henrietta stumbled as Connor pushed her aside but as she straightened she looked at the doorway, her face paling as she saw the man standing there.

Charis fell to the floor as she was released, coughing and choking as she dragged breath back into her body.

The fight between Connor and George went on around the room. Chairs and the table were overturned, the soup bowls and food flying onto the floor and being trampled underfoot. George recovered quickly from the first strike and returned the blows being landed on his face and body. Connor had been severely beaten and flogged during his days in prison. He was weaker than usual, but George was no match for the enraged seafarer.

Connor had him pinned to the ground, his hands around the other man's throat. "Luke!" he roared. "Stop him!"

Luke moved as if awoken from a dream. He looked down to see Richard Hardy on his knees, producing a small pistol from his inside pocket and aiming it at Connor. In two strides Luke reached him and kicked the weapon from his hand. He glanced at Connor, and with a movement almost economic with slowness and grace, he closed his hand into a fist and struck Richard a solid blow to his jaw that sent the older man reeling, joining his son on the floor.

The landlord and a couple of his men had, by this time been

alerted by the noise of shouts and crashing furniture. They came running in to the sight of the two well-dressed and unpopular gentlemen sprawled on the floor, one being held down by the young man who had entered the inn some twenty minutes earlier.

A young lady, recovering from what appeared to be a faint, struggled to stand. The other lady now stared, white-faced and shaking at the tall, dark-haired man standing over the prone figure of the older man, his hands still curled into fists.

Connor realised that Luke was in some kind of a daze and took command of the situation.

"Landlord!" he ordered, "Tie these two men up."

"What have they done?" the landlord demanded.

"Abduction!" Connor responded, going over to kneel beside the chair where Charis sat. She looked up into his face as he put out a hesitant hand to her cheek.

Connor helped her to stand, and the younger couple ignored everyone in the room as he pulled her into his arms and held her tightly. "Charis," he whispered. "Are you all right?"

Her eyes were swimming with tears as she looked up into his face. "Yes, oh Connor, yes, I am now."

She lifted her face to his and, with a groan, he kissed her lips. All trials and tribulations were momentarily forgotten as she returned his kiss and hugged his neck.

Henrietta shocked them all.

"Murder," came her soft, shaking voice.

The whole room was silenced by the word. Richard Hardy looked fit to murder her there and then. Charis turned in Connor's arms and held her breath as Henrietta pointed to Richard.

"He killed his wife and then my husband," she went on.

"Not your husband," Luke whispered.

The atmosphere was electric. The landlord and his men paused in their endeavours of tying up the two men on the dusty parlour floor to stare at them.

Henrietta put her hand to her throat and pulled a plain gold locket from beneath the bodice of her dress. Luke did the same, and a simple gold locket shone against the darkness of his coat as he walked forward, his legs unsteady, his whole body shaking.

Tears were in Henrietta's eyes. Tears of genuine wonder and emotion. Charis was astonished. She had never seen the hard-eyed Henrietta shed a tear in the three years she had known her.

Luke and Henrietta stopped inches away from each other. "They told me you were dead," she whispered.

"Your father told me you and Lily had both died," Luke replied.

"Lily died…" Henrietta's voice broke. "No one would help me, and our baby died…"

"Hetty…" Luke's voice was a groan, and he put his shaking hands on her cheeks, wiping the tears away with his thumbs.

"Lucas…"

At the sound of his name, Luke pulled her into his arms and kissed her. His arms went around her, pulling her trembling body against his own.

"Whore!" Richard Hardy was furious, watching all his careful plans unravelling. "Whoever you are – this woman was the most popular whore in London!" He spat the words out.

Luke lifted his head from hers and gazed into her eyes.

He frowned, but he did not release her. "Is that true?" he asked quietly.

She nodded. "It's true, Lucas. I had nothing left to sell, so I sold myself to survive." She stared into his eyes, her cheeks now stained with a deep redness. She swallowed but her voice remained steady, and she did not waver. "Richard took me out of the brothel and introduced me to Anthony Waverley. I thought you were dead so I married Anthony when he asked me."

A wave of emotions surged through Luke. He could not speak for a moment. His mind filled with memories and regrets. Hatred towards his wife's family, anger at his daughter's death, regret that he had not been there when she had needed him most.

His eyes were drinking in her face, her eyes, he pulled her close and lowered his lips to hers once more. She shook as he raised his head, her voice tremulous, husky. "I never forgot you, Lucas," she whispered.

"I never stopped loving you, Hetty," he replied. "Can you ever forgive me?"

"Can you forgive me?" she replied.

He lowered his head and rested his forehead against hers. "Oh, my heart..."

A movement from the floor interrupted them. The landlord pulled Richard Hardy to his feet, his men holding the bound George Hardy between them.

"I will lock these gentlemen up and send for the Magistrate, sir," the landlord said.

"Charis..." Connor was alarmed as the girl in his arms swayed suddenly. "What is it, my love?" he asked.

Richard Hardy was still furious. "You stupid bitch, Henrietta!" he shouted as he was dragged, protesting out of the parlour.

Luke had to be restrained by Henrietta from following Richard. She shook her head. "Leave him," she said. She withdrew herself from Luke's arms and turned to Charis. "My marriage to your father was obviously bigamous," she said calmly. "However, my only defence is that I truly believed my husband had been killed at Trafalgar."

Charis raised her white face to Connor as Henrietta continued. "I can promise you I had nothing to do with your father's death," she said, her voice breaking. "He found out about my past – in the brothel – and was going to divorce me. Richard tricked him into making a new Will. He wanted your money, and that meant disinheriting you and marrying you off to his son."

"You were going to let them kill me..." Charis managed to say at last.

Henrietta hung her head and sighed. Then, taking a deep breath, she raised her head again and stared at Charis and the two men. "Then my future lies in your hands, Charis. If you are to accuse me of attempted murder, then I can neither blame nor prevent you," she said. She straightened and stared at Luke. "And I will disappear from your life again Lucas," she said quietly. "Permanently."

There was a silence in the room, and Luke looked at Charis.

She knew then that all the power rested in her hands at that moment.

Luke spoke. "I have been a smuggler these last ten years so I cannot censure your life or what happened to you. You did what you did to survive. My love for you never wavered and I never found happiness with anyone else. "

"We have both changed so much, Lucas..." Henrietta's voice was barely a whisper.

"No..." Luke replied. "Our lives changed, circumstances changed, the world changed, and we were lost in it all. But one thing never changed. My love for you."

Charis stared from one to the other. Henrietta had been her most deadly enemy for the last three years, and her presence in her life had resulted in the death of a beloved father. She had hated the woman with a passion and had hated Richard Hardy even more for the influence he had over her stepmother. But did she want Henrietta dead?

Confused, she turned to Connor, who held her hand in his. His eyes were gentle, and he knew the decision she took now would influence their future lives forever.

Taking a deep breath, she looked at Luke. "Where will you go?" she asked.

"Virginia," Luke replied. "We will leave on the next tide, and you will never see us again."

Henrietta had not moved. She was holding her breath, awaiting her fate.

Charis nodded and slumped against Connor.

Luke strode over to her and took her hand in his. Raising it to his lips, he kissed it gently. "Thank you, Charis. God bless you. Goodbye."

He turned to Connor and placed his hands on the other's shoulders. Without a word, the two men hugged.

Luke winked at the young couple and swiftly turned away.

Henrietta had already put on her dark blue velvet cloak. Her eyes stood out wide and blue in her pale face. Her whole expression had changed, softened somehow. Charis thought her stepmother had never looked more beautiful.

"Goodbye, Charis," she said. "With all my heart I thank you."

Luke went to her and, with his arm around her shoulders, led her out of the parlour.

Charis and Connor followed them to the doorway of the inn. A few minutes later, a carriage left the courtyard, and they watched as the Waverley coach, wheel repaired, drove out back onto the road leading to Scarborough, the coast and a waiting ship.

"Will we ever see them again?" Charis asked, leaning against Connor, his arm around her.

"I hope not," Connor replied, his voice and demeanour entirely serious.

•

Two hours later, the parlour was restored to order and the curtains closed, shutting out the winter night. The Hardys were safely locked in the cellar, awaiting the arrival of the local militia, and Charis sat beside the cheerful fire blazing brightly in the hearth. Sitting alone, she looked up expectantly as the door opened and Connor stood in the doorway.

His wounds had been dressed, and with the assistance of the landlord, new clothes had been found for him. Breeches, a freshly laundered shirt and his boots brushed free of snow and mud. He returned to the parlour washed, shaved and presentable.

She stood as he entered and went to him. Inexplicably shy now they found themselves alone, a rosy blush suffused her cheeks as he took her hands in his and raised them to his lips.

"I have been waiting so long for this," he said softly.

"I've missed you, Mr McQueen," she said, her eyes smiling up into his.

He grinned and, releasing her hands, pulled her into his arms and kissed her. Her arms went around his neck and returned his embrace, feeling his arms, like bands of steel, holding her close.

"Charis…" He groaned as he lifted his lips finally. "There's so much I need to tell you."

"And I you, Connor," she replied. Removing herself from his arms, she took his hand and led him to the settle. They sat together, his arm around her shoulder, holding her close.

There was a table and tray in front of them. The landlord had thoughtfully provided a bottle of wine and two glasses, and she handed a glass of the ruby red liquid to him. He took a swallow and drank appreciatively.

"Where do we start?" he asked.

Thoughtful now, he frowned and looked into her eyes. "I am no fortune hunter, Charis," he said softly. "I fell in love with you when I thought you a penniless companion and I a common sailor. I gave no thought to the difference in our station in life then. I knew you were a lady and I wanted you despite our circumstances."

She waited, knowing he had to finish speaking.

"I love you more than I thought it was possible to love anyone," he went on. "I could not forget you. Your face was in my mind every time I closed my eyes. You were in my thoughts every time I awoke and the last thing I thought of before I slept." He paused, his eyes drinking in her face. "I was in agony thinking I might have hurt you. When Luke told me I had a reputation for being a womaniser, I cursed myself for even thinking I could be worthy of a lady like you."

She smiled then. "Luke told me he had lied to extract some kind of revenge against you," she said. "But he admired you greatly and spoke of your courage and bravery. And tenacity – you pursued him relentlessly through the worst storm he had ever encountered in twenty years, he said."

Connor shook his head as he recalled the circumstances of that night, the ferocity of the storm.

"I was a hot-headed fool," he said softly. "My arrogance and pride cost me my ship and the lives of my men. I should have just let him go."

The regret and pain in his voice caused Charis to squeeze the hand that held hers.

She shook her head. "You were doing your duty, Connor," she said softly. "He understood that and admired you for it."

He was silent for a moment, and she gazed into his eyes before lifting her lips to his and kissing him softly.

"I love you – whoever you were or are! Now tell me your history, my darling!"

Relaxing again, he hugged her close before resuming his story. "Oliver Connor Steele at your service, madam," he began. "Second son of Admiral Lord Tristan Steele. My brother Oscar is the heir and currently resides in Ireland. He is looking after the estate on our father's behalf, and my parents live in Portsmouth. We have a house in London, but my parents very rarely attend Court. I joined the Navy at sixteen and worked my way up through the officer's ranks. I was at Trafalgar – but not on Nelson's flagship, I regret to say. I was injured a year ago during the Battle of New Orleans and invalided home. My father secured a command for me in the Revenue service." His eyes clouded over momentarily. "I think my mother had something to do with his order," he said softly. "I suffered a bullet wound during the battle, and that was enough to get me sent back to England."

Seeing the frown, which creased her brow, he kissed her again. "I am fine now. Fit and healthy except for a bang on the head which addled my brain and caused me to forget who I was for a time. I have no sisters. There is just my brother and I. I am not a poor man. I have inherited my grandmother's house and estates in the West Country. I visit them regularly whenever my duties allow."

She gazed into his face, solemn and still as he recounted his history. She guessed his years in the Navy had been a lot more adventurous than he was telling her now but she knew they would discover everything about each other in the fullness of time.

"And no sweethearts?" she teased. "No girl in every port as Captain Vincent suggested?"

He shook his head. "I am nearly thirty years of age, Charis. My life has been dedicated to my duty in the Navy." He grinned at her, a twinkle in his eye. "I am no saint, however." He paused once more, took her hand and pressed a kiss to it. "Even as a callow youth I never fell in love with anyone. I can promise you my heart is yours, now and forever. If you will have me, my love?"

"I will," she whispered.

They did not speak for a few minutes. He held her tightly and kissed her once more.

Drawing a deep, shuddering breath, he lifted his lips from hers, pushing her away slightly, realising she was totally unaware of the effect her responses had aroused in him.

"Now, Miss Waverley," he said, with a mock seriousness in his voice. "Would you mind telling me – from the beginning, if you please – just why those people were trying to kill you?"

She laughed and rested her head on his shoulder. "It's a long story, my darling!" she replied.

Settled in his arms, in front of the blazing fire in that cosy room, she sighed. She looked up into his eyes, seeing the love reflected there, seeing the tenderness and the admiration, and she realised she had never felt happier in her life. From the look in his face, from the way he held her, from the kisses he pressed on her lips she knew, without any doubt, he felt exactly the same way.

Talking softly, making plans for the future, they sat contentedly, both knowing that this was where they belonged. The poor companion and the unknown sailor restored at last to their birthright, knowing that whatever trials may come they would face them hand in hand, together forever.

Outside, the blizzard stopped, and beams of dazzling moonlight sparkled on the serene virgin snow. The winter's night was an arctic tableau as the smuggler's moon shone down on two pairs of lovers, both setting sail on new voyages, new adventures, ready to face the world together, never to be parted again.